A Family
Scandal

Zoë
Miller

piatkus

PIATKUS

First published in Ireland as a paperback original in 2012 by Hachette Books Ireland
First published in Great Britain as a paperback original in 2013 by Piatkus

A CIP catalogue record for this book
is available from the British Library.

ISBN 978-0-7499-5229-7

Typeset in Bembo by M Rules
Printed and bound by CPI Group (UK) Ltd, Croydon, CR0 4YY

Papers used by Piatkus are from well-managed forests
and other responsible sources.

MIX
Paper from
responsible sources
FSC
www.fsc.org   FSC® C104740

Piatkus
An imprint of
Little, Brown Book Group
100 Victoria Embankment
London EC4Y 0DY

An Hachette UK Company
www.hachette.co.uk

www.piatkus.co.uk

Dedicated with much love and gratitude to my family

Acknowledgements

Heartfelt appreciation goes to the fantastic people I am privileged to work with, who keep me on track with unstinting encouragement and commitment: my wonderful agent Sheila Crowley and all the team at Curtis Brown; my super-talented editor Ciara Dooley, and the great people at Hachette Books Ireland, including Breda, Margaret, Joanna and Bernard; the lovely Piatkus UK team, including Emma Beswetherick, Donna Condon and Paola Ehrlich; and all who work on my behalf behind the scenes. I can't thank you enough for fantastic help and for having such great faith in me.

This book is dedicated to my family, without whose tremendous love and support there would be no book: Derek, Michelle, Declan, Barbara, Dara, Colm, and the wonderful and infinitely precious Cruz. I love you all far more than I can ever express. Thank you for everything.

Gratitude also to my extended family, and friends and colleagues, for happy times and for always being there whenever I remember that life exists beyond the storyline.

And thanks to my supportive circle of writer friends and all my lovely readers. I really appreciate the encouraging messages sent via Facebook and Twitter and to zoemillerauthor@gmail.com. I hope you enjoy *A Family Scandal*.

Zoë xx

Prologue

'And finally . . .' the newsreader pauses.

She holds her breath and silently urges him to get on with it. It might be just a two-minute, late-night news item, slotted between a summary of the newspaper headlines and the weather forecast, but, for the Morgans, it's the family skeleton stalking out of the cupboard and her heart leaps into her mouth.

The newsreader launches into the short report. 'Today marks the twentieth anniversary of the tragic death of the rock musician, Zach Anderson . . .'

She shouldn't be watching it. After all, ignorance is bliss. But she can't help herself, and her eyes are riveted to the plasma screen. She plucks a silk pillow off the bed, hugging it to herself as if it will cushion the attack on her senses.

Some hope.

'. . . fans from around the world have been gathering at Lake Antonia. They are marking the anniversary by holding a vigil at the spot where Anderson plunged to his death when his Harley Davidson went off the pier in questionable circumstances.'

A dramatic guitar riff spills out across the bedroom and resonates painfully in her head. His unique signature sound. She brushes away the ghostly image of him and looks at the grey, Canadian landscape filling the screen. The camera slowly pans across a scene still emerging from the long grip of winter; a sky so leaden it seems to press down on a dark, brooding pine forest. A scatter of seagulls wheeling into the sky, black silhouettes flapping against the breeze.

And, then, the deep, silent lake.

She recalls another news programme, twenty years ago. It had been sunny that day and the lake had resembled a sheet of blue, unblemished glass with not even a surface ripple to hint at the sad tragedy it had witnessed. Now, the choppy waters mirror the iron-grey sky, and the corrugated surface is dotted with colour from the bobbing flower wreaths. The camera slowly pans across knots of people gathered along the pier, huddled into coats, jackets, scarves, boots, some of them curving their hands around flickering candle flames, struggling to keep them alight in the playful breeze.

The music fades and the newscaster continues, 'Scottish by birth, Anderson was the father of Lucy Morgan, the successful, London-based fashion model. He moved to the Canadian lakeside retreat to concentrate on his songwriting when his relationship with Lucy's mother, the Irish actress Vivienne Morgan, ended, and it was there that he wrote the iconic, emotionally charged anthem 'Forever My Angel', which brought him global, posthumous success. His anniversary has sparked renewed interest in his music and a recently redigitalised version of his chart hit has become the fastest selling download this year . . .'

Just as she steels herself, there is a brief clip of Zach on stage. Strobe lights cast a purple hue on the dry ice writhing like a ghostly snake around his leather jeans. His guitar is slung low on his hips in his trademark stance. She presses her clenched fist against her mouth as a swirl of memories rise up inside her; Zach's smile, his laugh, his jauntiness . . . the throb of raw emotion in his voice as he sings to her, the look on his face as he leans over the bed.

Then the newscaster continues, 'In London today, Lucy Morgan was not prepared to comment on the anniversary of her father's tragic death.'

The footage changes to a busy London street and her heart squeezes at the sight of a girl jumping out of a cab. Long legs in skinny jeans and a ripple of flame-red hair against a faux-fur jacket, she sprints up the steps into the sanctuary of a Chelsea townhouse, head down as she runs the gauntlet of the waiting press and cameramen.

Zach Anderson's milestone anniversary was one of those events that spike briefly in the celebrity-hungry media. He'd been splashed across a weekend supplement, and she'd discovered that fans had set up a website dedicated to his memory, complete with video footage of his performances and links to Twitter and Facebook. Everything about him was up for grabs, including Lucy.

Then, it's all over. They have moved on to the weather forecast. Tomorrow will be dry and bright. She stares at tiny sun symbols marching optimistically across the map of Great Britain and Ireland and realises she is still holding her breath. She presses the remote control and the screen darkens. Her hands shake as she unties the ribbons of her satin dressing gown and turns down the duvet.

It has only been a short news item. By next week, the fickle world of social trending will have moved on, the insatiable celebrity hunger feeding off another victim, and Zach Anderson would be relegated to history, where he belonged.

Afterwards, she wondered how she could have been so naive ...

Because it wasn't all over. It would never be all over, considering Zach's ultimate legacy – ruthless ambition coupled with insatiable desire. And no matter how much she wants to ignore it, the question about whether Zach had deliberately driven his Harley Davidson off the pier, or if it had just been a terrible misadventure, or worse, some kind of foul play, is pulsing loud and clear like a steady drumbeat behind all the social commentary.

Only two people know the answer – and she is one of them.

Chapter 1

*E*llie Morgan had just lit a white pomegranate-scented candle and was looking forward to opening a bottle of Château Margaux and spending the evening wrapped in Johnny Tyler's arms when her mobile buzzed.

'I'm at Heathrow,' Lucy Morgan said, in a soft, quivering voice. 'I'm coming home to Dublin for a couple of days. My flight will be boarding soon. Can you pick me up?'

Ellie felt a sliver of annoyance as her hopes of a chill-out evening were dashed. Nonetheless, she summoned a smile and said, 'Sure, hon. What's up?'

'What do you mean, what's up? It's my dad. All this stuff about his death is freaking me out. I can't take any more of the paparazzi camped outside the front door.'

Listening to Lucy's quavering voice, Ellie's heart sank. Her youngest sister was no stranger to the tabloids, racking up column inches on a regular basis, and she often appeared to be in your face with her fearless and spunky attitude as she played to the cameras, so she must be quite rattled with the way her father's anniversary has attracted the glare of the media.

From their far-flung locations, all the Morgans had watched the news snippet that had aired two nights ago, and, afterwards, they had agreed that it meant nothing whatsoever and didn't deserve a second thought. Ellie had been putting on a brave face. She wondered now if Miranda, her sister, and Vivienne, her mother, had been doing the same. Even devil-may-care Lucy had insisted that she didn't give a damn.

'I thought you were okay when we chatted after the news,' Ellie pointed out gently.

'I *was* okay,' Lucy went on, in a whispery, slightly sobbing tone. 'Then something happened that sent me over the edge.'

'Tell me,' Ellie urged. Lucy was almost incoherent and it took a while for Ellie to grasp that a funeral wreath with Zach Anderson's name on it had been delivered to the door of Lucy's apartment in Chelsea.

'What did I do to deserve this?' Lucy's voice quavered.

'Darling, just ignore it, that's some fan out of his head on coke,' Ellie said, a prickle of unease at the back of her head. No wonder Lucy was so upset. With Vivienne on holiday, she would have to stay with Ellie – it was the least she could do.

'I don't care who it was. It scared me. I cancelled my appointments for the rest of the week, threw some stuff into a case and snuck out the back door into the laneway. One of my mates was waiting to smuggle me to Heathrow and I'm here now, hiding in the ladies' cubicles until the final call for the flight. Can you pick me up?' Her voice sounded a little stronger, Ellie thought, as she proudly recounted her dash to freedom.

'Of course,' Ellie said, 'Johnny's on his way over. Text me your flight details and we'll both be there.'

'I hope Johnny doesn't mind.'

'He won't,' Ellie said glibly.

'You're a star, thank you!'

Ellie suppressed her unease as she blew out her scented candle and inhaled the final puff of scent. To hell with whoever had decided to resurrect Zach Anderson and drag an old family scandal into today's ultra-intrusive limelight, never mind scare Lucy half to death. Ellie was finding it difficult enough to blank out her own memories of Zach's relationship with her mother without having to cope with the drama of Lucy coming home and raking over the bones of his death. Her half-sister was prone to hissy fits and it would take all Ellie's energy to cope with her. Energy she didn't have at the moment. Still, blood was thicker than water, and half-sister or not, Lucy was a Morgan, and no matter what was going on behind the scenes, the three sisters always stuck together in the face of the media. Johnny gave a half-hearted grumble when she told him of the change of plan when he arrived. 'I was looking forward to having a big glass of red and ravishing you,' he said.

'We'll save that for later,' she said.

'Why can't Lucy get a taxi?' he asked as he picked up his car keys and followed Ellie down the hall.

Ellie stabbed in the alarm code. 'She's upset. She doesn't feel like making small-talk with a chatty taxi driver. Would you, if you were in her shoes?'

'I dunno,' he said easily. 'Since I've never been in her glam Louboutins.'

'God.' Ellie shook her head as she shut the hall door.

'Hey, lighten up. You know your wish is my command.'

Ellie had timed things so that they would reach the airport just as Lucy came through arrivals, so when they were delayed in traffic on the northbound motorway, her stomach clenched with anxiety.

'Can't you go any faster?' she asked irritably, when Johnny's Mercedes eventually cleared the tailback.

'I already have six penalty points, thanks very much,' Johnny said, nonetheless careering across into the fast lane. 'What's the rush?'

'I don't want Lucy hanging around, attracting unwanted attention.'

'Relax. I don't know why you're so edgy. She'll love that.'

'Not tonight, she won't.'

Johnny drove right up to the terminal building and slewed to a halt in the tow-away zone. 'I'll hang on here, and be ready for a quick getaway,' he said roguishly.

'Thanks. We might need that.'

Whatever about Lucy, Ellie found she was the one attracting attention as she dashed into the brightly lit terminal, long legs in stiletto boots, her cream woollen coat swirling behind her, and her dark hair spilling from a careless chignon. As she hurried to the arrivals hall she made herself slow to a walk, hoping to be as inconspicuous as possible.

The downside to being the eldest of the feted Morgan sisters and a successful fashion designer – as well as being hailed as half of one of Dublin's golden couples, a label Ellie normally laughed at – meant she was instantly recognisable wherever she went. Her emerald-green eyes blinked as she looked up at the arrivals board and tried to focus on the data jumping in front of her, and she breathed easily when she saw that the Heathrow flight had landed fifteen minutes earlier. But she still had to wait another ten long minutes, keeping her face blank and composed, uncomfortable with the sidelong glances cast in her direction.

At last she saw the tall, slender figure of Lucy, caught up in the middle of a surge of returning holiday-makers. Her pale face was at odds with the straggling crowd boasting out-of-season suntans.

She might have left London in a hurry, but, Ellie noted with a swift glance, she still managed to look ultra chic in her faux-fur jacket, thigh-high leather mini-skirt and lace-patterned leggings.

'Lucy! Over here,' she called softly.

Her sister halted, her pointed chin raised in a defensive angle, as the crowd streamed around her. Her hair was scrunched up under a fedora hat, exposing her pale, luminous neck, and Ellie couldn't see the expression in her light-grey eyes as they were concealed by enormous sunglasses, but her body language said it all. Lucy had the graceful, yet guarded, stance of a deer sensing danger.

Or, Ellie thought irritably, a supermodel waiting for the best moment to launch herself down the catwalk.

'Lucy, over here,' she repeated.

Lucy finally saw her and hurried to the end of the barrier. With rather more spectacle than Ellie would have liked, she abandoned her luggage, whipped off her sunglasses and threw herself into Ellie's arms.

'Oh, God, oh, God, I'm so glad to see you. It's been awful.'

Ellie hugged her quivering body. 'I know, of course it has. Come on, let's get you out of here.'

Ellie looked for the shortest possible route as they hurried across the concourse towards the exit. She linked her arm through Lucy's, urging her along, but, just as she had feared, they weren't quick enough to prevent someone from jumping in front of them and raising his iPhone to take a quick photo.

Lucy immediately turned her face away and shoved on her sunglasses. There was a small flash and Ellie felt her cheeks redden with anger. 'Get out of our way,' she said, her voice shaking.

'Come on, give me a break,' he wheedled, aiming his iPhone again. He was about thirty years of age, with a casual, well-bred arrogance that inflamed Ellie. 'God, you Morgan sisters are even more beautiful in the flesh,' he said, his eyes slowly giving them an appreciative, head-to-toe stare.

'I'm calling security,' Ellie snapped, looking in vain around the terminal hall as she took a firmer hold of Lucy.

He kept pace with them as they scurried across to the exit. 'Hey, Lucy, did London get too hot for you? Why aren't you over in Canada keeping vigil with Zach's fans? Or is that too hot as well?'

Ellie halted and squared up to him. 'Why don't you piss off,' she raged, fighting the impulse to knock his iPhone out of his hand and annoyed that he had provoked her into using uncharacteristic language. Then, the exit doors whooshed open and Johnny marched through. At six foot two, in his leather military jacket, his appearance was more effective than any security guard. No matter that he had a big black frown on his handsome face and his short, dark hair had been spiked by his impatient fingers. His timing was perfect. Ellie felt a wave of emotion that took her by surprise and put it to one side because she'd no time to think about it now.

'Hey, what's keeping you two?' he said. 'My wheels are about to be towed away if I don't move pronto. And I don't fancy any scratches on my pride and joy.'

'Johnny!' Lucy squealed before hurling herself into his arms as though he was her saviour.

There was another camera flash and Ellie could just see it all in the tabloids: 'Lucy Morgan tries to slink into Dublin unobserved and comes home to a very warm welcome.' Johnny seized up the situation immediately and told the impromptu photographer where to go, using language that was even choicer than Ellie's.

'Who's that jerk?' he asked.

'Some asshole,' Ellie said, through gritted teeth.

Johnny grinned at her in amusement. 'Wow, Ellie, your aggressive side turns me on. You should unleash it more often.'

Even though anxiety was nibbling at her, she couldn't help but smile. 'Let's get out of here.'

Johnny bundled Lucy under one arm and pulled her case with his free hand as they dashed out through the exit. Ellie gulped in the chilly night-time air as they hurried down the pavement to where Johnny's Mercedes was diagonally slung across the tow-away zone, causing an obstruction. An airport official in a high-viz jacket was beadily eyeing it as he barked into a walkie-talkie. Lucy dived into the back of the car as Johnny threw her case into the boot and jumped into the driver's seat. Ellie jumped in beside Lucy and they had barely fastened their seatbelts before Johnny accelerated away from the terminal building in a squeal of tyres, waving cheerily at the beady-eyed official who hurriedly sprang out of his way.

'Are you okay?' Ellie asked, reaching for Lucy's hands. They felt cold, so she held them tightly in her own steady grip for a few moments.

'I'm okay now that I'm here,' Lucy said, shivering. 'But the past couple of days – Oh, God, I tried to pretend it didn't really matter, but it's been a nightmare. I haven't been able to put my nose out the door without being accosted.'

'I thought you were a pro at managing the paps, and that you loved being on the telly,' Johnny said. Ellie sent him a warning glance in the rear-view mirror, but unabashed, Johnny raised comical eyebrows.

'Yeah, well, it's one thing if I'm a bit wasted or having a bad hair day, I've no problem if it's my fault, but harassing me about my dad is totally out of line.' Lucy's voice hardened and Ellie squeezed her hand.

'Of course it is,' she said, glaring at the back of Johnny's head, but it was in vain for he was too intent on navigating the circuitous route to the airport's exit to notice.

'And did you see all that crap on Facebook and Twitter about how he died? Was it an accident . . . was it something else?' Lucy gulped. 'Mum always insisted it was an accident. I can't believe people are suggesting it wasn't. And where's all this coming from? He's been dead for twenty years, for crying out loud. Why is it suddenly being dumped on me now? I was barely one when he died. He never even bothered with me.' Her voice rose dramatically as she pulled off her hat and ran teasing fingers through her long hair.

'I dunno what to say,' Ellie sighed. In the forty-eight hours since the television coverage of Anderson's anniversary had been aired, it had been picked up by a couple of the tabloids, and images of the crowd gathered by the Canadian lake juxtaposed beside Lucy avoiding the cameras in London were splashed across both print and digital versions.

'His Facebook page was only set up a week ago but it has thousands of fans already,' Lucy said indignantly. '*Thousands!* I couldn't believe it.'

'Jesus, Lucy, you sound jealous,' Johnny said, with a trace of laughter in his voice.

Ellie ignored him. 'You can blame Facebook and the Twitterati for hyping it all up out of nowhere,' she said. 'Social networking has a lot to answer for, never mind the media. We all felt for you when we saw you on the news.'

'How come you were all watching it?'

'Miranda's researcher friend had tipped us off, but none of us expected the spotlight to turn on you. Were you talking to Mum? I know she wasn't happy with the way you were singled out.'

'I missed her call but she left a message on my mobile, telling me to ignore it. But I don't want her worrying about me, not when she's supposed to be having some rest. That's making me feel ten times worse,' Lucy said, slumping back in her seat.

Great stuff, Ellie silently fumed. She could do without Lucy adopting the role of martyr to add to her repertoire. Still, Lucy had been on her own in London when the story broke. At least she had had Johnny for support and, over in Hong Kong, Miranda was miles away. Vivienne was in the best place of all, pampering herself in the luxury of an eastern Mediterranean cruise after a health scare with her heart. None of them wanted the long-legged ghost of Zach Anderson marching back into their lives, or the sound of his gravelly singing evoking a time that was best forgotten.

Since the news story had exploded, she'd had to forcibly remind herself that she was a successful fashion designer and life was good. She was a long way from the sensitive teenager who had watched Vivienne bravely cock her elegant fingers at an inquisitive world when she had found herself unexpectedly pregnant after a brief, but much publicised, relationship with Zach just a year after her husband had died. She was even further from the seventeen-year-old who'd had to put up with the media eruption at the time of Zach's death.

'Relax, Lucy,' she said, keeping her tone light. 'It's just unfortunate that some crank fans decided to make something of your father's anniversary. And it's not very nice that someone took a pot shot at you. Unfortunately, you're in the limelight so much that you're an easy target,' she couldn't help adding. 'And Mum is fine. She's going to enjoy the rest of her break, and the weather in the Adriatic is lovely.'

'Please don't tell her about the wreath.' Lucy's voice dropped to a dramatic whisper.

'I won't. You've no idea, I suppose, who might have sent it?'

'It was just a plain white card with Zach's name on it, nothing more.'

'Obviously some prankster,' Ellie said. 'Forget about it. On the orders of your big sis. And with Mum on holiday, you're staying with me.'

'Staying with you? That's a first. I don't want to be in your way,' Lucy said stubbornly. 'I can easily go to Mum's as usual.'

'You're not staying on your own, and Mum's house is cold, empty and locked up. I phoned Mum to tell her you're coming home, without telling her why, and she said she'd feel much better if you stayed with me.'

Although Ellie wasn't entirely happy with the arrangement. Right now, she hadn't the energy to cope with Lucy's see-saw emotions on top of everything else. For apart from the fuss about Zach, she also had Johnny Tyler's recent marriage proposal swirling like a cloud of anxiety in her head.

'It'll be a change, staying with you,' Lucy said.

'So long as you don't mind doing your share of the cooking,' Johnny joked as the car surged around the looping slip road and down the ramp onto the M50. 'Ellie still can't boil an egg.'

'I can do lots of things with an egg,' Lucy flipped back. 'And beef, and chicken . . . I'm not just a beautiful bimbo.'

As they chatted away, Ellie sank back against the squashy leather and tried to regain some sort of calm. Traffic was light at this late hour and the Mercedes cruised comfortably along the M50. She took measured breaths and watched the long, curving necklace of motorway lights stream past as they headed south. Soon they were leaving the motorway and climbing into the lower foothills of the Dublin mountains, where housing estates became more scattered until they gave way to small villages.

Eventually, Johnny turned down a lane and in through wooden gates to Laurel View, Ellie's split-level bungalow.

Before heading to the airport, she'd left on welcoming lamps and the under-floor heating, so when she opened the hall door and ushered Lucy inside, her home was warm and cosy, the hallway scented with jugs of tall-stemmed lilies. Johnny took her case and Lucy followed him down to the en-suite guest bedroom, where Ellie had left out fresh towels, scented candles and a selection of magazines.

Ellie went into the kitchen.

Now that she had a moment alone, she thought about the rush of emotion that had washed over her at the sight of Johnny marching into the terminal just in time to rescue them. Had it been affection? Could it have been love? Or had it been pure and simple relief? She tried to recapture the moment in her mind and pinpoint the feeling because there was a big difference between affection and love. Then again, love was all about how you behaved, and not just a feeling. So how was she behaving with Johnny? Or he with her?

Did she love him enough to marry him?

The moment slipped away from her as Lucy strode into the kitchen, her heels beating a staccato on the tiled floor.

'Ellie, my room is amazing, you are a pet!'

'No prob.'

'Maybe I should make *this* my base for my trips home from London.'

Ellie stayed silent.

Even though she was supposed to be in a bad place right now, Ellie couldn't help but notice that Lucy exuded all the glamour synonymous with a celebrated catwalk model. A tight, black sweater hugged her pert breasts, and her trademark flame-coloured hair tumbled down past her shoulders. At five feet eleven, she stood slightly taller than Ellie. Her slender figure was perfectly toned, thanks to her strict regime of diet and exercise. No wonder she was one of Rebecca Grace's most successful models. Ellie was suddenly conscious of her much fuller, curvy figure. She wasn't twenty-one with a sylph-like body anymore, she sighed to herself. She was thirty-seven. And right then, she felt as though she was wearing each and every year.

'I forgot how pretty this is,' Lucy said as she went across to the window in the conservatory.

Ellie's home, situated in the hills south of Dublin, enjoyed a stunning view of the city. At night, out beyond the shadowy garden, the orangey-yellow lights of the city twinkled like a magic carpet of glittering sequins, unrolling in front of her as far as the eye could see, until it reached the horizon and met the deep, dark, velvet heavens.

Ellie loved this view. There was something spell-binding about it that lifted her spirits. It was as if God had emptied his pocket of a million sparkling gemstones and had lavishly strewn them from the heavens in order to brighten the dark night. If she ever felt anyway fraught or uptight about life, she loved to go outside in the garden and spend time soaking up the panorama, enjoying the beauty of it all and putting her problems into perspective, telling herself she had no real troubles at all.

Ellie handed Lucy a mug of tea generously laced with brandy. 'We could sit outside if you like? I could give you a warm fleece and turn on the patio heater. I find it very relaxing.'

'Ugh, no thanks, it's still freezing,' Lucy said, turning away from the window, instantly dismissing Ellie's suggestion. 'I can't believe it's almost the end of March.' She took a sip of her tea and wrinkled her nose. 'Hey, what's this?'

'My special concoction to help you sleep. I'm taking the day off tomorrow and we're going out for lunch to help you forget about the past few days.'

'Ha. I wish it was that easy,' Lucy said petulantly.

'Look, sis, all that stuff about Zach is just something that's hot at the moment but next week there will be another story trending all over the blogosphere.'

'I hope so. It's a big pain considering he was never part of my life, apart from the crucial moment of conception,' Lucy said, curling her hands around the mug and sitting down on a butter-milk-shaded sofa. She toed off her high heels and looked up at Ellie with big, light-grey eyes. With a mixture of Vivienne's classic bone structure and delicate Celtic colouring, and her father's soulful eyes, Lucy had the appearance of an angel.

'As one asshole pointed out,' Lucy went on, her voice brittle, 'I was just the result of a quick fling between Mum and Zach.'

'Ouch, don't tell me someone threw that at you?' Ellie's heart sank. How could people be so cruel? She couldn't believe that this snide comment had come round again and was now being fired at Lucy. It wasn't far off what she'd experienced in the class-room all those years ago when toxic classmates were only too happy to try and take the tall, reserved Ellie Morgan down a peg or two, murmuring cutting comments about her mother's brief and ill-starred relationship with Zach. She'd never thought it would come back to bite Lucy when it most hurt.

'Don't worry, sis, I told him exactly where to shove it.' Lucy giggled, showing a lot more bravado than Ellie had ever felt back then.

'Good for you. Don't ever give that kind of crap a minute's thought. Mum loved you from before you were even born and she has spent her life making up for Zach's absence,' Ellie pointed out.

'Yeah, and I know I disappoint her from time to time with the antics I get up to,' Lucy rolled her eyes in an exaggerated theatrical expression that would put even Vivienne's best performance in the shade. 'I can't help it if I'm not as successful as you or as clever as Miranda . . .'

Here we go again, Ellie sighed to herself. She was about to object but Johnny came into the conservatory in time to hear Lucy's comment and got there first. 'I thought all the Morgan sisters were bright, beautiful *and* successful,' he said.

'Ellie is beautiful in a classy way, and Miranda is bright, but I'm the bold sister,' Lucy beamed, as though she was granting herself an award.

'Bold? Ellie can do bold as well,' Johnny said, reaching out and lightly spanking her bum. 'But begging your pardon, darling, you might be a brilliant fashion designer and all-around fabulous, but I bet Lucy's blog has more hits than yours. Hey, Lucy, why don't you dump that tea and I'll get you a drink more suitable for your hour of need. Gin? Vodka?'

Lucy relinquished her half-full mug immediately. She curled her feet under her and tucked Ellie's raspberry chenille throw around her. 'Mmm, vodka, thanks. With lots of ice and cranberry, if you have it.'

'Ellie has everything in her cavernous fridge,' Johnny chuckled as he loped across to the kitchen. 'Everything you can cook at the touch of a microwave button, courtesy of Marks & Spencer. She's their best food hall customer. Isn't that right, darling?'

'Yes, darling, whatever you say,' Ellie shook her head at his retreating back.

'One vodka and cranberry,' Johnny said, returning and pressing a glass into Lucy's hand. 'Ellie? What can I get you?'

'I'll have the same,' Ellie said, joining Lucy on the sofa. Already there was some colour returning to Lucy's face, she noticed, as she watched her joke with Johnny. A break from London until the fuss had died down would sort her out. She was glad that Johnny was being his usual lively self and making up for her lack of spark. But she wished Miranda was here to talk to and, for a moment, she felt a flash of annoyance that her sister was away on the other side of the world and safely removed from it all.

Three months ago, Miranda, a highly regarded economist, had surprised them all by announcing she was spreading her wings and moving to Hong Kong, when her latest relationship had crumbled. Now she was working in the financial department of XAM, a large multinational company and, by all accounts, was perfectly happy and enjoying every minute of her new life. Ellie was pleased for her, but they were best friends as well as sisters and she missed her a lot. It was at times like these that she felt her absence.

Although Miranda was four years younger than Ellie, she'd been there with her when the gossip columns were crawling with the story of Vivienne Morgan's pregnancy and love child and, later, Zach's death. And Miranda would have been some kind of support in dealing with Lucy.

It was always better when the sisters were together. Sometimes Ellie sparked off Lucy and vice versa, but Miranda was the warm, affectionate sister, the calming one, the glue that held them together. She would have known exactly what to say to Lucy, how best to cheer her up and stop her from feeling sorry for herself. Sometimes Ellie felt years older than both of her sisters.

'What else is happening in your life?' Ellie asked Lucy. 'Any exciting trips on the horizon?'

'Not as much as I would have liked,' Lucy frowned and bit her lip. 'I just missed out on some Paris shows, but,' she paused, 'I'm hoping to be part of the autumn/winter promotion for the

House of Venetia, so it's fingers and toes crossed. I've seen some of the designs and they're fabulous. Glitzy party wear in lace and black velvet, as well as a lingerie range with balcony bras and matching briefs in chiffon and mulberry lace. A girl could feel really special in that stuff and it would be a good profile job to help to launch me into the big time.'

'Wow, sounds great, tell me more,' Ellie relaxed against the cushions and smiled encouragingly.

Johnny poured more drinks as Lucy outlined the campaign that would start shooting early in the summer. 'There will be a television commercial, with filming in the Swiss Alps, and lots of advertising in the glossy magazines. I'm up against stiff competition because everybody wants a piece of this action, but they're only choosing three Rebecca Grace models. A brunette, a blonde and a redhead. I suppose I could always dye my hair blonde if I don't make it in the redhead category.'

'Don't you dare. You're fabulous just the way you are.'

'Do you think so?' Lucy coiled her hair on top of her head, angled her neck and examined her reflection in the darkened conservatory window.

'Of course you are,' Johnny said. 'And so is Ellie,' he went on, ruffling Ellie's hair affectionately.

Afterwards, Ellie told herself that Lucy must have had too much to drink, or else her upset over the past few days ran deeper than Ellie had first thought, making her thoughtless, for Lucy sat back and combed her hand through her cascade of hair as she remarked heedlessly, quite innocent of the fact that to Ellie, her words were tossing the equivalent of a gallon of oil onto a smouldering fire, 'Hey, Johnny, if you think Ellie is all that fabulous, why haven't you made an honest woman of her? You guys are together – how long?'

There was a tense silence, broken eventually by Johnny.

'Two years and that's the million-dollar question,' he said evenly. 'But it's the other way around. I'm still waiting to see if Ellie will make an honest man of me,' he laughed, shooting Ellie a searching glance that caused her stomach to clench. 'Maybe she'll tell you what's holding her up, because I sure as hell don't know.'

'Ellie? I'm surprised at you,' Lucy said jokingly. 'What gives? Johnny's quite a good catch. Lots of women would love to be in your shoes – never mind bed,' she added wickedly.

'I think that's between Johnny and me,' Ellie said, flashing Lucy a meaningful look. 'And right now it's after midnight and we've all had a tough couple of days.'

'Oops, in other words don't go there,' Lucy pulled a face, interpreting the glance correctly and rising to her feet. 'Sorry if I spoke out of turn and thanks for putting me up – or putting up with me, whatever. I can't promise to be down in time to cook a five-star breakfast, but I know you guys are busy people, so I'll do whatever I can around the house while I'm here. Cleaning the plughole, recapping the toothpaste, ironing the tea towels, whatever.'

'Johnny was only joking with you earlier,' Ellie reassured her. 'Stay in bed as long as you want and have a good rest. Anyway, I still have Marta coming in three mornings a week and she's in charge of everything, including the ironing. She'd hate her nose to be out of joint.'

Johnny said, in a half-joking, half-serious tone of voice, 'I'm a bit like Marta. I come and go two or three times a week, and if I'm lucky, the weekend.'

Ellie ignored a pang of disquiet and forced herself to hold her tongue in front of Lucy.

'I'm off,' Lucy said. She slid her feet back into heels and tottered across the tiled floor to give them both a kiss on the cheek.

'I'll leave you guys to battle it out between you. See you tomorrow.'

'Sleep tight, Lucy,' Ellie gave her a hug.

Lucy's footsteps receded down the wooden-floored hall. Ellie could almost taste the tension in the air and she felt her heart pounding as Johnny gazed at her with his bright-blue eyes.

'Well?' his eyes gleamed. 'Will we go to bed and have ravishing sex? Which was our intention before Lucy phoned. Would you like it tender and sensual, or torrid and animalistic? I can do both. Or do you feel like telling me why you still can't give me an answer?'

'Johnny!' she laughed to take the sting out of her words. 'You know I'm out of sorts after the past couple of days and I can't take anything seriously right now. Stop being so mischievous.'

'Mischievous? Thanks a bunch.'

'With all the upset this week, I can't think straight—'

'For God's sake, Ellie,' he suddenly huffed, 'you're being ridiculous. What we all need is some good news. Like an engagement. Or a wedding. I can't believe you're still giving me the brush off.'

'I'm not giving you the brush off,' she said. 'Can't you see it's a bad week for me?'

'Yes, I know you've been upset but you're mad to let all that shit about some long-dead, crummy musician get to you. It's ancient history and it'll be over before you know it. You could make this the best week of your life. Hmm?'

She hesitated.

'I'm beginning to think you've no intention of marrying me,' Johnny said.

'Hush,' she said, leaning in close to him and silencing him by placing a finger across his lips. She was conscious that her green eyes were cajoling as she looked into his eyes. 'We'll talk about this soon, very soon, I promise.'

'Don't you believe me when I tell you I love you?'

'Yes, and it's great, but I just want to be sure we're making the right decision.'

'What could be more right than two people who love each other getting married?' He sighed. 'I just don't get you at times.'

'Maybe that's why you're still with me,' she said, softening her words with a smile. 'I'm a mystery to you.'

'Sometimes, I feel like I'm not with you at all.'

'Let's go to bed.' She put her hand on his thigh – sex always distracted Johnny – but he brushed it away.

'That's not the answer.' He looked at her steadily and said, 'Ellie Morgan, I'm asking you for the last time and I'm giving you two weeks to decide if you want to marry me.'

Chapter 2

Ellie's bedroom and en-suite took over the first floor of Laurel View. Her room was wide and spacious, and decorated in soft hues of oyster and pale blue. She had a big, king-sized bed with a pale-blue throw over the oyster-shade duvet, and expansive, mirrored wardrobes. Best of all, she had dormer windows that looked beyond laurel woods to the cityscape and skylights that allowed her to see the stars when she lay in bed at night.

When Johnny came out of the shower and joined her in bed, she didn't need to feign sleep or tell him she felt exhausted. He turned on his side and ignored her, showing her the full measure of his annoyance. There had to be something drastically wrong for Johnny to ignore the possibility of sex. Still, she was relieved. Emotionally drained, she didn't feel the least bit sexy or desirable.

His words echoed in her head. What could be more right? What was wrong with her? Why couldn't she commit? Vivienne would love to see Ellie settling down at last. Would love to see grandchildren on the scene. Lucy would be pleased. She'd said he was a great catch, and approval like that, coming from her careless, indifferent sister, was approval indeed. Even Miranda would be delighted. Miranda would come home for an engagement party and then the wedding. It would be a big family celebration, something happy to lift them up, far up and away from the long-legged shadow of Zach Anderson, wouldn't it?

All she had to say was yes. Simple, really. Yet, as she lay in bed, grateful that Johnny had fallen asleep, she had never felt more confused.

From the minute they had started to date, they'd captured everyone's imagination. On the one hand Ellie had been a little embarrassed with the gossip fodder and photo opportunities that she and Johnny Tyler had generated as they partied with Dublin's celebrities in the glitziest clubs and bars. On the other hand, she hadn't been willing to restrict her social life and be dictated to by the fickle media.

When they were described as the city's sexiest golden couple, Ellie found it hilarious, but she didn't need to look at their photographs in the social pages to know that they looked good together.

'Tall, beautiful Ellie, successful fashion designer,' was how she was frequently described, and sometimes her name was linked to her mother's star, 'Ellie, the daughter of Vivienne Morgan, the renowned Irish actress, and the eldest of the stunning Morgan sisters.'

She laughed when Johnny was described as the ultimate 'dress-hire maverick'. To her, Johnny was simply Johnny. He was fun to be with. He made her laugh and he was easy and relaxed. She had heard of Johnny before he had heard of her. Then again, everyone knew of the swashbuckling Johnny, his champagne-party nights and troop of gorgeous girlfriends, as well as his award-winning dress-hire business in Jervis Alley. But it wasn't until he was booked to supply the suits for the shoot of Ellie's autumn/winter collection that they got together.

The new collection was Ellie's big chance to cement her reputation. She'd already caused a ripple on the Irish fashion scene with her first two collections and she was about to launch her much-anticipated third collection. It would be showcased in Dublin Fashion Week and promoted in a leading weekend supplement spread, as well as a television fashion slot.

Her passion was for occasion wear. Dresses, coats and jackets that women would enjoy wearing, and that could be dressed up or down with a change of accessories. Her Ellie Belle label was elegant and feminine, softly tailored with an understated sexy vibe, and she was fast finding a niche for herself in a contracted market where women were conscious that every item in their wardrobe needed to work for them. Ellie knew that quality was the key and she worked with linen, tweed and wool, sourcing most of her fabrics in Irish mills.

Claire, Ellie's business manager who also took on the roles of stylist, marketing and production, overseeing a team of local seamstresses, had suggested using a couple of male models in formal jackets to contrast with Ellie's ravishing outfits and Ellie loved the idea. On the day of the fashion shoot, she found herself more nervous than excited as the hours progressed and she saw what had begun as a single idea in her head come to life, fully formed, real and fluid, on the models in front of her. Textured coats and curvy hour-glass dresses in autumn palettes of scarlet and gold, with cobalt blue and dramatic purple for contrast. She was impressed with Johnny's sheer professionalism. Beautifully dressed in a sharp suit and ice-white shirt, he seemed to know exactly what was required of his suits to best foil Ellie's work as dazzlingly as possible, and his energy was contagious.

'Hey,' he said. 'Why don't I kit out one of the ladies?' he suggested, going over to his selection of suits on a rail. 'Any one of them would look sensational in a tux. It would be an amazing way of drawing your collection together.'

'Yes, it's worth a go,' she said, even as Claire spoke to the models and they eventually agreed on the six foot, Tanya with the razor cheekbones and full, red lips.

Ellie watched Johnny's patient hands as he styled Tanya, giving her the keen focus of his attention as he adjusted the dress shirt, carefully fixed the bow tie, and almost caressed the lapels of the black, tuxedo jacket into place with seductive precision. She found herself mesmerised for a moment and wishing she could swap places with Tanya. He caught her staring at him and winked at her.

When the shoot wrapped up, a few of them went on to a cocktail bar on South William Street.

'Fantastic results,' Claire said. 'This collection will be a winner. I can feel it. Well done you.'

'Well done *you*,' Ellie tipped her glass to Claire's. 'I don't know where I'd be without you.'

'Nor me without you.'

Claire had studied with Ellie years ago, and Ellie trusted her completely.

'I'm heading off in a minute,' Claire said. 'And not before time. I think Johnny Tyler will burst with frustration if he doesn't get to sit near you soon. Seems to me like you've well and truly brought a committed bachelor like him to his knees – the way you do most men.'

Ellie smiled. She'd noticed Johnny's eyes raking in her direction several times, and she'd felt a steadily burning anticipation growing inside her. Sure enough, the minute Claire left, he slid onto the banquette beside her and she wasn't quick enough to prevent him from picking up her mobile phone, his fingers flying across the screen.

'What are you up to?' she asked, bemused.

'I'm making sure you have my private number,' he grinned at her with friendly blue eyes. 'So you'll have no excuse not to call me.'

'And why should I want to call you?'

'Because you have to allow me to style you some time,' he said, reaching out and gently twirling strands of her long, dark hair. Her scalp prickled. 'I can see your fabulous hair falling across the satin lapel of one of my jackets,' he said admiringly. 'As well as that, I think you and I could be good for each other.'

'Yeah, right,' she laughed self-consciously, having no intention of taking him up on his offer.

'I'm serious,' he said. 'I predict you're going to be big, Ellie Morgan, very big. You have the drive and the ambition. I have ambitions too, and I see no reason why we couldn't work together for our greater good. I could use some of your elegant creations in my own promotional material. Together, we could be a fantastic success. Dublin needs entrepreneurs like us to rise again.'

'Who said I was in this for the money?' she said, conscious that she was flirting with him, and liking it.

'Did I mention money?' he grinned. 'I should hope you're in this for the sake of your art. As I am, of course. Success is all about making the world a better place in big ways and small ways, and that includes creating an esteem-building gown or putting together a confidence-inducing look. Okay, there might be fringe benefits, but someone has to keep the top-of-the-range car dealers and fine-wine distributors in business.'

She laughed. 'I like doing what I do,' she told him. 'I love creating something out of nothing. I'm very grateful that I can do it full time and that it keeps the roof over my head.'

'You should have no fear of that. Don't you realise how talented you are?' Johnny said.

'The world of fashion is fickle and challenging,' she said. 'Even when I left school and started in the Academy, I wasn't sure if it was just an indulgent childhood hobby or something I could support myself with,' she admitted. She was too modest to tell him that she'd won Young Designer of the Year after she graduated from the Academy at the age of twenty-one. It helped to convince her that she was on the right road and answer any doubts she might have had, doubts as to whether she was merely indulging herself with her creative passions or if she was seriously talented.

'I spent a few years working with some of Ireland's and London's big names,' she continued, 'building up my skills and experience. But it wasn't until I was in my thirties that I decided to risk branching out on my own. So now I work from a studio that is annexed to my house and my range, Ellie Belle, is available countrywide, in most high-end boutiques. So that's me.'

She smiled at him and stopped short of admitting her real fear that she'd wake up some morning and not be able to think of a single idea, that a piece of cloth would feel like paper in her hands.

She also stopped short of delving into her family history – her late, beloved father, Edward Morgan, a respected barrister, who had been steady at the helm of the family and had provided a grounding force for his two daughters, and Vivienne, his colourful, extrovert, actress wife. Polar opposites, their passion for each other had been plain to see, and Ellie and Miranda's childhood had been warmly secure under the blanket of love showered upon them. Then, when Ellie was fourteen and Miranda just ten, Edward had suffered a massive stroke just before he left for his office on a bright, summery morning. It was a blessing, they murmured, when he passed away twenty-four hours later. A numbed, disbelieving Ellie didn't understand. What blessing could have taken her beloved dad away from her? He had been in his early forties, far too young to die. Only later did she understand that the brain damage the stroke had caused would have severely reduced her kind and clever father's quality of life if he had survived. At the time, it had been a cataclysmic event for them all.

Then, just a year later, Vivienne had met Zach.

Some people, the kinder ones, said Vivienne must have been unhinged after Edward's sudden death. And Ellie had long buried the memory of those painful days.

But all of this would keep for another time.

'I like the sound of you,' Johnny said. 'I want to hear more. A lot more.'

'I think it's your turn to do some talking,' she said.

She liked the look of him too, his blue eyes that were warm and sexy, the masculine nearness of him, and his citrus scent as they sat close together on the leather banquette and talked as though they were the only two in the cocktail bar. By degrees, their group dispersed and, after a while, she looked up and saw that they were, indeed, the only two left of their original group, and a couple of hours had gone by.

'Are you in a hurry home?' he asked.

'Um, not really,' she said, deciding she liked him enough to let the night unfold a little more.

Johnny brought her to his favourite Michelin-starred restaurant, securing the best table in the house even though he had no reservation. Ellie was amused with the stir of interest they caused as they followed the maître d' to their table, but she soon forgot about that, as she became even more amused with Johnny's charming, larger-than-life attitude towards everything. He made her laugh with his self-deprecating stories of dress-hire disasters. She was half aware of the glances of other diners being drawn to the good-looking couple at the prime table, and she had the best fun she'd had in a long time.

'I hope you're still not in a hurry home,' he said after their meal as he poured the last of a bottle of Bordeaux into her glass.

'Why, what else could I be doing?'

'I can think of lots of things,' he said, grinning wickedly. 'Unfortunately, they're not remotely suitable for a first date.'

They went on to the VIP area of a glitzy nightclub and were photographed sipping champagne as they looked into each other's eyes. Immediately, gossip journalists were calling them the hottest new couple in town.

There had been plenty of men in Ellie's life, but never anyone who tempted her long enough to consider supplementing her busy career with marriage and babies. In her twenties, her energies had gone into gaining experience for her career. In her thirties, she was busy making a name for herself and much preferred to hold on to her independence. Although she found Johnny attractive, she didn't think he was The One and she felt sure it would only be a short-lived relationship, given his bachelor reputation. Still, it would be fun for a while and it suited her – but she wasn't going to hop into bed with him too easily and be just another conquest.

When they were still together six weeks later, Ellie found it impossible to hold him off any longer, and invited him into her bedroom, where on clear nights the city gleamed through her dormer windows and stars peeked through the skylights. In the calm, dimly lit bedroom, he undressed her very slowly, deepening her desire with short butterfly kisses moving seamlessly into long, sensual kisses, while his hands ran across and around her curves with a firm, yet tender, touch.

Johnny's body was just as strong and hard and well endowed as she'd expected. 'You've been worth waiting for, Ellie Morgan,' he said, smiling at her as he pushed her back across the bed.

'Good,' she said.

When she finally opened her legs and wrapped them around him, feeling him surge deeply inside her, she smiled up at him, and through her skylight windows she could see the outline of the night-time heavens framing his face.

But she didn't see any glittering stars. Not that first time. Nor any time.

Although it was good – Johnny was a hungry lover and he always made her come, twice or three times, gasping for breath and weak in the aftermath – whenever they made love, there was still an empty space. When he pulled her into his arms, it was easier to snuggle into the breadth of his shoulders and go with the flow rather than look into the private depths of her heart.

Ellie didn't really know if she had any depth, or if this was it. Was she destined to be happy and successful in her career but always stopping short of that vital something inside her being touched?

As the months rolled by, Ellie and Johnny went from success to success. They were fêted and admired by their friends and the media, and they gave rise to endless speculation about when they would tie the knot. Ellie laughed it all off. Johnny was the perfect fun-loving boyfriend; warm hearted, generous and with a big appetite for life, including sex. It was all too easy to coast with him along the surface of everything, and not take their relationship too seriously. Johnny had a spectacular, four-bed penthouse apartment with even better views of the city's panorama about a ten-minute drive from Ellie's split-level bungalow. Sometimes, she spent the night or the weekend with him; other times he came to her. The arrangement suited Ellie perfectly. She had her own space, and sex with Johnny on tap. She thought it suited him equally well.

Before she knew it, two years had gone by in a flash. She knew other single women of her age were panicking about their ticking body clocks, but the few times Ellie stopped to think about it, she knew she couldn't even imagine bringing a baby into this world unless she was in a fully committed relationship. Which meant she didn't feel she was in a fully committed relationship with Johnny.

When Johnny began to talk about wanting to wake up beside her every morning, it was something she was able to ignore. But when he asked her to marry him, that was not so easy to ignore.

'I'll be forty next year,' he'd said, turning to her in bed one night recently. 'I'm not getting any younger. I think it's time I made an honest woman of you. What do you say, Ellie?'

'I hope that's not a proposal,' she'd joked, raising herself on her elbow and brushing her hair out of her face. 'I never saw myself marrying a forty-year-old man.'

'Not even a rich forty-year-old man?' he said hopefully.

'Especially not a rich forty-year-old man,' she smiled, moving in to kiss his cheek to take any sting out of her words.

But Johnny wasn't so easily distracted. 'Why do I feel you're only half-joking?'

Ellie pushed away her unease. 'It's a bit late to be having this kind of talk,' she said gently. 'We're both up at the crack of dawn.'

'Okay, it'll hold,' he said. 'But just for now.'

Since then he'd asked her again, and she'd brushed off that proposal just as easily for the simple reason that she didn't know how she felt about him as far as full commitment was concerned. Did she want to spend the rest of her life with him and have his babies? Was the sex between them the best it could be? Was there more? Was there really such a thing as feverish, explosive, exhilarating sex? Surely if she imagined it, it had to exist.

Or was she living in fantasy land?

Chapter 3

*I*t was early on Wednesday morning when Vivienne
Morgan strolled out onto the deck of the *Mediterranean
Enterprise*, plucked off her Ray-Bans, turned her face to the
rising sun and leaned against the rails. In this part of the
Adriatic, the sea was a crystal-clear turquoise, and she loved
they way the warm, seductive shade contrasted beautifully with
the blue-grey slate of the rocky islets around the Croatian coast-
line. As the cruise ship glided majestically up the straits north of
Dubrovnik, she secured her Dolce & Gabbana wrap a little
closer around her shoulders against the cool morning breeze.
For a nanosecond, the calming beauty of the morning was
soured when she compared the turquoise panorama unrolling
in front of her with the spooky, black waters of a Canadian lake
that had flashed across her television screen a couple of nights
ago.

She was glad her attention was snagged by a lone swimmer
powering energetically across the swimming pool on the nearby
deck. Her eyes narrowed when she caught a flash of his bronzed,

lean torso as he reached the end and double-flipped back the way he had come.

Carlos.

He was, no doubt, getting rid of his pent-up energy. Energy he had probably anticipated expending in her bed after his increasing efforts to entice her. It was, of course, out of the question, before even the damned news item about Zach had shaken her. She replaced her sunglasses and watched him covertly from behind her shades until he'd finally had enough and in a graceful leap, jumped out of the pool. He picked up a white towel, dabbing it roughly against his dripping wet, shoulder-length hair and sweeping it across his gleaming chest before securing it around his hips.

And then he saw her watching him. He waved, before disappearing from view and reappearing several moments later to join her by the railings.

'Vivienne!'

'Hi, Carlos.'

'It is early for you to be up and about.'

'I couldn't sleep.'

'I couldn't sleep either,' he said, his gaze dropping to her generous breasts.

She felt a spark of desire deep inside her and willed it to go away.

A casual flirtation had hummed between them from the first night they'd met on the eastern Mediterranean cruise, when they'd found themselves seated at the same dining table. As the ship took to the seas off Venice, Carlos had sat with his arm along the back of Vivienne's chair and had chatted quietly with her. A doctor based in Seville, his marriage had broken up but the cruising holiday had already been booked to celebrate his fiftieth birthday, so he was taking it alone.

'You have to be Irish,' he'd said, his warm brown eyes roving over her hair and sweeping down to linger on the paleness of her slender neck.

'How on earth did you guess,' she'd laughed, putting her hand to her hair, the once fiery-red now toned to a deep russet-gold. It was softly feathered around her face, which made her look a lot younger than someone approaching sixty-two.

They'd sparked off each other as the cruise got under way, Vivienne swiftly realising that he wanted to sleep with her. And goodness knows, she was tempted, but after her reckless dalliance with Zach, she'd sworn off men and sex for life. But having experienced lust and desire, from the warmth of married passion with Edward to the explosive desire that Zach had ignited within her, she found it impossible not to be tempted from time to time. And she'd had opportunities – even back in Ireland, there were lots of admirers.

And sometimes she met someone like Carlos.

But she'd learned to ignore her desires, and if Carlos had shaken her resolve a little, the news item on Zach had crashed into her world and brought her up sharply, plunging her back there again and tainting the prospect of any light flirting with Carlos. The seductive spell that he'd cast around her had burst like a bubble. She'd managed to avoid him since and had dined alone in her cabin the past couple of evenings.

'Not long to go now,' Carlos said, leaning against the rail.

'No, just two more nights,' she tilted her mouth in a rueful smile. She knew he'd sensed her withdrawal and was puzzled by it, but there was no way she could explain. She flicked her eyes away from his tanned arms and the way his biceps flexed as he grasped the rail.

'And then for you?'

'A short break in Venice, and then, home.' She didn't tell him that she was on the cruise to take time out of a hectic schedule on the orders of her doctor, or that she had a further month of enforced relaxation before she went into rehearsals for the leading role in *Big Maggie*, the iconic, John B. Keane play, in the Abbey Theatre in Dublin. That would be too much information.

'Home to my family, my daughters,' she said, deliberately bringing them into the conversation for the first time, and putting a wedge between them.

'I see. You have daughters.'

'Yes, three.' *And they mean the world to me, and I dare not risk hurting them again, so what was I thinking, flirting with you?*

'Are they as lovely as you?'

'No, they are far more beautiful.' She felt choked for a moment, thinking of them: tall, gracious Ellie, dark haired like her father, but with green eyes even more sparkling than her own; Miranda, the one in the middle, who most resembled her in looks, yet was quiet and introspective compared to her effervescence; and Lucy. Her heart clutched when she thought of her youngest daughter, who had the best of both her mother and father: Zach's height and thickly fringed eyes, although hers were a light, innocent-looking grey compared to his dark, brooding grey, and shades of her hair, but more beautiful again as her long tresses were a distinctive, bright gold – a Botticelli-angel gold, her hair was been labelled.

'You are lucky, to have three children,' Carlos said. 'I have a son, just the one.'

Now they were talking like polite strangers who had nothing much in common, the way you chat to people sitting next to you on an airline flight just before you land. Any excitement that had crackled between them had dissolved. Carlos' eyes were full of a respectful distance, instead of the warm anticipation they'd shown from the start. They chatted a bit longer and then, eventually, Carlos excused himself. She felt a slight pang of regret as she watched him lope off and take the stairs to the lower deck two at a time, but it was nothing like the regret she'd felt watching the news item on Zach.

She hoped her daughters hadn't been too upset. Her beautiful, attractive, gorgeous daughters; all different, yet equally loved. They meant everything in life to her. The last thing she wanted was Zach Anderson reappearing on the scene, reminding them all of the time that she had well and truly lost the plot. After the news item, she'd spoken to both Ellie and Miranda, deliberately making light of the whole thing, as though it was totally inconsequential. Not giving it any power was by far the best way to react.

Lucy hadn't answered her call, so she'd left a message, telling her in an upbeat tone that she'd been perfectly right to ignore those stupid reporters, that it would all blow over in a day or two.

If you ignored it, it would go away, wouldn't it?

She stood for a few moments, soaking up the sight of the rippling turquoise water. Sometimes, she still couldn't believe the mess she'd made of it all, or how the pain of Edward's death had blindly thrust her into another man's arms.

She'd met and fallen in love with the warm, intelligent Edward when she was twenty-one, and they'd married within a year, much to the disgust of his parents. Respected judges, who were horrified that their barrister son had become embroiled with an actress, they had never accepted her, especially when she'd gone on to secure a leading role in one of Ireland's most popular soap operas. But their marriage had been wonderful, and she'd felt blessed with happiness when first Ellie and then Miranda had been born. She would never have got through those lonely, tortuous months after Edward's sudden death if it hadn't been for the strong support of Florence, her mother, who, widowed herself, had some inkling as to how much she missed Edward. For a while, her daughters were without both parents, as Vivienne was lost to them, leaving her mother to pick up the pieces.

She began to put her life back together around the time of Edward's first anniversary, a day she'd been dreading so much that she'd asked her mother to take care of the girls.

'I'll look after them,' Florence offered. 'We'll go shopping and drop into White's on the Green for lunch. We'll have some fun. But after this, Vivienne, it's time to get your life back. I know things have been tough, but you've spent a year wallowing in misery and it's not fair on your daughters. I'll be here for you any time, but Ellie and Miranda have had it tough as well, and even if only for their sakes, you must return to the land of the living.'

At first Vivienne had been outraged. How dare her mother speak to her like that? Surely she must appreciate the depths of her daughter's grief? But it was the kick she had needed. As the day slowly progressed, she realised that spending it on her own in a flood of self-indulgent recollection, sitting in despair or crying at length into her pillow in a storm of loss and self-pity, wasn't going to bring Edward back. Nothing would.

She would, she realised in a sudden moment of clarity, have been far better off spending the long day with her daughters, going shopping for treats and enjoying a good lunch. In her total self-absorption, she wasn't being fair to them. Ellie was fifteen going on sixteen, quite tall and very self-conscious of her height. Vivienne knew that the last year had been very difficult for her, struggling through a clumsy teenage phase on top of missing her father, while her mother had been too dejected to help. Miranda was a quiet and reserved eleven-year-old, on the cusp of adolescence, and she needed a mother's guiding hand to get through the next few years.

Then, two weeks later it had been her fortieth birthday. She might rage that she was far too young to be a widow, but who was she raging against? Who was listening? Nobody. Fabulous, flirty, forty, some of her birthday cards encouraged. Life begins, they urged. Forty could, indeed, be her prime, and there was nothing to stop her life from beginning again. If she wanted.

And, she remembered, that had been the frame of mind she'd been in when she was invited to guest on a Saturday-night chat show, where she'd met Zach Anderson in the green room. An up-and-coming rock musician, he'd been ten years younger than her. Brash and outgoing on the surface, he was the total opposite to her modest, quietly spoken, late husband. She'd known she was on the rebound, but she'd fallen for him immediately. The liaison had lasted barely three months, and Lucy had been the result of that careless, unbridled passion.

At the time, her hungry infatuation had defied all logic, and she'd been heedless to the effect it would have on Ellie and Miranda. Then again, she reasoned, as her thoughts spiralled around, if she hadn't met Zach, she wouldn't have had the joy of Lucy. And in the next breath, she thought of the way Lucy had been left without a father – because soon after she'd discovered she was pregnant, Zach had gone to Canada and, around the time Lucy celebrated her first birthday, he'd died, without ever seeing his daughter.

Zach! Surely there would be no repercussions, after all these years. Vivienne leaned on the rails and gazed across to the spit of land where she caught glimpses of white-washed hotels and blue swimming pools sheltered behind landscaped grounds rimming the foreshore.

By now, more early-rising holiday-makers were up and about.

She heard splashes coming from the swimming pool and laughter from the games area. Ahead of them lay the turquoise swathe of the Adriatic and the shimmering horizon. Yet despite the beauty of the morning, Vivienne could do nothing to prevent an old seed of anxiety from bursting open inside her.

Chapter 4

The first time Miranda had attended a meeting in the board-room of the XAM Systems Inc financial division, a thick, grey mist had cloaked the view of Hong Kong beyond the floor-to-ceiling windows. Then, two weeks into her new job, a meeting had been held on a clear, crispy afternoon and as she'd crossed the threshold, she'd gasped aloud at the view of the city.

'Like it?' a tall, well-built guy had asked.

'*Like*? It's, God, wow. Spectacular. Has it been there all the time?' She'd flushed, realising too late how ridiculous she'd sounded. But she couldn't help it. From the thirty-fifth floor, the board-room windows had a bird's eye view down across the skyscrapers of Hong Kong island and, on a mist-free day, there was something almost mesmerising about the pattern of it all. The columns of steel and glass looked like silent sentinels and seemed to fall away gracefully as they followed the downward slope of the island. Far below, you could also catch a glimpse of the iconic harbour.

The tall guy was perfectly polite in the face of her embarrass-ment. He merely smiled kindly and said, 'Yes, on a misty day it's hard to believe the splendour that's behind the veil. I think it's beautiful.'

Beautiful it certainly was. Miranda had thought that the view of Dublin city from Ellie's back garden was fabulous until she saw this. Then again, there were lots of things about Ellie's life that she had found impressive, and bigger, and better than her own, until she'd come here and had begun to forge her own life in this vibrant city.

'Jesus! *Hong Kong*? Why so far away?' Ellie had asked, when Miranda first began to talk about it.

'It's not that far,' Miranda was annoyed that she'd immediately felt on the defensive. She'd expected objections because she knew Ellie would be unhappy and would try to talk her out of it. *Try* to talk her out of it – there was no way she'd succeed. Miranda's mind was made up. Even though she'd never been to Hong Kong and hadn't a clue what it was like, it would suit her purpose just nicely. The New York of Asia, someone in the office had said. So it couldn't be all that foreign.

'At least I have a job lined up,' Miranda pointed out in an agreeable tone of voice.

'A *job*?' Ellie had spluttered. 'With your financial expertise and experience in Ryan Johnson? I can't understand why you're giving it all up, especially during a recession. If you need a change that badly why not try somewhere closer to home – London or Brussels, perhaps? Somewhere I could pop for a weekend. Hong Kong is hardly a girly weekend destination.'

'Maybe I want to spread my wings,' Miranda pointed out.

'Now you're talking like a gap-year student instead of think-ing of settling down and—'

'Who says I should be settling down? And what about you? You're older than me, but you haven't settled down.'

'I'm not the domestic, happy-ever-after kind, but you are,' Ellie said in her pleasant-but-determined voice that couldn't be argued with.

'Why is it always one law for Miranda and another one for Ellie?'

'Don't be daft, I don't know where you got that idea from.'

Even though they were sisters, their lives were totally different. Miranda lived by the rules; Ellie seemed to write them to suit herself – and Lucy totally ignored them.

'What about Graham?' Ellie probed. 'I thought you were keen on him?'

'I was,' Miranda admitted, 'but he wasn't so keen on me.'

Ellie tipped her head to one side. 'Ah. So you're running away?'

'Now you're the one who's being daft,' Miranda said, managing to sound suitably annoyed with her sister even though she was dead right. As usual.

'Hey, sis, is this your way of telling me you've been dumped?'

Miranda stayed silent and gave her a rueful grin.

Ellie drew her in for a hug, in the way only Ellie could, a warm and meaningful hug. 'I hope Graham hasn't upset you,' she said. 'I don't think he deserved you anyway, so it's his loss and there's plenty more fish . . . bigger and better fish.'

'I'm sure there is, somewhere,' Miranda said, her voice muffled against Ellie's jumper, the expression in her eyes hidden, the scent of her sister's White Linen perfume in her nostrils.

Miranda thought how Ellie hadn't a clue what it was like to be dumped. Her tall, beautiful sister, with the glittering green eyes, seemed impervious to men, and the way she held them in thrall. Her attraction had something to do with her warm smile that promised you the world, but behind that smile you sensed she was like a shining star – beautiful to look at, but out of reach. A challenge for most hot-blooded men. She was even giving the charismatic bachelor, Johnny Tyler, a run for his money.

Ellie drew back, held her by the shoulders, and looked at her searchingly. 'But that doesn't mean you have to desert all of us and go to the other side of the world.'

'You're exaggerating. It's not that far.'

But it was too far for a weekend, which was just what she needed. Ellie would be shocked if she knew that Miranda wanted to spread her wings as far away from the bosom of her family as possible – for although Lucy was in London, she might as well be living next door. It wasn't just to mend her rejected heart, Miranda wanted time and space to be herself, to stop being one of the Morgan sisters for a while and start to be someone in her own right.

Ellie only realised Miranda was completely serious when she sold her car and rented out her apartment in Dublin's trendy docklands. Miranda only realised she was finally going through with this major life change when she stored some of her belongings and mementoes in the attic of Vivienne's house in Dún Laoghaire, the big roomy house the family had been reared in. Then feeling scared at the enormity of what she was doing, even though she was supposed to be clever and brainy, and most gap kids would do it in their sleep, she flew out to Heathrow on a Monday morning, and from there to a new life in Hong Kong.

On this Wednesday afternoon, three months after she'd arrived in Hong Kong, she made sure to grab a chair on the side of the oval table that faced the boardroom window. You were supposed to be at a disadvantage sitting on this side of the table, with the light falling across your face while the person opposite had their face in the shadow, but she chose it deliberately so she could look out at the view and remind herself that she was a million miles from Dublin.

The meeting had been called to inform the XAM Financial Unit of the full significance of the upcoming quarterly report and outline exactly what was required of them in terms of information and deadlines. The room was packed to capacity. Death by PowerPoint, she felt like uttering, as the detailed presentation proceeded. She was bored within a minute and stifled a yawn as best she could. Her eyes strayed across to the window and rested on the view.

But this afternoon, not even the spectacular view could stop her heart from plummeting to her toes as she recalled the way the old family skeleton had been dragged up out of its watery grave. Thanks to the time difference, she'd caught the late-night news programme in Hong Kong first thing on Monday morning. That had been a couple of days ago, and although her job had been a welcome distraction during the day, she'd slept fitfully since, worrying about how they were all coping – Ellie, Vivienne and Lucy.

Exactly the kind of thing she'd come to Hong Kong to avoid.

Even more worrying was the email from Ellie that had dropped, without warning, into her inbox soon after lunch that afternoon. Miranda had almost gasped aloud as she scrolled through it.

'Just to let you know that Lucy is home and spending a couple of days with me, as Mum is away. She left London in a hurry because – you'll never guess – some weirdo planted a funeral wreath with Zach Anderson's name on it outside the door of her apartment. I'm gobsmacked and furious, but trying not to make too much of it in front of Lucy. She's upset enough and doesn't want Mum to know. Lucy said the card didn't give any indication of where it had come

47

from, so she can't trace the asshole who sent it . . . rather scary stuff, don't you think?'

Scary stuff? It was absolutely horrible. Poor Lucy! Just as well she had gone home to Ellie for a few days. But who could want to distress her like that? Even though Miranda was already exhausted, she knew that thoughts of this awful wreath and Lucy's upset would keep her awake that night. As the meeting progressed, she tried to stifle another yawn, but the kind, well-built guy she'd first met in the boardroom all those weeks ago was sitting across the table and he caught her eye mid-yawn and winked at her. She coloured, and hastily looked away. She now knew him to be Christian Blake and his desk was down the floor from hers. Christian was Australian and, with thick blond hair, his broad shoulders filling his cream linen jacket, and tie slung rebelliously at half-mast, he was most definitely out of place. The majority of those in the boardroom were Asian, their slight frames impeccably clothed in razor-sharp suits, jet-black hair slicked back with not a disobedient strand daring to move out of place, and an air of focused energy that Miranda found impressive.

Across the table, Christian was trying to catch her eye, but she did her best to ignore him. He fidgeted with a sheet of paper and, to her amusement, he appeared to be making a paper aeroplane. She shook her head and threw him a sharp glance and his blue eyes glinted with mischief as he met her eyes and mouthed, 'Gotcha!'

When Miranda had first come to Hong Kong, it had been like being thrust into a strange but enormous melting pot of bustle and diversity. Compared to the reception rooms in the family home in Dún Laoghaire, or her docklands apartment, her living space in Hong Kong on the twentieth floor of a soulless

48

high-rise block was a tiny shoe box. Her job in XAM wasn't half as challenging as her financial consulting career in Ryan Johnson had been.

And Hong Kong was a million miles from Dublin in terms of culture, noise and activity. She hadn't ventured very far by herself, finding the pulsating city almost too much to get a handle on, but after a couple of weeks, when she'd felt more settled into her apartment and job, she'd begun to socialise with her colleagues at the weekends. They were a group drawn from all nationalities, though mainly Asian, along with a scattering of German and British twentysomethings who were working on contract with XAM, and, more and more, she was noticing Christian. There was always a reception of some sort to go to – a drinks party, a publicity promotion. She'd found it awkward at first, to be sitting in a foreign hotel or bar, miles away from home, surrounded by such a cosmopolitan mixture of nationalities, but Mai and Sara were friendly and chatty and, much to her surprise, Christian often singled her out.

She told herself he was just being polite and kind in helping her find her feet. Other times she was jittery with nerves when she found herself to be the sole focus of his attention, even though she loved the way he often drew her off into a corner where they could talk in peace away from the crowd. Those times, she kept expecting his gaze to wander over her shoulder, to someone else beyond her – to someone prettier or more outgoing or higher in the pecking order, but so far that hadn't happened. At thirty-four, he was a year older than her and had been in Hong Kong for six months.

'I'm here to gain experience in the general field of financial management,' he'd said. 'I could have done that back in Oz, but I want to see a bit of the world.'

'Same here,' she'd said. 'Just getting some experience.'

He'd slanted a disbelieving eyebrow. 'Hmm. I'd say you have brains to burn, Miranda Morgan, and could buy and sell the whole operation.'

'How did you guess?' she'd said, laughing as though it was a joke, congratulating herself on her nonchalance. No way was she prepared to reveal that she'd a Masters in Economics at Trinity College and had graduated top of her class, or that she'd sometimes appeared on Irish current-affairs television programmes, debating the state of the nation. She definitely was not going to tell him why she'd walked out of a high-flying career to come to work in Hong Kong at a level well below her capabilities.

Christian reminded her of her father at times, because even though he was a six-foot hunk and an all-Australian male, he was quietly spoken and charming, and made her feel looked after, as though she was someone important.

Her father! He'd been gone from her life for what felt like hundreds of years, but was still very much alive in her heart. Which was why she was finding it hard to cope with Zach Anderson being on the scene again, even as a ghostly presence. Forget it, a little voice said. You're miles away from all of that. And forget about Ellie and Lucy and the way they almost smothered you with their bright, confident personalities as they flitted about the home in Dún Laoghaire, taking charge, taking control, often ignoring you in their determination to score points off each other and come out on top. Look instead at the way Christian is smiling at you across the table. Feel his smile reaching into the dark corners of your heart.

Eventually, the presentation was over and Christian caught up with her in the corridor outside.

'Fancy a beer after work? Just us?'

She had to tilt her head to look up at him and his eyes glinted with expectation, but she didn't break her stride. He'd casually suggested a beer after work a couple of times already and she'd just as casually declined. Now she clutched her handouts close to her chest and wondered why she was behaving like a prim virgin. 'No thanks,' she said. 'I'm going straight home and having an early night.'

'An early night? Lucky guy, whoever he is.'

'An early night, alone.' She hoped she didn't sound too sad.

'Someday, Miranda Morgan, you'll agree to a date with me. I'll win my prize eventually.'

'A beer after work is hardly a date,' she smiled at him. *And I'm scarcely a prize – although maybe a consolation prize.*

'So that's where I'm going wrong. You want something more classy. Hmm. Let me think about that.'

She stepped into the crowded lift, Mai and Sara shuffling back to make space for her, but there wasn't enough room for Christian.

'I'll catch you later,' he said, and she watched as the lift doors whooshed together and shut him out, just like she had.

The best way.

The safest way.

Chapter 5

'*H*ey, big sis, too busy for that lunch you promised me?'

Ellie lifted her head from the sketches strewn across her table to see Lucy sticking her head around the door of her studio, a cheeky grin on her face.

For a fleeting moment, the sight of her sister's pose transported Ellie back in time to the family home in Dún Laoghaire. Lucy had been four or five, and pestering her to watch cartoons. Ellie had been working at her table in her bedroom, totally absorbed in preparations for looming Academy exams, as well as fighting the inner conviction that in believing she had any modicum of talent, she was fooling herself.

'Not now, Lucy,' she'd said, 'maybe another time.'

'That's no good,' Lucy had cried, stamping her foot. Her brows had drawn together beneath her fringe. 'You don't love me,' she'd announced grandiosely. '*Nobody* loves me.' She'd shaken her head vigorously so that her short red hair fanned out on either side of her cheeky face.

'Of course we do,' Ellie had said half-heartedly, her attention focused on the outline of the skirt she was sketching. In her mind's eye, she could visualise the complete design and the sensual, flattering way the material would flow across the model's hips, and she could feel the texture of it in her hand, see how it moved – but some elusive, key ingredient was missing in the translating of this vision from her head to the sketch in front of her. Damn and blast.

Lucy had given a disgusted snort.

'Look, darling, it's just that I'm very busy now,' Ellie had said, holding on to her patience.

'Huh. Why is everybody busy except me?'

As she'd trounced imperiously out of the bedroom, Lucy had pulled Ellie's door behind her with as much strength as she could muster, causing it to slam, and totally breaking Ellie's concentration. Enraged, Ellie had marched across the room, jerking it back open as she'd shouted at Lucy to behave, knowing even then that she was behaving as childishly as Lucy. She'd been marginally relieved to hear Miranda's soothing voice calling to Lucy from the hallway.

Now a grown-up, Lucy strolled into Ellie's studio, which ran the length of her house in Laurel View, and, in the blink of an eye, the vision of her young, truculent sister dissolved and was replaced by a hip, rock-chic twentysomething with gothic eyes, a carefully contrived tumble of hair and a thin, grey jumper over her black, skinny jeans.

'You must have been up early,' Lucy said. 'I think I'll skip brekkie and go straight to lunch.'

Ellie flipped her pencil so that it bounced across the table. 'I was up early, yes. How are you feeling?'

'Miles better.' Lucy stretched her arms over her head so that her pert breasts were thrust up along with the delicate curve of her rib cage, and her slender waist was exposed. 'I'd a great sleep.'

Ellie wished that she felt miles better and that she'd had a great sleep.

On top of her restless night, Johnny had left early that morning, barely muttering goodbye to her, not even pausing for a kiss or to give her a quick cuddle, which was a bad sign. When she'd heard the hall door close behind him, Ellie had felt so flat and depressed that she wanted to burrow under the duvet, close her eyes and stay like that all day.

In the end, with her thoughts going around in circles and her limbs feeling as heavy as lead, Ellie had dragged herself out of bed. Sipping hot coffee in her kitchen, she'd known there was only one way to make it all up to Johnny. She could stop being so elusive and agree to marry him. But marriage meant loving someone wholeheartedly and allowing them to love you equally wholeheartedly. She didn't think she'd ever be ready for that with Johnny – or with anyone. She'd gone into a relationship with Johnny, happily convinced that he wasn't the marrying kind, but thanks to a midlife crisis with his fortieth birthday looming, his goalposts had shifted.

And now she had Lucy sleeping in her guest room, and expecting Ellie to comfort her after the upset of the past few days. Ellie didn't feel she had it within herself to cheer up Lucy. Thoughts of Zach Anderson left another bad taste in her mouth. She'd emailed Miranda to tell her about the obnoxious wreath delivered to Lucy's door. In her studio, she'd made half-hearted attempts at outlining some preliminary sketches for her next spring/summer collection, finding it difficult to come up with any kind of theme. Then she'd found herself wondering about the wreath. Who could have sent it? The guy had been dead twenty years and it was kind of menacing. No wonder Lucy had jumped on a plane home to Dublin. That kind of stunt would upset the most stoic person, never mind a mercurial person like Lucy.

Still, it hadn't disturbed her sister's lie-in because it was after midday before Ellie heard the sounds of her moving around and the muffled roar of the shower, and it was lunch-time before she popped her head around the door.

'Thanks for getting the papers,' Lucy said. 'I had a good scan through them but it looks like I managed to give everyone the slip.'

'Yes,' Ellie smiled. 'The spotlight has moved on to Josh and Abbie and their celebrity marriage bust-up and there's enough shock factor in that story to keep the papers in juicy gossip for the next month. So you're safe for now.'

'But not for too long, I hope.'

'I thought this was what you wanted? That you'd had enough of the front pages?'

Lucy scowled. 'Only when it was about my dad. All that crap about how he died upset me. Wouldn't you be upset if it were *your* dad?' her voice rose as she walked over to the floor-to-ceiling mirror to check her reflection, widening her eyes to check her mascara. She pouted her lips. 'Thing is, Ellie—'

'Look, sis, please forget about it,' Ellie jumped in to reassure her. 'It's long behind you. He was never part of your life. You're doing great. You're making a successful life for yourself. Don't let anything about Zach Anderson drag you down.'

'I won't, but you see, Ellie, I never really gave it much thought before, like, you know,' Lucy's eyes were huge as she gulped, 'if it was a terrible accident or—'

'Don't go there,' Ellie urged, there was something forlorn about Lucy tugging at her heart.

'Yes, but all of a sudden I can't help thinking what it must have been like—'

'There's no point,' Ellie said briskly. 'Think of cheerful things instead,' she said, getting up from her desk. 'I'm going to tidy up here and we're going out to brunch or lunch or whatever right now. Then, tonight, we'll go to the new chick flick in Dundrum. I guarantee that'll have us both laughing. And after that, we'll come home and open a lovely bottle of Chablis.'

Outside it was a cold, but bright, spring day. The flowerbeds were awash with tulips swaying in the light breeze and the city was a grey sprawl in the distance. Ellie walked around to the side of the house and pressed the remote control to open the garage door. She backed out her car and waited while Lucy slid into the passenger seat.

'Wow, new car?' Lucy asked, stroking the cream upholstery. 'I'm dead jealous.'

'It's not exactly brand new, it's a couple of years old,' Ellie pointed out. 'I bought it second hand.'

'Still, a 5 series beamer is just that. And Johnny's driving a merc. You both must be rolling in it.'

Ellie winced at the sound of begrudgery in her sister's voice as she glided out of the gateposts and turned onto the road. Somehow, to Lucy, the grass was always greener. Even as a child, she had always hankered after anything Ellie and Miranda had had, comparing it more favourably with what she'd had – their clothes, make-up and perfume, even their social lives.

'I won the Lotto, didn't I tell you?' she teased.

'What?' Lucy's shock was comical.

'Only joking. When you've been working as long as I have, darling sis, you'll be able to afford a Ferrari.'

'I'll be ancient by then.'

'Yes, and when you're as ancient as I am,' Ellie said smartly, 'you won't have quite the same svelte figure or peachy bum. So it's swings and roundabouts.'

'Have I got a peachy bum?' Lucy asked.

'You certainly had when you were modelling that slinky thong in the lingerie shoot in *Cosmo*.'

Ellie's eyes had popped out of her head at the gymnastic angle of a near-naked Lucy poised over a bath, looking sensational with a sliver of black lace snagged between the wet, glistening curves of her bum.

Lucy giggled. 'I remember that. It took ages to get the angle right. I thought Justin, the photographer, was deliberately taking his time.'

Or maybe Lucy was deliberately teasing him, Ellie thought, sighing to herself.

They turned in at the gates of an old stone farmhouse set back from the road.

'Is this it? It looks nice.'

'Yes, and the food is great.'

The farmhouse restaurant was cosy with wooden floors and a huge rustic fireplace. Against a backdrop of soft music and appetising aromas, trade was brisk with several diners sitting in compact booths and along chintz-covered banquettes. The windows looked out onto a mountain valley rimmed in the distance by a thick green forest. It was a relaxed yet efficient kind of ambience that was perfect for an informal business lunch or a cosy get-together. Ellie felt the slight stir of interest that rippled around as she and Lucy sat in one of the private booths, but with the corporate nature of the clientele, she was happy that they wouldn't be disturbed. They both ordered mineral water and pan-seared fillet of hake on crushed potatoes and a side order of fried artichoke hearts with garlic croutons.

'Delicious,' Lucy said, 'I'm very impressed with where you lunch.'

'Yes, it's not bad,' Ellie said.

Then after a while, Lucy said, 'Sorry if I put my foot in it last night. With Johnny, I mean.'

Ellie's stomach tightened. 'You weren't to know.'

'My head is all over the place after everything that's gone on,' Lucy said, her fingers sifting through her hair and flicking it over her shoulder. Sleek and wavy, it looked almost freshly polished. Ellie was conscious that she was already concealing a few grey hairs, but Lucy had no such worry. 'I've missed a casting as well,' she went on, 'but I don't care – so long as I'm back in London by next week. That's the all-important deadline for the House of Venetia casting.'

'I'm sure you'll be up for it,' Ellie said. As far as her job was concerned, nothing fazed Lucy. Sometimes Ellie gasped at the sheer provocation lurking behind Lucy's angelic face as she strutted her stuff across glossy magazines.

'Do you think so?' Lucy asked, her eyes widening a fraction.

'Of course, you have it all – the looks and the ambition. The only thing, Lucy . . . ' Ellie hesitated, unsure how to phrase her concern.

'Go on,' Lucy frowned.

'Sometimes, I think you attract the wrong kind of publicity.'

Lucy laughed. 'There's no such thing as wrong publicity. You of all people should appreciate the need for constant visibility. I can't help it if the press are always waiting for me to slip up. If I put the tiniest foot wrong, it always seems to come to the attention of the lenses. *And* be magnified out of all proportion. And now,' she smiled, 'I know I shouldn't indulge, but after that main course I'm seriously tempted by the desserts.'

Ellie let the topic drop as they shared a dessert of white chocolate mousse and pink sorbet, topped with cream. And when their coffees arrived, Lucy rested her chin in her hand, gave Ellie a puzzled look and said, 'So getting back to last night, has Johnny really asked you to marry him?'

'He has ...'

'But?'

Ellie shrugged.

'Ellie, this is major, and you're sitting there as though it means nothing. What's up with my sister?' Lucy looked stupefied.

'What difference would a few words and a ring on my finger make?'

'What difference? Hello, you'd be *married*. What if you had kids?' she paused. 'Don't you want kids?'

'Lucy, whoa!' Ellie gave a laugh. 'These are big questions.'

'Yes, but two years – surely you'd have an idea of the answers by now?'

Ellie was conscious more than ever of the gap between them. She had never been as close to Lucy as she was to Miranda. Then again, not even Miranda would understand why Ellie was stalling. It sounded ridiculous that a woman of Ellie's age was looking for bells and whistles and star-spangled banners.

'Marriage is for life,' Ellie said.

Lucy shook her head. 'I don't understand you at all, passing up someone like Johnny.'

Neither do I, Ellie admitted to herself, as she called for the bill.

Chapter 6

$\mathcal{N}$othing could look greyer than Edinburgh when the weather was cold and wet.

Princes Street was full of scurrying shoppers with their heads bent, heedless to anyone else in their rush to get wherever they were going. He had to dive and duck from time to time as the spokes of their brandishing umbrellas almost threatened to take his eye out. The traffic swishing through the rain-washed streets was bumper to bumper, red tail-lights gleaming in the darkening evening. Bus windows were steamy with condensation and full of disembodied heads showing through where the steam had been wiped by an impatient hand. Up to his left, high up on the hill beyond Princes Street Gardens, Edinburgh Castle squatted like a powerful medieval king, surveying all beneath it. Sometimes, he found it an inspiring sight, filling him with the deep, warm certainty of being at home. Other times, like today, it made him feel horribly deflated and as though he had somehow failed the rich heritage it symbolised.

He was wet and cold as he trudged along the streets, and

raindrops trickled uncomfortably inside the upturned collar of his jacket. The day, he thought, reflected almost perfectly the mood he was in. For the swell of expectation that had driven him for the past few weeks, peaking during his recent visit to Canada, had suddenly disappeared, just like Zach Anderson's life and future promise had when he went into the cold, dark lake. Deliberate or accidental? Or something more sinister? No one seemed to know. Misadventure had been the official line. Out there, someone must know the truth. And he'd thought that all the recent publicity he'd managed to generate, including the lakeside vigil he'd planned, might have prompted someone to come forward.

The few things he had discovered, from a trawl through local press articles and the internet, was that the world had known about Zach's plunge into the lake thanks to an early-morning fisherman, sitting a half mile down the bank, who had spotted the rising sun sparking off the motorbike as it sped up the deserted pier, where it gleamed brightly for one moment, suspended between sea and sky, before disappearing from sight. Zach's remains had been brought to the surface, and a month later his ashes had been scattered on the waters off the pier, in accordance with the wishes of his adoptive parents, from whom he'd been estranged. They'd since passed on themselves, so that avenue had been closed to him. It had been a tragic end for the talented musician who'd spent much of his wayward life and stormy youth chasing a dream.

Hands thrust into his pockets, he tramped down the Lothian Road, and with every footstep, his resolve to uncover the truth strengthened. He was drenched to the skin but full of a hard determination by the time he reached Tollcross where he lived in a flat on the fourth floor of a Victorian housing block. The pervasive odour of stale cooking smells followed him up the stairs, along with muffled television sounds and the shrieking cry of a baby. Up on the top floor, patches of bilious green paint were peeling off the walls, revealing an equally sickly beige colour underneath. The skylight in the roof was broken. To his right, there was a blue door; a shining, rich, indigo blue door, that was so totally at odds with everything around it that it jumped out, startling you. Outside this door, he took out a key and paused.

He could suddenly see her there, her paint-smeared hand gripping the brush, and it brought a knife-like pain slicing through his chest.

'A blue hall door gives off positive energy and a sense of calm,' she'd said. 'It signifies abundance and prosperity. Wait until you see – our turn will come.' Her voice with its hint of joyous laughter echoed around the confines of the top landing. He imagined it bubbling up into the atmosphere beyond the ceiling of this dismal landing, up through the broken skylight and out into the clear air.

Our turn will come.

Problem was, she'd believed all that shite. Symbols, meanings, yin and yang and that crappy feng sway – or whatever the feck it was called. He put the key in the lock and felt the old famil-iar wrench in his heart as the door swung open to the empty apartment. He walked in, closed the door behind him and stood for a moment.

Inside, all was clean and shining like a jewel, a far cry from the dilapidated landing. From the neat living room-cum-kitchen, to the orderly bedrooms and bathroom, the flat echoed with a deep silence. He took off his wet clothes and showered.

As he towelled his hair, raking it back into dark spikes, he glowered at his eyes in the mirror. Eyes were the mirror of the soul and, right now, his were dark and empty. Dressed in jeans and a jumper, he went out to the living room, where the cushions were still perfectly aligned on the sofa exactly as she'd left them, and her novel with the pink, escapist cover on the coffee table still held the bookmark in place.

Four months. It felt like yesterday.

In one sense, his turn *had* come, because in place of a shabby thirty-two-inch television, he now had a state-of-the-art plasma set. His mobile had been upgraded to an iPhone. He turned on the television, pressing buttons on the remote control and scrolling through options until he located the news item he had optimistically set to record before he went to Canada. It had been one thing to tip off the news station about the anniversary vigil he'd carefully planned in the hope that they'd follow it up, but he'd been elated when he actually saw the camera crew turning up at the lakeside. No wonder he now felt depressed. Still, he had other options.

As the television screen filled with a cold, Canadian landscape and the choppy grey waters of a lake, he settled down on the sofa, careful not to disturb the cushions. He increased the volume, even though he knew it would never cover the empty feel of her absence. He heard the guitar riff and the opening lyrics of 'Forever My Angel'.

He was still humming the song to himself as he watched a flame-haired girl jump out of a taxi in Chelsea, and planned his next move. He was going to give himself six weeks. That should be enough time to find out the reason for Zach Anderson's death.

Chapter 7

*L*ucy sat cross-legged on Ellie's buttermilk sofa in the conservatory, going through some fashion and beauty magazines from cover to cover as she worked out how best to project herself in order to wow the casting director for the House of Venetia.

She had to get this job. Because for all her nonchalance with Ellie over her bad publicity, Lucy was beginning to think that Ellie might have a point. The career that had held so much promise at the outset wasn't quite hitting the heights she'd expected.

At eighteen years of age, Lucy had been spotted by a talent scout as she strolled out of Zara on a Saturday afternoon in Dundrum Town Centre. After taking some preliminary photographs, he uttered the magical words – she was a natural with a big future ahead. It was the stuff of dreams. Lucy, who still hadn't a clue what she wanted to do with her life and who felt she had no particular talents, had promptly dropped out of the intensive, results-targeted college that had cost Vivienne a fortune in fees, even though she was just three months off repeating her final exams.

Ellie had been horrified.

'What's the rush?' she'd said. 'There's no need to thumb your nose at your education. Surely the scouts would facilitate you? Three months will fly in, couldn't you wait?'

'I can't afford to take that chance,' Lucy had pouted. She couldn't believe that instead of sitting in the exam-focused classroom the following week, she'd be preparing to have her portfolio compiled. 'You followed your dream so why can't I follow mine?'

'If they think you're all that special, you could put your dream on hold for a few months. Your education is important, Lucy, I think you're mad to chuck it in. Modelling is a tough life, believe me. It's short lived, and far from everything it's cracked up to be.'

'Guess what, Ellie, I think you're jealous,' Lucy had laughed. 'You're stuck behind the scenes but I'll be out there in the bright lights.'

'Well good luck.'

Her mother had caved in easily enough.

'It's a golden opportunity,' Lucy had told her. 'The kind that every girl dreams of. I'd be mad to turn it down. Anyway, if I failed my exams first time around, I'll scarcely pass them this time.'

'Lucy, darling,' Vivienne had said, 'I'd much prefer you to complete your formal education, but I won't stand in your way. If that's what you want and it makes you happy, then I'm happy.'

She'd been prepared for more of an argument. Other parents would have had a difficult time accepting her plans, and would have promptly grounded their recalcitrant daughter, but Vivienne seemed to have the patience of a saint where Lucy was concerned. Nothing she did was outrageous enough to induce Vivienne to lose her temper or admit that her daughter drove her to distraction.

In a rare moment of introspection, the eighteen-year-old Lucy had found herself wondering why her mother always gave in to her. Lucy pushed these thoughts away without dwelling on them too much, when she was caught up in the exciting whirl-wind of photo shoots and castings.

But although she had the height, the looks, the focused atti-tude, the poised runway walk and lots of press calls, her career in Dublin didn't quite follow the orbital route she'd expected.

'You have all the ingredients,' Miranda had assured her, when she'd met her for lunch one day and Lucy had admitted she was a little dispirited. 'I think you need more confidence and expe-rience.'

'Confidence?' Lucy had said. 'I thought I had more than enough confidence.' At least she pretended to have, for that was the only way she'd learned to cope with the press and the cut-throat jealousy that seethed behind the catwalk.

'You're bursting with energy and spark,' Miranda had said shrewdly. 'I wish I could bottle some of your verve for myself. And you're very sexy. But you need to balance it with a relaxed type of assurance. Think ultra cool. In your head. It'll work wonders.'

It was Miranda who had spotted the advertisement for the open castings for Rebecca Grace Models when she'd been attending an economics conference in London's Canary Wharf. She'd called Lucy immediately. 'Your face and figure are perfect for this and your experience in Dublin will be a big help,' she'd said. And don't forget to think—'

'Ultra cool,' Lucy supplied.

It had worked. Lucy had been signed up and now she found

herself working on a more elevated platform. However, after two years in London, she was beginning to think it was Dublin all over again – she had plenty of work rolling in, but she wasn't achieving the European success she'd envisaged. And she was nowhere near attaining supermodel status. Her dream was to have her name up there in the same spotlight as Gisele, Heidi, Claudia and Kate.

But sometimes it was more difficult than she'd expected. And being Lucy Morgan, one of Rebecca Grace's glamorous models, she found she was always acting a part because life was a constant stage. People didn't realise that apart from the job itself with its long hours and gruelling schedule, you were always on show. And you never knew where the camera lens might catch you out and what tabloid or magazine you might find yourself in quite by chance. It was unsettling the way the slightest little thing she did could be pounced on and used to fill the gossip columns – depending on the mood of the day, the media could savage you or love you, painting you as a little girl lost or a career bitch.

There had been lots of fun too, but it had stopped being fun the day the horrible wreath had been delivered to her apartment door, because it had had a distinctly creepy feel to it. Whoever had delivered it had managed to bypass the press outside, or else they had smuggled it through in a plastic sack, because it had been sitting there, propped against her hall door. Waiting for her.

Then, on the flight home from Heathrow, she'd wondered if she should have gone to Hong Kong instead, to Miranda. Because if Lucy and Ellie were the top and bottom layers of a crispy apple pie (Ellie being the top, of course), Miranda was the soft, sweet filling in the middle, keeping them all together yet holding them apart so that they didn't collide and crumble.

But it was very pleasant here, relaxing in the conservatory in Laurel View. Ellie was out for the morning at a business meeting with Claire. Then she was dropping in to some boutiques. Marta was in, and it was her day for changing the bed linen, which meant Lucy would have fresh, lavender-scented, white cotton sheets on her bed with no effort required from herself. Marta was doing all the vacuuming as well, and she'd told Lucy she hoped the noise wouldn't disturb her. Marta had even made coffee with Ellie's state-of-the-art machine in Ellie's sparkling-clean kitchen and asked Lucy if she'd wanted any ironing done.

Lucy decided her sister had it made.

They were going out with Johnny for dinner that evening, although Ellie hadn't been too keen at first.

'I feel cabin fever setting in,' Lucy had grumbled the previous night.

'I thought that was what you wanted. Some privacy.'

'Apart from the asshole in the airport, I haven't been bothered by anyone.'

'That's because you've been staying here.'

'What about lunch on Wednesday?'

'That was a hand-picked restaurant where they know me well and never intrude.'

'Can't we go somewhere like that for dinner? Please?'

'I'll talk to Johnny,' Ellie gave in.

'This hotel is so exclusive that it's swarming with the rich and famous and no pap is allowed to darken the elegant porch, so we can all chill a little,' Johnny said as he turned up a long avenue bordered by magnificent scenery that was washed golden with evening sunlight about twenty minutes' drive from Ellie's south Dublin home. 'Ellie and I come here from time to time when we want to escape.'

'It's good to have somewhere to go where you don't have to put on an act,' Lucy said.

'Put on an act?' Johnny grinned at her in the rear-view mirror and Lucy felt uncomfortable.

'Yeah, well, you know what I mean.'

'Ellie and I would hate to think you're putting on an act in front of us. We're family – well practically.' He squeezed Ellie's hand.

They drew up in front of an imposing Georgian Palladian hotel, the car doors were opened, and Johnny handed the keys to a uniformed valet. Lucy stepped out to be greeted politely and respectfully. Johnny put his hand in the small of Ellie's back as he ushered her up the entrance steps and into a sumptuous foyer.

Lucy had been to lots of five-star hotels in London, New York and elsewhere, but usually as part of a frenetic modelling team or a well-publicised, high-octane party where you had to work hard to hang on to your place in the pecking order. This was a far more low-key yet more plush affair. The hotel reeked of genteel grandeur, the kind of place she would have once dismissed as being too stuffy, but now she sensed that it spoke of sheer class, understated luxury, comfort and solid reliability. The world that Ellie and Johnny inhabited, she thought, feeling a spike of jealousy that surprised her. She didn't even feel she was dressed appropriately, in a plunge neck, floral print, mini-dress and towering wedge heels. Ellie looked chic and classy in a softly draping, knee length, cream dress, from the Ellie Belle label.

She was still just feeling a little vulnerable because of the anonymous wreath and the fuss about Zach, Lucy told herself. It had certainly rattled the framework of her life, making her realise how shaky it was, and casting Ellie's sophisticated existence in a more favourable light.

Still, she was surprised by how much she enjoyed the evening; delicious food, expertly served, the opulent yet relaxed atmosphere in the dining room, where panoramic views outside the window gradually dimmed as night-time fell. She spotted an Oscar-winning film star and his wife dining with a movie producer, and the staff were quietly respectful as though they had celebrity guests every night of the week. She enjoyed the careless banter around the table, thanks mostly to Johnny who had a very quick wit and made a joke out of the smallest thing. Normally, a visit home to Dublin, although they were few and far between, meant staying with Vivienne in her old bedroom and meeting friends in a loud, city-centre bar or heaving nightclub, or Vivienne would invite Miranda and Ellie for a leisurely meal around the table so they could all have a catch-up over chicken curry or lasagne, wine and champagne. Being out like this as part of Ellie's social world was new to her and, to her surprise, she liked it.

Johnny was easy to talk to and he seemed to understand the pressures of her lifestyle.

'I want to make the most of it while I can,' she explained. She toyed with her luscious dessert, but in fear and horror of gaining extra weight, she decided to take just a mouthful or two. 'Don't know what I'll do when I reach the end of my modelling days,' she grinned.

'From where I'm sitting, Lucy, that won't happen for a long time yet,' he smiled, his eyes crinkling at the corners. 'Any boyfriends on the scene?'

'Lots. But no one special. I'm too busy having fun. And I have to be choosy about who I sleep with, because some guys are only interested in one thing.'

Johnny crooked an eyebrow. 'Mind-blowing sex?'

Lucy laughed. 'Selling their lurid story to the highest bidder. Mind you, I've been the victim of some fairytales.' And there were times when it wasn't funny, she thought soberly.

Later, Lucy excused herself. 'I'm off to the bathroom,' she

said, picking up her sparkly D&G clutch. 'If it's anything like the luxury of this dining room I might not come back.'

Ellie watched the admiring eyes that followed Lucy as she glided fluidly across the dining-room floor despite her wedge heels, and she knew by the way her sister threw back her shoulders that she sensed the appreciative stares.

'Lucy seems to be okay,' Johnny said. 'She's pulled herself together quite nicely. Which leaves us.'

'Us?' Ellie's hand shook as she lifted her glass. Not again.

'Yes, *our* future.'

'I'm happy, you're happy, what more could we want?' she said, attempting to sound light-hearted.

'There you go, fobbing me off again. Thing is,' he went on, fiddling with his napkin, 'I don't always know where I stand with you.'

'As in?' She twirled the stem of her glass. Apart from her call to Johnny suggesting they bring Lucy out, she hadn't talked to him since the night they'd collected Lucy from the airport when they'd gone to bed without resolving the words between them. A meal with Lucy acting as an unwitting buffer had seemed like a convenient solution. Only now they were having more words.

'Come on, you know what I mean,' he said, pushing his coffee cup aside so that he could rest his elbows on the table. With his chin in his hands, he examined her face. 'I want to marry you. As well as all that, I sometimes feel like you're holding back on me, that you're not really with me, and maybe if we were married and properly committed to each other, it would be different.'

She forced a smile. 'But how would it be different with a gold band and a ceremony?'

'It would tell the world that we have vowed to love each other, till death us do part. I think that's very significant. And it

71

would mean love and security for any children we might have. God, Ellie, it's usually the man who's the commitment-phobe . . . ' he shook his head.

Ellie felt cold inside. She'd always assumed that one day Johnny would get fed up with her and that their relationship would have run its course. Now, she was beginning to realise that her very refusal to take him seriously was a turn on for him. 'We're fine as we are. Why rock the boat?'

'Is that a "no" then?'

Ellie sighed. 'This is hardly the time or place, Johnny. Anyway, you're rushing me. I thought I had another nine or ten days or so.'

She felt a thud in her stomach when, instead of replying, he just stared into space.

Lucy could have lingered in the ultra luxury of the ladies, and when she returned to the table and noticed Ellie's strained face and Johnny's hurt look, she wished she had stayed. Some of the glow had gone out of the evening. Ellie was mad, she decided, stealing a glance at her sister, who was full of forced composure. Johnny was gorgeous and she should have whisked him up the aisle as soon as he proposed. Ellie didn't know how lucky she was to have this kind of life, her successful business, and Johnny too, Lucy thought, suddenly conscious of all the uncertain years that lay ahead of her until she reached Ellie's stage in life.

'Isn't Johnny staying?' she asked, when he dropped them home and turned back down the driveway, causing a scatter of gravel and a lurch of disappointment in her stomach. She'd hoped he'd come in and they would have had more banter over a bottle of wine.

'Not tonight,' Ellie said in a flat voice as she opened the hall door.

Lucy followed her into the hall, guessing immediately what their argument had been about.

'I don't understand why you're keeping him guessing, it must be hard on him, as well as you,' she said, going on down to the kitchen, where Ellie was pouring a glass of water.

Ellie gave a half-laugh and turned around to face her sister. 'Oh, Lucy, you don't have to worry your little head about Johnny and me. We're fine.'

She shouldn't be laughing casually like that, Lucy decided, as though it was of no consequence. Johnny looked at Ellie as though she meant the world to him, so it was clearly of major consequence to him. No man had ever looked at Lucy like that. Ellie didn't realise how lucky she was and Lucy felt another flash of envy.

'If I were you,' she said, 'I wouldn't leave him hanging on. Not at your age.'

There was a silence. Lucy could have bitten her tongue.

Ellie raised an eyebrow. 'And what's my age got to do with anything?'

Lucy shrugged. 'Well you might want to be married and start a family.'

'Did you stop to think that on the other hand I might not?' Ellie said smartly as she left the room.

After Lucy had gone to bed, Ellie went into her studio and stayed there for a long time, rifling through half-finished pencil sketches, samples of velvet, Irish linen and Carrickmacross lace, and boxes of accessories, all the tools of her trade. They were all so familiar that they were part of who she was, where she had come from, and where she was going. With her vision and dedication, her sketches and fabrics were transformed into beautiful garments. It was the one part of her life that she could depend on, that validated her, that gave her a reference point and was her passion.

And it was in her total control.

She went over to the mirror and looked at her reflection. She was wearing one of her own designs, a simple ivory column that skimmed her curves, with lace detail around the v-shaped neckline and inset into three-quarter-length sleeves. Tonight her face was a pale oval with jutting cheekbones, her eyes were huge and glittering green, and her mouth turned down at the corners. She forced a smile at her reflection and imagined she was smiling at Johnny.

Whatever happened, she didn't want to lose him. She couldn't imagine life without his friendship and support, his easy laugh, the way he brought a lot of fun into her days, lightening her serious moods from time to time. Then, there was the way he held her close in bed.

Yet why wasn't *he* her reference point, her lodestar, her all-consuming passion?

Chapter 8

*J*ohnny Tyler stopped by the reception area just inside the shop and angled the silver-framed photograph of the wedding couple on the small display table to better catch the spotlight. He stood back and examined the arrangement of photograph, scented candle and a crystal bowl filled with rose petals. He rearranged a plump cushion on the leather couch and tidied the already-tidy magazine rack that held a selection of trade and bridal glossies. It was important to get this right – the small touches were crucial when it came to first impressions and he wanted every customer to form the best impression possible from the minute they entered his dress-hire shop.

'Are you okay, Johnny?' Jane, his senior manager, stuck her head out of her cubby hole of an office, which was across from the reception area.

'Just taking an early lunch,' he said. 'Here, put these in the recycling bin,' he went on, thrusting some out-of-date magazines into her hands. There was nothing worse than a slightly dog-eared, tired-looking magazine to alter the whole tone of the shop.

'Sure. I was going to look after that as soon as I have the stock figures keyed in.'

'No worries,' he smiled, anxious not to rock the boat with Jane. She looked after all the boring paperwork, promotions, stock and cash control, as well as updating the website and social networking sites on a regular basis. He'd be lost without her. She was also dating his younger brother David, whom she'd hooked up with at Johnny's birthday party six months previously.

Johnny had been surprised. Jane was quick and energetic, and a go-getter, whereas David was a quiet and sedate solicitor. Opposites attract, he mused. So far, they seemed to be making a go of it. They'd even moved in together recently, a feat he hadn't yet managed with Ellie.

He went out onto the sunlit street, stepping into what was now trendily known as the 'Italian Quarter' of Dublin city centre. His father, who had died over fifteen years earlier, wouldn't have recognised the area. And he wouldn't have recognised his dress-hire shop either.

Johnny went into a convenience store and bought a chicken wrap and a bottle of water – something else his father would have found hilarious. He walked out onto the quays and strolled down the boardwalk by the river, having lunch on the go, the breeze on his face and the tangy scent of the river in his nostrils. Sometimes, he wondered what his father would have made of his beloved shop, or if he would have approved of the way Johnny had turned the whole business around, taking full advantage of opportunities those post-millennium, affluent days had provided. It had allowed him to take a gamble on converting the rather staid and conservative Tyler's Tuxedos, Dress Hire, into the hip and buzzy Johnny's Glad Rags.

Things were different now, the flash of those crazy affluent days were gone, but his careful investments remained intact.

Dublin had picked itself up a little, the fiery Celtic spirit determined not to be squashed. Business was still ticking over, although he'd trimmed his cost base by not replacing two senior staff who had left and by introducing a more competitively priced range of suits. He found that cost-conscious customers were more inclined to hire a suit now rather than buy. Kids were still going to their Debs and Trinity Balls, and he had the coolest dress-hire place in town. And people were still getting married.

But not him.

When he reached O'Connell Bridge, he tossed his sandwich wrapper into a bin and twisted the cap on his bottle of water, taking a long slug. Then he retraced his steps and asked himself what was really going on in Ellie Morgan's head.

She'd entranced him from the moment he'd met her. He'd never thought he'd be serious about a woman. He'd been having far too much fun enjoying a succession of girlfriends and milking all that the Dublin nightlife clubbing scene had to offer, with no shortage of willing conquests happy to enjoy no-strings sex. But from the start, Ellie had been different. Beautiful and classy. Alluring. He could only guess at her hidden depths but he knew they were there. He saw promises of them in the sensual way she moved, and spoke and smiled. He stopped looking at other women, because he loved being with her. And he enjoyed the way they had taken the social scene by storm. Separate, they were high profile in their own right, but together they seemed invincible as they climbed the heights of the celebrity ladder.

And they had fun in bed. Great fun. Sometimes Ellie surprised him by appearing out of the dressing room in his penthouse apartment wearing nothing but a tuxedo, the lapels barely covering her rosy nipples. Sometimes, if she was feeling adventurous, she tied him to the bedposts with his silk ties, leaning across him provocatively to allow her generous breasts to brush along his chest. Another time, unknown to him, she had plucked a measuring tape from the glove compartment of his car and had shocked him by producing it in bed. It would have been enough to make most men wilt, but he had passed the test, she'd told him, dropping a kiss on the top of his rock-hard penis and giving him a sultry smile.

Then, one day, Johnny looked around and realised that all of his mates were married, some of them had families. He was asked to be godfather once too often. Men coming in to be fitted for wedding suits with excited brides-to-be in tow caused a pang of longing in his heart. He'd tasted success, he'd made his money, he'd thought he had it all, but he had the gut feeling there had to be more to life – marriage and babies perhaps. A wife and kids.

And with Ellie, of course.

Only problem was, she didn't seem to think so. And he didn't know what more he could do to persuade her that it was the perfect step for both of them.

Chapter 9

'Are you glad I finally managed to talk you into a date?' Christian asked.

'Are you serious? This is really your idea of a date?'

'Yeah, why? What's wrong?'

Miranda laughed and put up her free hand to stop the breeze from ruffling her hair. 'It's unusual, that's all.'

'You haven't been to Hong Kong until you've crossed the harbour on the Star ferry. I find it downright disgraceful, Miranda Morgan, that you haven't had that experience.'

She looked around her and took a long, slow breath, soaking it all up. She felt she could stay here forever. It was just a journey across Victoria Harbour on a packed ferry boat, the regular commuter ferry that chugged forward and back, taking an endless stream of passengers across what was a short distance between Hong Kong Island and Kowloon, but it was unforgettable. The cost was negligible, just a few paltry coins, but out on the metallic grey water, the dipping and swaying of Chinese junks silhouetted against the towering skyscrapers, which were, in turn, backdropped by the mountainous peak of Hong Kong, totally enraptured Miranda. The medley of sights and sounds all around her was spectacular.

'You're right,' she grinned. 'I can't believe I've been here over three months and I've missed all this.'

He shook his head, his eyes affectionate. 'Shame on you. You should see it at night.'

'Is that our next date?' she asked, emboldened.

'So you want a follow up? Good.'

'We'll see how the lunch goes first,' she said, a little alarmed with the way she was stepping out of the comfort zone she'd ring-fenced around herself.

Up to now, she'd steadfastly ignored Christian's offers of a beer after work, as flirtation of any description was not on her agenda. The safest way to keep her heart intact was to keep all men off limits. But, suddenly, that had changed. She'd finally accepted a date with him, primarily because she'd needed to do something to take her mind off her family back home, and the phone call from Lucy.

'I'm staying in Ellie's for a few days until the fuss of Dad's anniversary has died down,' Lucy had told her earlier that week.

'Yes,' Miranda had said. 'Ellie emailed me to explain what happened. I'm sorry it upset you that much. It must have been very difficult for you.'

'I don't think anyone knows how I really feel,' Lucy had said quietly, which was rather enigmatic for Lucy, who rarely attempted to make a secret of her feelings. 'Oh, Miranda, I'm sorry you're not here. I miss seeing you. Why did you have to go so far away?'

'I miss you too, Lucy, but you didn't see that much of me when I was home,' Miranda had pointed out. 'Anytime you were back from London you were busy catching up with your mates.'

'Yes, but I always knew that if I needed you, you were there. All those years I was growing up and fighting with Ellie or Mum you were there for me, in the background.'

'In the background' – that just about summed it up. Miranda had fumed with annoyance after the call. By moving to Hong Kong, she was supposed to have severed the umbilical cord that had been firmly attached to her family. An unexpected bubble of rebellion rose inside her. It hung there, in her chest, and the next time Christian asked her out, she said yes.

'Even if it's just a beer after work?' he'd said, clearly surprised.

'Yes, that's fine.'

'I can do better than that,' he'd smiled. Then he'd suggested a ferry trip across the harbour followed by lunch on a floating restaurant.

And as she sat in the restaurant, Miranda acknowledged that it was lovely to have this big, handsome man sitting across the table from her, laughing and joking about office politics, looking sexy and relaxed in a white cotton shirt and khaki chinos. Looking as though he was enjoying her company and wanted to be there. She didn't know whether to be glad or sorry that she had played it safe by sticking to a pair of black jeans and an emerald-green jersey top - an outfit no more alluring than her office suits. He moved on to tell her about his family back home in Byron Bay, Australia.

'Dad's in the sailing business, yacht charter,' Christian said. 'It's very successful and when he eventually retires, which knowing his zest for life, will be in about ten years' time, I'll be taking it over.'

A yacht business. No wonder he looked like he'd just clambered off a surfboard having conquered the waves. 'Does that suit you?' she asked.

'Does it heck! Sunshine and the sea, and Byron Bay? I grew

up with it and I can't think of anything or anywhere better, but I want to get a handle on the financial end of things, and that's one of the reasons I'm here. We have an accountant, but it helps to have some understanding of a balance sheet and a profit projection if you want to manage a successful business. Dad worked hard to build it all up, and in time I'll make it even better. How about you?'

'Me?' She was caught by surprise at the swiftness with which he turned the tables.

'Yeah,' he sat back in his chair and gave her a penetrating look. 'I've a feeling I'm only seeing the tip of the iceberg where Miranda Morgan is concerned and there's a helluva lot of interesting stuff going on under the surface. Which I'm keen to find out about.'

She laughed. 'You make me sound very enigmatic. I'm afraid you'll be disappointed.'

He shook his head and waggled his finger. He had nice hands, she noticed, with square-tipped fingers. His blond hair gleamed in the sunlight flooding through the restaurant. He was, she realised, quite gorgeous. All the more reason for her to safeguard her heart.

'No.' He shook his head. 'You're not allowed to even talk like that. See, Miranda, I don't think you realise how lovely you are. Especially when you blush. I quite like it when you blush.'

Her cheeks reddened immediately. He wouldn't be saying these things if he knew her sisters, Miranda thought coldly. Back home, she'd never been a person in her own right. She'd always been one of the Morgan sisters, the brainy redhead caught between Ellie's sensual beauty and Lucy's Celtic prettiness, and there was no avoiding her destined role. Everyone knew tall, elegant Ellie, and her successful fashion label, the woman who had Johnny Tyler eating out of her hand. Everyone knew Lucy, the vampish, fantabulous model who was rarely out of the gossip pages. And Miranda? Well, she was the boring, serious sister, who uttered grave pronouncements on the state of the country's economy. As Lucy had so accurately remarked, she was the background foil to her two extrovert sisters, and although she loved them to bits, Miranda was tired of being sandwiched between them.

But far from Dublin, this was something that Christian hadn't a clue about, she realised, feeling a lift of gratitude. And feeling something else . . . a definite loosening of the umbilical cord. He didn't know the rather dull Miranda who lived quietly in the shadow of Lucy or Ellie. He only knew of the Miranda who worked in XAM, the Irish girl with the red hair. She could be anybody at all. Anybody she wanted to be.

'What have I said wrong?' he asked. 'Or don't you like a compliment?'

'I do, it's good,' she said, tasting a new freedom, an unexpected zest for life.

'I'd like to tell you more,' his blue eyes searched hers, 'but I don't want to crowd you on a first date. Or come on too strong.'

'That's okay. I'll think I'll survive.' She was curious to know what he saw in her.

'Right, so.' And he leaned across the table and softly told her about the kind of woman he saw in Miranda as she dutifully sat at her desk in XAM in her charcoal-grey suits. Warm and charming, and always ready to smile. A little shy, but quick-witted, with an attractive, sexy vibe simmering beneath her calm reserve. The kind of woman he wanted to get to know a whole lot better.

Now that, she hadn't expected, and despite her determination to protect her heart, it was thumping wildly by the time he had finished.

Chapter 10

$\mathcal{S}$itting in the bedroom of her five-star hotel in Venice, Vivienne phoned Ellie's landline and was surprised when Lucy answered. 'Lucy! Lovely to hear you!' she said. 'But this is Ellie's phone, isn't it? I haven't pressed the wrong button, have I?'

'No, Mum, I'm still here in Ellie's, just for another couple of days.'

Vivienne closed her eyes and saw Lucy hiding her face from the cameras as she dashed up the steps of her Chelsea home. A side to Lucy she'd never seen before. How was the best way to approach this? Surely to reassure her that Zach Anderson's anniversary was nothing to be anxious about. 'Good,' she said cheerily, shying away from mentioning it at the last minute. 'It's nice to think that two of my daughters are having some bonding time together, especially you and Ellie.'

A silence; then, 'That's not the only reason I got out of London,' Lucy said, a slight note of challenge in her voice.

'If you mean the interfering paparazzi, you were perfectly right,' Vivienne said staunchly. 'They must have had nothing better to do. But I'm sure all that fuss has blown over by now and my advice is not to waste a single minute worrying about it. Besides, Lucy,' she went on encouragingly, 'your life is full of good things, it's exciting and busy, and they're the positives you need to focus on.'

'I know you don't want to talk about it,' Lucy said.

'There's nothing to say, darling,' Vivienne gave a half-laugh. 'It's a bit unfortunate that someone or some people decided to make a talking point of your father's anniversary, and the media dragged you into it. I know the fuss is bound to have affected you, and that's why I'm glad you're with Ellie. But don't let it get to you. Just ignore it.'

'Yeah . . .' Lucy's voice was faint. 'How is your cruise?' she went on.

'That's why I'm calling. I've disembarked and I'm now in Venice. I'll be home next Wednesday.'

'I'll not see you so. I'm going back to London on Monday evening.'

'Ah, no. I can't believe we'll miss each other. What a shame. I'd love to have seen you.' She would have liked to satisfy herself that Lucy was okay. She could have looked her in the eye, given her a hug, made absolutely sure that she wasn't suffering any ill effects on account of the way her father's death had been thrust into the limelight. 'Any chance you could postpone your flight?' she asked.

'Sorry, I'll miss you too, but I can't, Mum. I need to get back to London. Did I tell you about the new campaign I'm hoping to be part of?'

'No, tell me,' Vivienne encouraged.

Lucy went on to chat about the new campaign, sounding much like her normal, spunky self, and Vivienne breathed a silent sigh of relief. Maybe she was worrying needlessly. Lucy was well used to the limelight. It was run-of-the-mill for her, a central part of her carefully profiled career, she often told Vivienne. And she usually laughed off any gossip column critics who remarked on her hair and shoes, or painted her in an unflattering light or made her out to be a victim of her own success.

So her mother's blood ran in her veins, Vivienne thought as she ended the call. Lucy showed much the same indifference to the callous side of the media as Vivienne had after they'd reacted to her announcement that she was pregnant following her short but torrid liaison with Zach.

It was an announcement she almost didn't make.

For Lucy was the daughter she almost didn't have.

To her eternal shame, Vivienne's first reaction had been sheer panic when she'd discovered she was pregnant with Zach's baby. She was forty. She was widowed. Zach was just a brief fling. She couldn't have this baby. And so she made the same journey that many an Irish girl had made in similar circumstances. She flew to London, to an anonymous clinic.

At the last minute, as she lay on the cold, hard trolley, feeling desperately unhappy as she waited to have this minute scrap of life sucked out of her, she had a sudden vision of her beloved Edward, and imagined what he might say to her. In that moment, some kind of inner strength came to her and, without saying a word, she climbed off the trolley and got dressed.

It was an inner strength that had helped her get through the next few months, but even though she hadn't gone through with the abortion, her guilt at even considering it had swelled up inside her as soon as the tiny, wriggling mite of Lucy had been placed in her arms. And since then, as Lucy grew from impudent childhood, through turbulent teenage years into sometimes unruly adulthood, she'd done everything in her power to make it up to her.

Vivienne felt a little stiff as she got up off the bed. She crossed the room to the ornate Italian mirror and stared at her reflection, her eyes critical and judgemental as they stared back at her.

But no matter how hard she tried, there were some things she could never atone for.

Chapter 11

*E*llie was surprised when Lucy pranced into the kitchen on Sunday morning swaddled in her velour dressing gown.

'It's so warm and cosy I hope you didn't mind me sneaking into your bedroom to borrow it,' Lucy grinned.

With her face devoid of make-up and her hair caught back in a loose scrunchie, Ellie thought she looked very young and oddly angelic. A wave of nostalgia washed over her at the thought that, even for her little sis, youth was all so fleeting. 'No problem,' she said. 'I'm glad you like it, but I thought you preferred sleek and slinky as opposed to baby white velour.'

'I do, usually, but this feels so snuggly I couldn't resist pinching it any more than I could resist having a relaxing soak in the bath with your Jo Malone bath oil. Far more therapeutic than a quick power shower.'

She sat down at Ellie's pine table.

'Coffee?'

'An espresso would be lovely, ta. Having lived with you for a few days,' Lucy went on, 'I'm beginning to take a fresh look at the way you run your life. Compared to my mad Chelsea apartment, there's something very soothing and restful about your home and your lifestyle, and you can switch on the glamour as well, whereas I used to think you were—' Lucy wrinkled her nose, apparently lost for words.

'Boring?' Ellie supplied.

'No, I never found you boring, maybe just a little un-cool – apart from Johnny, of course.'

Ellie stayed silent as she made Lucy's coffee and passed it across the table to her.

'Oops, sorry for mentioning the war,' Lucy grimaced. 'Anyway I'll be out of your hair tomorrow evening.'

'Mum will be home on Wednesday, don't you want to stay and see her?'

Lucy shook her head. 'I can't pass up my chance to be part of the Venetia job and it means getting back to London tomorrow night The casting is happening on Thursday morning and I'll just have two days to get ready.'

'You'll be fine. Do you feel ready to face London again?'

Lucy's face was shadowed as she pulled off her scrunchie and combed a hand through her rippling hair. 'Sort of. I can't stay away forever.'

'What about the – you know, the wreath? I'd hate to think it's still there waiting for you.'

'Ugh, no way. I stuck that straight into the refuse bin. It was horrible, even just putting my hands on it . . .' Lucy shivered and wriggled her fingers as though she could still feel traces of it clinging to her hands.

'At least it's gone,' Ellie said firmly.

Lucy sat with her elbows on the table and her face in her hands. 'Although I'd like to have talked to you some more about

Zach. Even just to suss out if there was any reason for someone to play a prank on me like that. I can't ask Mum in case it upsets her. I can't even contact the florist because there was nothing on the card beyond his name.'

'Relax, Lucy. If I were you I'd just forget all about it,' Ellie said briskly. 'I'd pretend it never happened.'

Since she'd collected Lucy the previous Tuesday night, Ellie hadn't allowed Lucy to dwell on the whole unfortunate incident. She flicked through a weekend newspaper, spreading the pages across the table, before smiling at Lucy, 'And, see, there's no more mention of Zach's anniversary, things have moved on and everyone is caught up with Wills and Kate and the latest soccer-star bust-up, so you're probably safe enough going home.'

'Hey, why don't I cook for you and Johnny this evening, seeing as it's my last night?' Lucy suggested. 'We could have a cosy night in with my five-star beef dish. I need to thank you guys for looking after me. You really came to my rescue when—'

'There's no need to thank us, that's what we're here for,' Ellie swiftly interrupted her, the prospect dismaying her. The last thing she needed was the three of them sitting around the table and another night of Lucy on hand to witness the strain developing between her and Johnny.

'I'd like to do this,' Lucy said. 'I'm not sure when I'll be back in Dublin again.'

'I've a better idea. Let's have a few friends around to ease you back into things. I could make some phone calls, order in hot food, wine and beer . . . what do you say?'

Lucy's face was clouded.

'Thought you would have jumped at the chance of a party,' Ellie prompted.

'Yes, but I would have liked a chance to talk as well . . . ah, what of it?' Lucy's expression cleared. 'We'll have a party.'

Ellie rose to her feet. 'Right. I'll get on to it straightaway.'

Later that evening, Ellie congratulated herself for turning the prospect of a tense night sitting in with just Lucy and Johnny to this. Her party was in full swing, with a dozen or so people turning up, including friends of hers and Johnny's, and a couple of Lucy's Dublin-based model friends with their boyfriends. It was one of those rare evenings in early April, when the days have started to stretch and are full of the promise of summer and good things to look forward to; a capsule in time when the air was mild enough to move around outside, the slight breeze scented and benign as it ruffled the late-flowering tulips in Ellie's patio planters, and, in the west, the sun lingered as though it wanted to stay at the party for a while, casting a golden wash over the swathe of Dublin city skyline. Ellie pointed everyone in the direction of the beer and wine, and encouraged them to help themselves to the canapé slivers, beef dish and vegetarian curry that had been delivered from the catering company in the village.

'Mmm, delicious. This is a nice surprise for a Sunday night.' Claire moved across to the table and picked up a plate and a napkin. 'And it's good to have a chance to catch up with Lucy. I haven't seen her in a while.'

Ellie glanced outside to the patio where Lucy was chatting to her friends, looking as though she hadn't a care in the world and every inch the successful model in her thin stiletto heels and figure-hugging, metallic mini-dress.

'It's been nice having her here,' Ellie said, taking a large sip of her cold white wine, unable to admit she sneakily felt relieved that Lucy would be going home the following evening and that there would be no more need to walk on eggshells. Johnny came through into the kitchen and filled his glass of red wine. Wearing black jeans and with a black leather waistcoat over his plain white shirt, he looked gorgeous.

'Great night, Ellie, but let's get some decent music on,' he said.

Shortly afterwards, music pumped through the speakers Johnny had set up outside on the patio and the impromptu party moved up a gear. Lucy looked like a silvery column of light as she twisted her svelte figure around, squealing that she'd never realised quite how good Johnny's taste in music was. Johnny caught her hand and twirled her around even faster until she collapsed in a fit of giggles. Johnny's mate Colm started the conga around the back garden as it fast turned out to be one of those unplanned, care-free, silly kind of nights where everyone was in high spirits.

Until Jane, Johnny's senior manager, turned up with David, Johnny's younger brother, flashing a brand new engagement ring. The first Ellie knew of it was when Johnny drew Jane into the middle of the group dancing haphazardly on the patio and shouted for quiet.

'Hey, everyone, can I have your attention?' Johnny roared, 'I'd like you all to congratulate the bride-to-be.'

Standing outside the group for a moment, Lucy only heard his words and didn't see that Johnny was holding up Jane's left hand, and she burst through the gathering, shrieking joyfully, throwing herself at Ellie. Everyone's eyes followed her. There was a frozen moment in time before Ellie quickly shook her head; Lucy clapped her hands to her mouth, her eyes huge. Somehow, Ellie recovered herself enough to go across to Jane and give her a hug.

'I hope we're not taking over your night,' Jane gabbled excit-edly. 'It's just that David proposed today and it seemed the perfect opportunity to break the news while we had everyone together. We can't keep this a secret!'

'Of course not. It's brilliant news,' Ellie said, turning to David and hugging him too.

Jane's face was glowing with happiness. Ellie wondered if her face would look so radiant if she were engaged to Johnny. So far, she hadn't dared to look him in the eye. David popped the cork on a couple of bottles of Moët and everyone toasted the happy couple. Johnny played a special request as Jane and David did a sexy dance in the middle of the patio.

Still, Ellie didn't dare look at Johnny, who was bound to feel aggrieved that Jane and David had made a commitment after just six months of coupledom, when Ellie was still holding him at arm's length. He was drinking too much as well, she noticed, knocking black glasses of her best Bordeaux as though it was water. This wasn't the time to check him, however. Anything she said would be like a match to a powder keg.

The evening seemed like an eternity. Most of the conversation revolved around Jane and David. Yes, the wedding would be sooner rather than later ... maybe a candle-lit winter wedding ... Synan O'Mahony for the bridal gown ... Ellie, of course, for the bridesmaids ... Dromoland, Leslie or Ashford? So hard to choose ... but all great fun.

Ellie gradually realised they had moved on to possible wedding venues. Suddenly, she wished the party was over and that everyone had gone home, including Johnny and Lucy. She just wanted to sit quietly on her patio and shore up the sudden sense of foreboding in her chest as she absorbed the panorama of Dublin city lights glittering in front of her.

But no matter how brightly they shone, not even they could shake off the uneasy feeling that she and Johnny were free-falling somewhere, whirring into space as though their moorings had become adrift, and she didn't know where they would land.

Chapter 12

 L ucy stuck out her hand from under the warmth of the
duvet and groped across the bedside table for her mobile.
Her head felt woolly and her mouth was as dry as sawdust. Jesus
Christ. What had she been thinking? Going on the batter two
days before an important casting was usually a no no. She eventually fished out her mobile from under some tissues, squinted at
the display and half fell, half rolled out of the bed when she saw
it was almost eleven o'clock.

 She dragged herself across to the mirror and stared in horror
at her hungover reflection of mascara-streaked face and slits of
bleary eyes. Why had she done this to herself? Had she been in
some kind of self-sabotage mode last night? Hazy images of the
night passed across the front of her fogged-up brain. Dancing to
some hot new band and being whirled around the patio by
Johnny, his black waistcoat flying open, the scalding-with-mor-
tification moment when she'd thought Ellie had got engaged,
Johnny filling her glass, and filling it again, and yet again ... Lots
of laughter. Lots of silly dancing. Gallons of wine.

Ellie had said she'd just invite a few friends. Yeah right. Lucy had realised quite early on that it was an enviable, A-class guest list, including well-known socialites, the lead singer of one of Ireland's most popular rock bands and his girlfriend, a British actor and his wife. The paps would have given an arm and a leg to be a fly on the wall, and the guests were floating between Ellie's kitchen and patio as though it was their second home. People left soon after midnight, and the rest of the party moved in to the warmth of the kitchen. She dimly recalled that she and Johnny and his celebrity restaurateur mate Colm had opened another bottle of wine after Ellie had gone to bed.

She had no recollection, however, of eating any of Ellie's lovely food, which might have been some soakage for the wine. She couldn't recall sipping any water. Neither had she bothered to take off her make-up before she went to bed. Cardinal sins each, never mind all three together.

Talk about being her own worst enemy.

She went into the en-suite, filled the basin with warm water, then, with cotton wool and cleansing milk, she began to clean her ravaged face. The house was silent. She recalled Ellie telling her that she had an appointment at ten o'clock that morning with her lace supplier. Then she was calling on Claire and dropping in to a couple of boutiques. She'd be home later in the afternoon and would have something to eat with Lucy before she drove her to the airport.

It meant that Lucy would be back home in London that evening, no wiser about who had tried to rattle her with the macabre funeral wreath. And no wiser about Zach Anderson, thanks to Ellie deflecting her questions and making light of her uneasiness. It was all right for Ellie, Lucy thought grumpily, she was secure in her comfortable home, with her fantastic career, celebrity friends *and* Johnny dancing attendance on her. It seemed a warm life, full of love and friendship, the things Lucy felt her own life was lacking. Boyfriends flitted in and out of her life, only interested in fun and sex, and there was so much cut-throat competition on the modelling circuit that the people she met and mingled with were afraid to let down their guard and be friends. They went out clubbing and drinking, of course, but the fun they had was all very frenetic and meaningless. Even with Sasha, the nearest Lucy had to a best mate, who had a flat near her in Chelsea, it was a friendship of convenience more than anything else. Sometimes, deep in her heart, she felt very much alone. Usually she could ignore it, but spending time in Ellie's had shown her the side of life she was missing.

To her enormous disgust, Lucy felt tears prick the back of her eyes. This wasn't her. Lucy Morgan never, ever felt sorry for herself. Whatever crap she faced, she usually picked herself up straightaway and battled on.

Feeling achey and annoyed with herself, Lucy brushed her teeth. She stepped into the shower cubicle and stood under the warm spray for ages, carefully buffing her body. After she had dried herself, she slathered on loads of her favourite body butter. She couldn't believe how stupid she'd been considering all the things she had to do between now and Thursday. She needed to treat her hair to a deep conditioning, have a facial, a manicure and a pedicure. She'd have to drink gallons of water and make sure she got her proper quota of sleep. And go on a crash diet. She patted her tummy and thighs trying to judge how many extra kilos she'd put on during her stay in Ellie's, thanks to rich desserts and last night's binge drinking. She looked in the wall mirror but it was all steamy and placed too high to see her full figure.

There was only one way to find out, she decided as she put on a black lacy thong and matching bra. Ellie had a bathroom scales in the cupboard in her en-suite. It wouldn't take two minutes to find out what she was up against. And she could have a good look at her body in Ellie's floor-to-ceiling, mirrored wardrobes as well, to see where it needed attention. She got dressed and pulled on Ellie's baby white velour robe before she headed upstairs.

Johnny was dreaming. In the dream, Ellie was walking along the edge of a cliff, her arms stretched out on either side of her for balance, like the wings of an aeroplane. Far down below, an angry, grey sea seethed and boiled against the jagged rocks supporting the base of the cliff. One small slip and Ellie would be gone. He had to save her, but no matter how hard Johnny tried to run towards her, something kept holding him back. His legs were pumping furiously but it was as if they were pumping in midair, for he was making no progress at all.

And then she disappeared.

He knew he was screaming her name, but no sound came out. He woke up to feel his heart pounding in his rib cage. He realised immediately that he had been having a nightmare and he was in Ellie's bed. He knew by his dry throat and pounding head that he had an almighty hangover. He checked his watch – just eleven o'clock. There was a bottle of water on the bedside table and flipped open the cap and swallowed it all, feeling marginally refreshed. He had a vague recollection of Ellie disturbing him as she'd slipped out of the bed, and by the time he'd reached across to her, she was gone and his hand was flailing against the empty edge of the bed. Maybe that's where his nightmare had originated.

She'd been fast asleep by the time he'd fallen into bed after the party.

The party. What a load of bollocks. It all came back to him in a fresh rush of jealousy. The proud glint in his brother's eyes, the happiness on Jane's face. It wasn't surprising he had a hangover. He'd needed a skinful of drink to blot out the violent stab of jealousy that had streaked right through him when his brother had announced his engagement. Worse, he'd felt as though his balls had shrivelled when Lucy had immediately assumed it was him and Ellie who were engaged. Now their friends would be speculating about what was going on. Not that it mattered what they thought in the grand scheme of things. The only thing that mattered was what was happening between himself and Ellie – or not happening. David hadn't been rejected by the woman he loved. His pride hadn't been wounded. He was in the happy place of knowing that Jane loved him enough to make the commitment to spend the rest of her life with him.

At least he'd had the wits to tell Jane he'd be in late today. By the time she'd headed home, he knew he'd had too much to drink. A sour streak of envy jabbed through him all over again. What was wrong with him that Ellie was still holding off? What x-factor was he missing? Didn't he satisfy Ellie enough? It felt like there was an aching hole in his heart and he moved over to her side of the bed and burrowed down beneath the duvet, trying but failing to find the scent of her.

'Yes, I like these,' Ellie said, gently stroking the delicate hand-crafted lace with the pads of her fingers. 'They're beautiful and very traditional, which is what I prefer.' She couldn't help noticing that across the other side of the table, Linda Connolly smiled with relief. An order for her speciality filigree lace from Ellie would be worth a lot to her both in terms of the financial rewards and the recognition it would bring.

Ellie sifted through the samples, wondering if she'd have any flashes of inspiration about how the lace might be incorporated into next year's spring/summer collection.

'I'll leave them with you,' Linda said.

'I'll certainly use some of this, it's beautiful, but as of now I've no idea about designs or quantities.'

That was putting it mildly, she sighed to herself, as she painted a smile on her face. She hadn't the faintest clue, and couldn't even begin to think of outline sketches. It wasn't surprising considering all she'd had to deal with in the past few weeks. Johnny and his proposal, then Zach's anniversary, followed by Lucy's visit to escape the media. Combined, it had turned her brain into a seething, jangling mess. And that was before the bombshell of last night, something she knew she was going to have to reconcile with Johnny. His ego was bound to be crushed after his brother's news.

After her meeting with Linda, Ellie drove across town to Claire's house, to go through the repeat orders for dresses and jackets that had come in from the various boutiques. She had turned a spare room of her home into her office, and it also housed a cutting table, sewing machine, and ironing press; by now it was as familiar to Ellie as her own studio. Except one of Claire's walls was haphazardly covered with a day-glo collection of her children's drawings.

'Don't rush off,' Claire said, pouring more coffee after they had discussed a work plan for the orders and agreed on delivery dates. 'The little monsters are safely in school until three o'clock so I have time for a break.'

'Did you enjoy last night?' Ellie asked, wondering how she was going to approach the whole subject with Johnny.

'It was some night! Did you have any idea about David and Jane?'

'Not a clue! They took everyone by surprise.'

'It sounds as though they're not planning to hang around too long before they tie the knot. Just as well.'

99

'Why do you say that?'

'I think the older you get, the harder it becomes to make a serious decision, such as marriage. If Andrew was to ask me again, I don't know what I'd say. I'd find it all a bit terrifying. Don't get me wrong, Ellie, I love him lots and the kids are precious to us both, but I've definitely lost a lot of that carefree optimism of youth, the kind that helps you to throw caution to the wind and expect life to turn out wonderful. I find that now I'm in my early forties, I'm more set in my ways, and a helluva lot more wary than I was in my late twenties. Although maybe it's less a sign of age and more to do with having the responsibility of kids. Who knows?' she shrugged. 'These croissants are delicious, Ellie, and I don't care what damage they're doing to my waistline.'

'Me neither,' Ellie said, nibbling on the last crumbs as Claire's words seeped into her head.

Was that it? Maybe it was nothing but simple, age-related caution that was preventing her from accepting Johnny's proposal. Yet that hadn't stopped him from being willing to take a leap of faith. Although, in his case, it also had to do with the need to finally put down roots as he approached his fortieth birthday. Did that matter more to him than being with Ellie? Was she just a habit with him? And supposing the babies didn't arrive, what then?

Marriage was a risky business. Then again, life was a risky business. But unless you are willing to take some risks, the chances are you'll remain in a dull, boring old rut. She needed to talk honestly to Johnny before it was too late. She'd left him in bed that morning, sleeping off his hangover. Which was unusual for him, but it meant he was probably still there.

When she opened the door to Ellie's bedroom, Lucy saw the mound of a sleeping figure snuggled under the duvet on the side where Ellie normally slept, and immediately guessed that her sister had decided to postpone her meetings that morning.

She closed the door quietly and tiptoed across to the en-suite. She opened the cupboard where she knew the bathroom scales were kept. She placed the scales on the floor and let her dressing gown slip down off her shoulders. She stood on them in her black lacy underwear. Hmm. Not bad – just an extra half a kilo. She'd have no problem getting rid of that. She bent down a little to make sure she was reading it correctly. Satisfied, she straightened up, stepped off the scales and picked them up to put them back but they slipped out of her hands and crashed noisily to the tiles, hitting off her toes. It was then that she saw the tall figure of Johnny standing silently in the doorway.

'Aargh! I thought you were Ellie,' she squealed, hopping around with her injured toe.

'How could you think I was Ellie?'

'The way you were in bed, under the duvet.'

'I thought *you* were Ellie when I heard a noise in here,' he said, glowering at her. Silence stretched between them and she saw his face change as he eyed the curves revealed by her scanty underwear. 'Wow,' he said, giving her an appreciative look. 'No wonder you were snapped up by Rebecca.'

He was just wearing a pair of black boxer shorts and as her eyes automatically gravitated towards his groin, she saw an unmistakable twitch beneath the fabric. To her mortification, she felt a hot rush deep inside her and made a grab for the dressing gown.

'Jesus, Johnny, tell me this isn't happening.' She gave up trying to find the sleeves with her shaky hands and bundled it haphazardly around her.

'This isn't happening,' he said, crossing his arms across his chest but making no move to get out of her way.

'Johnny, come on,' she said, turning sideways and trying to sidle through the doorway without coming into contact with him.

'Am I that awful?' he asked, his voice challenging.

He caught her off-guard. 'No, don't be silly. You're gorgeous, but you're my sister's boyfriend.'

'I'm not sure about that anymore,' he said. 'Ellie doesn't seem to want me.'

He was right. Wasn't he? Lucy remembered her sister's words about not wanting marriage and kids.

'I think she's being awfully stupid,' Lucy said, wondering how best to get out of this moment. Then, in the next breath, she wondered if she did want to extricate herself. Johnny was looking at her with hot lust in his eyes and she allowed herself to feel a wash of excitement. Ellie didn't want him, she reminded herself. Ellie, her confident, successful sister, who had always had everything she'd ever wanted, and knew her own mind and exactly where she was going, didn't think she wanted to marry Johnny.

'Do you?' he looked as though her opinion mattered to him. 'Of course, you think I'm a good catch, isn't that right? Marriage material,' he went on, a mocking edge souring his tone. 'Ellie keeps laughing me away, dismissing me out of hand.'

'She keeps dismissing me as well,' Lucy said, finally finding the armholes of the dressing gown and slipping her arms into them. She drew the edges together and tightened the sash. She tried to ignore his naked chest with the pattern of dark hair. He reminded her of Pierce Brosnan in the James Bond movie *GoldenEye*, and they could have been in the infamous spa scene together.

'You, Lucy?' he asked. 'When does Ellie laugh you away?'

Lucy was silent for a moment, feeling as though she was on

the edge of a precipice. Then she spoke, words suddenly bursting from the hard knot that had been sitting on top of her chest for days. 'Every time I try to talk about my dad, Ellie brushes it off as though it's not important.'

Johnny looked at her as though he cared and she felt something warm swell inside her.

'But of course it's important,' he said. 'He was your father. Even though you never knew him.'

She was a little surprised by the way she'd laid bare her feelings and he'd immediately empathised. She tried to reconnect with her perky, couldn't-care-less self. 'Okay, he was too busy to bother with me,' she said, lifting her chin defensively. 'But—' she hesitated, the lump in her chest suddenly unbearable.

'But?' he encouraged softly.

'There are things I'd like to know about him.'

'What things?'

He made her feel as though it was okay to talk about this, no matter how stupid or silly it might sound. 'What was he like? Was he kind and good humoured? Was he still in love with my mum?' she asked tentatively. Then a little emboldened, 'Look at his song, 'Forever My Angel'. Where did that come from? Sometimes, I wonder if he wrote those lyrics for me. They must have been written just after I was born, because the song was released months later and became a mega hit when he died. It would mean that at least he'd thought of me in a special way. I can't talk to Ellie about it and I'm afraid to talk to Mum in case she gets upset. She did her best to make up for everything and I can understand that it's not a brilliant topic of conversation for her, but still . . . ' She hung her head so that he wouldn't see the sudden sheen of tears in her eyes.

He reached out and gently lifted her chin. 'Hey, you're crying.'

She backed away immediately and came up hard against the door jamb. She blinked away a sudden tear. 'Don't touch me.'

'Why, what's wrong with me?'

'Johnny, come on . . .'

He moved in closer and she stayed absolutely still as, with a gentle finger he caught her tear before it ran down the side of her nose. Then locking his gaze on her eyes, he brought his finger to his mouth and licked her tear. 'I bet you're all soft on the inside behind that prickly front.'

'What prickly front?' she asked, suddenly dizzy. The air was thick with suggestion. They were playing a game, she realised, a game of cat and mouse. Right then, she knew she was the cat. Even though she was backed against the door jamb and her insides were quivering like jelly, she knew she had control. One tiny movement and her dressing gown would slither to the floor, and everything would change again. She imagined his hands caressing her and it sent an electrical jolt right through her.

This man wanted her and, with a sense of shock, she realised that she wanted him. Apart from good sex, she needed to feel close to him, to have his arms around her, to have him hold her tight and drive away the questions hurting her chest. But a long, dark shadow fell between them, bringing her back to reality.

Ellie! Jesus, what was she thinking of? She couldn't do this to Ellie.

Could she?

'Ellie doesn't want me,' Johnny said huskily, as though she had voiced her name out loud. He lifted a tendril of her hair and pushed it back from her face. 'These past few weeks . . . she's been treating me as though I'm some kind of bad joke. I'm not hanging around any longer to be made a fool of. We've reached the end of the road. So I guess you and I . . . we're like two lost souls.'

She swallowed hard, unable to say anything. She looked at him for a long moment, recognising everything in his eyes; the pain of rejection, injured pride, hurt. All of these sang a resonance inside her. She wanted to cling to Johnny like she'd never clung to anyone before and weld her body to his. Her need for him overwhelmed her and she moved away from the door, pulled at the sash and allowed the dressing gown to slip off her creamy shoulders and slide to the floor.

Johnny was amazing. She sensed he was full of coiled up tension but he held off the main event for as long as possible. He began by kissing her, slowly and deeply, at the same time as his hands reached around to cup her backside, meshing their hips together so that she could feel every inch of his arousal. Then he moved behind her, pushing her hair aside and gently nuzzled her neck as he unclipped her bra. It sent lots of lovely shivers down her spine. He slowly turned her around to face him, and spent a long time staring at her breasts, touching them with infinite tenderness before he bent and took her nipples in his mouth, sucking at them until they were fully ripened.

She was still standing when he nudged her thighs apart and she had to reach behind her and grip the towel rail for balance when his fingers slipped in under her lacy thong.

'Hey, what's this?' he growled. He pulled down her thong. She saw his eyes widen in surprise then darken with lust as he stared at her thin strip of red, pubic hair.

'I'm a model,' she gasped as she stepped out of the tiny scrap of lace and felt his fingers softly rove around her naked folds. 'I have to be prepared, like a girl scout.'

'Wow. I knew you were all soft.' His voice was hoarse as he tenderly circled her nub with his thumb. Then he looked at her face as, very slowly, he slid a long finger inside her.

Jesus! This guy could do sex. Big time.

She grunted, aware of nothing except the twisting and grinding of her hips against the pressure of his fingers as pleasurable sparks ricocheted around her body. Just as she was ready to explode, he pulled away from her and carried her across to the bed. Before she had time to notice the sharp absence of his touch, he lifted her hips and buried his tongue where his fingers had been.

She wasn't here, in Ellie's room, in her bed. This wasn't Ellie's boyfriend. Her whole life had distilled to a delicious whirl of touch and feeling, the gasp of her short breaths, the heat of his skin, the urge to dissolve into this man. His tongue moved up along her body, she felt strong flanks pressing against her thighs and she looked down to see his huge erection springing from a nest of dark hair. The sight of it liquefied her insides.

'Please,' she begged, grabbing him and feeling the silky hardness pulse in her hands.

'Want me?' he growled.

'Oh, yes ... quickly ...' she twisted beneath him and opened her legs wider, hungry with desire. She was dimly aware of him kneeling up on the bed, opening a drawer and scrabbling for a condom. Then mercifully, she felt his hands under her thighs, and then, at last, the thick length of him pushing into her. She screamed and dug her nails into his shoulders as he thrust, slowly, deeply, taking his time and building on her excitement until her aching nerve endings swelled and exploded in bursts of pleasure. Shortly afterwards, he gave one final lunge and she felt every spasm of his long climax.

Spent, they lay on the bed, her legs coiled around his, her head still spinning, all her insides throbbing with bliss.

And that was how Ellie found them.

Chapter 13

*E*llie heard a scream echoing around her head. It seemed to go on forever. Then she felt the noise tearing out of her own throat. She was staring through the wrong end of a telescope that thrust her back in time to a misty tangle of naked limbs, and her mother's contorted face . . .

What?

Her vision cleared and she saw the pale-skinned bodies of Johnny and Lucy. Together. On her bed. How could this be?

There was a moment when everything was frozen, and then Johnny vaulted off the bed and bounded towards her. She felt hands gripping her shoulders, shaking her. She heard someone shrieking hysterically, realised it was her and knew he was trying to stop it. She tussled with him, her initial moment of blank shock giving way to a cold fury. It gave her a new strength and she dislodged his hold, then drawing back her arm as far as she could, she swept it forward in a wide arc and slapped him hard across the face.

'Get away from me!' she screamed. 'Get out! Go!'

In the background, she saw the wiggle of Lucy's naked breasts and the curve of her bum as she jumped out of bed and scrabbled around, looking in vain for something to cover herself with. She scurried across her bedroom and into the en-suite, returning a minute later muffled in Ellie's white dressing gown, scraps of black lace in her hands.

The pain in Ellie's head was unbearable.

'You! Get that off and get out. Now.' She ran at Lucy and yanked at the dressing gown, hearing it rip at a seam as Lucy clung to it valiantly, trying to cover her body.

'Ellie, please.'

'You *bitch*. Get the fuck out of my house.'

It didn't sound like her voice. It was high and strained, like an animal convulsed with pain. She pushed Lucy towards the door, thumping her between the shoulder blades, making a super-human effort not to claw and scratch or pull at her hair. Beside her bed, she could see Johnny pulling on the shirt and jeans he'd worn last night.

Just last night. Her heart thudded. How had life changed so quickly?

In the doorway, Lucy hesitated and looked back towards him.

'Get out.' She marched over to Lucy and gave her another shove.

To her surprise, Lucy stood her ground, 'You didn't want him,' she said, her eyes expressionless and as dark as coal in her pale face. 'You told me so yourself.'

Ellie trembled. 'How dare you!' she cried. 'Fuck off. Go on, fuck *off*. I don't want to see your face as long as you live. Bitch.' Once more she lunged towards Lucy and Lucy gave a yelp before she scurried out of reach and ran down the stairs.

'Ellie, I'm sorry.'

She whirled around. Johnny was holding out his hands in an

open, conciliatory gesture that was so ridiculously futile she almost laughed. 'It wasn't Lucy's fault,' he went on.

His words were even more preposterous. 'Screw you,' she yelled.

'I thought it was you at first . . . when I heard the noise in the en-suite . . . and then it just happened.'

How dare he. How *dare* he stand there and look at her like that. She felt so enraged she could hardly see his face. Bile rose in her throat. 'Oh, yeah? Your dick stood up by all itself, did it? And then it jabbed itself into my sister. As if. I'm going to be sick. Get out of my house and don't dare come near me again. We're over.'

'We already were,' he said. For a moment, his face swam into focus and the sad look in his eyes plucked at her heart. Everything they'd ever been to each other rose up inside her for a moment, almost choking her before it dissolved. He walked out her bedroom door without a backward glance.

Ellie went into the en-suite and doubled over with pain. She struggled to take slow, deep breaths, but her teeth were chattering and there was no relief from the knife-like twist in her stomach. It lodged there, a solid block of pain. After a while, she heard the hall door close. Her eyes darted around the en-suite, and she plucked Johnnny's toiletries from the shelf and the cabinet, flinging them to the tiled floor. His bottle of Versace cologne crashed and splintered, sending a bubble of the fragrance wafting into the air. It reminded her of the smell of his skin when she moved in for a kiss and her stomach heaved.

She strode back into her bedroom, her lovely room with the soft blue bed under the skylight to the stars. It would never be the same. It was tainted now, with the revolting image of Lucy and Johnny splayed across her bed. With a howl of agony, she dragged the duvet to the ground and yanked off the cover. She pulled sheets and pillowcases off the bed until she had a heap of soiled linen on the floor. She trampled on it, wanting to set a match to the bundle and watch the flames gobble it all up, but she had to console herself by dragging the bundle of linen downstairs, and squashing it into a plastic bin liner, which she brought around to the side of the house and into the bin.

She stood on her patio for a moment, images of the night before burning across her vision. Johnny in his white shirt, setting up the music. Lucy, young and carefree, her body undulating seductively in her silver dress. She realised with a sense of shock that it was a beautiful spring day, with the panorama of the city a silent, soft, grey blanket in the distance, dotted with tiny glints here and there where the sun sparked off random windows. She drew in ragged gulps of air, thinking how crazy it was to feel warm, bright sun on her face when everything else inside her was pulsing with dark, unending rage.

Johnny was very quiet.

Lucy was afraid to talk to him as his Mercedes surged up the hilly road. She snuck an occasional look at his rigid face but, apart from the hum of the engine, there was a thick silence between them. They seemed like strangers to each other and she couldn't believe that less than an hour ago they'd been having urgent sex.

She would never, ever forget the moment when Ellie had opened the door. At first, Lucy had been too horrified to feel anything at all. Raw instinct had mobilised her enough to get her out of Ellie's bedroom and down the stairs to her own room, where she'd put on some clothes and dumped stuff into her case. She'd almost forgotten her passport and mobile phone – for a blank, panicky moment, she'd been unable to recall where they were, seizing on them in relief when she spotted them on her bedside table. God knows what she'd left behind in her rush to get away. She hadn't even asked Johnny if she could come with him, but he was waiting for her outside with the engine running when she hauled her case out of Ellie's front door. And like the evening he'd met her at the airport, he'd lifted her case into his boot and accelerated away before she'd had time to put on her seatbelt. She hadn't even asked him where he was taking her. She presumed they were going back to his apartment.

They drove through a small village and she saw a coffee shop and convenience store where people were going about their normal, innocent business and she would have given anything to be one of them. Now that her horror had subsided a little, Lucy felt a hot, scalding shame crash through her and the dull crump in her chest had started to throb, sending slivers of pain around her body. She couldn't cope with this. No way. It was far too excruciating.

'You'll be fine,' Johnny said gruffly.

His voice took her by surprise. Something wet slid down her face and tasted salty in her mouth, and she realised she was crying and he had spotted it. 'No, I won't. How could I be fine after this?' Her tongue felt thick.

'I'm sorry. It was my fault. I wanted to get back at Ellie in some way, but I'm sorry you were dragged into it. I know you're feeling like shite, but it'll pass.'

'Yeah, in about thirty years' time. Ellie will never speak to me again. Did you see her face? How could I have done this to her?'

'Ellie and I were finished. When she calms down, she'll realise that. I'll make sure she knows what happened between us was my fault.'

'It doesn't matter if you guys were finished,' Lucy gulped. 'What I did was despicable. My sister's boyfriend! I'm to blame. If only I hadn't taken off that dressing gown.'

'Do you think I was going to let you escape that easily? The minute I saw you standing there in that sexy frilly stuff, your fate was sealed.'

She didn't answer him. The corner of her brain that wasn't on fire acknowledged that her fate had been sealed because he'd wanted to get back at Ellie in some way – not because he'd found her totally irresistible. What had made her think for one moment that he might have found her ravishing and seductive? She stared out the window at the sunny day, feeling black inside. After a while, he turned in through the high pillars of a gated entrance and drove down an avenue where low-rise apartment blocks and duplex houses were so tastefully arranged around aesthetically landscaped grounds that they sickened her.

'Chez moi,' Johnny said needlessly, driving to the apartment block at the end of the avenue and jumping out of his car.

Under any other circumstances, Lucy would have revelled in the affluence of it all. Wheeling her case, he led the way into a luxuriously appointed marbled foyer and across to the lift. He slotted in his key card and pressed the button for the penthouse. His apartment was full of natural light that hurt her gritty, red eyes. It flooded through floor-to-ceiling windows and reflected off ivory walls and cream furnishings. On another kind of day, the long, galley kitchen would have been a dream, with walnut presses and gleaming chrome and glass. Through an open door, Lucy saw his bedroom, all cream and taupe, with a balcony overlooking the lush parklands of a golf course, and a high, wide bed.

Money, money, money, the sour thought came unbidden. Another secure, comfortable side to Ellie's life. She'd probably been here lots of times, enjoying the luxury of it all as well as great sex with Johnny. Until Lucy had torn it all asunder. She'd never forgive her.

Lucy sank down on the long taupe sofa in his living room feeling dazed.

'Strong coffee, I think,' Johnny said. 'Although looking at your face, brandy would be more like it, but it's too early even for me.'

'Why, what time is it?'

'Just half past twelve.'

Would this day ever be over, she fretted, closing her eyes as he went into the kitchen and she heard the sound of a kettle being filled, a fridge being opened, the rattle of mugs. Normal domestic sounds, but even they made her feel sick and tense because the day was anything but normal.

Her lips felt rubbery against the mug as she tried to sip the coffee, needing the comfort of it in her jangling stomach. 'My flight is at six o'clock,' she said. 'I don't want to be in your way. I'll just hang loose here for a while and get a taxi to the airport.'

'No way, I'll take you. I was supposed to go into the shop for a couple of hours but after what's happened . . . that's out of the question now.'

'Don't change your plans on account of me,' she said. 'The less time we spend together the better.' She'd be quite happy to see the back of him. Yet at the same time, she didn't want him to leave her on her own, not today, when she felt as though she was trapped in a dark, black hole. When she made it as far as tomorrow, in London, she would try to pretend it had never happened.

'Christ, Lucy, what difference does it make now?' Johnny's voice was hoarse. He ran a hand through his thick dark hair. 'We could spend the afternoon in bed and it wouldn't change what's happened.'

'How can you say such a thing?'

'It's true. We've already done the dirt.'

'Do you have to put it like that?'

He sighed heavily. 'I don't know what I'm saying. Bugger it. I'm the biggest fucker going. Ellie messed me about, laughing in my face about marriage, but she didn't deserve to find us in bed together. How could I have been so fucking stupid?' He slammed his fist against the coffee table, alarming her.

'Thanks. That was me you were in bed with,' Lucy said.

He looked at her for a long moment. 'Sorry,' he said quietly. 'I didn't mean that to sound the way it did. If you forget about Ellie for a moment, what you and me had Lucy, just us, it was good. You gave me something that made me feel great . . . for a while.' He lifted her chin and wiped her tears, reminding her of the moment that had started it all. It had been great, she agreed silently. If you disconnected it from everything, for that short bubble in time, it had been the best sex she'd ever had. What a pity it had all turned out so horribly.

'No matter how good it was, the price was too high,' she said, her tears falling again.

He sat down beside her and folded his arms. 'I don't know how I'm going to live with myself knowing how much I've hurt Ellie. And I wish to hell I hadn't messed it all up between you two.'

'So do I,' Lucy said miserably, feeling a cold tremor run through her. A fresh, terrible knowledge was swelling in her head and her heart. For it wasn't just about Ellie and Lucy. What about Miranda and her mother? They were bound to find out and God knows what they'd have to say. They'd both hate her for doing this to Ellie. This was what happened when you made mistakes. It trapped innocent people as well. How could she live with this?

'Our family will never be the same,' she said. 'This is going to pull us all apart and I'll never be able to come home again.'

'Come here,' Johnny said gruffly, holding out his arms.

This was where she was now, here, in Johnny's arms, in his apartment, on his sofa. It was a haven of sorts. In the horror surrounding her, it was all that mattered right now. She fell against his chest like a child seeking sanctuary after a terrifying nightmare, ignoring, for a precious short while, the adult inside her who whispered it was only beginning.

Chapter 14

On a bright April afternoon, he got the train from Edinburgh's Waverley Station to King's Cross, instead of a flight. He wanted to retrace the steps of his childhood, when life had been far more innocent. He found something soothing in the rhythmic movement of the train as it travelled down the length of the country, and in between watching the countryside flash past the window, he nodded off occasionally; brief, hazy dreams taking him back in time and unsettling him further. He knew he could never go back to that blissful innocence. Not now that Heather Douglas was gone, so shortly after she'd talked about Zach Anderson behind the closed curtains of her hospital bed.

He was no stranger to London. He'd first visited it years ago, on a school trip, and he'd marched along with his classmates around by the front of Buckingham Palace, feeling that for all its grandeur, it hadn't a patch on Princes Street. Later on, as a young teenager, he'd come with the school again, this time to visit the museums and he'd been bored silly.

Since then, he'd been in the city a few times. He found it vastly different to Edinburgh. Bigger for starters. More cosmopolitan. More frantic. A lot less friendly. His best visit of all had been last year, when, early in the summer, he'd taken Heather on the London Eye.

He'd paid extra for a champagne flight, and it had all sounded very grand. But in reality it had just meant they'd had a shorter queue to contend with, and halfway up they'd been given one thin flute of cheap and cheerful champagne. Still, she'd smiled brightly and clinked her glass to his as though it was Mouton Rothschild. He could still see her excited face as she sipped the champagne and gazed down at the wide estuary of the rippling Thames far below, and she'd laughed at the different view of the Houses of Parliament from the vantage point of their bubble suspended in the sky. She'd been so happy! It had made him feel all powerful and proud that he could treat her like this. There had been no sign that day of the cancer that was about to invade her body and dull her bright, blue eyes. He hadn't been all-powerful against that. He hadn't been able to make it go away or ease her pain. Or stop it from ravaging her body.

Life was bloody unfair.

Outside King's Cross, he jumped into a cab. The weather was warmer in London and spring was evident in the massed ranks of flowers brightening the broad, tree-lined avenues and parks of the city. Another simple pleasure that Heather Douglas had loved – the flowers each spring.

'Imagine they were waiting in ground all winter,' she used to say. 'And now look at them! Nature is amazing.'

He wondered what right they had to be bursting with colour and life when Heather wasn't around to see them. So much for her amazing nature. It stank like hell.

The flat in Fulham was smaller than the flat in Edinburgh. It was basic but clean and had everything he'd need, except WiFi. No worries. There were plenty of internet cafés in the neighbourhood, so that shouldn't be a problem, and he was only renting it for a month.

A month should be long enough.

Most importantly, he was within easy walking distance of Chelsea.

Chapter 15

*I*n her Georgian, double-fronted house quite close to the sea in Dún Laoghaire, Vivienne switched on lamps in her main reception room, creating cosy pools of light that glowed against the Venetian-marble fireplace, reflected in the family photos grouped above the mantel, and gleamed against crystal and silver on display in the cabinet.

She sat down on her chesterfield sofa, picked up a magazine, and waited for Ellie to arrive. She hadn't seen Ellie in the week since she'd returned from her cruise. Ellie had said she was far too busy to meet up, that she was rushed off her feet with orders and appointments, but her phone calls had been so short and brusque that Vivienne had sensed something was wrong. She had always been finely attuned to the nuances in Ellie's voice, and knew when she was having good days and not so good days. She always soaked up Ellie's humours and took them on board. She felt this was wrong in a way; she couldn't live Ellie's life for her and should have disengaged long ago.

She'd phoned Miranda for a chat and her middle daughter

seemed to be fine. Miranda had never given her any cause for concern, except when she'd headed off to Hong Kong quite out of the blue. Still, she seemed to be happy, which was all Vivienne wanted. She hadn't managed to talk to Lucy as her calls had gone to voicemail, but that wasn't unusual. Later in the week Lucy had made contact, but it was just the usual bland text.

When Ellie arrived, her face was pale and taut, her eyes ringed with shadows.

'How are you after your cruise?' she asked, in a forced cheerful tone. 'Feeling any better?'

'I'm fine, darling,' Vivienne said. 'Don't mind what those doctors said. The little scare I'd had was just that – a little scare. Nothing to worry about. I'll be around for a long time yet. I've lots of living to do.'

She might have been fine, but Ellie clearly wasn't. As she sat on the sofa opposite her, her expressive green eyes were full of something dark that Vivienne couldn't define, except it was far from Ellie's usual confidence. There was a tense, fragile air about her that Vivienne found unsettling.

And then Ellie told her she was off to New York for a while.

'I don't understand,' Vivienne said. 'If you're that busy, how come you're going on holiday to New York?'

It was the wrong thing to say. Sitting on the sofa, knowing there was something wrong, Vivienne felt powerless and realised too late that feeling ineffectual had made her sound nagging and critical.

'It's not exactly a holiday,' Ellie said, her voice defensive. 'I'll be away for a few weeks. That's why I've been so busy. I've been working around the clock prioritising my orders and getting as much work ready for Claire to complete as I could.' She fell silent.

'Are you going to tell me what's sending you over there?'

Vivienne asked, regretting that they didn't have an easy mother-daughter camaraderie. Vivienne knew that if Ellie had a personal problem, she'd be the last to know because their relationship had been strained and Ellie had always kept a careful distance from her.

Ever since Zach.

Sometimes, in her nightmares, Vivienne still saw a vivid picture of the fateful moment that had fractured the relationship between herself and Ellie – the crumpled bed, a tangle of naked limbs, the consternation on Ellie's face. It was an image cast in stone that memory would never soften nor time erase. She still felt something shattering inside her as she remembered Ellie bolting like a startled colt. She still heard Ellie's raw voice as she screamed at Vivienne to leave her alone and felt the sickening dread that had gripped her stomach as the reality of it all slammed home.

'How could I have let this happen?' Vivienne had cried, hardly recognising the thin sound of her own voice. Her shaking hands tried to gather her blouse around her.

'It's not your fault,' Zach had said. By now he was shrugging into his jeans and the sound of him pulling up the zip had caused her blood to run cold. His face had been pale but his dark-grey eyes held a sleepy trace of satiated lust. She didn't know how she resisted the tremendous urge to slap it off his face.

'Of *course* it is, you fool,' she'd said, bile rising in her throat. 'I've failed Ellie. We both have. How could I have let myself be so blinded by you?' Her voice had hardened as she continued, 'I never want to see you again.'

'Okay, maybe it shouldn't have happened,' he'd said, finally looking a little shaken, 'but it's not the end of the world.'

'It is for me and Ellie,' she'd said.

'Take it easy, Vivienne. Ellie will be fine. You can't wrap her in cotton wool forever.'

For a moment, words had failed her as she stared at him, wondering what exactly she'd ever seen in him or how it had come to this. 'You insensitive bastard,' she'd said through gritted teeth. 'She's barely sixteen and she's in a vulnerable place right now . . . Oh, God,' she cried. 'I wish I'd never laid eyes on you. I must have been totally deranged.'

'Hey, come on, that's a bit much—'

'The hell it is—'

'Don't worry, I'll be out of your hair soon.'

'Good. You can't go far enough away from me.'

There had been many more angry words hurled between them.

She'd never seen Zach again after that morning. Later, in the weeks that followed, she'd tried several times to talk to Ellie, but her daughter had been totally unresponsive and blanked her completely. For a long time afterwards, Vivienne had agonised that she should have persisted in getting through to her.

Now, to her surprise, Ellie shook her head and gave a bitter laugh. 'You'll find out soon enough. It's Johnny. We're finished. I need to get away for a while. I don't fancy being in Dublin while grossly exaggerated stories about our private lives are splashed across the gossip columns.'

'Oh, darling, I'm so sorry to hear that,' Vivienne immediately went across to give her a hug, and she was crushed that Ellie felt stiff and unyielding in her arms. 'How are you feeling? No, that's a stupid question. When did it happen?'

'Just before you came home. I've been keeping my head down, working my ass off to get on top of things before I go to New York. Johnny seems to be keeping a low profile too, but word of our split is bound to get out soon and I don't fancy being around when it does.'

'God, Ellie, I wish there was something I could do to help.' She knew by the look on Ellie's face that she wasn't even listening to her. Ellie was miles away.

'I finished with him after he cheated on me,' Ellie said, her green eyes glittering. 'That's all you need to know.'

There was a cloud of darkness in her eyes that told Vivienne there was a lot more to the story, but Ellie wasn't going to tell her. Her heart swelled with anger at Johnny. Her children might be grown up, and her relationship with Ellie might be far from perfect, but she still felt like an avenging tiger protecting her cubs. 'It's your business and I'd never dream of intruding,' she said. 'I know how you feel though. Breaking up is horrible and no matter the circumstances, you're left scarred for a while—'

'You mean like you were after Zach,' Ellie said bluntly.

Vivienne felt startled at the mention of his name coming from Ellie. No doubt that wretched news programme had brought it all back to her. Would he ever be truly gone? The only good thing that had come from her short-lived relationship with him had been Lucy. By the time Vivienne had finally plucked up the courage to break the news of her pregnancy to her daughters, Zach was in Canada and she was four months pregnant. Ellie's face had been a mixture of shock and disgust. And whereas now it might be cool and fashionable to be pregnant by a rock musician, especially if you were forty years of age to his twenty-nine, back then it had raised many eyebrows.

'I wasn't scarred after Zach. Not compared to how I felt after your father died,' she said gently, making the most of the opening Ellie had unwittingly given her to talk about the difficult subject. 'That was ... absolutely devastating. But I'd hate to think that all the publicity about Zach's anniversary has upset you, Miranda or Lucy. Time heals, Ellie. It really does. It brings a different perspective. Life is all about change and nothing stays the same. Sometimes, it's very unfair. But you can only carry on, otherwise there's no point in getting up in the morning. And I think that women have a great capacity to be strong and resilient. There's nothing like the support of friends to help.'

Ellie shook her head. 'Sorry, Mum, I just can't take any of that female solidarity crap right now.'

Vivienne sighed. How painful for Ellie, who was so used to being the one laughing off her admirers. Ellie had dated a succession of men down through the years, taking all of them for granted and none of them seriously. She'd been with Johnny for a couple of years now and Vivienne had hoped they'd make a go of it.

'Ellie, darling, the rotten feelings will ease,' she said. 'I promise. Is there anything I can do to help?'

'The best thing you can do is forget that I ever knew anyone called Johnny,' Ellie said crisply. 'I'm not talking about it again and I don't want any sympathy. I'd prefer you to carry on as normal. Pretend if you have to, that things couldn't be better. And get well yourself. The cruise must have agreed with you, as you look better than I've seen you in a while.'

Ellie had neatly changed the subject, erecting a barrier around her heartbreak that excluded her, and Vivienne decided it was best to go along with it. She picked up her mobile. 'I've some great photos I must show you,' she said. 'I had a brilliant time. There's nothing to beat being waited on hand and foot, plenty of sunshine and good food.'

It was only later, as Ellie prepared to leave, that Vivienne tentatively asked, 'When are you heading off?'

'Early next Sunday,' Ellie said. 'And if Johnny comes here looking for me, you don't know where I am, okay?'

'Of course, darling. I understand. Hopefully I'll see you before you go. Are you staying anywhere nice?'

'I'm staying in an apartment belonging to Claire's cousin,' Ellie said. 'It's near Central Park.'

'That sounds much more relaxing than a hotel,' Vivienne smiled brightly at Ellie's taut face, trying to conjure up something positive, and knowing she was failing dismally to lift even a tiny fraction of Ellie's gloom. She kept up her bright face as they went into the hall, making it sound like Ellie was off on a fabulous holiday. She continued to keep her smile in place when Ellie made a desultory attempt to air kiss her cheek, and only when her daughter had gone, tripping down the flight of granite steps outside as though she couldn't wait to get away, did Vivienne allow herself to crumple.

Chapter 16

*J*ust before she moved to Hong Kong, Miranda had told her family it was best to keep in touch through email.

'What about Skype?' Lucy had asked.

'Nah. Too awkward with the time difference. Email is the easiest way,' she'd said. 'Better than dragging someone out of bed or staying up late to catch you in the evenings. And if I have any news, you'll all hear it together.'

The time difference was a very convenient excuse, Miranda realised, as it helped to keep a distance between herself and her family. She called Vivienne most weekends, but only called Ellie occasionally, and Lucy, who kept such mad hours anyway that it was impossible to keep track of her, even less.

So she was a little uncomfortable when Ellie texted her and asked when would be the best time to call her for a chat. What kind of chat? Surely all the fuss with Zach Anderson's anniversary had died down by now and Lucy was back in London? How was she going to chat to Ellie without bringing Christian's name into the conversation?

Surely Ellie hadn't guessed something was up with Miranda?

Already, in the space of ten days, since their first lunch together, they'd been on several dates, cementing the tentative relationship that had already formed in the months she'd spent working alongside him. And it had gone far beyond dating him just to keep her mind off her sisters. She wanted to spend time with him and enjoyed his company. They'd gone for drinks after work, then for a meal and they'd spent a day on Repulse Bay, strolling by the glittering sea along a promenade with a carnival atmosphere, staying on to have a meal in one of the restaurants as the night softly fell. She was loving the way he kissed her at the end of the evening, and held her close, and generally looked after her, spoiling her with flowers and chocolates and champagne. He told her he'd been waiting months to spoil her.

'Months?' she asked, feeling fearful and excited, and as though she was wrapped in a warm glow.

'Yes, ever since I saw you staring out the conference room window at the view.'

'Oh. That time.'

'Yes, you blushed so prettily that I couldn't take the piss out of you. Then I realised I didn't want to.'

He was such a part of her life already, it would be difficult to pretend he didn't exist. Her colleagues in the office were beginning to notice that something was happening between them, particularly Sara and Mai, who sat adjacent to her. From Singapore, and years younger than Miranda, they were working their way around the world and enjoying her burgeoning romance, so they just smiled at her indulgently when from time to time Christian lingered a little too long by her desk.

'This really brightens up our day,' Sara said.

'Yeah,' Mai chimed in, 'looking at you pair is better than watching a movie.'

'And what movie would you cast us in?' Miranda asked, surprised at the way she was encouraging them. Surprised also that she was indulging in such gossipy chit-chat at her desk. It was something she'd never have had the time or inclination for back in Dublin. Then again, her normal restraint would have prevented her from becoming so friendly with the likes of Mai and Sara. And she was secretly curious to know what they thought of her and Christian.

'*Casablanca*,' Mai sighed.

'Oh, no,' Sara objected. 'We need a happy ending. Like *Four Weddings and a Funeral*. Or *Love Actually* – but with Matthew McConaughey in the lead.'

Miranda smiled. She'd heard of those movies but had never watched them. She wondered what Matthew McConaughey looked like and what kind of happy ending Sara imagined.

But in the interests of self-preservation, she didn't want Ellie to know about Christian just yet. It was too soon. She would ask millions of questions and maybe raise doubts in Miranda's head. Before she replied to Ellie's text, she feverishly re-read the last few emails she'd sent, but there were no clues in them to hint that her life had changed completely.

However, as she sat in her apartment in Hong Kong on Wednesday evening and listened to what Ellie was saying, full of a shocked disbelief, she realised she'd been worrying unnecessarily.

'Ellie, hang on a minute . . . you're not making sense,' she interrupted. So far, she'd gathered that Ellie and Johnny had split up, which upset her greatly for a number of reasons, but then Ellie had brought Lucy into the story. What did Lucy have to do with all this?

'What doesn't make sense?' Ellie said. 'It's simple really. I caught them in bed together – *my* bed.'

'You're joking.'

'Do you really think I'd joke about something like this?'

'I don't believe you.'

'Well, it happened.'

'But it's total crap, Ellie! Where's Lucy now?'

'I don't know and I couldn't care less. I presume she's back in London and I'm sure we'll see her bimbo body plastered across some tabloid sooner or later. I should have scratched her eyes out when I had the chance.'

'God, Ellie ... I can't take this in. It's unbelievable. Does Mum know? She never mentioned a word to me when I called her the other day.'

'She doesn't know anything other than that me and Johnny are finished, which I told her last night. I didn't tell her who he was fucking in my bed. She doesn't need that information.' Ellie's voice was caustic.

There was a long silence and Miranda spoke into the silence to make sure Ellie was still on the line. 'Why didn't you tell her?' she asked gently, mindful of Ellie's raw pain.

'It hurts too much,' Ellie said in a flat voice. 'I didn't want to see the look on her face. It was enough to deal with her sympathy. It's one thing to be betrayed but ten times worse when it's your own sister ... the little bitch made a right fool of me. They both did. But it's not even my pride ... I don't care about that,' she gave a strangled laugh that upset Miranda ever further, 'It's like – I feel as though everything has just collapsed inside on me.'

Another long silence.

'Yes, I can only begin to imagine how tough that is,' Miranda said. 'Christ. What are you going to do?'

'Obviously I'm never talking to Lucy again,' Ellie's voice shook. 'I don't want to see her or hear from her. She made her bed and she can bloody well lie in it. With Johnny. They're welcome to each other. I'm clearing out of Dublin for a while.'

Miranda found she was holding her breath and painfully gripping the phone as she scanned her small apartment. With a main living room, a small kitchen and bathroom, her bedroom, and a tiny spare room that just fitted a single bed and which she used for storage, it was all very compact. But it was *her* space, belonging to Miranda Morgan, and somewhere her sisters hadn't ventured. She still couldn't get her head around what Lucy had done, it seemed so terribly cruel, as well as being unlike Lucy, for all her devil-may-care attitude. And what about Johnny behaving so badly? But although she knew Ellie must be hurting terribly, and she empathised completely, the last thing she wanted was a broken-hearted Ellie landing in Hong Kong to cry on her shoulder, just when she felt she was making a new life for herself.

If that made her a really horrible person, she told herself shakily, well so be it.

She wasn't sure how long her fragile resolve would have held out before being replaced by guilt, and she tried to recall if she'd ever told Ellie she had a spare room. She was searching around in her head for a cast-iron excuse, when she grasped that Ellie was talking about going to New York for a few weeks.

New York? Thank God. Miranda was horrified with the surge of relief that flooded through her. This was her *sister*, after all. And she was in trouble. But still ... everything with Christian was all so new that she didn't want to share it with anyone, least of all a vengeful Ellie.

'What about your work?' Miranda asked, feeling it was safe to talk again.

'That's all sorted. Thankfully, the shows are over and lots of the orders are in. I've spent the last week working sixteen-hour days so that Claire has enough to keep her going for a few weeks and I can take the break.'

'I think you're right to get away for a while and New York would be perfect. With all the bustle and bright lights, it's so constantly full on that you won't feel too much alone.'

'That's what I'm hoping,' Ellie agreed.

Long after Miranda had finished the call, her head was still whirling as Ellie's news sank in. What had happened was unthinkable. Lucy and Johnny. Johnny and *Lucy*? Her little sister? *Ellie's* Johnny? How had they ended up in bed together? What the hell had been going through Lucy's mind to make her fall into bed with her sister's boyfriend? She'd gathered that there had been some kind of party the night before – a going-away party for Lucy, Ellie had told her bitterly. Had it been too much drink? Or was it something that had blown up in the aftermath of the publicity surrounding Zach Anderson's anniversary? That was, after all, the main reason Lucy had gone home.

And there was another question niggling her – if she'd been there, back home at the party, would it have happened? Could she have prevented it? She'd often felt caught in the middle between Ellie and Lucy when they clashed over silly things. But if she'd sensed something building between them, she might have been able to ease the tension.

If she hadn't run off to Hong Kong in the first place, she might have prevented this awful thing from happening.

She had to forget about it and pull herself together because she was seeing Christian that evening. It was hard to get away from the habits of a lifetime, from always being prepared to ease the tension between Ellie and Lucy. She wondered how Lucy was getting on in London. But most of all, she couldn't stop wondering how Ellie would cope, now that she knew what it felt like when your sister caused the break-up of your relationship.

*

Before she had left for Hong Kong, Miranda had just about managed to stop herself from admitting to Ellie that Graham's interest in her had fizzled out when he'd finally met her older sister. It was something she'd gone through with each and every boyfriend.

The Ellie test.

She'd kept Ellie and Graham apart for as long as she could, but when her birthday celebrations had come around, it had proved impossible. Lucy had come home from London and Ellie had insisted on bringing them all out for a meal, overruling Miranda's objections in her usual I-know-what's-best-for-you manner.

'I'm treating you for your birthday, Miranda, no arguments,' she'd said. 'It's the least you deserve. Both Lucy and I appreciate the way you always look out for us. I've booked the new Italian on South William Street. And I just have to meet Graham. I can't believe you've kept him to yourself without my seal of approval for . . . how long?'

'Three months,' Miranda had said. What will be, will be, she told herself in an attempt to be philosophical as she and Graham jumped out of a taxi outside the restaurant. It was more than time to give him the Ellie test. But they hadn't even finished their main courses before she'd noticed Graham staring at Ellie with something akin to adoration in his eyes, despite the presence of Johnny at the other end of the table. Graham had tried to hide his slack-jawed admiration, but she'd known they were finished at that moment.

Happy birthday, Miranda.

Other boyfriends hadn't been so tactful, either letting slip that they'd dated her just to get close to Ellie, or asking her for Ellie's mobile number – just in case.

'In case of what?' she'd glared at one unfortunate.

'In case I need her help to organise a special treat for you sometime.'

Yeah, sure.

Yet another, who'd looked as though he was a pillar of society, hadn't even got as far as bed with her before he'd asked, in the middle of a cosy, intimate meal, if there was any chance of a threesome. Miranda had lifted the bottle of Sancerre, poured it into his lap and stormed out of the restaurant.

But, naturally, Ellie knew none of this. So although Miranda had used the break-up with Graham as a reason to get out of Dublin and spread her wings, she couldn't tell Ellie the real reason they'd split. If Ellie knew the truth, she'd be horrified to think she'd been unwittingly responsible for a lot of Miranda's failed relationships. Even worse, she'd be embarrassingly aware of it with any future boyfriend.

So although she'd come to Hong Kong because she was tired of always being the one in the middle, Miranda had also had to get away because she was even more disenchanted watching her so-called loving boyfriends fall under Ellie's sultry spell.

But, she vowed, whatever she had to do, that wasn't going to happen with Christian.

Sitting across the restaurant table, Christian said, 'You're very quiet, Miranda. What's bothering you?'

She wavered. She wanted to keep it to herself. She didn't want to bring her sisters into the equation and mess up the tentative dynamic that was growing between them, or the new side to her life that was slowly emerging, especially after her firm resolve to be free of them all and just enjoy being with Christian.

'Is it us? You are tired of me?'

'Oh, no,' she said, horrified he would think this.

'Then, what is it?'

133

She bit her lip, realising it was better to be honest with Christian, no matter how much it cost her, than have him thinking he'd done something wrong.

Eventually she said, 'There's been a big row, at home, between my sisters.'

'That's a pity,' he looked sympathetic. 'It's not pleasant when a family falls out.'

'This is very serious,' she said. 'Something really awful has happened and I don't think they'll ever talk to each other again.'

'And you're worrying about it.'

'Yes.'

'You probably feel you're too far away to be of help.'

'How did you guess?'

He took her hand in his. 'I know what you're like, already,' he said warmly. 'You tip the taxi drivers far too much. You fret about the cost of a restaurant meal when families are struggling to survive on small wages in tiny apartments. Kind and caring about strangers, I can imagine how deeply you care about your sisters.'

She couldn't care all that much if she didn't want Ellie in Hong Kong though, could she?

'Do you want my advice?' he said.

'Depends on what it is . . .' she glanced at him, but nothing had diminished between them. If anything he looked more affectionate towards her.

'It's out of your hands, Miranda. There's nothing you can do, my pet.'

Out of her hands . . . she heard that part first. He was telling her there was nothing she could do. Then she allowed herself to hear it again. *My pet?* A great warmth surged through her.

'I'm not being hard,' he went on, 'but this is between your sisters, and only they can sort it out. You have to let it be. It is, I think, the best Beatles song. Let it be.'

134

She mulled over his words for a short while. It wasn't easy to shake the habits of a lifetime and just let it be. She could try, though, couldn't she? And — *my pet*. She hugged the words to herself, feeling them twirl around inside her chest like a glittering ball.

This was one relationship she had to keep well away from Ellie.

Chapter 17

'Lucy? You are ready to rock?' Sasha's voice came through Lucy's intercom a week after the Venetia casting call.

'It's open. Come in,' Lucy called.

Sasha opened the door and popped her head around, all big, doe-like eyes and mane of pale blonde hair. Her eyes widened in dismay as she stepped into the living room, and she waved an admonishing finger. 'What is this? Why aren't you ready?'

Lucy sat up a little straighter on the sofa, put down her bottle of beer and hugged her soft fleece blanket a little tighter.

Another model in the Rebecca Grace agency, Sasha was a tall Scandinavian, and Lucy couldn't help admiring her. She was a professional to her fingertips, had an apartment close to hers, and was the nearest thing she had to a friend in the competitive melting pot of her profession. This evening Sasha's svelte figure was showcased in a tiny white mini-skirt and lacy blouse. Six foot in her stocking feet, she was a little taller than Lucy and her legs seemed to go on forever from her slender thighs down to her sequinned heels.

Sasha frowned at her. 'Lucy? What is it?'

'I don't know if I'm going.'

'*What*?' Sasha's eyes were like saucers and in spite of herself Lucy smiled. 'Lucy! This is not you. To miss lots of champagne and photo opportunities? And a free sample of the new perfume? All Rebecca's girls have been invited. You have to show your face.'

'I don't feel like it.'

'You are down in the dumps?'

'Mmm. Yeah.'

'Good. Then you must cheer yourself up and come to the launch party. You can't hide in your apartment with a beer. Look at you!' Sasha went over and pulled off her blanket. 'You're still in your pyjamas. This is bad. Very bad. Now go into the shower,' she ordered, 'Get dressed and when you're ready I'll call a cab. We have no calls tomorrow so it's a night of champagne and free food.' She let Lucy know she meant business by leaning over her, catching the end of her pyjama top and pulling it up over her head as if she were a child.

'Hey!' Lucy scrambled off the sofa, clamping her arm across her bare breasts.

Sasha laughed. 'I've seen your boobies more times than any guy ever has.'

'You don't know how many guys I've had,' Lucy said, trying to sound playful as an image of Johnny rose up in her head and sent a shockwave through her. But Sasha was right, for in the scrum-like scenes behind the catwalk, where you were lucky to have a square metre to change in and boobs and bottoms frequently collided, there was no place for modesty.

'And I don't look at you the way guys do. I think you are pretty with a nice figure and lovely boobs, but they want to ride you because they think you are sexy.'

She didn't feel the least bit sexy. Lucy nibbled her lip – it was as if all the sexiness had drained out of her when Ellie had opened the door and stared at her in horror.

'Get your bottoms off and go shower. I'll take them off myself if you don't move.'

'There's beer if you want some,' Lucy gestured to where bottles of beer were sitting on her kitchen worktop along with several empties.

Sasha frowned. 'Drinking all by yourself? That's not good.'

'Yeah, you're right,' Lucy said, before she disappeared through the bathroom door. She stripped off and stepped into the shower cubicle. She stood under the warm spray and closed her eyes, feeling the water pour all over her, from the crown of her head to her toes. After a while she felt marginally better. She wrapped herself in a towel, scooping her hair up into a turban, and padded out to her kitchen to get the hairdryer.

'I never saw you in the dumps before,' Sasha said. 'Is everything all right? Are you worried about the Venetia campaign?'

'Nah, why should that worry me? We won't know until next week anyway.'

Lucy switched on her hairdryer and was saved from having to talk to Sasha for a few minutes because of the noise of the dryer. Sasha flicked through a magazine while Lucy stared at her reflection in the mirror as she angled the brush against the nozzle, stroked it down the length of her hair, and wondered if life would ever get back to normal.

She didn't expect to make the cut in the Venetia campaign. She'd turned up at the casting feeling low and out of sorts, instead of confident and sparky. No matter that she'd prepared well with a moisturising facial and with her hair professionally conditioned, she'd felt so depressed inside that she couldn't drum up the necessary confidence and she knew it had affected her performance when they'd asked to see her walk.

It was now ten days since Johnny had dropped her off at Dublin airport, and apart from the casting last week and her preparations, and a couple of studio shoots for a make-up advertisement and a lingerie promotion, she'd moped around the apartment thinking of little else besides the moment Ellie had discovered them. She'd texted Ellie, twice, hoping against hope that Ellie might respond and praying that her response might halt her downward plunge. She'd told her how sorry she was for what had happened, how she wished she could turn back the clock, but there was deafening silence from Ellie.

In an attempt to save herself from spiralling into despair, she told herself that maybe, just maybe, she'd done them both a favour. There must have been good reason why her go-getting sister felt unable to commit to Johnny. Surely Lucy had helped her to make up her mind for once and for all? And Johnny had enjoyed their romp, because he'd already known it was over between him and Ellie, so she'd boosted his injured pride. In the next breath, she told herself she was being ridiculous. There was no way to justify what had happened. She didn't know how she was going to pick herself up. Neither would she be able to vindicate herself to her mother and Miranda. She hadn't spoken to them yet because she was afraid to. Ellie had probably got them on her side already, so they would all really hate her – even Miranda. As she stared at her light grey eyes in the mirror, she had never felt so alone and despondent.

She picked up her GHD and finished styling her hair. Funnily enough, all that stuff with Ellie and Johnny had put Zach Anderson and that horrible wreath to the back of her mind. And besides her family and her shocking behaviour, she'd other things to concern herself with, like her career and the real threat of younger and greedier models stalking up behind her and passing her out. Especially if she couldn't focus properly on her job with her head running around in endless circles.

She would have to try putting her problems behind her, otherwise her career would hit the skids. And really, her career was the most important thing, wasn't it? It was separate to everything else and the one thing she had that gave her life meaning. She went into her bedroom and sifted purposefully through her wardrobe.

'What's keeping you?' Sasha called.

'Two minutes,' Lucy said, wriggling into a pair of silver hot pants that were cut high, and putting on a metallic see-thru top. Then she slipped her feet into a pair of Charlotte Olympia peep-toed purple-suede ankle boots. She put on her make-up hurriedly, blending Mac Studio Fix across her nose and cheeks and achieving a gothic look in less than sixty seconds by layering on the Kohl and applying several coats of volumising mascara. She then scraped her hair back into a ponytail, showing off the contours of her pale face, and a slash of Urban Decay crimson lipstick finished off the look. She picked up a purple Prada clutch, stood back and examined her image in the wardrobe's mirrored door. How was that for making a statement?

'Hey, where have you been hiding!' Sasha said, her eyes admiring when she sashayed out into the living room. 'Don't know if I'm glad or sorry I called for you.'

The paparazzi were corralled behind crash barriers outside the Belgravia hotel where the launch party for a new, luxury perfume range was being held. Lucy carefully stepped out of the taxi and paused to allow an explosion of flash bulbs to capture her image. She imagined Ellie or Johnny seeing her in a tabloid and she lifted her chin and threw back her shoulders as if to tell them that Lucy Morgan was back to her usual self, and she hadn't a care in the world.

For a moment she almost believed it.

'Hey, love that ass, Lucy,' someone called out. 'It puts Kylie in the shade.'

Lucy smiled and wiggled her butt for the camera, eventually joining Sasha in the hotel foyer. They were met by security and whisked up in a lift to the third-floor ballroom where the party was being held. It was thronged with the usual celebrities, and as the music thumped from the speakers, Lucy drank Cristal and mingled with them all, forcing herself to relax into the zone.

He'd taken a chance on getting into the party and on her being there tonight.

Facebook and Twitter were great. In the past few weeks, he'd become cyber friends with lots of London fashion photographers and models, including her, building up his contact list by degrees. He was using a fake name and profile of course, and he was amazed at how easy it as to put two and two together and figure out what was happening in the world of fashion shoots and launch parties, a world he'd never before inhabited. He'd noticed, however, that her Facebook page had been unusually quiet in the past couple of weeks, as though she was staying close to home, and he'd wondered if it had had anything to do with her father's anniversary.

He'd rented a tuxedo for the evening and arrived at the hotel in a cab, spotting the Rottweilers with the guest list patrolling the foyer just in time. He'd stalked down the lobby as though he belonged there, slipping into the gents to give himself time to work out a game plan. Then he'd gone back to the foyer to sit in the deep cushiony armchairs nearest the elevators, glancing at his mobile every so often, looking as though he was waiting for someone. His chance came when one Rottweiler went into a corner to take a call on his mobile and the other one escorted a couple towards the lift, but hurried away as a party of six came laughing and chatting through the entrance doors. It had been a simple enough matter to dash into the lift just before the door closed, smiling warmly at the couple as though he had every right to be there.

And he had, he told himself. If things had been different, this kind of ambience could have been part of his life; the elegant ballroom with the subtle lighting playing across the ceiling, the enormous flower displays, and sumptuously dressed tables around the side of the room full of tempting finger food, rivers of champagne and expensive goody bags. And all around him the crush of scented, designer-clad bodies. Tall, stick-thin models and good-looking men in sharp suits. He recognised Emma Watson and Florence Welch, and a member of The Killers, and then Holly Willoughby, and realised he was rubbing shoulders with celebrities he'd never expected to meet in his life.

If things had been different, Heather Douglas could have had all of this.

He imagined how her excited face would have looked and his frail composure faltered. The room was a lot warmer than he'd expected. He could feel himself perspiring in his suit.

And then she arrived, taking his breath away as she made an entrance along with a blonde chick. Now that he was this close to her, his heart thumped. She was taller than he'd expected. And stunning in real life. The confidence she oozed as she smiled and wiggled her fingers at people was like a magnetic aura around her. Is this what beauty and fame did? Gave you an indelible stamp? He watched her play the room in her sparkling hot pants and lacy blouse, and she seemed to be on top of the world as she mingled with celebrities, chatting as though they were good friends, helping herself to champagne as though it was water.

Rich bitch.

'Sir? May I offer you refreshment?'

He jumped as a waiter appeared beside him, half expecting to be lifted by the collar and forcibly ejected. 'Just water, please,' he said, casting his eyes desperately around the phalanx of glasses on the silver tray.

'Would that be sparkling or still?'

'Still, please.' God, anything would do. And why was he feeling so nervous? It must be that seeing her at last in the flesh was unsettling him. He would have to get over it.

'I'll be right back, sir.'

He spent a few interminable moments wondering if he should move from the spot and let the waiter run after him like a spoiled celeb probably would. But the waiter was back with the glass of water before he had a chance to make up his mind.

He spent the next half an hour drifting around the edge of groupings, thinking he could get good at this. All you had to do was to look interested and laugh a lot at the punchlines, some of which you could hardly hear, thanks to the booming music. And all the time he was aware of her circulating, flirting, fiddling with her ponytail, pulling down the edges of her tight shorts over her curvy arse. He thought she was drinking too much and wondered if the paparazzi would be waiting for her outside the hotel in case they'd catch her staggering on her sky-high heels.

And at last, out of the corner of his eye, he caught her looking at him through the crush of people. She had obviously sensed him watching her and there was a puzzled look on her face as though she was trying to place him. Someone moved and got in the way and he saw her angling her creamy neck so that she could give him another glance. He made himself smile and nod slightly, as though they were acquainted. Then someone else caught her attention and she looked away.

It was a start.

Chapter 18

'Did you pack this case yourself?' said the shiny, sparkling attendant at the check-in desk. She looked up automatically, a flash of recognition in her eyes as she saw Ellie standing in front of her.

'I did,' Ellie confirmed.

There were long moments of waiting while the attendant tapped on her keyboard. Then she asked, 'Have you any hand luggage?'

'I have,' Ellie said, lifting up her matching Vuitton wheelie case for inspection. She tried to curb her impatience and silently urged the attendant to get on with it as she went through the tiresome security questions. Ellie was so self-conscious it was as if a spotlight was shining on her from somewhere up above, illuminating every step of her getaway. She turned up the generous collar of her sheepskin jacket and wished she could beam herself onto the aircraft. At last the attendant handed Ellie her boarding pass along with a warm smile, 'Enjoy your flight.'

'I will,' Ellie said with feeling. The sooner she was through security and immigration and boarding the flight to New York the better.

Thank God Claire had come to her rescue. When she'd called to see her a couple of days after the great betrayal, Claire had known immediately that she was deeply upset. Ellie had spared the details, merely telling her that she had finished things with Johnny.

Claire had looked incredulous. 'You're joking. I can't take this in. Did he ... or you ...?'

'I threw him out after he ... did something he wouldn't have done if he'd really loved me. It all happened so suddenly that I'm still in shock.'

'Oh, Ellie, God, this is awful. I'm sure you'll sort it out between you.'

Ellie had laughed. 'No. Absolutely not. Not after ... what happened. I just wish there was some way I could get out of Dublin for a while. It's too small for both of us, especially when the news gets out, as it will. It's not that I care about our split getting out, but I dread to think what kind of scandalous spin will be put on it.'

She didn't think Johnny would talk – not under these circumstances – but she wouldn't put it past Lucy to drop some hints in her downward race for column inches.

Claire had given her a thoughtful look. 'Are you serious about getting away?'

'Yes, even for three or four weeks. I'll have to look at the orders on hand and see ... and then find somewhere to go. Preferably somewhere Johnny and I have never visited together, so that rules out half of Europe,' Ellie had felt more mirthless laughter caught in her throat as various cities slid through her mind like a roll call – Paris, Rome, Madrid, Vienna ... 'I'd love somewhere I could quietly disappear to without talking to a single living soul.'

'We'll look at the orders in a minute, but, Ellie, I have keys to my cousin's apartment in New York,' Claire had said slowly.

New York. She'd been there lots of times, but, funnily enough, never with Johnny. The city that never slept, where you could anonymously blend with the bustling crowds.

'It's not exactly a luxury loft in Tribeca, it's a one-bed apartment and probably not quite the style you're used to,' Claire had continued, a little more enthusiastically now that Ellie hadn't refused out of hand, 'but the beauty of it is, you wouldn't have to talk to anyone, or fill out any references, let alone any registration details. You know Laura? You met her the last time we were in New York for fashion week and we all went out for a meal.'

Laura. A friendly, bubbly, thirtysomething, who was a creative director in a large PR firm, Ellie had remembered. They'd had a good laugh together over a meal and drinks.

'She's away for three months, working on some campaign in Australia,' Claire had continued. 'She sometimes travels for work so she gave me a spare key in case Tom and I ever want to make use of it. At the moment Tom is up to his tonsils in work, so we won't be haring off for a weekend, but if you want a bolthole for a couple of weeks, no questions asked, it's yours . . . I can give Laura a call about it but I know she'd be glad of your having the use of it. How does that sound?'

'Sounds good,' Ellie had said, her mind already made up. A bolthole with no questions asked. 'And if you see anything in the papers, will you let me know immediately? Day or night?'

'Of course. But I can't see Johnny doing the dirt—'

'He already has,' another mirthless laugh. Funny how you could still laugh when your world had caved in.

'And at least the autumn/winter collection has been launched,' Claire had said. 'A break away would fit in with taking some time out to gather ideas on the next collection. You're bound to be inspired by New York.'

Inspired? I don't know about that, Ellie thought as she shuffled through security and immigration, feeling as though she was sticking out like a sore thumb and it was only when the aeroplane lifted clear of the Dublin tarmac and banked into the sky to give her a bird's eye view of patchwork fields below that she relaxed a little.

Johnny didn't know of her plans. Right up to that morning, he'd been inundating her with texts and voicemails, none of which Ellie had acknowledged.

'Ellie, please talk to me . . .'

'I can't believe what I did . . .'

'I never meant to hurt you . . .'

Go to hell, Johnny.

He'd also called to her house several times, almost every day, but she'd refused to answer the door and had put her fingers in her ears trying to block out his entreaties as he shouted through the glass.

'Ellie, I know you're in there, please let me explain.'

Piss off, Johnny.

She'd had to rid the en-suite of the toiletries she'd flung around in the heat of rage as she couldn't leave that telling mess for Marta. Getting down on her hands and knees and scrubbing the floor clean of his aftershave had been a catharsis of sorts, as though she had been scrubbing her heart and soul clean of him.

She hadn't cried. Not once. Not even after she'd talked to Vivienne and Miranda. Instead, she had harnessed her anger and fury and used that energy to tackle a mountainous workload, working long into the night to prepare work for Claire and her team of seamstresses, and falling asleep on her studio sofa for a few hours' fitful sleep. She hadn't been able to sleep on her own bed, feeling that it was tainted, but in the space of a week, she'd accomplished more than she usually did in a month.

She'd scanned online editions of the tabloids, relieved to see there was nothing in the gossip columns – yet – about her and Johnny and she was grateful for that. Yesterday, she'd spotted photos of Lucy at a party in Belgravia. She'd been photographed going into the party looking sparkling and assured, wearing an eye-catching pair of shorts. Unfortunately, she'd let herself down as usual because she'd been pictured coming out, quite clearly the worse for wear, lifting her shorts to expose a bum cheek. There was the usual attention-grabbing caption and it was obvious that Lucy was merrily getting on with her life as though she'd never torn Ellie's apart. The penitent texts she'd sent Ellie, which Ellie had ignored, had clearly been a joke, because there was no sign of a guilty conscience in those photographs.

'Screw you,' she'd muttered under her breath, closing the screen.

She put Lucy out of her mind as she sipped the complimentary champagne in business class and settled in for the flight.

Ellie didn't know what she'd expected to feel when she landed at JFK. She'd never run away from anything ever before and she'd always thought you'd feel liberated, relieved, freed from a burden as though it was lifted from you, especially in New York, arguably the most exciting city in the world where even the air was vibrant. She walked out to the line of yellow cabs, handed the address to the driver and sank inside, waiting to be caught up in the sparkle of the city and whirled away from her troubles as they headed into Manhattan.

It never happened. Instead, as she got out of the cab in front of the four-storey, pre-war brownstone on the Upper West side,

Ellie's limbs were like lead. It was drizzling rain and she shivered with cold after the heat of the cab, in spite of her sheepskin jacket.

'You okay, lady?' the cabbie asked, obviously surprised at the generous tip Ellie had pressed into his hand, when the reality was that Ellie couldn't have summoned the energy to look for a smaller bill. She forced a smile and told herself she must be suffering from jet lag, even though it was just the afternoon in New York and only evening time in Dublin.

Laura's apartment was a renovated one-bed on the fourth floor, full of high ceilings, charmingly exposed brick walls in the living room, and a kitchen full of cherry wall units and stainless steel. It felt strange to her, as though she was trespassing on someone else's life. Still, it was perfect – and meticulously tidy. A bolthole made just for her, where no one knew her, never mind what had happened. There would be no distractions and she could do exactly as she wished, without anyone looking over her shoulder. It made her feel untethered, like a balloon that had been cut loose and was drifting in the air. Right now, all she was really interested in was the bedroom with the comfy-looking, old-fashioned bed. All her limbs ached for the luxury of sleeping in a proper bed again. The bedroom window looked out over the quiet, tree-lined side road outside, and she pulled the curtains, kicked off her boots, and sank, fully clothed, under the duvet. Peace and quiet was what she wanted and exactly what she was going to get.

When she first heard the thumping noise, it took her a while to realise where she was and, as the noise continued, she groaned and put her head under the pillow. Bloody great. Maybe Laura's apartment was fab, but Claire must have forgotten to mention the noisy neighbours. After a while, the thumping stopped and she drifted off to sleep again, dreaming fitfully of Johnny. Then the noise disturbed her again, crashing into her dreams, and she thought in that hazy dream-like state that it was Johnny banging on her door. She burrowed further down the bed, gradually realising that the noise was coming from the hall door of Laura's apartment.

She ignored it for as long as she could, but the noise continued and, eventually, she dragged herself out of bed. Her limbs were just as heavy as when she'd climbed into bed, her head was woolly and weird, and it took an effort to tiptoe across the living room to the door. It was still bright outside, which meant she'd only been asleep for three or four hours. All she could see through the peephole was a wash of green so, whoever it was, they were standing very close to the door or using some kind of camouflage. Then she heard her name being called.

'Ellie, are you in there? You don't have to open the door, just tell me you're fine. Ellie, are you okay?'

She couldn't believe it. Who was on her case like this? She yanked open the door, forgetting she'd put on the security chain and it held fast, allowing a gap of six inches, enough for her to see that the green smudge was actually an Irish football top and, tall as she was, she had to raise her eyes to see that it belonged to a guy with curly black hair, hazel eyes and a worried-looking face. Her heart sank.

'Oh.' He seemed surprised she'd opened the door. 'You must be Ellie. Hi. Are you okay?'

'I don't believe this,' she said through the gap in the door, heedless to the sudden puzzlement sweeping across his face. 'I've come all the way over here for some peace and quiet. And what happens? I've been disturbed from the first decent sleep I've had in weeks.'

'Hey. Chill.' He backed away immediately and put his hands up in a defensive gesture. 'Look, lady, I was just asked to see if you're all right. Your doorbell isn't working so I had to knock.'

'What do you mean, am I okay? Of course I'm okay. Why wouldn't I be? And who the hell are you?'

He looked uncomfortable. 'I'm a friend of Laura's. She told me you were arriving on Sunday afternoon and asked me to say hello and point out a few things ... the nearest subway, shops ... I've been keeping an eye out for you, but this is the first time you've answered. So—'

'Yeah, well, I'm fine.' Then, when his words filtered into her head, 'Hang on, the first time?'

'Sunday night, Monday morning, then afternoon ...' he said, his eyes honest and direct.

'Hold on, what time is it?' She was beginning to think she should be asking what day it was.

'It's Monday evening, just after seven o'clock,' he supplied, second guessing her.

She tried not to let the shock show on her face. She'd slept for over thirty hours. No wonder she felt so weird.

'So? What's the big deal?' she asked, apprehension twisting in her stomach.

'I'm not making a big deal,' he said. 'Laura called me when she talked to her cousin in Ireland ... who was concerned when you didn't answer your mobile, and she thought there might be a problem ...'

Ellie remembered that she was supposed to have texted Claire as soon as she arrived. Great, she fumed. She was already on the back foot, instead of feeling liberated and away from it all. It seemed her baggage had followed her all the way across the Atlantic.

'What kind of problem?' she snapped, feeling hot that he might know what she was doing there. He was younger than her, thirty-one, maybe thirty-two. This must be what it felt like, she realised, if you had a younger brother who had discovered something humiliating about you. Mortifying. Ignominious.

'Look, lady, that's all I know,' he backed away from the door and shrugged. 'It's your business. I'll let Laura know you've arrived okay. There's a great little diner on the corner to your left, the nearest subway is one block away and full garbage and recycling facilities are down in the basement. So that's my job done.'

He turned on his heel and, after a minute, she heard his footsteps clattering down the stairwell.

She closed the door and leaned against it for a minute, feeling weak.

Well, of course she was feeling weak, she'd had nothing to eat for days, Ellie snapped at herself, jolted out of her temporary vacuum. She needed to get out of these clothes, have a shower, then go get some food. After that she'd have to unpack and phone home. Although it was too late to call anyone now, she realised, as it was after midnight in Ireland.

The following morning, she sat on the dark-green sofa, took a deep breath and went through her mobile. There were zillions of missed calls and texts, including lots from Johnny that she discarded straight away, and some from Claire. She texted Miranda and left a message on Vivienne's voicemail to let them know she'd arrived, and then she called Claire.

'Jesus, Ellie, you had us all worried,' Claire said.

'So I gathered,' Ellie said, keeping her voice level.

'Ben texted both Laura and me last night to say you were fine. We told him to get in touch, no matter how late it was. We didn't know if you'd even reached the apartment—'

'Ben?'

'Yeah, Ben Farrell from Leitrim, Laura's neighbour. He's staying in the apartment underneath. She emailed him and asked him to put out the welcome mat for you and make you feel at home.'

Ben Farrell from Leitrim. There would have to be a neighbour on hand to remind her of Ireland, Ellie thought glumly. She didn't want to be made to feel at home. She wanted to feel as though she was worlds away.

'I was asleep, Claire. I hit the bed on Sunday afternoon and he woke me up on Monday evening.'

'Wow. Sleeping beauty has nothing on you. How are you feeling now?'

'Not so bad. I might go out for walk soon and get my bearings.'

'Talk to Ben. He'll point you in the best direction.'

'I want to avoid all contact with men, especially Irish men,' Ellie said, feeling a little uneasy now as she remembered how she'd ranted at him.

'You needn't worry about Ben.'

'Why? Is he gay?'

'What do you think?' Claire scoffed.

She thought of his almond-shaped, hazel eyes. Serious and intent, and despite the thick dark lashes, they had looked like they belonged to a hot-blooded alpha male. 'Hmmm, no.'

'I think he has a soft spot for Laura, so he won't even spare you a glance. She's very fond of him too. Just so you know, though, in case something strikes you as odd, he's illegal.'

She'd sensed there was something not quite right about him, Ellie said to herself with a hint of satisfaction, managing to refrain from saying it out loud.

'And another thing,' Claire went on, her voice a little strained, 'Johnny called here, looking for you, but I wouldn't entertain him.'

'Thanks.'

'Ellie, he knows you've gone to New York.'

'*What?* How? Who told him?'

'Someone saw you at the Aer Lingus check-in desk and contacted the shop for a comment because you looked all out of sorts. Johnny took the call and said you were on business. So, of course, he came straight to me trying to confirm what had happened and find out if I knew where you were staying, but I didn't engage with him at all.'

'Thanks, Claire. Even if he does try to follow me,' Ellie said stonily, 'he'll never find me here.'

She still found it hard to believe that it had just taken a moment in time for everything to change. But that was life, wasn't it? She could no longer bear to think about the man with whom she had shared so much of her life, so much intimacy, plenty of laughter and silly, ordinary, everyday things.

Yet, despite all they'd shared, it hadn't been enough. And she still couldn't figure out if she'd been chasing a fairytale.

Chapter 19

*L*ucy tried to hold still as her hair was tweaked and twisted and sprayed by two pairs of hands at the same time as the make-up girl leaned in close and did her magic to Lucy's face with a palette of glittering eye shadow and dusty sparkle. It was bedlam all around her, with models in various stages of undress, surrounded by a bevy of stylists, make-up artists and hairdressing people. People were yelling and reaching over each other, someone was barking orders, someone else was pushing through with a rail of clothes. From the hall outside, she could hear the seductive beat of the music and she longed to get out there and lose herself in another world.

She was so lucky to have been booked for this show. Xenia was a new designer and rising star, and her casting director had decided that Lucy's eyes had the soulful depth she wanted to portray the vibe of the debut collection. Lucy had also been chosen to open the show, which was a huge prop to her ragged self-esteem.

At last it was time, she was ready, and the minute she stepped onto the runway and into the bright heat of the spotlights, in a sequinned, body skimming mini-dress, she felt the adrenalin pumping through her. Barely aware of the gasps of admiration coming from the crowd of people on both sides, she strode down the length of the catwalk, totally in the zone, chin slightly lifted, hands by her sides, then a pause and slight angle of the hips when she reached the end, and the explosion of flashbulbs from the bank of waiting photographers. Then it was back along the ramp and into the bedlam to be whisked this time into a slinky column of a gown, and have her make-up touched up before she walked down the catwalk again.

She loved the palpable excitement, the high-octane glamour of it all. It gave her such a high that she forgot about the long hours getting ready, the interminable hanging around waiting for phone calls, sleepy-eyed, early-morning starts, and the dashed disappointments when someone else got the coveted bookings. More importantly, she forgot for a precious short while the unholy mess she'd left behind in Dublin. Before she knew it, the show was over, and her sensuous clothes were replaced by comfortable leggings and a loose grey top over a cotton vest, an outfit she had worn to ensure there were no strap marks on her body.

'Are you coming for a drink, Lucy?' Carla asked, as they removed the worst of their heavy make-up. 'There's a few of us meeting up in the new bar around the corner. I could murder a raspberry mojito. But just the one, of course,' she smiled at Lucy. It was a cold, sweet smile that set Lucy's teeth on edge.

'Not tonight,' Lucy said. 'I've something else on.' She slicked on some lip gloss to keep her hands from wanting to smack the smile off Carla's face.

Now that her full-on adrenalin rush had subsided a little, she felt fidgety and out of sorts and she sensed the beginning of a low setting in, something she was finding difficult to shake these days. The after-show drinks session would be a good place to unwind, but she needed to stay out of the limelight for a while, and she didn't fancy spending any time in Carla's company. Carla was another red-haired model in Rebecca's stable and she was another hot runner for the Venetia promo, which meant she was Lucy's nearest rival.

Besides, she had an appointment with Rebecca, something she wasn't going to admit to Carla. She knew Carla's smart comment referred to the latest pictures of Lucy to hit the tabloids, taken outside the perfume launch party in Belgravia. Lucy's heart had plummeted when she'd seen herself described as 'Hot Botty'. Obviously, Rebecca hadn't been pleased – and that was surely why she wanted to see Lucy for a chat.

Outside, the London evening was dark with threatening clouds, and she managed to flag a cab straightaway to take her to Victoria Embankment and Rebecca's office. On the way, she felt like a schoolgirl about to see the headmistress.

Several times, during her less than stellar academic career, she'd worn a trail to the headmistress's private office. It had always been the same old story. Each end-of-term report bore the legend that she could have done a whole lot better.

'Lucy Morgan, what will we do with you?' the headmistress had said, when Lucy was sixteen. 'You have brains to burn, but you're just not applying them.'

'I'm not anywhere as good as the clever, dedicated pupils who are going serious places,' she'd said, unable to admit that it was far more fun hanging out with the clique of dizzy, hopeful *It* girls who had no academic aspirations. And brains to burn? Her headmistress was surely dotty to think that Lucy was academically talented.

The headmistress had been wise to her. 'I know it might seem dull to apply yourself to your studies, but your behaviour is a little short-sighted. A good education is an investment for the future and will stand to you all your life, irrespective of the path you choose. And you shouldn't, ever, sell yourself short.'

'What do you mean?' she'd asked.

'You should have more trust in your abilities, Lucy. People will treat you the way you treat yourself and what you get back in life is mostly up to how you choose to put yourself out there.'

'Where I'm going I won't need academic kudos,' she'd uttered frivolously. 'Although I've no idea where I'm going except it won't be university.'

The headmistress had looked disappointed and, to her surprise, it had taken Lucy a while to get that look out of her head. And now, it suddenly popped into her mind as she sat in Rebecca's office with a view of the Thames and, in the distance, the twinkling curve of the London Eye.

Rebecca had been a celebrated fashion model during the eighties, working with all the high-wattage fashion houses, including seasons for Chanel and Valentino, and now she ran her own successful agency. She regularly gave pep talks, advising her girls that, to be on top of their game, early nights, good nutrition and minimum booze should be the norm. But this was the first time she'd taken Lucy aside privately like this. Rebecca thanked Lucy for coming and went through her usual advice, with Lucy only half-listening until Rebecca fell silent and let the silence stretch long enough for Lucy to feel uncomfortable.

'I signed you up because I like you, Lucy,' Rebecca said, her blue eyes cool and appraising. 'You have the ability to make it big in Paris or Milan, but that hasn't happened yet . . . ' she paused and let her words sink in for a moment. 'The reason it hasn't happened is totally down to yourself, or rather the way you're choosing to behave.'

Here we go again, Lucy sighed to herself. But it was galling to be listening to this when she was twenty-one years of age. And not nice when it concerned her heartfelt dreams.

Rebecca was watching her. But she didn't launch into the tirade Lucy had been expecting, asking her instead, 'Why do you think that is, Lucy?'

Lucy's head whirled. 'I dunno, I'm not sure where you're coming from.'

'Come on, Lucy, you're a smart woman. I don't have to tell you that you're generating a lot of publicity but not all of it is positive, and casting directors don't like that. It's not good marketing for starters. You could end up becoming more of a bad advertisement for yourself than a brand ambassador for a particular product. I want you to ask yourself why you feel you need to behave like this. Why are you letting yourself down? You could be great, an international name, but the only person who's stopping you is *you*. And I can't understand why you're damaging your career prospects like this – and you most certainly are. Think about it, will you?'

'I will,' she said.

This was a new approach, Lucy grimaced. Self-analysis. Or navel gazing, neither of which she was remotely interested in. And she needed this like a hole in the head. She just wanted to draw a thick heavy veil over the past few weeks and her damaging behaviour.

In the gathering darkness, she took a taxi home to Chelsea and sank into the back seat, telling herself firmly that if she wanted to keep her career on track, keeping a low profile was an absolute must for the next few weeks. It began to rain as the taxi trundled up King's Road. After making a couple of turns, it drove by the top of the lane running behind the house where Lucy had her apartment. Lucy glanced down, remembering the night she'd made her escape through the back gate. Her eyes widened as, just before the taxi passed the top of the lane, she could have sworn she saw someone standing in the shadows, just across from the rear garden that her bedroom looked out onto. It gave her a creepy feeling and, for an inexplicable moment, she thought of the wreath that had been delivered to her door.

Her imagination was surely playing tricks on her.

When the cab pulled up in front of her house, Lucy was still staring into space.

'Are you okay?' the driver asked.

She pulled herself together and rummaged in her bag for her door key and the taxi fare. 'Would you mind doing me a favour?'

'That depends on what it is, luv,' he laughed.

'Don't drive away until I have the hall door closed behind me,' she said, feeling a little silly.

'Of course, luv, no worries,' he said amenably.

The street was quiet as she got out of the cab, but nonetheless as she hurried up the steps and in through the hall door, closing it securely behind her, she was suddenly chilled and felt very much alone.

He wasn't sure what he was doing here.

Wasting valuable time, surely. She'd been very quiet in the past few days, probably after that picture in the paper. It had looked more silly than hot to him. She didn't seem to be going out much and then she'd tweeted that she was opening a fashion show that afternoon. But as she hadn't given any details, he couldn't follow it up. Rather than pace the floor of his apartment or idle his time sipping weak coffee in an internet café, he'd spent the evening strolling around Chelsea, walking by her front door, and then around the block, feeling the need to get close in some way. He'd strolled down the lane behind the road she lived on, counting off the posh houses backing onto it, and he had just reached the one he figured her apartment was located in when it began to rain.

He wasn't sure where to go next, or what to do. The burst of energy that had brought him to London had disappeared. He could have coped with the weak and tepid coffee in the internet café. He could have coped with the rain. What he couldn't cope with was the fact that the Zach Anderson internet site he'd so carefully put together had had no hits in the previous twenty-four hours. Not a single one. Worse, people had lost interest in the Facebook page he'd set up too. He was nearly back where he'd started. No wonder he felt beside himself with anger.

And then his patience was rewarded. Just when he was about to trudge back to his flat, a light sprang on in a window on the top floor, and he shrank back into the shadows as a figure approached the glass. He saw the pale oval of her face, haloed with her flame-coloured hair, stare out into the darkness.

Almost as though she sensed him there.

Good.

Chapter 20

'Excuse me.'

'Excuse me.'

Ellie dodged from left to right to avoid colliding against the broad width of Ben's green-jerseyed chest. He did the exact opposite to her so that they ended up doing a silly sideways dance to avoid bumping into each other in the doorway to the basement. She had thought it would be safe enough to venture down with her rubbish during the day, figuring that most of the occupants in her building would be out at work, but if anyone was to be around, it had to be Ben, of course.

'Sorry,' he said, moving back from the doorway. He didn't look at all sorry. His hazel eyes were cold, telling her clearly that he disliked her.

'No prob,' she said, finding her voice, embarrassed that she'd been caught with a couple of empty wine bottles to dispose of along with her small bag of rubbish. This time, his football top had gold stripes and it boasted a Leitrim logo.

Tribal, she thought.

She wondered, oddly, if he had parents back in Leitrim, a father or a mother who were bound to be worried about their son living illegally in New York. Or a brother, perhaps, who made sure to keep him supplied with football jerseys as a link with home. For the briefest of moments, she felt they had something in common, both refugees in a sense, away from their homeland. Then, without saying a word, Ben edged through the doorway, his exaggerated attempts to stay as far away from her as possible almost comical. Ellie held his cold stare and gave him what she hoped was an equally chilly look. Then he was gone, leaving her to the mercy of the intimidating-looking rubbish bins.

She had been in New York for a couple of days, and, if anything, she felt worse instead of better. Totally fatigued, her spirits flat, she found it hard to summon the energy to pop down to the nearest food store, never mind grab a coffee and muffin in the diner on the corner. She'd no real appetite anyway, so she hadn't ventured out much, flopping around Laura's apartment and staring at daytime TV, images of Lucy and Johnny superimposing themselves on the wall, on the screen, on Laura's bed, and even grinning at her from the side of the bin. She dumped her rubbish and recycled her bottles and stalked back out to the basement foyer, summoning the lift to bring her back to the fourth floor.

She'd always considered herself unsentimental, but now she couldn't bear to look at happy-ever-after movies, or anything remotely romantic, changing the channels the minute any mawkish, heart-tugging programme came on. Music of any kind was torture. From the time she woke in the morning, until she fell into a restless sleep, thoughts of Johnny ran through her head in an endless loop, gouging out fresh tracks in her heart each time. How had it happened? Why had it happened? And worst of all, if she'd been a bit later coming home would she ever have known it had happened? Had she sensed all along that, deep down, he couldn't be trusted? And, if so, was that why she'd been unable to commit to him?

She reached the top floor, the lift doors slid back and she walked across the corridor to the apartment that was beginning to close in on her. How had she thought a spell in New York would be the answer, as if it would distract her from what had happened? And as for bringing along her sketchpads, that was a laugh. They were still neglected in a side pocket of her case, pristine and untouched. Even the thought of sharpening her pencils made her feel panicky, never mind actually facing the blank page.

She was keeping her mobile switched off, just checking in once a day in case there was anything from Claire, her mother or Miranda. Johnny was still trying to reach her, deluging her with voicemails, texts and emails, all of which she immediately deleted. There was nothing he could say or do to make up for the way he'd betrayed her. And nothing on earth would persuade her to talk to him. In the middle of the fog of exhaustion and numbness that blanketed her, one hard bright certainty shone like a diamond – they were finished.

But Lucy, being family, was another problem.

Later, Ellie phoned her mother, gathering that Vivienne was still unaware of Lucy's treachery.

'I never got a chance to ask you if Lucy was okay after all the hassle,' Vivienne said.

'You mean over Zach?' Ellie said brusquely.

'Yes, it must have been difficult for her on her own in London with that rabble of photographers. She must have felt very exposed.'

Ellie almost laughed, her breath catching painfully in her throat. 'Why don't you ask her yourself?' She stared out the window and saw that branches of the trees outside were swelling with bud. Spring. Why had she come to New York in the springtime? The exciting city pulsating with new beginnings and fresh hope. Surely there was nothing worse to aggravate a troubled soul?

'You know what Lucy is like,' Vivienne was saying. 'It's always hard to pin her down, but she's worse than ever lately. All I'm getting is occasional texts in response to my calls, so I'm assuming she's very busy. Or else she's avoiding me. Sometimes . . .' her mother's voice caught. 'Oh, Ellie, I know I shouldn't be bothering you like this, but sometimes I still feel she blames me over Zach never being around.'

Her mother must be very concerned to voice this, Ellie thought grimly. It was the sure sign of a guilty conscience. 'She's probably very busy,' Ellie said, wondering if by some stretch of the imagination that Lucy was also suffering from a guilty conscience and was avoiding Vivienne. Not that her audacious sister had ever worried before about anyone's opinion of her.

'If she's talking to you, will you ask her to give me a call? It doesn't matter what time of the day or night it is,' Vivienne said.

'Aren't you in rehearsals for *Big Maggie*?' Ellie avoided answering the question.

'We start next week,' Vivienne said.

'And you're feeling up to it?'

'I'm grand. It'll be a challenging role but I'm up for putting my own stamp on it. And I want to see you all there on the opening night, even Miranda, if we can lure her home from Hong Kong for a few days. You should be back by then and it'll be something to look forward to. It would be lovely to have my daughters all together and we could go up to the Shelbourne afterwards for post-theatre champagne. That means more to me than all the encores, no matter how rapturous.'

After chatting some more, Ellie put down her mobile with a heavy heart. That kind of family get-together was out of the question from now on. Birthdays, Christmases, all those celebrations would be tainted. Ellie's injured pride would keep her away and Lucy probably wouldn't give a damn. And Miranda would be caught up somewhere in the middle.

Maybe she should have gone to Hong Kong instead of New York. At least she would have had Miranda to talk to and go for meals with. There was nothing worse than dining on your own in New York, especially when you were crying inside. But Miranda hadn't offered her a refuge, which was unusual for her normally generous sister. Maybe she was afraid of being caught in the crossfire between her two sisters.

Ellie forced herself to get out of the apartment the following morning before she was driven crazy from lack of exercise. She approached the diner on the corner, on the brink of going in for a skinny latte when she did a swift about turn in the doorway – Ben from Leitrim was sitting inside with a gang of four or five others, aged from twenty to forty, and, judging from the laughter and hilarity coming from their table, they were having great fun. He was wearing a grey tracksuit and he looked fresh and energised and carelessly happy, and on another planet compared to the way she was feeling. They were all wearing sports gear, she noticed, as she strolled by the plate-glass window and gave the group a sidelong glance.

Ben was looking out the window in her direction but he didn't acknowledge her at all – in fact, he looked right through her. She continued on down the street feeling invisible, wishing she'd never left the apartment and thinking how silly she'd been to imagine they might have had anything in common.

The rest of the day dragged by. Ellie fidgeted about the apartment and cleaned the already spotless bathroom. She checked

Laura's bookshelves to see if there was anything to tempt her, totally alarmed to find that nothing appealed to her at all. She was normally an avid reader. How come her break-up with Johnny was reducing her to this? It seemed as if every single part of her life was infected with a sweeping despair.

Was this what it felt like when you reached the bottom? This mindless kind of stupor that was all fidgety under the surface and made you feel agitated and unable to settle to anything?

Ellie was facing into another long, lonely, restless evening and she made a half-hearted attempt at tidying the kitchen cupboards when she realised there was no coffee left in Laura's ceramic jar. For a disjointed moment as she stared into the cupboard, she forgot where she was.

Johnny loved his cup of coffee in the evenings. He enjoyed relaxing with an espresso after a meal. She saw him quite clearly, as though he was right in front of her, leaning back in the kitchen chair, shirt collar opened, stretching his arms back behind his head in satisfaction after they'd shared an Indian take out. She heard his laughing voice.

'Ellie, even if you can't boil an egg, at least you can make a darn good coffee, even if it is out of a machine. And for that, I'll excuse you anything.'

Hard reality crashed over her like a cold tidal wave, sucking the shifting ground away from beneath her. She didn't have to concern herself with Johnny and his espresso ever again. She would never again see his face smiling at her in that careless way after a shared meal. He'd never lean back across the kitchen chair looking at her with the light in his eyes that meant he was pic- turing them in bed together, or try to grab a playful feel of her breast as she leaned across to pick up his empty coffee cup.

Something white exploded behind her eyes, the apartment was suddenly stifling, and she knew she had to get out straight away before she lost it altogether. She thrust her arms into her jacket, grabbed her door key and slammed out the door. She didn't even wait for the lift, but clattered down four flights of stairs, only pausing when she found herself standing outside on the pavement, gulping mouthfuls of cool evening air into her tight chest.

Instinct told her to keep away from nearby Central Park and the sight of arm-in-arm couples enjoying the romantic beauty of that oasis in the early evening. She darted across the road in the opposite direction just as the lights changed, causing a sudden cacophony of honking car horns from oncoming traffic surging around a blind corner to her right. Just in time, she reached the pedestrian island in the middle of the intersection, her heart thumping wildly, her whole body trembling.

And with a leap, Ben was beside her, his chest rising and falling rapidly beneath his navy fleece, his eyes blazing. She realised he'd just sprinted across the road right behind her.

'What the hell are you up to, lady?' he raged. 'Have you some kind of death wish?'

'What do you care?'

'I don't care what happens to you,' he retorted, his breathing ragged, his eyes boring right through her, the pupils angry, like flints. 'But I'd rather not see your mashed-up body parts being scraped off the road.'

'Then why did you come after me?'

'I heard you running down the stairs as if the devil himself was after you. You even gave me a fright,' he stopped to catch his breath. 'Then I see you racing across the road like you want to get killed. I thought I'd have to push you out of the way . . . so, what the hell is wrong with you?'

'Is there no privacy in this wretched town?' she asked defensively, horrified with her reckless behaviour. 'I thought New

York was supposed to be anonymous. Anyway, I don't have to answer your stupid questions.'

As the traffic snarled around both sides of the pedestrian island, he stood there, hands by his sides, the blaze of fury in his eyes turning to hostility. Then, his breathing back to normal, he said, 'No, you don't. It's just that if anything happens to you, like being attacked by a murderer with a cleaver, which is what it sounded like, or if you end up in a body bag, which you could have with that friggin' stunt, I'd have a helluva job squaring it with Laura. How do you think she'd feel?'

'And neither do you want to risk being dragged in as a witness,' she sounded scathing.

It didn't seem to bother him that she was aware of his illegal status. 'I've no intention of putting my neck on the line for you,' he said, 'but I'd prefer it if you stayed out of trouble while you're in New York. For everyone's sake.' There was a gap in the traffic and he stalked back across the intersection towards the apartment building, his shoulders rigid with anger.

Ellie stood for a couple of moments, trying to slow her racing pulse. Then waiting for the pedestrian lights, she marched off towards the Hudson river.

Even that was a mistake. She wanted to avoid slushy, romantic things, anything with a layer of sentimentality, or any situation at all that would attempt to trace a light finger across the tenderness of her aching heart, but she reached the river-front esplanade just as the sun was setting. And, silhouetted darkly against the immensity of the Manhattan sky, like matchstick figures in a Lowry painting, there were more than enough couples and lovers to taunt her, as they gathered along the boardwalk to watch the sunset.

What was the big deal? she glowered to herself. It was an ordinary moment. It happened most bright evenings. Feeling irritated, she was about to turn and stalk back to the apartment when something about the hushed beauty of the evening stalled her.

Even though New York was bustling and busy, the larger-than-life city was dwarfed by the immensity and splendour of the evening sunset Across the opposite bank, the sun was a bright shining disc on the edge of the marmalade sky – looking, Ellie thought, like a beacon of hope. Because no matter what happened in the dark of the night, it would rise again in the morning, sure and steadfast. Puffy clouds were tinged with reflected colour and whatever way they lay in patchwork shreds across the lower heavens, they made her feel that up beyond them, the sky was endless. The sun sent a glowing trail across the slate-blue waters of the Hudson, a bright column of light tinged with yellow that streamed in her direction. Just for a moment, Ellie fancied it was reaching across to connect with her, like some kind of grounding force.

Grounding force. Yeah. Still, in that moment of pause, everything else seemed unimportant, including the dark jumble in her head. After a while she strolled home, her breathing back to normal, knowing she wasn't going to lose everything after all. Not this time anyhow. Inside her apartment block, she stopped the lift at the third-floor landing, recalling that look of angry concern and the way he'd sprinted across the road in her wake. Summoning her courage, she rang the bell of the apartment underneath hers.

A twenty-something girl with dark wavy hair opened the door. Her warm expectant smile and attractive face made Ellie feel ancient. And puzzled.

'Hi,' Ellie said, thinking furiously. She was at the right door, wasn't she? So much for being head over heels in love with Laura. Obviously, she had no sooner left for Australia than he'd moved someone else in. She heard music in the background and she recognised Muse. Memory flashed of the time she'd brought Johnny to see the group play at Slane Castle. He'd hated all that alternative rock and electronic stuff, he'd said, whereas she'd loved it. It made her feel creative, she'd said. It sounds like shite, he'd said. She wiped it from her mind and looked into the hall where a couple of fleece jackets hung from wall hooks, still holding the impression of his body shape, and two or three pairs of Converse sneakers were lobbed in a heap underneath. There also a green and gold flag curling out from the wall. She didn't need three chances to guess that it had 'Liatroim' emblazoned across the centre.

'Can I help you?'

She had an Irish accent, Ellie noticed. Was there no getting away from her homeland? There was a faint drift of cooking smells, beef and garlic, and for the first time since she'd landed in New York, she realised she was hungry. 'I was – em – looking for—'

'You mean Ben? Hey, you must be Ellie. Welcome to New York. Come in—'

'No, er—' Ellie was about to change her mind but Ben must have heard her voice because next minute he was there, on the threshold, arms across his chest defensive style, his hazel eyes hostile. Sensing conflict in the air, the girl melted away.

'I wouldn't have disturbed you if I'd known you had company,' Ellie said, backing away from the door.

'I don't,' he said, 'Megan lives here, it's her gaff.'

If it was Megan's place, she was obviously very understanding, allowing Ben's stuff to take over. He was even in his stocking feet, wearing thick, grey sports socks.

'What do you want?' he asked.

'Just to say, look, I'm sorry we got off on the wrong foot—'

He shook his head as though she had cracked a dismal joke. 'You mean *you* got off on the wrong foot,' he said levelly. His eyes were accusing and they made her flinch. 'I didn't do anything to deserve your little . . . tantrums.'

'Yes, well, I was wrong, I'm sorry,' she said, wondering why she was finding the words so difficult.

'Is this your way of saying there'll be no more kamikaze stunts?'

'I wasn't thinking straight.'

'I hope not.'

She didn't like the dismissive way he was looking at her. 'It was just that I wanted to go for a walk.'

'A *walk*?' he said in disbelief. 'You think that mitigates almost getting splattered across the road?'

'I know.' She bit her lip, quietly appalled at how close she'd come to doing herself an injury. 'It won't happen again because I'll be more watchful from now on. I forgot about the traffic being on the other side of the road.'

He shifted position, leaned against the door, looked her up and down in mock despair as though she was a nuisance. 'I hope not. I don't want to have to answer to Laura and she doesn't want a call from the cops asking her about her death-wish tenant. Okay?'

'Okay.' She turned away and began to climb the stairs to the top-floor flat, her legs like jelly.

'Next time, Ellie, wait for the green man,' he called after her, but he said it patiently, as though to a child.

She was surprised to find it warmed her a little.

Chapter 21

*A*fter her talk with Rebecca, Lucy was on her best behaviour.

She stayed off junk food, drank gallons of water and got to bed early. She thanked her lucky stars when a booking for a photo shoot for one of London's major high-street boutiques was confirmed and she spent three days on Brighton beach patiently waiting for breaks in the rain along with the rest of the crew so that she could stand by the pier in tight denim jeans and floaty chiffon as she splashed by the edge of the sea. The two-page spread featuring a capsule of the store's summer range would be appearing in the national papers and used for in-store marketing. Not exactly the international exposure she dreamed of, and hardly Vogue, but it was good bread-and-butter work, even though it had been long and tiring and she felt like she'd been put through a wringer by the time the day's shooting was over.

On Friday evening, the word that she'd been dreading came through. She was just back in her apartment emptying her small travel bag when Sasha called.

'Hi, Lucy, have you heard any news?'

She gripped her mobile. She sensed immediately what Sasha meant by news, but Lucy hadn't heard anything and a wave of disappointment surged from her chest right into her mouth. She could hardly talk for a minute but she forced herself to sound cheery. 'I've been in Brighton the past three days, waiting for gaps in the rain, that's all the news I have. I presume the House of Venetia have made the announcement? You might as well tell me the worst, I know it isn't me.'

'Sorry, Lucy. We heard yesterday.'

'Who got the job?'

'Well me, along with Beatrice and ... um ... Carla.'

Even though Lucy knew she wasn't one of the chosen ones, it still hurt to hear it spelled out. 'Congrats, Sasha, I'm delighted for you. I knew Carla would get the redhead slot.'

'They picked the wrong girl,' Sasha said loyally. 'Carla does not work with me like you do.'

'No matter. She was chosen along with you and Beatrice.'

'And another thing, Lucy ... Carla's having a party tomorrow night and all of us are invited.'

'What kind of party? Wait – don't tell me – a champagne party to celebrate your wonderful success?' She knew she sounded petulant, but, so what, she was entitled to. Carla had swiped the golden opportunity that Lucy had longed for.

'Her daddy wants to throw a little party for her.'

Her daddy. A well-known chat-show host. Proud as punch of his daughter, no doubt and dying to show her off. 'Why didn't she ask me personally?' Lucy said, unable to hold back. 'Oh, I know, she mightn't want me there. I could show her up.'

'Don't talk like this, Lucy, it's not good. You can't let this disappointment get you down,' Sasha said.

'I'm not disappointed,' she said airily. 'Try keeping me away.'

Lucy went into the bathroom, tied her hair back and began to cleanse her face, pulling a forced smile. There was nothing wrong, she was fine, her mouth said. But her eyes told a different story. It wasn't just the sting of rejection at losing the hot contract. It was everything. It was her whole messy life.

Some days, she couldn't stop thinking of Johnny. She couldn't help remembering the careful way he'd made love to her, as though every inch of her skin was adorable. It hadn't been just a quick shag like she'd had with guys of her own age, who were too impatient for the main event to give her proper attention. Johnny had even given her the best orgasm ever, and she squirmed inside when she remembered the exquisite rapture of it, but then she remembered how her lovely afterglow had been cut short when Ellie had come home early.

Ellie!

Lucy patted her face dry and picked up a face mask she'd got in a Chanel goodie bag. She chucked on dollops, heedless of where it was going, almost sticking it into her eye. She couldn't bear to think of Ellie right now. She still didn't know if word had reached Miranda or her mum. Her mum had sounded a little desperate the last time she'd left a voicemail, urging Lucy to pick up the phone and talk to her. But how could she? If her mum didn't know, how could Lucy talk and pretend everything was all right? And if she did know, how could she put up with the shame of her mother's disgust? This wasn't just a bad school report, to be lightly brushed aside. Her mother would be incandescent with fury.

And the same went for Miranda, and she couldn't bear to think of her disgust.

Worst of all – and she laughed to herself at this because it was so ridiculous – she felt an incredible urge to see Johnny again. She wanted to look at his face and hold his gaze as she told him that just for one, ecstatic moment, she'd known what mind-blowing actually meant. And that just showed how sad she was, Lucy grimaced, because he'd only been getting back at Ellie. She lay down on the bed while her face mask refreshed all her pores and rejuvenated her skin. Pity she couldn't get something to refresh the inside of her head.

Imagine, though, if Johnny had said she wasn't just a substitute for Ellie. That he'd told her she was a brilliant lover. That their love-making had meant something to him . . .

She sprang off the bed. Yeah, Lucy, get real.

The following night, she prepared carefully for Carla's party. She took up every space available in her Chelsea apartment laying out a selection of clothes and underwear, lining up her make-up on the dressing table. She was going to take it easy on the booze because she didn't want to see herself plastered across the tabloids and being described as 'hot totty gone wrong', or something equally cringeworthy. She had a funny feeling she was on her last chance with Rebecca and if she messed up, her career was in tatters. No other agency in London or Europe would touch her with a ten-foot barge pole. So she had to be the model of perfection, and she laughed at her own pun.

She'd already phoned Sasha to see what she was wearing.

'Just do your own thing, Lucy, without going over the top,' Sasha had said.

'What do you mean, "over the top"?'

'Better to dress down than flaunt it. There might be people there, you know. Carla and her father have invited everyone from what I've heard.'

'People?'

'Yes, contacts, casting directors, PR, paparazzi . . . as many as they could get together at short notice.'

A fresh thump of jealousy in her chest, just when she didn't think she could take any more. 'So it's not really a party, it's a publicity stunt. Carla has some neck. Why didn't you tell me this yesterday?'

'Would you have changed your mind?'

'Nope.'

She was able for this. It was publicity for her as well, albeit reflected. She would show them all that the House of Venetia had backed the wrong horse. She slid on a vintage Jenny Vanders dress she'd bought in Dublin. It had a black taffeta skirt and sequinned top. Her long legs in plain opaque tights and black patent Jimmy Choo ankle boots completed the look. The sexy side of sophistication. It gave her instant confidence.

Ellie got a buzz from this, she thought with a pang. Her life-long passion was less about herself and more about giving women something beautiful to wear. She squirmed when she remembered the time she'd laughed that Ellie would always be behind the scenes. She pictured Ellie bent over her drawing table in the quiet isolation of her studio, the intensity on her face as she committed her ideas to paper – there was something so inherently honest about it that her heart bled.

Something dark still clutched at her insides when she caught herself remembering what she'd done to Ellie. Before she lost her nerve, she picked up her mobile and texted her again. Any kind of contact with her sister would be preferable to this horrible dark silence between them, even if Ellie told her to get lost. She waited a few moments, her heart pounding, but, once more, there was no answering text from Ellie.

Lucy finished applying her dramatic eye make-up and helped herself to a gin and cranberry while she waited for Sasha's call to say the cab was outside. She took a last look in the mirror and told herself she was fabulous, even though she knew she was lying through her teeth. Fabulous, fabulous, fabulous, she repeated like a mantra as she went downstairs and glided out to the cab.

'Wow, you look amazing,' Sasha said, sitting in the back seat, immediately lifting Lucy's spirits a little.

Maybe it was time she grew up a little and moved away from the rock-chick grunge look, Lucy thought as the cab pulled away from the kerb. Problem was, even at twenty-one, she still hadn't decided what her own style was all about, and she was always chopping and changing.

The party in a Park Lane hotel was buzzing. Lucy couldn't help another shaft of envy at the turnout, all to celebrate Carla being part of the Venetia campaign. She spotted Erin O'Connor, standing out from the crowd with her urchin cropped hair and black tuxedo, a striking look only she could carry off to such perfection. She felt a curl of jealousy when she saw her chat to Carla. Carla even had the gall to put her hand on Erin's arm in a friendly but personal gesture as she threw back her head and laughed, a pretty tinkly laugh, of course.

'Get a load of that crap,' she said to Sasha. 'You'd think they were bosom pals. You're up there too, you know. You should go over and steal some of her thunder. Carla seems to think she's the star of the show. You're on the team as well.'

'No, that's not me,' Sasha said. 'And it's not the team tonight. Carla and her dad organised all this.'

As though Carla heard herself being gossiped about, she beckoned Sasha over for a group photo. Lucy watched the trio posing for the camera, Carla looking like the cat who licked the cream. If things had gone differently, it could have been her, she agonised quietly.

Yeah right. She'd never have had the hard-necked confidence

of Carla. Besides, she was missing an important ingredient. She didn't have a daddy to treat her like his little princess. She glanced quickly at her mobile, but there was still no response from Ellie, so she took another champagne cocktail from a circulating waiter and sipped it, looking around the room to see if there was anyone she could talk to without watching every word coming out of her mouth.

He'd had a stroke of luck, being able to wangle his way into this hot-shot gathering, he decided, as he moved around the edge of the crowds, trying to blend in. Although he had just as much right to be there as Lucy Morgan.

He'd seen it on Facebook, a posh bash to celebrate some contract or other. He'd gathered that lots of media would be there and important people, whoever they were. He'd guessed that Lucy might turn up. This time, he'd been better prepared. He'd had some business cards printed, making out that he directed a PR company, and he held his head high, shoulders straight, keeping his face bland as he approached security along with some photographers, and he congratulated himself on his cleverness when he was waved through. He accepted a glass of wine this time, as he figured he'd look out of place sipping water. The trick was to sip it very slowly, and not allow his glass to be refilled.

He saw her immediately, chatting to the same tall, blonde chick she'd been with before. She was dressed differently tonight. More polished and sophisticated than the last time he'd seen her. The black thingy she was wearing suited her. It screamed money and her whole outfit probably cost more than Heather Douglas had spent on clothes in a year. He pushed away the familiar sense of loss that gripped his chest. He wasn't going to think about his mother tonight. He needed to stay calm and level-headed.

Especially when her friend was called away and Lucy swept her eyes around the throng, pausing when they came to rest on him.

He smiled and lifted his glass in a silent toast. He forced himself to relax, almost overcome with stage fright as she sidled through the crowd in his direction. This was just what he wanted. All was going exactly to plan. It was just that he felt so fucking nervous it wasn't funny.

'Hey, do I know you?' She paused, putting her head to one side, looking at him quizzically.

'I don't think we've met,' he said.

'Haven't we?'

Up close, he was in awe of how incredibly beautiful she was; the perfectly contoured face, eyebrows delicately arched, the crescents of her long, spiky eyelashes and those smudgy grey eyes – softly grey, not dark, inky grey like his. He caught her expensive fragrance. An intangible sense of glamour clung to her, and she carried herself so confidently. All that came with success, of course. They were poles apart. She was studying him, clearly waiting for him to introduce himself.

'Ian Douglas,' he said, 'I'm in PR.' Although he gave his real name, he had a fake resume ready to trot out should it be needed, although he knew better than to start shovelling on too much information.

'I'm Lucy Morgan,' she said, extending a slim, manicured hand. It felt cool in his and her handshake was relaxed. Her voice was softer that he'd thought it would be. It had an Irish lilt, different to the London accents he was getting used to.

'You're Irish,' he said, pretending he was surprised by this discovery.

'Yeah, I'm from Dublin originally.'

'And you're a model, I'll bet.'

'That's right. For my sins,' she gave a self-deprecating laugh that grated on him. What did she mean, "for her sins"? Didn't she realise how jammy she was?

'I can't see you having too many sins.'

'Oh, you'd be surprised.' Another little self-indulgent laugh.

'Would I?' Yeah, I can imagine. Her top sin was probably sprinkling too much sugar on her cereal. 'All the same this isn't a bad set-up. Just an average Saturday evening for you, I suppose.' Fuck it. He was blowing it. Surely she had picked up the tinge of resentment in his voice? She was looking over his shoulder as though she was ready to move away. 'Would you like another drink?' he said quickly, as a waiter passed by.

'Ah sure, why not,' she said.

He plucked a champagne flute off the tray and handed it to her, their fingers touching again, and he wondered how long he could play this out for and hold her attention, and how many flutes of champagne it would take to get her drunk.

'And where are you from?' she asked, her huge eyes appraising him once more as though she was trying to figure him out.

There was no point in side-stepping this one. 'I'm from Edinburgh. Scotland.'

He watched her response as the information registered. A quick flash followed by a hasty blink of her eyes. So she wasn't immune. Scotland meant something to her.

'Ever been?' he asked.

'No ... no, I haven't.'

She didn't look like she was anxious to visit. 'It's a beautiful country, Scotland, winter or summer. I think you'd love it,' he said deliberately pushing the button.

'Maybe sometime,' she said evasively. Then, much as he had feared, she gave him a polite smile, 'Could you excuse me?'

'Of course,' he said. 'It was lovely to meet you, Lucy.'

'And you, Ian.'

She knew by the way she was talking that she'd downed too many champagne cocktails. When Sasha introduced her to Stella McCartney, she knew her greeting was far too effusive, words tumbling out of her mouth with a life of their own, her laughter too loud. Then she found herself gabbling away to Carla, but she was sober enough to make a monumental effort to contain herself, in case she revealed the full extent of her low spirits and came across like a bitchy cow.

Of course, she *was* a bitchy cow. She took another gulp of champagne.

'Hey, Lucy, relax,' Sasha urged, taking her by the arm and drawing her away.

'It's all right for you,' she snapped, unable to keep up a front. 'You're one of the chosen ones.'

'Lucy. Stop it. Did you ever ask yourself why you weren't picked?'

'Huh, I suppose you know.'

Sasha seemed to be casting around for inspiration, then she said, 'Someone should tell you that you're getting a reputation. Not a good one either. And this doesn't help,' Sasha plucked the flute of champagne from her fingers and plonked it down on a table.

'I just don't feel on top of things tonight,' Lucy found herself admitting.

'That doesn't matter. You have to be professional. You can't be negative or let important people see this is getting you down.'

'Who's important?' Her eyes scanned the room. There was no sign of the guy with the Scottish accent. He seemed to have melted into the crowd. She must be on a knife edge if mention of Edinburgh had thrown her that much. Just because it had been Zach Anderson's home town. Then again, there had been something about the way the guy had looked at her as though he knew all about her, and the niggling feeling that she'd met him before but couldn't place him. He was a couple of years older than her, mid twenties, she guessed. If he was in PR they'd probably been at some functions together but never introduced. Hadn't he been at the perfume bash? And of course he'd know all about her. She was well known on the modelling circuit. Too well known in some ways.

'There are lots of big names here tonight and it's water for you for the rest of this evening. And here come two of my favourite photographers,' Sasha beamed in their direction as two photographers advanced on them. She linked arms with Lucy. 'Come on, Lucy, chin up! Smile and look like a million dollars! We'll get some good press for you, hmm?'

Sasha was too good for her. Too good for Lucy Morgan with her shitty behaviour and self-destructive attitude, never mind her unforgiveable mortal sin. She felt herself sliding into a dark depression until the music changed and the sound of Madonna's 'Into the Groove' pounded across the room. The rhythm pulsated down to her toes, reminding her of the way she stalked along the catwalk in time to the beat. She held on to that image, as a drowning man would clutch at a raft, letting the music flow through her, pushing away the dark moment as she straightened her shoulders and smiled brightly at the camera.

Chapter 22

The Felix restaurant, in the Peninsula Hotel, Hong Kong, enjoys magnificent views of the harbour at night. Better again, it boasts ringside seats at the Symphony of Light, a stunning light show that takes place between Hong Kong Peak and Victoria Harbour and is best viewed from along the Kowloon promenade.

Miranda sighed with inner longing as she fastened her eyes on the fabulous display of glittering lights, flashing and beaming in turn like a fantastic dance sequence. Christian had excused himself for a few minutes while he went outside to take a business call. As soon as he came back, they would order dessert. Then after that . . . she wasn't quite sure. But she did know Christian's kisses weren't enough anymore. They'd been dating solidly for three weeks now, and their friendship had been slowly deepening for most of the four months she'd been in Hong Kong, but was she ready to make love? Could she put her heart on the line yet again and risk disappointment?

Yes, she couldn't ignore the frisson that had been clamouring silently between her and Christian all evening. As though it was time now . . .

For a moment, she revelled in the fact that she was sitting here at all, feeling quite at home in this vibrant city, working with such an eclectic group of people and being fully accepted for who she was, instead of being judged and found wanting in the context of having a well-known fashion model for a younger sister and a beautiful, successful designer for an older sister. Even enjoying her job, for which she was more than capable, as well as the social aspects of it, instead of working long, challenging hours to prove something to herself and being too circumspect to let her hair down or go for gossipy lunches with the girls, was something to savour.

And added to all this, there was Christian.

Looking at the scintillating lights and entranced by the magic of it all, she suddenly felt like a child at Christmas, as though something wonderful was about to happen. She recalled her father and the way he had always made magic at Christmas with his stories and traditions, and, her emotions touched, she felt a gush of tears in her eyes.

She didn't see Christian coming back to the table until his voice broke into her thoughts.

'Sorry about that,' he apologised, slipping into the seat opposite her. 'It was a critical call, and with the time difference I had to take it. Sometimes, it's hard to synchronise stuff with the New York office and they're working around the clock this weekend, signing off on a report, so it was urgent. Hey, what's up?'

She knew he had seen her tears and with anyone else she might have brushed it off and pretended she had dirt in her eye, but Christian was different. 'I was just thinking about my father,' she said, her voice husky.

He clasped her hand in his. 'Tell me about him.'

'Where do I start?' she smiled.

'At the beginning. I want to know all about you, Miranda.'

She began to describe her idyllic childhood, growing up in the big house in Dún Laoghaire, which was the scene of many a party, her quiet father and flamboyant mum gathering an eclectic assortment of friends and colleagues quite easily. There were mid-term breaks in Kerry and Mayo, summer sunshine holidays in the south of France and Portugal, magical Christmases, and then suddenly when she was ten years old, that part of her life was over when her father died.

'I can't explain what it was like. I felt as though a shutter had come down on all that warm wonderful life and, for years afterwards, I thought a terrible mistake had been made.' She hesitated and checked for his reaction, but Christian was still watching her quietly, his blue eyes kind, and somehow the champagne bottle was drained and two balloons of brandy were on the table.

'I thought there had been some kind of mix-up, that Dad was still alive and well but just gone away somewhere. Then I made a pact with God . . . ' she half-laughed as her voice wobbled and she wondered if she dared tell him something she'd never told anyone before.

'What kind of pact?' Christian's hand squeezed hers. He was looking at her as though she was the only thing that mattered to him.

'I promised to be the best girl in the whole wide world if he'd bring Dad back,' she gulped. 'But, of course, no matter how hard I tried, both at home and in school, that didn't happen.'

She dared to meet his eyes, but there was nothing except loving concern in them. No mockery, no hint of laughter. No suggestion that she was a sad case. 'Even when Mum started seeing another man, a year later,' she went on, a little stronger, 'I didn't pay too much attention to him. He was just like any of the family friends who regularly visited our house. I only found out afterwards that he was a rock musician. Then he disappeared off the scene, and a little later I found out Mum was expecting a baby.'

'How did you feel about that?'

'The funny thing is, Christian,' she said, feeling a weight shift inside her, 'in my state of limbo, I thought it was my father's child, that somehow he was around somewhere and my mother was still seeing him, and that comforted me. I know this sounds mad, but it wasn't until Lucy was about three or four that the truth had gradually dawned on me. Or maybe it was that I couldn't face the truth until then. I was a bit shocked when I realised, but by then the rock musician was dead so I just pretended in my head that he had never existed.'

There was a long silence.

'Did you resent Lucy?' he asked.

'Not at all,' Miranda smiled. 'As a baby, Lucy was tiny, and incredibly beautiful. A perfect doll. She had enormous eyes fringed with thick lashes, a button nose and a pink, rosebud mouth. When her eyes fastened on me, they seemed to be begging for love. I couldn't help but love her back. So that's me, where I've come from. Well, mostly.'

She wasn't going to think about Ellie. Not here. Not yet.

He looked at her for a long time, his eyes soft. Then he spoke. 'I want to make it all up to you. All that childhood pain and unhappiness. If you'll let me.'

She caught her breath and held it, afraid that if she said something it would be the wrong thing.

'Hey, you're gone again,' Christian said.

Miranda shook her head. 'Um, sorry. Just – you took me by surprise. I'm thinking about . . . what you said.'

'Nice thoughts?' he said hopefully, lifting her hand and

looking at her as he gently kissed her palm and then the tender inside of her wrist.

As she caught his eye a spark shot through her. The look on his face was unmistakeable. Something hot rose inside her.

'Hey,' he said softly. 'Am I rushing you?'

Rushing her? She hesitated, thinking of the men she'd been to bed with already. Not too many, just a few. Their faces drifted through her mind like a kaleidoscope of images, some fuzzier than others. Men she'd given herself to only to find she wasn't enough. Not exciting enough, not sexy enough. She thought of how fresh, new desire had so often turned sour. How rejection and disappointment had set in, leaving a hollow ache in her heart. It wasn't easy to move on from that, to trust again, to take another chance and risk being cast aside once more.

But that was past, wasn't it? The old Miranda.

Christian was still looking at her, his eyes full of desire for her. She smiled. 'You're not rushing me at all.'

He booked a room with a view of the shimmering harbour. This first time was too important, too special for his place or hers, he said. Her legs felt wobbly as they walked down the corridor so she was glad he curled a warm arm around her shoulders, and she was glad he kept up a light conversation because her throat was dry. In the bedroom, the wide, sumptuous bed swam in front of her vision, and through an open door she saw a marbled bathroom with huge mirrors reflecting a deep bath and an inviting pile of white, fluffy towels.

She watched as Christian slid off his tie and undid his cufflinks, dropping them on a side table. He opened the top buttons of his pale grey shirt. He caught her looking at him and straightaway put his hands on her shoulders, 'Miranda? You're sure?'

'I am, yes,' she said, even though she felt a sudden spike of anxiety. What made her think she would be good enough, exciting enough, for him?

As soon as he started to kiss her, threading his hands in her hair, her little fears melted away, like a patch of lingering ice disappearing under the glow of the sun. She was carried away with his warmth, his deep kisses, the slow way he undressed her, stopping to plant kisses on every inch of her creamy skin, and then swept away even further when he finally sensed she was ready for the full blast of his desire and swiftly shed the rest of his clothes. He laid her across the cream cotton sheets very carefully, as though she was precious to him. He tucked a pillow behind her head and kissed her again. Then she parted her legs for him, gasping with pleasure as he slid up inside her until they were locked together, and she held his gaze and clung to him as they fell into a perfect rhythm, each looking in wonder at the other, as though the spiral of pleasure they were giving each other was beyond anything they'd tasted before.

At some point during the night, they moved into the bathroom. Later, as she stood up in the bath, Miranda saw her blurred reflection in the huge, steamy mirrors; her green eyes so like Vivienne's and Ellie's, now shining with lust; damp tendrils of her red hair framing her face, her pale, gleaming breasts. Then the reflection of Christian in front of her, his back to the mirror; she saw his hands spanning her rib cage, and the back of his blond head and broad sweep of his shoulders as he leaned and fastened his mouth to her beaded nipple and exquisitely teased it with his tongue.

The erotic reflection thrilled her almost as much as the delicious sensations darting through her body. And above all that, the feelings inside: free, exciting, as though a new, liberated version of her life was unfolding in front of her, thanks to this man. Then Christian stood up and blocked her view. He lifted her out of the bath, picked up a sponge and led her into the waterfall shower.

This was her, Miranda Morgan, she told herself. She felt warm soapy water slide down her tingling body and smiled up at him.

Chapter 23

O n Monday morning, after almost a week of being cooped up in the apartment and scarcely venturing out beyond the local store, the bright spring morning finally tempted Ellie enough to dress in her Chanel jeans and a navy blazer and grab her tote bag and stroll into the heart of Manhattan.

On the way, she couldn't resist a peek into the diner, and they were there again, Ben and his mates, looking all very friendly and as though they were having a good laugh and a chat. This time, he definitely saw her, she knew by the way his eyes flickered in recognition, but she looked away immediately, embarrassed at being caught.

She took her time strolling along, angling her face to feel the light breeze and hazy sunshine, obeying the traffic signals this time, and allowing herself to tune into the energy of the city and feel the constant undercurrent of excitement that thrummed in the air at every street corner. She wasn't headed anywhere in particular. For now, she just wanted to re-engage with something – life, she supposed, ordinary, everyday living. And maybe, by revisiting places she'd never been with Johnny, she might somehow connect with the Ellie she'd been before him.

She strolled past elegant hotels where uniformed concierges stood to attention on the pale grey sidewalk and tipped their hats to her. Her thoughts flew back to the time she'd celebrated her thirtieth birthday by splashing out on a weekend in Fitzpatrick's with both Miranda and Claire. Lucy hadn't come, she recalled. She hadn't been allowed to because at fifteen years of age she would have badly cramped Ellie's style.

'We'll be nightclubbing until dawn,' Ellie had explained, annoyed with Lucy for throwing a teenage tantrum. Surely she realised she'd be in the way? She knew she was underage so there had never been any question of her joining Ellie's adult, glitzy party weekend. Lucy would have put a damp squib on the whole thing.

'It'll be no fun for you hanging around a hotel room by yourself while we go out on the tear,' Ellie had said, striving for patience.

'Yes, but, hello, Ellie, a luxury hotel room in *New York?*' Lucy had wailed. 'I could go out with you during the day and then at night I could soak in a fancy bath and read American magazines and eat grapes, and pretend I'm rich and famous. Like Madonna—'

'That wouldn't work. How could I enjoy myself properly thinking of you left behind in the hotel? We'll do something different together. Promise.'

'Don't care. I want to go to New York,' Lucy had said sulkily.

'When you're older, we'll go.'

'I hope you *don't* enjoy yourself,' Lucy had scowled. 'You can think of me stuck at home all on my own when I could have been with you and Miranda. How come I'm always the odd one out?'

'You're not the odd one out.'

'I *am* the odd one out. And you don't like me. If you did, you'd have arranged something to include me, instead of leaving me out.'

In the end, Vivienne had pacified Lucy by offering to take her to Paris for the weekend. No nightclubs, she had decreed, but plenty of shopping and sightseeing.

Ellie had shaken her head, 'You have her spoiled, Mum. She already has twice as much designer stuff as Miranda and I ever had, put together.'

Now when she looked back, Ellie wondered if she could have been more understanding with Lucy. Her youngest sister had been right in pointing out that Ellie hadn't even paused to consider her when she'd been making her thirtieth birthday plans. But it hadn't been the first time she and Lucy had clashed, nor the last. Right from the time Lucy had been small, demanding attention in a way Ellie or Miranda never had, there had been some kind of friction between them, in spite of their age difference. Even when Lucy had announced her grand plans to drop out of school and take the modelling world by storm, they'd clashed. Was it possible that all those confrontations had finally added up in Lucy's head, and spilled over so as to goad her into bed with Johnny? But surely it had been more Johnny's fault? Getting back at Ellie for not wanting to marry him? And what about all those texts that Lucy had been sending her, each one sounding more heartfelt than the previous one?

This wasn't supposed to be happening, Ellie reined in her thoughts. She had to stop thinking of Lucy and Johnny. When she reached Times Square, she deliberately stood for a moment, soaking up the overwhelming vibrancy of the place with the iconic neon signs, the constant rumble of the traffic, the flowing tide of people, and the expectant queue already waiting in line for half price Broadway tickets. She strolled across to the Rockefeller Center, where she went into a café and had a light lunch of coffee and a panini.

Even that plunged her back in time. The year before last, she'd been here with Miranda, and they'd gone up to the observation deck to marvel at the view. Lucy was modelling in London by then and Ellie had brought Miranda to New York, thinking she'd cheer her up after yet another failed relationship. Her third or fourth by now.

'I thought you guys were brilliant together,' Ellie had said. 'What went wrong?'

'I don't want to talk about it,' Miranda had sobbed. 'I want to forget he ever existed.'

Ellie had hugged her blotchy-faced sister. 'Right. As soon as you feel up to it, we're having a weekend away, just the two of us. We'll go to New York like we did for my birthday and paint the town red,' she'd said. 'We'll stay in the Plaza this time, and dine in the Palm Court. We'll go shopping and sip cocktails in Manhattan. By the time we've finished, you'll have forgotten all about him, I promise.'

How insensitive she had been, Ellie thought uncomfortably, pushing her panini around on her plate. As if a weekend in the Big Apple with her was going to make it all better for Miranda. Her sister had smiled bravely and said she was having a great time, but through the whirl of shopping and cocktails, she must have been broken up inside.

Now it was Ellie's turn to try and get over a mangled heart and it took a lot more than a luxury weekend, she thought wryly. She wondered if Miranda was seeing anybody in Hong Kong. She hoped she was. Her kind, considerate sister deserved nothing but the best.

Ellie felt a bit shaky as she rose to her feet. She was reluctant to go back to the apartment just yet, given that her midtown stroll wasn't exactly bringing her good memories, reconnecting her instead with slightly unsettling thoughts. Thoughts of herself being a little hard and tactless.

Or else, she mused, she was seeing it all from a different perspective because she was coming from a place where she was freshly hurt herself, and could only now fully appreciate how Lucy and Miranda must have felt. Still, she'd been hurt before, hadn't she? Her life had shattered into a million pieces after her father had died and her mother had taken up with Zach. However, she thought a little proudly, she'd dealt with that hurt quite efficiently. She'd buried it so deeply that no one, not even herself, could ever reach it. Maybe she hadn't been the best sister in the world, but she wasn't perfect. Nobody was. And nothing excused Lucy's betrayal.

Ellie headed up Fifth Avenue even though for now, she couldn't summon the enthusiasm for shopping. She paused by the windows of small exclusive boutiques and large gleaming stores, displaying international designer clothes and accessories. She should feel at home here, the exclusive names all so familiar to her – Bergdorf Goodman, Saks, Tiffany's, Henri Bendel – but her eyes glanced over them as though they meant nothing. She recalled of the previous February, when she'd been over with Claire for the Fall/Winter Fashion Week, admiring the chic couture and wondering if her collections would ever feature.

'What do you mean, *if*, Ellie? You should be saying *when*,' Claire had decreed optimistically.

'When, not if,' Ellie repeated to herself, grasping the words to herself like a talisman. There was more to Ellie Morgan's life than Johnny and Lucy and a crappy betrayal. She just had to learn to rise above it all and get back to herself, which she would. She eventually headed back to the apartment, passing the

Plaza Hotel and strolling along Central Park South in the bright, crisp afternoon.

She made coffee and pulled a chair and a small occasional table over to the window. She took out her pencils and sketch pads, and made herself comfortable. She held her favourite pencil between her fingers and took a sip of coffee. Just a few doodles would be enough to get her started. She thought of the energy and life of the New York streetscapes and wondered how she could tap into that to infuse and colour the shape of material skimming off a form.

Nothing. It was just as if a great blank had descended upon her, wiping clean any budding ideas before she had a chance to capture a silhouette and shape it on the page. She sat there, giving herself time to relax. She looked down and saw her fingers totally rigid around her pencil and realised her head had started to throb. Throughout her career, she'd had good days and bad days, but she couldn't ever recall feeling like this, as though everything in her mind and heart had been totally wrung out, leaving a blank except for the taste of sour nausea in her mouth. In a wave of panic, she flung her pencil across the floor and bundled her sketchpads into her laptop bag.

Jesus, what was wrong with her? Was this it, her career down the tubes because she couldn't get it together? Was it a temporary block or had one of her greatest fears come to pass?

'I sometimes wonder if I'll wake up some morning and I won't be able to come up with a single sketch,' she'd once said to Johnny. They had been in her big, wide bed and were enjoying the kind of relaxed chit-chat that comes after making love, her head nesting in the curve between his neck and shoulder. By now, they had been together nine months and Ellie had felt secure enough to voice her fear.

'Don't be daft,' he'd chuckled.

'No, really,' she'd insisted, turning so that she was resting on her elbow. 'Imagine if overnight, I went completely blank. That I had no ideas, no concepts, no passion . . . or no sense of where to even start.'

'Relax, Ellie, forget it, that will never happen,' he'd said. His hand had plunged between her thighs. 'If you're looking for passion, I think we should start again, right from the top . . . or maybe the bottom,' his hand had wriggled in further.

And now the very thing she'd feared had happened. As Ellie stood there breathing hard, there was a knock at the door. A gentle knock.

'Yes?' her voice was shrill.

'It's Ben.'

Damn. She couldn't face him just now, feeling as downright scared as she was. It was bound to show on her face. Then again, she couldn't very well pretend she wasn't in – she'd already answered him.

'Hold on a minute.' She squared her shoulders and forced a smile onto her face. Then she opened the door.

He was wearing the same grey sports top he'd had on earlier that day. She let her eyes fasten on that bulk rather than meet his eyes.

'What is it?'

'Are you okay?' he asked, before laughing and putting his hands up in surrender. 'Sorry, we seemed to have had this conversation already. You just looked a little spooked and I hope I didn't disturb you.'

'You didn't.' And what exactly did he mean by 'spooked'? Did he still think she was some kamikaze stunt woman?

'I was just thinking . . .' he paused. Despite her best intentions, she found herself drawn to those hazel-coloured, almond-shaped eyes. They looked totally at ease. Comfortable. Friendly.

She waited.

'Just getting back to the other evening,' he said. 'If you're all that keen on walking, but you want to stay out of danger, I'll allow you to join my walking group.'

'What's that?'

'I'm making this offer strictly so you'll stay in one piece and I don't have to answer to Laura.'

'Well, naturally,' she responded a little testily.

'A few of us meet most mornings to go walking in Central Park, so come along if you want.'

She thought of the gang she'd seen in the diner that morning. 'When does this happen?'

'Usually Monday and Wednesday, sometimes Friday. Starting at eight. We meet up by the 79th Street entrance. It's just a couple of blocks from here.'

'And you're inviting me?'

'Hey, it's not a big deal. I don't send out gilt-edged invitations. Whoever turns up, turns up, simple.'

'I'll see.' It would get her out of the apartment, wouldn't it? So far her days had been long and aimless. Her bolthole, far from being a refuge, had turned out to be a little suffocating. But it was far too soon to go home and risk running into Johnny or mention of their split in the papers. And exercise was good – something to do with the endorphins. She needed that.

'Five minutes before eight am,' he reminded her. 'Bring water and good sports shoes.' His glance flicked to her ballet flats and instantly dismissed them. 'Your first walk is free.'

'*Free?*'

'Yep,' he looked pleased with her reaction. 'You hardly think I do this for nothing. I have to earn a crust somehow. And I'm putting you on trust that you won't go running to immigration.'

'I won't.'

When she closed the door after him, she realised that even for those few minutes it had been good to talk to someone, even if it had just been about a walk in the park. And good to talk to Ben without any animosity fizzling between them.

Chapter 24

A walk in the park, Ellie had thought. It was turning out to be anything but a walk in the park.

She'd visited the nearest Foot Locker the previous day, picking up a tracksuit and sports shoes. She didn't know what kind of miracle the shoes were supposed to perform. According to the sales assistant, they boasted some kind of heel technology to reduce impact, and featured superior traction and movement, so that she'd feel as though she was walking on marshmallows.

Marshmallows? Every step required exertion. She couldn't believe how unfit she was. Although to her shame, she'd never incorporated much in the way of exercise into her life. Vivienne had her treadmill at home and Miranda visited the gym, but Ellie's exercise had been confined to sporadic Sunday afternoon strolls, which scarcely prepared her for a military-like stride around Central Park.

She could drop out at any time. Simply leave the group and limp her way back to the apartment – but she wasn't going to give up or give Ben the satisfaction of seeing her crawling home with her tail between her legs. Not that he had paid any attention to her. Funnily enough, that annoyed her. She'd made a huge effort to be here, but he'd barely noticed her arrival at five to eight on that Monday morning as she joined the half a dozen or so people waiting by the entrance at 79th Street. Promptly at eight o'clock, they headed into the park. There was no sign of Megan, though, she noticed. The walking group comprised four guys and four women, including herself and Ben, and they ranged in age from mid-twenties to mid-fifties. Ben led the group around along with a young twenty-something blonde whom Ellie disliked on sight.

You're just envious, she told herself. Envious of her perfect, petite figure in slim-fitting gym pants and a cropped top, the four-inch gap between both garments revealing a smooth, toned midriff. Her hair was tied up in a ponytail that obediently swished from side to side with every step she took. She was the clichéd all-American blonde who had been the class prefect as well as chief cheerleader in college. She looked carefree and optimistic as she chatted easily to Ben, looking as though the world was her oyster and would bring only good things.

Ellie was happy to hang back and bring up the rear, along with another woman around her own age. She felt she screamed novice in her so pristine-they-were-light-reflecting sports shoes and fresh-from-the pack-looking tracksuit.

'Does it get any easier?' she asked the woman striding along-side her.

'Is this your first time?'

'Yeah.'

She gave Ellie a big, bright smile. 'Hi, I'm Tina.'

'I'm Ellie.'

'It takes a few outings to find your marching feet, Ellie, depending on the walk. This is one of the easy ones. It takes about an hour and a half,' Tina grinned at her.

Easy? Ellie was already out of breath and they'd only been walking for about twenty minutes. Tina looked perfectly comfortable in her navy leisure suit as they marched down the side of the meadow in the blowy morning. Up in the soft, dove-grey sky, where the cloud was lightly fragmented, glimmers of pale sunlight shafted through. Only for the iconic view of New York skyline beyond the trees bordering the far perimeter, they could have been in a large meadow in Ireland. Ellie couldn't help being intrigued with the sense of seclusion in the corner of this great park, given that they were a stone's throw from the heart of a big, bustling city.

'So how many other walks are there?' Ellie asked.

'Three altogether that Ben arranges. This one takes you around Sheep Meadow and the lake, there's another one that starts at The Pond, but the best of all is hiking around the woods in Central Park North. Bit more of a challenge. Ben tries to vary the route every so often, but he always guarantees a full hour and a half workout,' Tina said.

'Workout? I thought this was a walking group.'

'Power walking,' Tina clarified. 'Not quite boot camp, but not far off it when you keep pace with Ben. He's a hard taskmaster. Do you think you'll stick with us?'

'I'll see,' Ellie said, realising she was having her first near-normal conversation since coming to New York. 'Is it always the same group?'

'Nah, people come and go and about a dozen of us are regulars but we don't all manage every outing. I'm on shift work, so it suits me to come most Mondays and Fridays. You?'

'I – um – I'm on a short holiday,' Ellie said.

'So lucky you, you're free to come whenever ... you'll find this sets you up for the day. We meet in all weathers, unless it's monsoon-like rain or a snow blizzard. We'd lots of snow last winter, and the park was gorgeous.'

Even now it was gorgeous, Ellie decided, feeling a little energy springing from somewhere as they headed up The Mall, and she admired the beauty of the American elms lining the wide avenue. She even found herself searching and finding those first fat buds of spring. Maybe this was her endorphins kicking in at last.

'Hey, swing your fists, Ellie,' Ben's raised voice came at her. 'Bend the elbows.' He had doubled back to where she and Tina were soldiering along at the rear of the group. So he knew she was there and he remembered her name. Her pride was a little restored now that he was seeing her in a positive environment and not as an incompetent basket case. He kept pace with her for a few minutes, swinging his arms in an arc from his waist to his chest. 'Look, like this. It'll keep your fingers from swelling and get more from your workout,' he said.

She felt a self-conscious prickling along her hairline as he studied her while she copied his arm movements.

'Yeah, that's it, you have it now ... good, keep it up. Tina, tuck that butt right in. Remember the dollar bill?'

'Yes, sir!' Tina saluted.

Ellie continued to swing her arms enthusiastically as they headed up the tree-lined avenue and Ben loped back to the top of the group, rather glad that he hadn't been examining her butt.

'And you, Ellie, same thing,' he turned around and roared. 'As soon as you get comfortable with the arm movement, I want you to pretend you're clenching a dollar bill between your butt cheeks. Really work them glutes. Right?'

'Jesus,' she felt a little embarrassed. 'Is this guy for real?'

'Yeah, he's a personal trainer,' Tina said. 'He can't get a full-time job though he picks up a few shifts in one or two Brooklyn gyms when they're stuck. So he knows what he's talking about.'

'Do you work in the industry yourself?' Ellie asked.

'I wish!' Tina laughed. 'I'm a nurse in Mount Sinai.'

Ellie was intrigued. 'I'm impressed. That must take dedication.'

'It's busy,' Tina said, her matter-of-fact tone belying the seriousness of her job. 'That's why I like to walk. It takes me away from all the stress. I'll think of this tomorrow, the feeling of the breeze on my face, the loveliness of the park, when I'm up to my neck in hypodermics and bed baths.'

'It must be very demanding – but satisfying,' Ellie commented.

'Mmm. It has its good days and bad days, but whatever happens I get to take off my uniform, walk out into fresh air, and go home to my comfy apartment at the end of my shift,' Tina said. 'And you?'

'Nothing as worthwhile, I'm afraid,' Ellie admitted. 'I'm a fashion designer. Ladies occasion wear.' She thought of the contrast between the luxury, designer stores in Midtown and the non-stop bustle of a hospital ward. Compared to Tina, surely her job was superficial and frivolous? It was something that had occasionally nibbled at her self-esteem. In what way was she contributing to society? Making the world a better place, like Tina and all of those who soldiered out there at the coalface of humanity? And was she being totally self-indulgent in her absorption to her career?

'Don't dare knock yourself, Ellie!' Tina grinned. 'That's a highly competitive field. You must be hard-working and talented to make that happen.'

'It's all I've ever wanted to do,' Ellie said honestly.

'There you are, it's your gift. You must exercise it. We long-suffering nurses rely on people like you to help us feel feminine and good at the end of a day's work. We need you to dream your dreams and use the best of your inspiration and creativity so that we can dress in nice clothes, look in the mirror and feel glamorous. I know confidence comes from within, but a beautiful dress sure helps.'

Ellie felt a lift of gratitude. In a few simple words, Tina had given her something special, a nugget of validation that meant a lot to her. She would remember this, she thought, whenever she felt unsure about the value of her career.

By the time the power walk had finished, and Ben had led them through a few stretches, Ellie had aches in parts of her body that she'd never known existed. She noticed that their petite blonde leader was milking the stretches for all she was worth, stretching her arms as far behind her as she could and shoving out her boobs, almost into Ben's face. He smiled at her and said something that made her laugh. Naturally, she had a sexy, tinkly laugh.

What was it about men and women and sex, Ellie thought sourly. Was there no getting away from it, even on a power walk?

'Some of us go for coffee afterwards, are you interested?' Tina's voice broke into her thoughts.

'No, thanks, not this time,' Ellie said, knowing she'd had enough for now. Apart from her aches and pains, her fragile endorphins hadn't lasted too long because she suddenly felt exhausted with the sheer effort it had taken to climb out of her fog and behave like a normal human being. She knew she wouldn't be able to keep it up much longer. Especially not with the blonde cheerleader and Ben ogling each other across their coffee. It was all so irritating.

Had Johnny ogled Lucy like that? Without her noticing? The few times he'd met Lucy, he'd treated her like a kid sister. Had anything been going on behind her back? And, if so, for how long? More stuff to torture herself with, she sighed. Still, for almost two hours that morning she hadn't thought of Johnny.

She knew she had a long way to go before he and Lucy stopped gnawing at her head, but that had to mean something.

'So, see you another time?' Tina said brightly.

Ellie smiled back. 'Yeah, probably.'

She hung back as the group exited the park, surprised to find herself a little piqued that Ben strode out without a backward glance in her direction. Then, in the next breath, she told herself she was being ridiculous. He didn't owe her anything. So why would she have liked some token of acknowledgement from him?

Chapter 25

On Thursday evening, as soon as the last customer had left and the doors of Johnny's Glad Rags had closed, Johnny told the staff to go home before they'd completed his strict tidying regime. There was a half-hearted chorus of objections from the junior staff.

'What about the shirts for the laundry?'

'Nah. Don't bother.'

'And the suit bags?'

'And the kitchen?'

'Leave them.' This came out so much like a growl that the two junior assistants who usually carried out these tasks backed away and bumped into each other.

'Are you sure, Johnny?' they asked tentatively.

'Yes, I'm sure. Now get going before I change my mind.'

There was a flurry as they grabbed their jackets and legged it, anxious to be out downing pints in the buzz of a Dublin Thursday evening, which was often seen as the start of the weekend.

'Are you okay?' Jane asked, hanging back.

'What do you think?' he gave her a lopsided smile.

'I dunno. I know something has gone wrong with you and Ellie.'

'How do you know?' he asked cagily. It was the first time she'd brought it up. He'd thought he'd behaved very much as normal over the past couple of weeks, throwing himself cheerfully into the job, almost too cheerfully to counteract the long, silent evenings at home. But someone who knew him as well as Jane was bound to have spotted that his world had caved in around him.

'She doesn't call looking for you, you haven't mentioned her name in ages, and you've been hiding away from the gang. She's not just in New York on business, is she? Also,' she took a deep breath and gave him a level look and he knew what was coming next, 'you've hardly talked to David since the party night, the night we got engaged.'

'Sorry about that, I had other things to think about.'

'That wasn't hard to figure out. But why don't you talk to him, call him, tell him what's wrong? He's your brother. He doesn't know we're having this conversation, by the way. But I'm concerned for the both of you. You and Ellie, and you and David. And—' she faltered, looking embarrassed.

'Go on.'

'Me and David are having a party to celebrate our engagement next Saturday night. We know you're in a bad place right now, but we'd love you to be there,' she said in a rush, her cheeks pink. 'So think about it, will you? And talk to David.'

'Sure,' he said. Her face was so earnest and honest that it endeared her to him. His sister-in-law-to-be. Fancy that. He'd never had a sister before. 'Now off you go. I'll call David soon. Promise.'

She turned back to him in the doorway. 'Johnny, look after yourself, won't you?'

He gave her a half-hearted smile as she left. He locked the entrance door and pressed the button to bring down the window blinds dulling the evening brightness that was pouring into the shop, shutting out the street outside, leaving him alone with his guilty conscience. He'd been shabby and small minded in the way he'd ignored David in the past couple of weeks. He'd barely congratulated Jane, even though she was his chief assistant and deserved far better from him. He should have organised some flowers, champagne, a present. That seems to have been the story of his life lately – behaving shabbily, getting it wrong.

Getting it wrong? How the hell did that describe the brutal way he'd betrayed Ellie? What demon had possessed him?

Jealousy of his brother, an urge to hit back at Ellie in some way, coupled with a weak moment in time. But there was no excuse for what he'd done. No way.

Johnny fetched a laundry bag and stuffed it haphazardly with returned dress shirts. He realised too late that he should have been keeping tally. It should have been second nature to him, he'd begun his little empire at fourteen years of age by helping his father during school holidays and on Saturdays. Almost twenty-five years ago, he thought, shuddering at how swiftly the time had flown. He'd never envisaged how it all would turn out or the way he'd become a successful part of the Dublin celebrity scene. 'An unstoppable force', he'd been recently labelled in a 'Sunday Diary' page and he'd boastingly read it out to Ellie.

She had laughed.

He closed his eyes. He saw her sitting up in bed sipping orange juice with sheets of newspaper crumpled between them.

'Let's see how good this unstoppable force is,' she'd said, putting down her glass and shoving the paper out of the way, laughing as she reached for him.

'Don't you dare tell me you have a tape measure under your pillow.'

'This works just as well,' she'd said, fastening both hands around his stiffening penis.

Ellie had laughed a lot. Problem was, she'd laughed too much. Way too much. At him and his proposal. He opened his eyes and saw his glowering face in a lighted mirror. Dark, saturnine, unhappy.

Shite. Bloody, bloody shite.

He went over behind the reception desk and snapped a switch so that all the strategically focused spotlights were extinguished, leaving just the overhead lighting. He pulled back dressing-room curtains and fixed them around the curtain hook, scoured the small sink in the kitchen, washed the tiled floor and emptied bins, needing the basic satisfaction of light physical labour and putting everything back to rights for the following morning.

He'd been shabby, too, with Lucy. He'd only met her a few times and he'd thought her too spoiled and indulged to have the perseverance necessary to make it as an international model – which, she'd told him during their first meeting, was her main ambition in life. But that morning had been different. She'd looked at him with a childlike trust. She'd been full of a soft, yielding warmth that surprised him. Worse, he'd felt her cling to him as though she was desperate for love and affection. As she'd stood before him, stripped of her clothes and her usual spikiness, he'd sensed a wild and hungry neediness about her that went beyond sex, and, gradually, in the chill of the night, during all those dark, beating-himself-up hours, it had made him realise two things:

Ellie had never really needed him like that, not in a deep, down, feral way.

Lucy was vulnerable and susceptible behind her spiky front and he should never have taken advantage of her.

He was all fingers and thumbs as he set the alarm and locked up. He stood in the porch, aimless for a moment as all around him Thursday evening swung into gear, and the beautiful people clattered down the street, heading for pubs and restaurants. It was the kind of bright Thursday evening that he and Ellie would have enjoyed, with a pale, apricot light casting a golden glow in the sky and the city alive with the anticipation of summer. They would have sat over drinks on a pavement terrace before going back to his or hers to make love. But tonight he was going home alone to mop up his feelings of despair with a bottle of vodka. Anything to blur his mind and prevent him from calculating the damage he'd done.

Chapter 26

Despite Ellie's resolve to pick up her life again, she found herself lingering in bed on Friday morning instead of joining Ben and his group for the power walk. She needed more time to get her act together before she ventured out again. She sat down on the dark green sofa, placed her laptop on the coffee table and spent a half an hour catching up on emails. She steeled herself against a surge of panic when she saw more emails from Johnny invading her inbox and she deleted them unopened. She checked progress with Claire, pleased that things were running smoothly in Dublin. How grateful she was to have Claire, holding the fort for her, allowing her this precious down time. She answered business emails, including one from her accountant. That hadn't been too bad, had it? At least some part of her was back in the land of the living.

Then feeling sick with nerves, she took a deep breath and turned to her sketchpad and pencils, handling them slowly and carefully as though they were about to bite her. Nothing. Still nothing, except the beginnings of another headache. Rather than sit there and have the blank page mock her, she made coffee, rummaging in the cupboard as the kettle boiled when the craving for something sweet couldn't be ignored, but even that was a waste of time. She threw on her jacket to head to the nearby store for some comforting chocolate.

And as if she wasn't stressed enough, she bumped into Ben coming into the building. 'Hi, Ellie! Missed you this morning. It was a great workout. Pity you weren't there.'

'Why, do I look like I need to lose some weight?' she asked tartly. 'Preferably off my butt cheeks?' Even as she uttered them, she wished she could take back the childlike words. Ben jumped back and held up his hands in defeat, the friendly smile draining from his face.

'Wow,' he said, 'I don't know what your problem is. I thought you enjoyed the other day. And I wasn't being personal about your – ahem – butt. That's the way I operate. It's a workout and I like everyone to get the most from it.'

His hazel eyes were clouded with a mixture of disappointment and angry pride. Suddenly, she wanted him to like her. He had done nothing to deserve the unfriendly tone she was using, and neither was her childish behaviour doing her battered self-esteem any good. She was going to need to be a lot more positive if she wanted to drag herself out of this limbo, starting with small things. 'I did enjoy it,' she said, sounding as earnest as possible. 'I didn't mean to slag it off. It was good fun.'

To her relief, his face brightened. 'No worries. Off anywhere nice?'

'Just to the shop down the block,' she said.

'Hey, sure, I'll walk down that far with you,' he offered. Before she knew it, they were strolling together, Ben with his hands in the pockets of his grey sports top. She resisted the temptation to tell him to remove them and walk with his elbows bent. She didn't dare check out his butt.

'This isn't a power walk,' he said. 'I'm using this opportunity to figure out why a posh Irish girl like you is slumming it in Laura's apartment,' he said.

She snuck a glance to see if he was joking but he was looking straight ahead. Posh! How dare he! He scarcely knew her. She wondered if Claire had let something slip to Laura, and she in turn had dropped a hint to Ben.

'You mean you don't know already?' Even she disliked her haughty tone, but she couldn't help it.

'Nope. I just figure you don't look the type to be hanging out in Laura's cramped place.'

'What makes you think I'm posh? And Laura's apartment is lovely.'

'Hey, come on, it suits Laura as she's a crazy, fun-loving babe. Herself and Megan are a scream when they get together. But you, Ellie . . . hmm, I sense a more refined, sophisticated Ellie in there, behind the lunatic woman who frightened Upper West Side traffic, the classy kind who would normally be hanging out in the Plaza or Fitzpatrick's.'

'I've stayed there so often I'm bored with it,' she said jokingly. 'I'm here for a few weeks and it would be rather a push to stay in the Plaza. It's a sort of sabbatical for me,' she said, congratulating herself for her clever thinking. A sabbatical covered a multitude. 'And I thought I'd get me a slice of proper New York life.'

'Complete with noisy, door-bashing neighbours.'

'Absolutely.'

They reached the corner shop and paused outside.

'After you,' he said, standing to one side of the door.

Just as she smiled before she moved past him, she became

aware of him in a different way. She'd already registered that he was a little taller than her and his dark curly hair was slightly too long and permanently tousled. Up to now, she hadn't paid much attention to his face, but in the pause between one moment and the next, she felt as though she was seeing it for the first time, and there was something in the arrangement of it all – dark brows under the tumble of hair, those clear hazel eyes with the dark lashes, the long nose and full, generous mouth – that whispered sensuality and slammed into her chest.

She swallowed hard. Ben from Leitrim looked sexy in a young, Daniel Day Lewis way. No wonder, she thought in the next breath, he had women all over the place. Between Laura, Megan and the blonde cheerleader, this guy had a number of notches on his bedpost. Not that she'd ever be one of them. Her sudden confusion embarrassed her and she almost closed the door in his face.

'I'm going in too,' he said.

Great. And she was here for some comfort-eating chocolate. She went across to the confectionery counter and helped herself to a selection of chocolate bars, both milk and plain. She saw his glance of amusement as she paid for her calorific, fat-inducing haul, but he refrained from passing any comment.

At first. He picked up a magazine and paid for it, a sports one, of course. Then outside on the pavement he cocked an eyebrow, 'Midnight feast?'

'Good guess,' she said. 'But you're wrong. I need to put back the calories I lost on Monday morning.'

They strolled back along the pavement, an ambulance siren cutting through the air, preventing them from chatting for a minute as it roared past, the wail eventually receding into the distance.

'Pity you didn't come this morning,' he said, 'you would have loved the trail through the woods.' He spoke as though she'd really missed a treat.

'How do you know?'

'Because it's beautiful,' he said. 'Like a microcosm of Ireland. Particularly Leitrim.' The look he gave her was so self-satisfied and totally confident of her agreement that he rubbed her up the wrong way.

'Yes, of course, lovely Leitrim,' she knew her voice was a little mocking, but, hey, he was boasting.

'Have you ever been there?' He turned around to face her, walking backwards along the pavement and keeping pace with her so that he could see her face while she answered.

Leitrim. She recalled her map of Ireland. It was somewhere near Sligo and Roscommon, wasn't it? Somewhere you might drive through en route to Donegal, where you didn't even stop for coffee because there was nowhere to stop. Unless Carrick-on-Shannon, was that in Leitrim?

'Of course, lots of times, it's fab,' she said airily. Then she realised she was taking a dig at his native county and she wasn't being fair.

'So come on, where have you stayed?'

He wasn't letting her away with this, she realised. Tenacious about his county. Loyal as well.

'I've just passed through a few times,' she admitted. 'Carrick-on-Shannon mostly, on the way to Sligo.'

'Next time don't just pass through. Linger a little in Rossinver, Dromahair or Lough Allen. Stand by the Drowes river at Tullaghan, where you catch the best salmon in the world. It's a beautiful county.'

He wasn't just sports mad, she thought. He had heart, even though he'd look more at home shooting baskets rather than standing on the pavement pronouncing Irish place names in a musical accent. Here in New York, it was a piece of Celtic soul and it plunged her back home to weekends spent in welcoming country hotels, a soothing medley of green fields surrounded by dry-stone walls and Atlantic breakers off the coast of Mayo.

They reached the apartment building, hurrying together the last few yards as the rain began to pelt in big fat drops.

'Next week? Monday morning?' he said, inside the hallway.

She felt suddenly shy. 'I'll think about it. I have to – em – pay you. How does that work?'

'Ah sure, no bother. I'll put it on the slate and you can fix up with me later. I trust you.'

'Really?'

'Aren't you a friend of Laura's? That's good enough for me!'

Laura. Megan. Blonde cheerleader. She wondered how he managed to keep them all going. She jumped into the lift, glad that he'd opted to take the stairs and spare her from standing next to him in that close spot. Not that it should worry her in the least . . .

The following night when she heard the crump of loud music coming from Megan and Ben's apartment, she slipped out onto the landing and listened for a couple of minutes, long enough to hear their apartment door open to a cacophony of hellos and welcomes. Shrieks of laughter mingling with music wafted out the open door, before it closed over again, muting the sounds. Party central was obviously going on.

So what if she hadn't been invited? She told herself she was silly to feel annoyed.

Ellie had a shower in the tiny bathroom and put on cotton pyjamas and a dressing gown. She tied her hair up in a ponytail, poured a glass of white wine and sat down to watch a spy thriller, raising the volume to drown out the party noise. Saturday night in New York and, all of a sudden, she felt lonely, with nowhere to go and no one to go with. This must be how Cinderella had felt – although she hadn't had much of a choice, whereas Ellie had deliberately chosen this to get away from Dublin and Johnny.

Johnny!

She felt a sharp wave of longing for him, so painful that it took her breath away. For once she didn't brush it aside, but allowed herself to remember the feel of his skin against hers, the familiar sight of his head beside hers on the pillow at night. Even his light snores and the comforting hump of his body under the duvet had become woven into the routine fabric of her life. She'd taken his presence for granted in lots of ways.

For all his talk, she'd never thought he was really serious about marriage. She liked her space and independence and thought he liked his. They had all that, as well as sex in regular doses. It was the best of both worlds. She needed a certain amount of peace and solitude in order to create, and he knew all about that and had always been supportive. At the weekends they made up for it, and had fun as they whirled round Dublin's hotspots – night-clubs, soirées, private parties, they had always been inundated with invitations.

She wondered how many of those would come her way now that they had split. It was a consequence of their bust-up she hadn't considered until now. A lot of the A-list celebs they regularly socialised with as a couple were Johnny's friends. Ellie wasn't one of those who had kept her friends since her school-days. She'd been only too glad to see the back of school and some of the bitchier classmates, and wipe the proverbial dust from her feet. Art and design college had followed, where she'd met Claire, and then there had been many years of hard work behind the scenes, putting in so many long hours to establish her career that it had limited her time to develop new friendships.

It had been easy to slot in with Johnny and his friends, and they had gladly accepted her – after all, Ellie Morgan was fast making a name for herself, one to be reckoned with. But if it came down to a choice on the invitation list between fun-loving, larger-than-life Johnny and successful, career-driven Ellie, she knew who they would choose. All the invitations would be flying in his direction. Even if word got out about Johnny sleeping with Lucy – he'd be forgiven, in time. There was no such thing as equality. Not when it came to sex. Thanks to the double standards that still existed, Johnny's betrayal would be indulgently viewed as a little peccadillo. Men were men, after all. Wild oats and all that. Fair play to him for getting it off with a hot model who was years younger than he was. And although she was the one who had sent Johnny packing, Ellie, the singleton lurching swiftly towards forty years of age, would be a sort of embarrassment, while Johnny, the unattached and very eligible bachelor with the horny reputation, would be on everyone's invitation list.

But that was no help to her now, on a Saturday night in New York. Missing him. Wanting him, even though jealousy cut through her like a knife at the thought of him with Lucy.

The bastard! She felt the familiar lump gathering once more at the back of her throat but she was still too angry to let it out and cry. She didn't realise she was sitting in semi-darkness with just the glare coming from the television, until there was a knock at the door.

It was Megan.

'Hi, Ellie, I'm just up to apologise for the noise, hope it's not driving you mad,' Megan said in a chatty voice. 'You're very welcome to join us, if you like. I thought Ben would have invited you, but apparently he forgot.'

Ellie blinked and pulled herself together. Megan looked fab.

Her dark wavy hair was tied back and flowing over one shoulder and she was wearing a floaty Grecian-type dress and funky, silvery boots. Her make-up was exotic, eyes emphasised with glittery shadow and smudged, navy liner. Megan had obviously left her apartment door open because the sound of riotous laughter and raised voices floated up the stairs. Her Saturday night was obviously as lively and sparkling as she looked, and, in comparison, Ellie felt drab and flat and boring.

As she found her voice, she realised she hadn't uttered one word to anyone that day. 'It's okay, Megan, don't worry about the noise.'

'Why don't you come down? We're having a party. It'll give you a chance to meet some of the gang.'

Ellie shrank back. The prospect of meeting some of the uproarious gang filled her with nerves. She gave a self-deprecating laugh and indicated her nightwear. 'I'm not exactly in party mode,' she said.

'So? You'll be in the mood for plenty of craic after one glass of my punch.'

When Ellie made no reply, Megan went on, looking slightly disappointed, 'If you change your mind you know where we are.'

'Hey, what's keeping you two?' Ben's voice came up the stairs, roaring to make itself heard over the noise.

Megan leaned over the stairwell. 'I'm coming, but I'm not sure about Ellie.' She turned back to Ellie. 'Seriously, you're very welcome.'

'Tell Ellie to get her butt down here, or else I'm coming to get her.'

Megan grinned. 'There you are, orders from the boss himself. And he doesn't care if you're not in party mode. We'll give you ten minutes, Ellie. You don't need to get all dressed up, just throw on a pair of jeans, you're the kind who looks great in a plastic sack.'

Megan went downstairs and Ellie closed the door. She stood with her back against it for a moment, her heart thumping. Ten minutes. One part of her wanted to dive under the bedclothes and stay there. Another part of her felt like Cinderella again, only this time she'd been told she was going to the ball. The noise from downstairs grew louder. She pictured Ben hammering on the door and as if galvanised, and with a lift of excitement, she flew around the apartment, casting off her dressing gown and PJs, pulling on her Chanel jeans and a crisp white shirt. She put on some make-up, looking at her flushed face in the mirror. Then she loosed her hair from its ponytail, letting it fall to her shoulders in a dark, raven cloud. Grabbing a bottle of white wine as her contribution, she felt a frisson of giddiness and a wave of anxiety as she locked her apartment door and ventured down the stairs.

What was she letting herself in for?

Still, it was better than sitting in the dark, thinking of Johnny. Anything was better than that.

A wall of music, shrieks of laughter and heat hit her when Megan opened the door. It wasn't really her scene at all and she was plunged into a different world when Megan made swift introductions as she dragged her through a raucous throng reeking with testosterone and glamour out to the kitchen and the bowl of punch. Glamour from young women in mini-dresses, maxi skirts, jeans and designer tops. Testosterone oozing from what seemed like the entire Leitrim GAA expat contingent crowding out the apartment, to judge by their jerseys. This was obviously the 'gang' that Megan had referred to. And all of them so lively and carefree and younger than her, ranging from Lucy's age up to early thirties.

She was in the midst of them all before she realised it. The apartment was bigger than Laura's, from what she could see. It had a comfortable, lived-in feel, with throws on the sofas and shelves full of books, magazines and CDs. The kitchen surfaces were awash with beer bottles, glasses and bottles of wine.

Ellie didn't have to worry about producing bright conversation because no one could be properly heard above the pulsating music. Megan introduced her as a friend of Laura's and she was accepted immediately. No one was too interested about what she was doing in Laura's apartment. If she'd wanted a perfect antidote to her lonely Saturday night, this was it.

She was on her second glass of punch when Ben pushed through the crowd towards her.

He put his hand on her arm in a welcoming gesture. 'Nice to see you here, Ellie,' he said, looking as though he meant it. 'Feel free to help yourself to whatever's going, especially Megan's punch. She's determined to pour every last drop down our throats even if we all suffer tomorrow.'

'What are you celebrating?'

'A match, of course.'

'What match?'

'Leitrim, back home. Great match against Roscommon. We were beaten by just two points.'

Ellie smiled to herself. 'So you keep in touch with what's going on?'

'What do you think? Thanks for coming,' he went on. 'We couldn't have you sitting up there all by yourself listening to this racket.'

There it was again, that feeling of pique prickling in her stomach. Was that the only reason she'd been invited? Because they didn't like the thought of lonely Ellie in the apartment up above and felt obliged to include her?

'Hey, cheer up,' he said, looking at her as though he could read her thoughts. 'That's not the only reason you were asked.'

'No?'

He grinned. 'Megan and I thought you might add a bit of class to our boisterous gang.'

Megan and I. He spoke her name with a fond familiarity and Ellie immediately chided herself for noticing. What business was it of hers? Still, they'd been talking about her. Together. And class. Did she wear it like a badge? How come she didn't find it appealing?

'I meant that as a compliment,' he went on, his hazel eyes warm. 'You're a little different from the rest of us crazy people.'

She didn't know if she was happy about that, it seemed to set her apart and, funnily enough, she wanted to belong and feel part of this friendly gathering. Someone called to him above the din, and he pressed through the crowd to the front door, reappearing a minute later with Blonde Cheerleader by his side. She looked sparkly and minxish and Ben made a great fuss of the cascade of silky green ribbons she had tied in her hair. Clever. So Megan had competition, and where did that leave Ben with Laura? He sure got around, that was certain.

Men had it every way, Ellie decided. She was going to have more punch and join in the singing that had started up. Above all she was going to ignore the sight of Ben chatting away with his blonde girlfriend because it didn't mean anything to her.

All the same, she couldn't help her eyes flicking across the angles of his super-fit body as he leaned against the counter, noticing the warm tilt of his mouth and the way his eyes were all absorbed in blonde cheerleader and whatever she was saying. She told herself she only wanted to swap places with her, and have those hazel eyes to smile warmly at her, because she desperately needed some kind of basic human friendliness after the hammer blow both Johnny and Lucy had dealt her. And for all her expectations of seeking anonymity in New York she had to admit she was feeling lonely, and scared that she'd never be able to design anything ever again – not even a plastic sack.

As for the quiver that hummed through her body when he turned and caught her looking at him? Ellie determinedly told herself it was scarcely sexual attraction.

Chapter 27

$\mathcal{S}$he was looking at him with her red mouth slightly open, as though he was the sexiest thing alive, and Johnny basked in it, allowing that look to seal over the dark space where Ellie and Lucy constantly tumbled.

Karen. He even remembered her name.

'K for Karen,' she'd said, giving him a full-on look. So he couldn't be too drunk. An actress, she'd told him, who had finally landed a part in a daytime soap and was determined to blaze a trail for herself. He slid closer to her in the black velvet booth of the VIP bar of Purple Space, one of Dublin's most exclusive clubs. He lifted the bottle of Stoli Elit vodka out of the ice bucket and sloshed more liquid into their glasses. His Rolex gleamed and he saw it was half past two in the morning. He reached through a fuzz to recall how he'd got here.

Earlier that night, Jane and David's engagement party had kicked off with a meal in l'Ecrivain and moved on to the Shelbourne for more drinks, where Johnny found himself chatting up a petite, attractive blonde with a friendly, sympathetic face.

Everyone else seemed to be part of a couple and, without Ellie, he felt as though half of him was missing, so it was all too easy to chat to her. Then someone suggested they finish off the night in Purple Space. He'd been to the club with Ellie for the extravagant opening night six months earlier and they'd had great fun laughing at the blingy ostentatiousness of it all. He pushed that memory out of his head and asked his new blonde friend to join the party.

By now, most of the group had gone home, all partied out, including Jane and David. They had tried to persuade him to come with them, but he had shrugged off David's arm, taking Karen's outstretched hand instead and allowing himself to be dragged into the secluded, black velvet booth.

He knocked back vodka while Karen murmured away, her red mouth opening and closing on brightly bleached teeth, her blue eyes pools of adoration, her tits swimming in front of him as they strained against the soft white silk of her top. After a few more drinks that slid down all too easily, his back was glued to the soft, comfortable booth and no way was he ever going to get to his feet, never mind stumble his way home.

She was fiddling with his shirt buttons.

'That's very sad about you and Ellie, from what you told me,' she said.

What had he told her? He couldn't remember.

'You must be missing her,' Karen's voice was soft. Her finger eased in behind the opening of his black shirt and scratched his bare skin. He looked down and gazed at her cleavage, his index finger itching to slide into that dark cleft in the creamy swell. It was right under his nose, just within touching distance of his hands. They were smaller than Ellie's generous breasts but just as inviting. He reached for her glass to top it up again, and when the back of his hand brushed across the seductive swell, he pretended it was an accident.

'Naughty Johnny,' she whispered provocatively, inching closer to him on the banquette.

And that was what Johnny saw screaming from a tabloid newspaper when he fell out of bed the following afternoon and lurched down to the local shops for a pint of milk and a filled baguette. He grabbed a copy, waiting until he got home to check out the grainy photo of him locked in a clinch with a blonde babe, his fingers splayed across a silk-covered breast.

Je-*sus*. Some opportunist with a mobile phone, he guessed, his eyes skimming the text underneath:

'Naughty Johnny is getting over his bust-up with fashion supremo Ellie Morgan by checking out another bust. Sources say that Ellie has gone into hiding in New York while the millionaire entrepreneur is larging it up in Purple Space, Dublin's hottest A-list watering hole. Or larging it down, as pint-sized Karen Newbury is no match for curvy, Nigella-like Ellie in the bust department. Still, a bird in the hand is worth a double D bird in the bush. And from the look on his face, Johnny's not worrying about a storm in a B cup.'

He rubbed his tired, scaly eyes, glad his head resembled a wall of thick cement that prevented him from taking this on board or thinking too deeply of Ellie.

Who the hell was Karen?

Some fragment of memory prickled icily in his head, the image of him sucking on a breast that wasn't Ellie's, a body cuddling down under the duvet, and in a dizzy stupor he mounted the stairs, pulling back the bunched up duvet, relief washing over him at the sight of the empty bed. For a moment there ... He heard a click behind him and spun around.

A petite blonde padded out of his en-suite wearing nothing but a smile.

Shite. In spite of his thick head, something hit him right between the eyes. Whatever slim, vestige of hope he'd clung to that Ellie might find it in her heart to forgive him even a tiny little bit, melted away.

'You must be Karen?'

'Mum?'

'Hi, Miranda! What time it is in Hong Kong?'

'It's just half past seven. In the evening.'

Miranda almost smiled in spite of her tension. Her mum always asked the time, as though to gauge how long the call might be. Short, if it was late in the evening, shorter again if Miranda was calling from the office, but any other hour meant time for a decent chat, and she knew Vivienne would take the phone to her sofa and relax while she talked.

'I can never figure out the time difference,' she often said. 'And now with my three daughters in all corners of the world, I'm more confused than ever.' It sounded more like a boast and Miranda knew it as a comment she probably voiced regularly with her friends and colleagues.

'Well, Lucy's the same time as you,' she said. 'I'm seven hours ahead and Ellie is five hours behind.'

'Oh, it's far too difficult to do the maths.'

Miranda could almost see her mother waving her hand with exaggerated dismissal. 'Are you going out to lunch?' she asked.

'Yes, I'm meeting some friends later. We're trying out a new restaurant in the village. Six of us. The maître d' will have a heart attack when he sees us coming! They do a Sunday special until 4 o'clock, but we'll be looking for the best of attention and a couple of freebies.'

Miranda took a breath and then plunged right in. 'Did you see any of the newspapers?'

'Don't tell me Lucy's splashed all over them again!' Vivienne said. 'I'm worried about her, Miranda, I've heard very little from her since – since I came home from the cruise. What's she been up to now? Drunk and disorderly in Mayfair? Or falling around Soho? It's a wonder she still has a job.'

Miranda was silent for a minute. She had to forcibly remind herself that Ellie hadn't told Vivienne about Lucy's part in the break-up so her mother only knew the half of it. 'Well, no, Mum, it's Ellie. Or should I say Johnny. Word has got out about their split.'

'Are you sure?'

'Yes, Claire has been on to me. She's been watching out for this. Actually, we both expected the news to break sooner. Johnny's been keeping a low profile since the bust— since the split, but it sounds like he's made up for it.'

'Don't tell me. Or maybe you should in case my friends have seen it and I need to refute the evidence.'

'Sorry, Mum, there's no refuting this story.'

'Oh dear. Poor Ellie. You'd better give it to me straight.'

Miranda took a breath. 'According to Claire, Johnny was photographed in a clinch with an actress called Karen Newbury in Purple Space, some new nightclub. I can't remember the exact text that Claire read out, but it wasn't very pretty.' She didn't want to remember it, never mind give her mother the gist of what Claire had told her.

'Oh no. That's too bad. I've heard of Karen Newbury, I've run into her a couple of times. She seemed nice enough. Oh dear, what are you going to tell Ellie? It'll have to be you, Miranda. I couldn't bring myself to tell her. Or do you think she needs to know?'

'I've talked to Claire and we both agree that it'll find its way onto Facebook or Twitter if it's not there already, and it would be better for her to hear from someone in the family. I don't fancy telling her either. She's bound to react angrily. I thought maybe . . . ' Miranda groped for words.

This was where she'd half-hoped Vivienne might take over and say, *I'll do it, I'm her mum, I'll talk her around and break it as gently as possible, even if it means I have to put up with her anger and annoyance* . . .

'I hope you weren't thinking of me, Miranda,' Vivienne said, sounding worried. 'Far better if you spoke to her, you have the soothing touch. Ellie won't get cross with you.'

She sounded nervous of her eldest daughter. Miranda sighed.

Afterwards, she asked herself how come she was always the one to soothe over the troubled waters. Even now, miles away from them all, she was piggy in the middle, this time between her mother and Ellie. But now that she *was* miles away from them all, Miranda could see in sharper focus that there had always been a strain between Ellie and her mother. They just hadn't the relaxed, comfortable relationship you'd expect to see between a mother and her eldest daughter.

Years earlier, in a drunken late-night conversation with Ellie, her sister had admitted that she'd had a difficult time when Zach came on the scene.

'I couldn't believe that Mum found someone to take Dad's place like that – so soon. I was totally shocked and felt she was being disloyal to his memory. And, even though he was dead, unfaithful to him. Does that make sense? I was really angry with her and it messed up my head big time. And that was before I found out they were actually *sleeping* together! Did you know what was going on? That they were – God . . .!'

'Not until a while after Lucy was born. I was only a very

sheltered eleven, so a lot of the finer details went over my head. At that age, you can't imagine your parents having sex, never mind your mother and her boyfriend. But it must have been tough for you. I remember sensing the tension between you and Mum, the atmosphere. I tried to ignore it because it made me feel sick.'

Ellie had shuddered. 'I didn't know at first. Then I found out . . . what they were up to by accident. And I hated Mum for it. But I never talked to her about it. Then, after Zach had left, she told me she was expecting Lucy and tried to explain she was so wrapped up in grief for Dad that she didn't really know what she was doing. But I still wouldn't talk to her. I wasn't having any of her excuses.'

'And now?' Miranda had prompted. 'Do you still hate her?'

Ellie had stared into space, her eyes blank as though she didn't want to go there. 'Nah. What's the point? I was an angry teenager then. We still don't talk about that time, but it's all water under the bridge.'

Miranda went into her tiny cubby hole of a kitchen, where the small window looked out onto other high-rise buildings. The sun had gone down an hour earlier, the sky was inky blue, and lights were shining here and there in the nearby tower blocks. Far below, down on the street, moving cars looked like matchbox toys, red tail-lights gleaming like tiny gems. It might be foreign to anything she'd experienced in Dublin but it was a scene she now felt totally at home with. Up here, looking down from the twentieth floor, she felt weightless and free in a funny kind of way.

She was sorry she'd remembered all that tension between her mother and Ellie, because it made her sad. It was such a waste of emotion really, and had done neither of them any good. Now Ellie needed to be told about Johnny. More upset, she sighed. It was too early in New York to call Ellie. And this wasn't something you could text or email. She would wait until first thing in the morning and catch Ellie on her Sunday evening. She'd break the news as gently as she could. There was no getting away from family, not really. Not when it was stuff you carried around inside yourself. Until she learned to let go of it for once and for all, and she was beginning to think that it might take longer than a few months in Hong Kong – and that thought didn't bother her in the least.

Last night she'd gone out on the town with a gang of women from XAM, celebrating a thirtieth birthday, and she'd had great fun kicking up her heels in the frenetic nightclubs in Lan Kwai Fong. Great fun just being her, without being bothered by questions about Lucy's latest exploits or Ellie's exciting social diary – or wondering if people were simply chatting to you because they were curious to find out more about your glamorous sisters. Miranda looked at the crystal wine glasses ready and waiting on her worktop, and her heart lifted because there were two glasses waiting to be filled with fine wine. Two glasses meant Christian was coming. She picked one up and twirled it by the stem, watching the facets glint in the light. He'd bought the set of glasses for her, because she deserved to drink wine out of a beautiful crystal glass and not just the plain glasses that formed part of the apartment's standard stock.

She was cooking for him that evening, there was a casserole in the oven and a pavlova in the fridge, and they planned to have a relaxing night in. She knew they'd end up in bed, and she very much wanted it. Since the night in the Felix, he'd stayed over a couple of times and she'd also stayed in his plush apartment in Kowloon.

It was all very new and tentative. When he looked at her with his warm blue eyes he made her feel sexy and voluptuous and as though she was the best thing that had happened to him. He was certainly the best thing that had ever happened to her. She tried to imagine how she'd feel if she caught him in bed with Lucy, but even though she'd only known him a few months, it didn't bear thinking about.

And, she asked herself, supposing it became serious with Christian? How would she square that with Ellie? How would she cope if they came face to face? She couldn't risk bruising her heart again. It might mean, Miranda realised, not going home to Ireland for a long time.

Chapter 28

*B*ecause the party in Ben and Megan's apartment had gone on until the early hours, Ellie stayed in bed until one o'clock on Sunday, treating herself to a long lie-in and feeling curiously at ease for once rather than veiled with anxiety. She went into the shower, realising it was the first time she'd woken up without that clutch of dark apprehension.

She could thank the party for that. The mixture of Megan's soporific punch and the lively yet undemanding atmosphere meant she'd been able to mingle with the crowd and join in the singing, without even having to make the effort of conversation. Outside it was raining, spilling down from a charcoal-grey sky, so she spent the afternoon listening to Muse on her iPod at full volume, then relaxing with a novel. But her fragile peace of mind vanished when Miranda phoned at seven o'clock that evening with the news about Johnny. Ellie listened in stunned silence as Miranda haltingly told her about the newspaper article.

'Don't leave anything out, trying to spare me,' Ellie ordered, eventually finding her voice. 'I want to hear it all. We're so over it won't make any difference.' And who was she kidding? Of course it made a difference. The difference between Johnny having some basic respect for her feelings or trampling them into the ground.

'I don't have it word for word,' Miranda said. 'I haven't seen it myself. Claire read it out to me and it more or less said Johnny was getting over your break-up, that you had gone to New York, and he was partying in Purple Space with Karen Newbury . . . '

Ellie listened. Thoughts of Claire having to regale Miranda with this kind of script, so that it could be passed on to Ellie, seemed so ignominious, yet it was nothing compared to what Johnny had actually done – announced their break-up in the most public way possible. She knew the press would have latched on to it sooner rather than later, and she'd expected that Johnny would have been noticed socialising without her, but to be seen out with someone else already . . .

'Why didn't Claire contact me straightaway?' Ellie snapped, her head beginning to pound.

'Would you prefer to have been disturbed at five o'clock this morning to hear all this?' Miranda asked with unaccustomed impatience. 'Claire called me because she was going out for the day, to a christening in Mullingar, and wasn't going to be home until late. And, Ellie, it's not the kind of news you'd pass on by email or text. I told her I'd look after it and when I phoned Mum we agreed that I'd be the one to talk to you.'

'So you were talking to Mum about it as well!' Ellie rapped.

'Of course I was, Ellie, someone is bound to mention it to her and at least she was forewarned. She was as worried about you as I am. It's Monday morning in Hong Kong and I'm not long out of bed, but I wanted to catch you before I left for the office.'

'Okay, look, sorry for being—'

'No prob. *I'm* sorry to have to break this kind of news to you.'

'What's she like – this Karen Newbury? I presume there was a photo?'

A silence. Ellie's nerve endings trembled.

'Come on, Miranda. Don't let me find out the hard way.'

'There was also a photo. I'd say it was taken on a mobile phone.'

'What kind of photo? You have to tell me.'

'The unvarnished truth?'

'Yes.'

'They looked very cosy.'

'You mean he had his arm around her?'

'Not exactly. Oh, shite, Ellie, you'll probably find out eventually – his hand was on her boobs.'

A light inside her went out. Even though it was over, and he'd already trampled her feelings into the ground, this plunged her into some dark spot. She'd expected headlines, but not this. If he'd ever had any feelings for her, why couldn't he have kept his hands to himself instead of being so careless in public? *To hell with you, Johnny.*

'Hey, sis, I'm really sorry,' Miranda said, her voice gentle. 'There was a small photo of you as well.'

'It's okay. I'd rather know the worst so I can deal with it,' Ellie said. She was determined to put on a brave face but she felt her emotions seesawing wildly and suddenly her spirit crumpled. 'Actually, on second thoughts, why pretend I'm feeling brave? I'm finding all this incredibly tough.' She laughed, trying to make light of her admission and wondered why she was trying to spare Miranda the worst of her feelings. 'I'm sorry I came rushing over to New York,' she admitted. 'It's not what I expected. Maybe I should have gone to you in Hong Kong.'

'I'm sorry that hasn't worked out for you on top of everything else. I suppose whatever city you're in, it's bound to be difficult.

You know the old saying, Ellie, wherever you go, there you are. Although I know that's no consolation. Look, I'll call you later this week, I have to get ready for work now.'

'And how is life in Hong Kong?'

'Fine, it's great.'

Something about her ultra-bland tone alerted Ellie. 'Any sign of you coming home?' she asked.

'Umm, not just yet.'

'Good. That might give me a chance to go over and visit ... '

If she'd expected a warm invitation from Miranda, she was sadly mistaken.

'I'm late, Ellie, gotta fly and get organised for work! Talk soon,' Miranda said.

Ellie thought Miranda suddenly sounded as though she couldn't wait to get off the phone. But she'd other things on her mind besides her sister's brisk manner. She sat for a while on the sofa, trying to soothe her raw nerve endings and keep the pain at bay as she thought of Johnny in Purple Space snogging someone called Karen Newbury. Then, telling herself he didn't deserve another minute of her time, she went out for some fresh air, getting some grim satisfaction as she slammed the door behind her, pretending she was slamming a part of Johnny's anatomy in the door jamb.

In the diner on the corner, her eyes slid over the gleaming serving counters without really seeing them and she ordered the first thing that came into her head, a milky latte and a chocolate muffin. When she sat down, she couldn't remember how she'd got there or why she'd come. It seemed as though her life had shrunk to this moment, the plastic table top in front of her, the neat container of sauce sachets, the hard seat of her chair, and she felt totally removed from everything else. She broke her muffin apart on her plate and speared lumps of it with her fork, pretending she was damaging Johnny's anatomy again, but it gave her no satisfaction whatsoever and she wished she had stayed in the apartment instead and opened a bottle of wine.

Had he ever really loved her? Yet how could he have, considering everything he'd done? But what about her? She hadn't really loved him, had she?

After a while, she lifted her head and looked around, wondering what the hell she was doing here, and feeling suddenly homesick, because it was all so different from the normal life of Ellie Morgan. The diner was quiet, it had that muted Sunday evening feel with just a few tables occupied and the only spark of energy coming from the couple sitting close together in a booth by the window. With a cloak of detachment, Ellie watched the way they laughed in unison and whispered sweet nothings as though they had recently discovered each other and were now trying to show everybody else how happy and wonderful and how very much in love they were. We're great, their body language said. We're going to sleep together tonight and it'll be brilliant. Ellie glared balefully and wondered how long they'd last and which one of them would hurt the other first. Love! Who wanted it or needed it? Not her.

She'd been right all along to pour her energy into her career. At least she knew where she stood with that.

'Hi.'

Her career was totally within her control. It would never leave her feeling as though she was helplessly drifting. Or cut clean in two.

'Hey, Ellie!'

Or useless and insignificant. Then something cold ran down her back. What about the other day, when she hadn't been able to hold a pen in her hand, let alone outline a shape? What did that mean? Sitting there, she began to feel dizzy and her heart started to pound. When a man stopped at the other side of her table, she hadn't the energy to tell him to go away and leave her alone. A hand waved in front of her face.

'Ellie? Are you with me?'

Totally disorientated, she blinked and dragged herself back to the diner, and looked at the person in front of her. She knew him. She recognised those hazel eyes and the dark curly hair that needed a trim.

'Ben?' Her voice came out like a whisper.

'You were miles away,' he grinned. 'Have you recovered? From that dreadful punch? I made Megan pour the rest of it down the sink. Hope it didn't affect you too much.'

At first, he seemed to be talking in a foreign language and then in the time it took him to pull out a chair and sit down, images rushed back to her: the sharp tang of the punch, smoothing her insides, Megan, twisting her way through the heat and crowds of the party, the escalating noise and laughter, and blonde cheerleader waylaying Ben in the kitchen. Her name was Susan. In the middle of the frenzy, Ben had introduced her to Ellie.

Then the moment when Ben stood on a kitchen chair and sang 'The Fields of Athenry' into an empty bottle of beer, accompanied by a raucous out-of-tune chorus from everyone else and in her heart she was crying; she knew the song but now the lyrics about love and loss resonated deeply, causing hairs to rise on the back of her neck.

Lots more punch.

And after that, the smell of frying sausages someone had brought from Dublin and hands diving on the heaped plate that Megan held aloft. Biting into the hot, juicy spiciness and really tasting it like she'd never tasted an Irish sausage before.

'Hi, sorry about that,' she grappled with words. He was sitting opposite her. He seemed too close for comfort.

'No sweat. I hope you're not suffering too much from the after-effects.'

'No, I'm fine,' she said, thinking how ridiculous she sounded. How stupid to pretend, when she really wanted to put her head down on the table and bawl, only she knew the tears would refuse to come because they were caught in a bind at the back of her throat. 'It was a great night,' she went on. 'Thanks for asking me.'

'No bother. Besides, we couldn't risk you calling the cops to complain about the noise,' he grinned. 'Anyway, sorry for disturbing you. When I saw you sitting here I just wanted to make sure you didn't need a hangover remedy.' He pushed his chair back and gave her a lopsided smile as he rose to his feet.

'Wait.' The words were uttered before she realised it. She didn't know exactly what she meant, but she didn't want him to leave her on her own with just her black thoughts and cold coffee for company.

'So you do want some of that remedy?' he said with an easy smile.

'Well I just . . . ' Oh, God, why had she stopped him? 'What's it like?' she asked, making a huge effort to put everything else on hold and drift along the surface.

'A mixture of raw egg and garlic, with a spoonful of cod liver oil,' he paused. 'Joking, of course. There's a great little wine bar around the next block and they do a really smooth Chilean red that I guarantee will counteract any remnants of the punch. Are you up for it?'

Again, that friendly warmth in his hazel eyes that suddenly seemed important to latch on to.

Before she knew it, they were sitting on high stools by a bright gleaming bar, behind which bottles of wine were arranged in white wooden racks all the way up to the ceiling. A row of spotlights suspended low down the length of the counter threw off pools of light and a smiling bartender was pouring a rich red wine into two glasses.

'Cheers,' Ben said, tipping his glass to hers.

'Thanks,' Ellie said, bemused that she found herself here. She had the odd thought that if she could somehow lean in a little closer to Ben and get a picture of the two of them hotwired back to Ireland, it might restore her pride a little. She wondered if it would upset Johnny.

'So, how's New York treating you?' he asked.

'It's okay.'

'How long do you plan on staying?'

'I dunno yet.' Even though she'd felt homesick and had been wondering what she was doing in New York, thoughts of going back to Dublin were anathema to her. During the long, lonely nights she had begun to imagine never going home, winding up her business in Ireland, putting her house on the market and starting afresh in the fashion capital of the world. It would be difficult, she thought, but not impossible. And it would keep her well away from Johnny. In some logical part of her mind, she was beginning to come around to the idea that what had happened had been more his fault than Lucy's. He was supposed to be the mature adult. He knew Lucy had been in a difficult place. If anything, he had taken advantage of that. And look at how quickly he'd hooked up with this Karen Newbury. Not that she could bring herself to forgive Lucy just yet. But still . . . she thought of her sister's texts and she mentally pushed them aside. 'What about you?' she asked Ben. 'Or is it okay to talk about it?'

He looked at her for a long moment, his face suddenly shadowed, and he picked up both their glasses and said, 'Let's sit somewhere more comfortable.'

After they were settled on the white leather sofas running

along by the wall, he said, 'I can't go home, unfortunately. I've overstayed a holiday visa by about six months, so if I tried to leave, I'd be caught and, at the very least, barred from ever returning again.'

'That's a mess, isn't it?'

'It is, and I'm only one of thousands, but it's nothing like the mess I left behind.'

She looked at him questioningly. She hardly knew him, yet she felt a strange affinity with him and now it seemed they were both on the run from something.

'Oh, Ellie,' he laughed ruefully, 'I'm afraid my story is one that's repeated the length and breadth of Ireland. I owned a chain of leisure and fitness clubs in the northwest of Ireland. I started off with one club in Leitrim and expanded into Sligo, Roscommon and Donegal. I stretched myself finance wise, and for a while business was booming.'

She could guess what was coming next. An all-too-familiar story thanks to the cruel way the recession had decimated many of the country's businesses and people's livelihoods.

'Then when the crash came, gym membership was the last thing on anyone's mind.'

'I can imagine,' she said quietly. She forgot about herself, or why she was there, tuning in to him instead, her heart going out to him as she knew the sorry conclusion before he'd even voiced it.

'I struggled for a while, cut the membership fee, reduced the overheads, but I was just kidding myself. It turned into a nightmare of lurching from crisis to crisis, bank payment to bank payment. I'd no choice but to close them down one by one, hoping I might scrape by if I consolidated and managed to hold on to first three clubs, or even two and then even one outlet. The last one to go was really a killer as it was the first club I'd opened, pouring all my passion and my dreams into it.'

'Oh, Ben, that must have been so difficult . . .'

He gave her a sad look that cut her to the quick. 'No, the worst part of it all was telling the staff that their jobs were gone, seeing the shock and anxiety on their faces, knowing that they had little or no hope of alternative work. I still have nightmares,' he said, looking at her honestly. 'Even now, a year after it all went belly up, I often wake up drenched in sweat around four in the morning.'

'Jesus, a nightmare is right. It must have been horrendous.'

'You're better off not knowing,' he grinned. 'Hey, we're supposed to be fixing your hangover, I didn't bring you here to listen to the crap story of my life.'

'I'm glad you told me,' she said simply. 'I'm glad you didn't just pretend that everything is fine.' It meant he trusted her enough and it gave her back a measure of dignity. 'And how did you end up in New York? Or am I allowed to ask that?'

'Megan's flatmate moved out and she invited me over,' he said. 'I was doing nothing back in Ireland so I came over on a holiday visa and stayed on. I get casual work to cover my day-to-day stuff and pay something off my debt back home. But now I'm here illegally and caught between the divil and the deep blue sea.'

'So you knew Megan before you came over?'

He gave her a funny look. 'Of course. Don't you know?'

'Know what?' They were married? Engaged?

'Megan's my youngest sister. She's been working here for the past two years.'

'Ah. That explains it.'

'Explains what?'

'Nothing,' she said swiftly. How could she say it explained that he wasn't necessarily a serial womaniser, now that Megan was out of the picture and there was only Laura and Susan to contend with.

243

'I'd love to know what you meant by that, but I'll let you away with it,' he said. 'I'm sorry I didn't organise myself better. I could have been in a more legitimate situation and earning a more regular income. Sometimes I think I should have stayed at home, been more positive and worked through the crisis somehow. Ireland's a fab country with great people. There are different opportunities back home if you're willing to adapt and think outside the box. Now, I have a confession to make, but I want to get you another drink first.'

He signalled the bartender, who poured more wine, and then Ben gave her a look that sent alarm bells shrieking as he moved a little closer to her and said, very carefully and very gently, that he knew who she was and had a sort of an idea as to why she came to New York.

At first Ellie didn't react. She searched his face, refusing to acknowledge what she was thinking. She swallowed hard and fought down panicky waves, and when he gave a little apologetic shrug and all her insides were clamouring loud and clear about what he meant, she still refused to believe it.

And then she picked up her bag, and tripped over the leg of her chair, but held her head high as she walked out.

'Ellie! Come back.'

She walked faster, ignoring his running footsteps behind her. He was delayed settling the bill, so she'd had a head start, but within minutes she heard him catching up with her, coming alongside and felt him putting his hand on her arm.

She wrenched her arm away from his grasp. 'Go away,' she said, thinking that of all the stunts she'd ever pulled in her life, this had to rank up there as the silliest. Stalking up the New York street as a purple dusk settled around the city, and rain started up again and dripped down in soft spikes, feeling like an angry child as she shook off the arm of a man who'd just told her about his worst nightmares, and who seemed to know all about hers. Miles away from home and a life that had given her a certain contentment until it had fallen apart in front of her and lay like cracked eggs at her feet.

Ben did his trick of moving in front of her and half running backwards so that he could see her face as he talked to her. 'Ellie, please, don't ignore me.'

'Leave me alone.'

'I'm sorry if I said the wrong thing—'

'Are you still here?' she glared.

They came to a junction and he had to turn around and watch for the pedestrian light. 'How could I pretend I didn't know?' he said. 'Would you rather I had been dishonest with you?'

She didn't answer him. He was right, of course, she realised grudgingly.

'And why aren't you wearing a jacket?' he frowned. 'You look frozen. And wet. Did you leave it behind in the diner?'

'No, I came out without one,' she admitted, feeling obliged to answer him in case he ran back to look for it.

He unzipped his sports top and handed it to her.

She waved it away. 'It's okay, thanks, we're nearly there anyway.'

The lights changed and they crossed the road, Ellie staying silent until they reached the apartment building.

'Good night,' she said, feeling raw and stupid and wondering how to get out of this without losing more face.

'Why don't you come in for a beer?' he asked, smiling at her hesitantly. 'We've truckloads left over from last night. And it's just me and Megan. All those wild GAA men and women are long gone home. So no hassle. And I won't ask you a single question, promise. You don't have to talk at all. We can just have a beer and look at mind-numbing TV.'

It was an olive branch of sorts. And decent of him to hold it out considering the childish way she'd behaved. And better than going back to an empty apartment. Where she would just be thinking of Johnny and Karen in Purple Space.

'Okay,' she said. 'Yes . . . thanks.'

Now that the crowds from the party had gone, she could see that the apartment was much bigger than Laura's and, peeking into the two bedrooms as he ushered her down the hallway, it was clear that one was Ben's and the other belonged to Megan.

'Guess who I found,' Ben said.

Megan jumped up from the couch. 'So you found her? Good!' She gave Ellie an embarrassed smile. 'We were a bit worried when we heard you slamming the door. Ben insisted on going after you instead of—' she stopped and Ellie intercepted a warning look from Ben.

So he'd come looking for her. On purpose.

'Hey, Ellie doesn't need to know all that,' he said with a good-natured smile. 'Beer, Ellie?' he asked.

'Instead of what?' she asked.

Ben ran his hand through his dampened hair. 'I was half-supposed to be meeting some mates, but it's no sweat, I'll catch them again.'

'I'm sorry if I spoiled your night.'

'You didn't,' he insisted, turning to face her. 'I can see them anytime. I wanted to make sure you were okay and that you weren't about to pull another kamikaze stunt.'

Then Ellie saw the open laptop on a table in the corner and put two and two together. In one way, it was a relief not to have to put on an act. And at least Ben had been honest with her. Someone else might have strung her along, pretending not to know.

'I suppose you've read all about it,' she said, a wave of fatigue allowing her to flop onto the sofa.

Megan gave her an empathetic smile. 'We couldn't help seeing it, Ellie. We always keep up with the online news and gossip, especially at the weekends, as it's an important link to home. So you get the good news and the bad news and everything in between. Don't worry, we'll look after you, and I promise we won't be emailing any x-rated photos back to Dublin or divulging your whereabouts,' she laughed, her eyes sparkling. Coming over to Ellie, she gave her a warm hug.

'Scouts honour,' Ben said. 'Apart from the raunchy photos we took during the session last night, when you were drunk and disorderly after far too much punch. And now that we have that out of the way, will you have a beer, Ellie?'

'Yes, thanks.'

'And will you stay and watch a movie? Megan has at least three or four that she's nagging me to look at.'

'Sounds good.'

'We'll even let you pick. How's that for being neighbourly?'

'I have to give you full marks,' she said.

There was something warm and cosy about the apartment that Ellie found soothing, but it was everything to do with Ben and Megan and the casual way they accepted her and relaxed with her that evening. Ben slotted in the comedy DVD and passed around bottles of beer and Megan put a pizza in the oven and at no stage did either of them show any curiosity about Johnny or what had happened, or comment on Ellie's lifestyle or background. They were kind and careful around her and included her in their sibling slagging, not out of pity, she was glad to sense, but from genuine consideration and kindness, and it eased her jangled head and as the evening went on, put a buffer between herself and the cruelty of Johnny in a clinch with someone else, his hand on her boob.

Eventually the DVD was over and Ellie rose to her feet.

'Thanks to both of you,' she said. 'You got me out of a bad spot this evening and took my mind off everything.'

'Anytime you want to pop in, you're more than welcome,' Megan insisted.

'I'll see you home,' Ben said.

'It's fine,' she laughed.

'I insist,' he grinned. 'It's not too much out of my way.'

It was comforting all the same, having him beside her as she walked up the flight of stairs. He held out his hand for her key and opened the door for her. 'Right, there you go,' he said, standing in the doorway.

'Thanks. I mean it,' she said. 'And thanks for not asking any questions.'

'Ah, sure, we're just softening you up. Megan's dying to get her hands on all the juicy gossip but we're a great believer in the carrot approach rather than the stick.'

She sighed, letting her guard down a little. 'It's not all that interesting.'

'Look, Ellie,' he said gently, 'I'm not going to pry, but whatever has happened in your life I'm sure you've been hurting ...' he hesitated and gave her a questioning look as if unsure whether to continue.

She bit her lip and silently nodded as a wave of sadness filled her chest.

'... but you're here now in New York, for however long or short a time, and the best thing you can do is to look after yourself. Speaking as your personal fitness instructor that means getting back to the basics of good food, plenty of sleep, fresh air and exercise. I had my dark nights of going on the binge and wishing I could turn back the clock, but it got me nowhere and I soon realised that the only person I was hurting was me. I certainly wasn't solving my problems. There's nothing to be gained by letting your anger or hurt get the upper hand. If you ever feel you're losing it, take long, deep breaths. Believe me, it works. And,' he grinned, 'sorry if this sounds like a lecture, but letting your hair down at the odd party, especially if it's a wild Irish one, is compulsory.'

'Good.' She smiled, unable to resist his natural warmth.

'I'm not quite sure why you picked New York if you were looking for a bolthole,' he looked at her quizzically. 'It's a great city, but you have to be in form for it. I came for the work, I'd no choice really, and Megan was here already, but it's big and clamorous if you're all alone and trying to mend a broken heart.'

'I just grabbed the opportunity of borrowing Laura's flat and getting away with the least amount of fuss.'

'At least you have me and Megan,' he said. 'We'll keep an eye out for you.' The look he gave her was honest and direct and she felt something inside her lift in response to it.

It was slightly alarming having him all to herself after the way she'd watched him the previous night, laughing and joking with friends, and flirting with Susan. From a safe distance, it had been easy to think he looked sexy and attractive, that he had the kind of sensual yet caring face you'd like to see on the pillow beside yours, and eyes that you could easily imagine flickering from laughter to desire as they looked at you. Up close, it was a lot more difficult to take all this in, especially when he was standing right beside her, within touching distance, now even closer still, until she realised with a little shock that he was moving in to kiss her goodnight.

He pulled her in for a hug and she fitted into the curve of his neck. She hugged him back, his body unfamiliar but amazingly easy to lean into. She stayed perfectly still for a long moment, absorbing the warmth of his hug. Then he drew back a little, but only so that he could kiss her on the cheek, gently, like a feather kiss, and then, equally softly, on her forehead.

He smiled, his hazel eyes caring. 'Goodnight, Ellie. Have a good sleep. I'll give you tomorrow morning off, but you'd better be outside Central Park on Wednesday. We'll be doing the northern area of the park and, to my mind, it's the best thing next to Leitrim. So no excuses.'

Her face, where he'd kissed it, still glowed long after she heard his footsteps receding down the stairwell.

Chapter 29

'Come on, Lucy! Gimme some attitude,' Justin, the photographer yelled as he knelt on the grass in front of her.

Attitude! She knew how to do that, didn't she? She'd been doing attitude all her life. Lucy allowed herself a quick pout before she draped her body against the tractor and stared moodily into the camera. At least she hoped it was moodily, because clad in short dungarees and a thin, floral blouse, she felt every little flurry of the chilly April breeze and was sure she looked as though she was freezing to death. It was an outdoor shoot on a Surrey farmland for the Jakki summer collection, the newest, high-street, budget-conscious label. More work she'd been glad to get.

'Wait a minute.' The stylist darted forward and adjusted the angle of her floppy hat by a centimetre and the make-up girl took advantage of the short pause to pounce with her brush and layer on another brushful of lippy onto her already glossed-up lips. Lucy looked enviously at the make-up girl's parka jacket and wished she could snuggle into it. What about her goose pimples, she felt like asking. They were so prominent they would surely have to be airbrushed out of the photos.

Justin fired off a few shots as Lucy angled herself against a wheel of the tractor, and then lounged across the bonnet, and she finished up by sitting on the engine for a few playful shots.

'Gimme some fun, Lucy!' Justin yelled.

She stuck out her tongue and grinned at him. She liked working with Justin, he was one of the most sought-after photographers in the game right now but he was down to earth and knew how to get the best out of her. They sometimes hung out with the same crowd, and she'd even slept with him a couple of times, when they'd found themselves together at the end of a night, strictly no strings, though. Just when she thought her face was going to be permanently stuck in a cheesy grin, the creative director said they had enough material and it was time to organise everyone for the shots by the bubbling stream. Lucy privately groaned. From the brief, she'd known that she would have to pose by a stream looking ethereal and feminine in a selection of floaty maxi dresses, as though she was cooling down in the heat of a midsummer's day. And, just as she had feared, they wanted her out on the wet-slicked stepping stones with flowers in her hair while the cold stream frothed all around, chilling her bare feet and soaking the hem of her dress. Great. Still, it was keeping her busy and it had taken her out of London for the day, which pleased her.

Because for the past week, Lucy had had the funny feeling she was being followed. It was more of a fleeting impression than anything else, a sense of feeling unsettled, of hairs rising on the back of her neck at odd moments. It wasn't that she heard footsteps coming along behind her or anything frightening like that. Sometimes she felt she was being watched when she jumped out of a taxi at the end of a day's work, but the street always looked normal enough, just a couple of pedestrians going past and no sign of anyone melting into the shadows to avoid being seen. She'd berated herself more than once as she dashed up the stairs to her apartment. Her flat was fine, there was nothing hiding under the bed, and she'd chided herself more than once as she'd peeked underneath, laughing at her own foolishness.

She *was* being ridiculous – how would she spot anyone if he'd already ducked for cover? It was just her imagination getting the better of her, after the night she thought she'd seen someone hanging around on the lane that ran by the back of her building. She told herself she was being paranoid when she began to close her bedroom curtains while it was still bright, so she wouldn't have the eerie feeling of being watched as she crossed the room to pull them across the shadowy darkness lurking beyond.

Now, out in the bright and breezy April day where sunlight flickered across the undulating acres of farmland, and birds chirped happily, her fears all seemed so laughable. She took a deep breath and looked around at the crew, some sipping coffee and chatting, others rushing around with clipboards, and it was all so familiar to her that it felt reassuringly safe. There was nothing like routine normality to chase away the shadows of the night. She was hardly Kate Moss, so who'd want to stalk her anyway?

Someone, the unwelcome thought fluttered, who thought she was worth the expense of a funeral wreath. But that had been about Zach, not her – a mad fan who thought they were making a personal contribution to his anniversary. All that fuss had died down now and even the re-released single had long fallen out of the charts. Ellie had been right, she had to admit grudgingly; it had just been a one-week wonder.

Ellie! They still weren't talking and it made her feel all sick inside.

'Now, Lucy, cheer up. Let's see if you can conjure up sexily shy,' Justin called, winking at her.

Sexily shy? It immediately made her think of Johnny, because if she blocked Ellie out of the picture, she knew that was exactly how she'd feel if she saw him again.

'Perfect, Lucy, you're a natural, keep it coming.'

She must be some kind of monster that she hankered after Johnny like this, she decided uncomfortably, finding it incredibly easy to give the camera all she could. She was exhausted but sorry in a way when the shoot wrapped up and most of them piled into a minibus for the drive back to London.

'Hey, Lucy,' Donna, one of the stylists said, twisting around in her seat to face her, 'isn't Ellie Morgan your sister?'

'Yeah, why?'

'I see it's all off with her bloke and she's hightailed it to New York.'

Her breath almost froze. 'Where did you see that?'

'It was on Twitter this afternoon and in one of those online celeb mags. Didn't you know? You'd imagine Ellie would tell you first,' Donna giggled, 'after all she *is* your sister.'

'I did know, of course,' Lucy said. 'But it's not something I was going to gossip about.'

'Ah, well, he wasn't long finding a replacement.'

'No, he wasn't.'

Something cold ran through her. A replacement? Had word got out about her and Johnny? Scarcely, Donna would never have kept that juicy tit-bit to herself. She couldn't believe that Johnny might have hooked up with someone else already. And Ellie in New York! It was the first she'd heard of it though. Lucy still hadn't talked to her mother, or Miranda, simply sending the occasional bland text. All the way back to London, her mind churned as she wondered what exactly was on Twitter and she itched to grab her iPhone and check it out. As they neared the city, she heard some of the crew talking about going for a drink, and Justin invited her along, but even though she was gasping for a vodka and shot, and Justin looked hurt at her refusal, she had to get home and check out the news in peace.

Her fingers skidded across the keys as she logged on to Twitter and entered Ellie's name in the search box, hoping against hope that she'd find nothing too damaging. But no such luck. In amongst a raft of comments, some commiserating with Ellie, others slightly mocking, she found a link to the online magazine article. Her eyes devoured the short piece, and the photo sent a quiver across her stomach. She couldn't begin to think how Ellie must be feeling if she saw it. Or how incredibly angry she must be with Lucy, who'd caused it all to happen in the first place. She'd never talk to her again, Lucy fretted. Although Johnny had played his part too. And now it looked like he was really going all out. A flicker of irrational jealousy rose up inside her at the sight of Karen Newbury, with Johnny's hand on her boob.

She texted Sasha, praying she'd be up for a couple of mind-numbing drinks in the local pub.

'I'm taking it easy on the booze,' Sasha said, twirling her straw around in her cocktail with her blood-red fingernails, a legacy from her shoot earlier that day, she'd said. 'And I'm not staying out too late. Especially on a Monday night.'

'Yeah, not now you've landed the Venetia job,' Lucy said. 'Only joking. I'm still very jealous. But I agree with you, I'm taking it easy myself. I just thought a couple of hours out would take the sting out of the week.'

'So how did it go, down on the farm?'

Lucy sat back in the booth and enjoyed having a moan about her freezing cold feet, feeling more relaxed, the photo of Johnny and Karen and thoughts of an angry Ellie disappearing behind a soft veil of alcohol. She was on her third drink when she glanced across to the bar and realised a guy was looking at her. She was well used to being gawped at, it happened all the time and she and Sasha together were prime targets for attention, but there was something studied about the way this guy was looking at her that alerted her. He smiled and lifted his glass as though he knew her, and Lucy felt a prickle down her spine as she tried to place him. Then she realised in a rush of recognition that it was the cute, Scottish PR guy. She smiled back.

'Hmm. Not bad at all,' Sasha said approvingly, following her gaze.

'Yeah, he's okay,' Lucy said, deliberately taking her eyes off him in case she appeared too interested. 'I was chatting to him at Carla's party.'

'I think he's coming over. He *is* – nice one, Lucy. He must fancy you.'

'Fancy me?' Lucy scoffed, a ripple of interest going through her when she saw that he was making a beeline for her. He looked rather cool and sexy in black jeans and a dark shirt. He carried a leather jacket.

'Hey, Lucy, isn't it?' He gave them both a tentative smile that she found endearing, 'I'd love to buy you both a drink, if that's okay.'

'I'm fine,' Sasha said, putting her hand over her glass in a gesture of refusal, 'I've an early start in the morning, but Lucy . . .'

Sasha turned her head away from him so that he couldn't see her face, and she looked questioningly at Lucy, as though to ask if she'd said the right thing. Lucy hesitated. Her head told her to refuse politely, go home and have a good night's sleep. Still, she was off tomorrow and intended to go for a mani and pedi and a massage, nice relaxing stuff. And she needed something to take her mind off Johnny and Ellie and everything else. This cute guy looked like he'd fit the bill just nicely. She'd liked him instinctively the first time she'd met him. She gave Sasha a look coupled with an almost imperceptible nod, which translated as, *I am interested, very much, but hang around for a bit, just in case.*

'This is my first time to drop into my local,' he went on. 'I couldn't believe it when I saw a face I recognised. I'd love a chance to have a chat with you away from the flashbulbs and the bedlam as I'm new to the business, but if it doesn't suit . . .' he half-turned away.

'No, wait,' Lucy said. 'Ian, isn't it?'

'That's right, you remembered,' he smiled warmly, holding his jacket awkwardly, like a buffer in front of him, and Lucy felt another lift of interest. There was something engaging about him, so it was easy in the end to introduce him to Sasha, move up on the banquette and invite him to sit down, exchanging a glance with Sasha behind his back to indicate that they might as well have a bit of fun and see what happens.

'I'll get some drinks first,' he said, folding his jacket clumsily on the seat as though he was marking his spot, and taking out a wallet. 'Lucy?'

'I'll have a mojito, please,' Lucy said. It was her fourth. Very bad behaviour for a Monday night, but, hey, who was counting?

'And a water for me please,' Sasha changed her mind. As soon as he was at the bar and out of earshot she said to Lucy, 'Just the one for me and then I'm off. Okay? It should be long enough for you to find out if you want to stay on with Mr Sexy—'

'Mr Sexy?' Lucy was amused.

'Well, isn't he?'

'Hmm . . . I find him more cute than sexy.'

Ian was boy-next-door cute. Johnny was sexy in a dark, sensual way.

Ian was easy to talk to, and the perfect antidote to everything in her life right now. They chatted about Carla's party, who had been there and who hadn't been there, Ian explaining how he'd moved from a head of marketing position with a Scottish textile business to set up his own public relations company and was still finding his feet. 'I'm aiming to specialise in media relations.'

'And what brought you to London?' Sasha asked.

There was a slight pause. 'Sorry?'

'Why London? I'm sure you find it a big change.'

'This is where it all happens, isn't it?' he said. 'It's heaving with possibilities, and about the best city in the world to kick start a career in public relations. Everything passes through here. I know it will take me a while to build up a client list, but I'm ready to put in the long hours. As well as that . . .' he paused and flicked Lucy a glance.

'Yes?'

'Someone very close to me passed away, and it was a bit difficult . . .' He paused. 'So I'm trying to find my feet again and move on.' He smiled self-deprecatingly as though to reduce the seriousness of his topic of conversation.

Or as though he was trying to make out it didn't matter all that much, but Lucy instinctively sensed it had rocked his world. God, how she knew that feeling.

'I'm very sorry to hear that but you're right to keep going,' Lucy said, wanting to put a hand on his arm, but something defensive in the way he was looking at her stopped her. Instead, she smiled at him empathetically. Was that what clicked with her? Vulnerability behind his friendly front because of his loss? He'd obviously had his life pulled from under him. She wanted to tell him that he shouldn't be trying to make light of it to spare them, because anyone who'd ever lost a special person could identify with him. He was staring at her, she realised, as though he was equally drawn to her. She was used to appreciative looks from men, but this was different. It was more intent, as though he was trying to see behind her perfect model face to the person underneath. Just for a moment, she felt a tiny sliver of unease, but it was so minute that she wondered if she'd imagined it.

Sasha looked embarrassed at the way their light-hearted chatter had shifted into something more personal. 'I'm sorry to hear that as well,' she said, 'it hasn't happened to me yet but it must be terrible to lose the people you love. I'd like to wish you the best of luck with the new career, however I've an early start in the morning . . . ' She nodded conspiratorially at Lucy.

'You go on ahead,' Lucy told her, making up her mind to stay for a while. 'I'll just have another drink with Ian and give him some advice from our point of view. Steer him in the right direction and make sure he knows the kind of publicity we prefer as well as the rubbish we don't want to see!'

'If you're sure.' Sasha was frowning slightly.

'I *am* sure,' Lucy insisted, all the more determined in the face of Sasha's reservation. Sasha hadn't lost anyone she loved, so she didn't know what that ache was like. After Sasha had left in a cloud of disapproval, Lucy chatted to Ian, telling him about some of the jobs she'd worked on, the events she'd been to and how they had been handled.

'The worst nightmare for someone like me is not being able to let your hair down in public,' she admitted. 'I can never really relax. I know it comes with the job and I can't really complain, but you never know who is going to be out on the prowl with a telephoto lens. I could do with a personal minder like you to keep the relentless media off my back and counteract my bad public profile,' she laughed at her joke. Rebecca had a PR firm working on behalf of the modelling agency, but Lucy wasn't a big enough name to warrant a personal spin doctor.

'I'd love to be of help,' Ian said, taking her seriously. 'I'd see that as a powerful launch platform and a fantastic opportunity—'

'Hang on, I have a very good agent to represent my business interests and look after my contracts, and we do have a media firm who oversee publicity,' she said, hoping he wasn't getting too carried away. 'But I'm sick of being misrepresented. I've missed out on good contracts because I've been in the wrong tabloid at the wrong time. I could do with some positive publicity. And I only have finite time left in my modelling career to make a mark, so I can't afford to put a foot wrong too often.'

'If there is anything at all I can do, I'd be happy.'

She grinned, warming to his enthusiasm. 'I'll think about it. It might be nice, having a personal publicist.'

'I'd have to know, of course, what's going on in your life, anything that might make tabloid news and damage your career prospects. Would you be okay with that?'

She stopped, appalled at a sudden thought that shook her. A wave of dizziness washed over her.

'Are you okay?'

She started to laugh hollowly. Maybe she'd already wrecked her career. For now that the news had broken about Ellie and Johnny, what was to stop her sister from denouncing Lucy as the main culprit? If the part she'd played in Ellie's break-up ever got out, it would be picked up like wildfire and the British media would have a field day. Her career and reputation would be in tatters. Why had this side of it never occurred to her until now? If Ellie wanted to put the boot in and exact revenge, this was her golden opportunity. For, sure as hell, if the situation was reversed, that's what she'd be doing.

'I think we should do lunch this week,' she said to Ian. 'I'd like another chat with you. You never know, this might work.'

'Sounds good,' he said, opening his wallet and taking out a business card.

'Oh, don't bother with that, I'll surely lose it.' She picked up her mobile. 'What's your number?'

Shortly afterwards, they left the pub and he walked her home, stopping at her building.

'Hey, how did you know I lived here?' she asked, a little bemused.

He smiled sympathetically. 'I saw you on the news a couple of weeks ago. You were running up those very steps, trying to get away from the cameras. I remember feeling annoyed that they were hounding you. I didn't mention it when we were sitting in the pub in case I upset you.'

'Oh.'

'I guess all the stuff about your father was difficult.'

She swallowed. 'It was, rather.' She was glad he seemed to understand. She'd known, somehow, that he would. He seemed to be as vulnerable as she sometimes felt, behind all the bravado.

A silence fell.

'Look,' he said eventually, 'have a think about what I said and call me during the week. I know we could be good for each other.'

'Yeah, maybe.'

She didn't have to ask him to wait while she hurried up the steps. He stood there anyway, giving her a little wave before she closed the hall door.

Chapter 30

*H*e couldn't believe how easy it had been.

He flung himself down on the narrow bed in his Fulham flat, stared up at the ceiling and tried to contain his surging emotions. Although a couple of times that night he'd thought everything was going to go pear shaped.

Firstly, when she came out of her building and stood on the top of the steps, looking up and down the road. He'd thought she'd spotted him. He'd had to kneel down hurriedly and pretend he was checking a tyre on a parked car. One of these evenings he'd get caught if he wasn't more careful. Then the blonde chick from the building next door had clattered down her steps – how they walked on those skyscraper heels he'd never know – and they'd met up on the footpath hugging and air-kissing as though they hadn't seen each other in a month.

His mother had loved her heels as well. Even though they were from a high street chain store and cost a fraction of what those rich babes were wearing. She'd called them her ultra-glam heels and often had to hang on to his arm so she wouldn't fall over. If she'd had the money to splash out on a really expensive pair, they might have hugged her small foot better or been more comfortable.

He'd never know the answer to that now.

And she used to laugh at all that air-kissing on *Desperate Housewives* and *Sex and the City*.

'It's so false and insincere, a bitchy kind of kiss if you ask me. I'd rather not be kissed at all than kissed like that.'

It seemed air-kissing was the rage all over London, particularly at the high-octane gatherings he'd gate crashed. He could imagine his mother rolling her eyes in amusement. She'd stopped rolling her eyes like that long before she died, and the thought of it made his chest crump, like a bomb had imploded, so he tried to focus on the questions that nagged him by day and lost him sleep at night. Ever since his mother had whispered her confession to him from her hospital bed.

He'd found it easy enough to follow the girls down the street, as they were so busy chatting to each other they hadn't notice him strolling behind at a slight distance. He'd hesitated outside the door of the pub, his nerves suddenly jangling, and then he'd taken a deep breath and gone in.

And then she'd smiled at him and, after that, it had been like a roller-coaster ride where he'd been petrified and elated and then brought up so sharply that he couldn't catch his breath, especially when he'd nearly wrecked it all at the end by stopping outside her house. It was a bad mistake to have made. He hoped he'd covered his story well, but that bit about pretending to be annoyed with the paps for hounding her had been genius. He'd known by her face that he'd struck home.

Little had he known that, when he'd said he was in PR, it would potentially open all the doors for him. He stared at a crack in the ceiling, still unable to believe the way it had fallen into his lap like a ripe plum. He checked his watch and jumped off the bed. He'd no time to waste. He didn't know when she'd call or when they'd meet. So he was under pressure to get his background sussed out and find out what media relations was all about. Then he had to work out the best way to get her to talk.

He was humming the lyrics of 'Forever My Angel' to himself as he powered up his laptop.

'*In my dreams I feel you close/I see your perfect face . . .*'

Chapter 31

*O*n Wednesday morning, Ellie sat by the window having orange juice and yogurt for breakfast as a veil of rain drifted down from soft grey skies and left a wet-slicked sheen over the city. When she left the apartment at a quarter to eight, pulling up the hood of her tracksuit top against the light rain, she felt more than self-conscious at the thought of seeing Ben again, and hoped she wouldn't bump into him en route to Central Park. She hadn't seen him since Sunday evening and knew it would be easier to engage with him within the buffer of the walking group.

She'd taken his advice, finding it hard initially to switch her thoughts away from Johnny during the previous two days, and even more difficult to make herself focus on something positive instead of her anger and hurt. But giving all her attention to ordinary things helped her to feel better about herself. Even though she wasn't a great cook, she took a little more care with her food and made sure she ate well, cooking fluffy omelettes and simple, herb-filled chicken dishes. She sank into a deep, lavender-infused bath instead of showering hurriedly, and she went to a local hairdresser for an invigorating head massage followed by a blow-dry. She still needed a couple of glasses of wine in the evenings to help her sleep, so she lit scented candles and sipped a good cabernet sauvignon straight from Napa Valley, feeling that by being extra good to herself, she'd made a start at digging herself out of a deep chasm of anger and self-pity.

She'd even taken more care with her make-up that morning.

Of course, as luck would have it, on the very morning she was hoping for a crowd, there were only five people waiting outside the entrance to the park, two couples in their forties whom she hadn't seen before, and Ben. Neither Tina nor Susan were there, to her dismay.

'Hi, Ellie, you showed up just in time,' Ben said, giving her a warm smile. At least he greeted her this time, she thought with some satisfaction. There were brief introductions all around and then he said to her, 'For a minute, I thought you weren't coming, but I'm glad you're here. You're walking up front with me.'

'Am I now?' she threw him a glance, surprised at how much that pleased her. She straightened her face, hoping she didn't look too enthusiastic. Then she felt panicked at the thought of chatting to him for the next hour or so.

'The others have walked this route before and I want to make sure you don't get lost at the back,' he said. 'We don't chatter too much, by the way. Not on this walk. It's better to absorb the sights and sounds. Just focus on your breathing, remember? Slow and regular. And your posture. Shoulders back and relaxed, tuck the tailbone in. Keep your stride comfortable. Oh, and let go of your hands.'

'My hands?'

'Yes,' he said, taking her by surprise as he lifted one of her arms.

Ellie looked down to see her white knuckled fist clenched tight. She immediately let go, releasing the tension, and she laughed, wiggling her fingers. 'Okay, right.'

'Much better. Same with the other hand, please, and off we go, folks.'

She realised very quickly how much better it was to refrain from chatter. The group moved quietly up through a sweetly scented meadow, where they might as well have been transported to the heart of the countryside, as all the sounds of the city were obliterated. They headed down a grassy slope into a valley, and on through to a forested landscape that took Ellie by surprise, and was stunningly beautiful and even a little mysterious under a veil of misty rain. Ancient trees, seemingly as old as time itself, provided a canopy as they walked through the woods to the backdrop of birdsong and the sound of rushing water gurgling over a stony bed, and the sweet earthy scents drifting on the air. They paused on a small wooden bridge to watch the swift flow of a stream passing underneath. Hiking through to a hilly area strewn with boulders, Ellie found it strange to think that the rocks had probably been lying there in the same spot for centuries, while visitors passed along and the endless cacophony of New York life ceaselessly played out outside the perimeter of this magnificent sanctuary.

Ellie felt the soft rain on her face as she drank in the peace and serenity of the morning and images fell gently into her heart; a quiet grove of cheery trees, bursting with signs of spring; raindrops clinging like sparkling jewels to bud-swollen branches, a hidden pool, secluded and soothingly peaceful, the gush of water cascading over a rocky incline, a burst of yellow forsythia. Beyond a light touch on her arm to draw her attention to an unusual bird, a cache of hidden bluebells, a blossom tree fat with buds, Ben didn't break the spell of tranquillity that gradually wrapped around Ellie with the gentleness of the rain.

Then away from the acres of natural woodland, a wrought-iron gate into another world again, where a landscape of formal gardens was a different type of oasis, flaunting ornamental fountains, a beautifully constructed pergola, and mingled scents from dazzling displays of spring tulips.

When it was all over, and the group exited onto the city street noisy with passing traffic, she found herself blinking hard and almost light-headed. She felt in a trance as the two couples said goodbye and headed off in the opposite direction to her and Ben. It didn't even matter that she was left on her own with him, or that her face was slightly damp with the rain and her hair, where it had escaped her hood, was a mass of frizzy tendrils.

'Well?' he looked at her carefully. 'Did that do anything for you?'

'All I can say is wow,' Ellie shook her head, bemused. 'How can you describe that experience?'

'A good one, I hope?'

'Good ... fantastic ... rejuvenating. I enjoyed the other walks, they took me away from myself for a while, but today was ... almost magical. I was in a completely different space.'

'That's my favourite one,' Ben said. 'You're really back to nature in those North Woods. And it helps not to break the atmosphere with too much chatter, although there was lots of stuff I wanted to point out to you and tell you about. Some of the trees are very old and quite rare, and if you were here in May, the lilac blossoms and cherry trees are spectacular.'

'I might be, you never know,' she said, half-joking, but at the same time not able to visualise herself returning to Dublin.

'And when you get back home, there's always Leitrim. A few days up there would soon sort you out.' Ben stared at her, and she had the odd thought that he was picturing her there already, maybe by the River Drowes, watching the flicker of salmon, or hiking though misty green valleys and along by silvery, mirror-surfaced lakes.

Then he asked her to go for coffee.

'So, Ellie. Fashion design. Where did that come from?'

They were sitting in Starbucks. Ben had ordered a fruit juice and Ellie a skinny latte.

'It started when I was a child, believe it or not,' Ellie said, teasing it out for herself. He was the kind of person it was easy to be totally honest with. Not only easy to be honest with but necessary, because Ben would see through her straightaway and she already sensed he'd no time for any kind of bullshit. It was totally refreshing because it meant she didn't have to try and be funny or enigmatic, or put on any kind of successful, sophisticated Ellie act.

The realisation startled her. How often had she been putting on an act? How about with the successful and sophisticated Johnny? And, if so, did that mean their relationship had been doomed from the start, with her tacitly playing along with the notion that they were one of Dublin's golden couples?

Ben was talking. 'Most burning passions begin in childhood. The first Christmas I got a proper GAA football, I took it everywhere, even into the bathroom never mind my bed. Were you always drawing stuff?'

'I was always taking apart dolls' clothes and putting them back together, and making stuff out of pipe cleaners, empty loo rolls and tin foil. Later, I was attracted to the whole artistic feel of costume design. My mother is an actress,' she explained. 'Vivienne Morgan, she does theatre and some television.'

His eyes softened. 'Yeah, Megan figured that out when we read the, um—'

'It's okay,' Ellie waved her hand. 'When I was old enough to be trusted I'd be allowed to drop into her after school whenever she was rehearsing in a Dublin theatre. I also hung around the dressing rooms during Saturday matinees in the holiday times. I had to stay very quiet, of course, and be on my best behaviour, but I loved going through the wardrobes behind the scenes ... the feel of the fabrics – velvet, chiffon, lace – it fired my imagination. The other kids in my class used to make up pop songs and stories, but I used to draw fantasy women in beautiful clothes.'

For a moment she was thirteen again, delighted she was mature enough to be allowed the freedom to drop into her mother's rehearsals, while nine-year-old Miranda was looked after by Florence, Vivienne's mother. 'They were happy times,' she said, her thoughts turning inwards. 'I might start some homework if it was school term, and one of the stage assistants would get me lemonade and sweets, but I was quite happy pottering around, checking out the wardrobe, knowing I'd be going home with Mum afterwards. She was always on a high after a matinee or rehearsal and she'd collect my sister from Granny's and we'd all go off for something to eat. They were good days,' she said, and suddenly daring herself to creep out of her normal barrier around this topic she elaborated, 'They were some of the best days, in fact, because my father died when I was fourteen and, after that, everything changed.'

'Oh, God, sorry to hear that,' Ben said. 'It must have been awful for you. And your family.'

'It was.' She swallowed a lump.

He asked gently, 'Do you want to talk about it?'

'Not really,' she smiled at him to show she wasn't shutting him out. 'It seems a lifetime ago. I was a different person then.'

'I'm sure it's something you never forget, though.'

'No.'

He didn't rush to fill the space with patronising words and she was comfortable with the silence that dropped between them.

After a while, Ben asked if she wanted more coffee.

'Yes, please.' She was in no rush. She watched him walk up to the counter and for the first time since she came to New York, she felt relaxed. Smoothly contented. Almost happy.

When he returned with fresh coffee and fruit juice, he told her how he moved into the area of fitness and trained to be an instructor in tandem with playing Gaelic football for his local club. 'From the time I was young, it was all I wanted to do. My heroes were the sporting legends in the All-Ireland finals. As a young teenager, the excitement on the football pitch really got to me. I don't think anything else in my life has ever beaten that feverish kind of excitement. At that age, the whole world is opening up for you and life hits you with a bright intensity.'

'Is this more of your psychology?' she asked, her smooth contentment suddenly disturbed by the realisation that when he spoke of the world opening up with a bright intensity, it touched a nerve deep inside her.

'I've studied lots of stuff as part of my qualifications,' he said. 'I'm interested in people. The whole make-up. You must be very talented and disciplined to be where you are, but behind that at a deeper level, I guess you're linking back to happy memories of your childhood.'

'That's a very sweeping statement,' she said. 'I never looked at it like that, but I don't feel the need to recreate memories. I like to think I'm a happy, successful and well-adjusted adult.'

Even she heard the note of defensiveness that coloured her tone. It put a barrier between them, because, as Ben spoke he looked apologetic. 'I'm sure you are. Sorry, I'm getting off my soapbox now. Just ignore my amateur attempts at working out what makes you tick.'

'And don't mind my huffing and puffing,' she said, laughing, conscious that she was taking herself far too seriously. 'There is some truth in what you say.'

Afterwards, as they strolled back to the apartment, the sun came out and glittered on the wet pavement so that it looked like they were walking on sparkling jewels, and Ellie found herself marvelling that a shower of rain could cause such ordinary magic, and wished she had an excuse to prolong the morning and suggest they go walking in the park all over again.

'It was a lovely morning, thank you,' she said, when they paused in the hallway of the apartment building. 'I'm glad I came, and,' she felt her face reddening and fidgeted with strands of her long dark hair, 'I took some of the advice you gave me the other evening and I feel the better for it.'

'Hey, good stuff. Look,' he said, touching her arm in a friendly gesture, 'I'm sticking my neck out here and tell me to go shove it if you like, but the big thing you have to remember is that you're still you, no matter what your boyfriend has done. His behaviour is all about him, not you. You can decide to step away from it so that it won't drag you down. I had to do that with my business. I had to remember that I was still me, and step away, at least in my messed-up head, from the debts and all the crap.'

'That must have been a challenge.'

'It still is.' He gave her a rueful look with his hazel eyes. It went straight to her heart and for a long, charged moment she wanted to reach out to him in some way. Touch his face. Kiss his cheek, the way he'd kissed hers. Put her arms around him and take that look out of his eyes. Kiss his mouth ... She swallowed hard and looked away in embarrassment at where her thoughts were taking her.

'Stairs or lift?' he asked.

'Lift for me, please,' she said, her voice husky. 'Hey, it *is* four floors,' she went on, in answer to his mocking glance.

He pressed the button to summon the lift. 'Be warned. This is the last time I'm letting you off the hook!' Then she watched his long legs taking the stairs two at a time.

Ellie rode on up to her apartment in the lift, still recovering from the electrifying moment in the hall. Where had it come from, that tremendous urge to stroke Ben's taut face, lean in and catch the scent of him, put her arms around him, hug him, kiss those lips, and – she closed her eyes and felt hot and cold when she thought of this – follow the feeling right through and take him to bed?

The alarming thing was that she couldn't recall ever feeling this intense longing for Johnny.

Chapter 32

*F*or Miranda, life in Hong Kong had taken on a magical quality. The days were becoming longer and brighter. It was warmer, with temperatures in the high teens most days, and the winter fogs that had lingered into April, blanketing skyscrapers like a ghostly mist, gradually disappeared. There were days of sunny blue skies, but, now and again, heavy downpours of rain. Sometimes she woke in the mornings to the unexpected brightness of spring sunshine pressing behind the blinds, and it immediately gave her a lift. Other mornings were even better when she woke to find herself in Christian's arms and memories of the night before rushed back to her. Either way, she was filled with sheer happiness.

By now they were spending most of their free time together. Christian introduced her to Harbour City in Kowloon, laughing with her surprise at the extent of the shopping complex, with its hotels and cinemas and designer shopping malls. She gaped at the fantastic views of the harbour through floor-to-ceiling windows, and the sight of elegant cruise liners berthed alongside.

She found it hard to believe the whole area had once been a cargo dock lined with nothing but warehouses.

Sometimes they dined sumptuously in high-class hotels, the table heavy with crystal and silver cutlery; other times they used their fingers to enjoy crispy Peking duck or seafood in a quirky Tsim Sha Tsui restaurant. Saturday night was often spent sipping beer in the nightclubs of Wan Chai or cuddled upon the sofa in one or the other's apartment.

She found it easy to distance herself from Ellie and Lucy and the mess they had created. And she hugged her new-found bliss to herself, unwilling to share it with anyone. Least of all, Ellie. Little by little, she knew she was moving away from the old Miranda Morgan and all her baggage, and becoming this new person, who was surprising even herself with the way she now felt totally at home in this cosmopolitan city.

Never mind in Christian's bed.

'I hope you don't mind me saying this, Miranda,' Mai began one morning as she sat across the workstation in XAM.

'But?' Miranda's heart quivered, just for an instant. This phrase usually preceded someone announcing that she didn't look a bit like her sisters, and was accompanied by a puzzled look, as though they were trying to figure out if she actually came from the same gene pool. But Mai had never met Ellie or Lucy, or even seen a photograph of them.

'Sara and I were saying that you look a lot younger than the day you started here,' Mai announced.

'Good. I certainly don't mind you saying that,' Miranda laughed.

'There you go, it has something to do with your laugh. You looked worried and anxious at the start, we thought you were going to be hard work, but we were wrong. Now you laugh more and it makes you look pretty. We can see you're a lot happier in your life.'

275

'I love living here, and I enjoy my job,' Miranda said, finally admitting it to herself.

'Because of Christian?' Mai smiled with delight.

'It's more than Christian,' Miranda said.

From the MTR underground to the Star Ferry, the energy of the city had swept her up and whispered freedom to her – freedom from old habits and restraints, from old ties and patterns of behaviour. She fitted smoothly into the exciting flow of it all. And although she had told herself in the beginning that she could be anybody at all, she felt even happier that she wasn't pretending to be anybody, but was simply herself.

Even the undemanding nature of her work pleased her. She might be busy, but she was off the hectic treadmill she'd trudged back in Dublin with Ryan Johnson, where she'd put in long hours and felt obliged to live up to her clever reputation and Masters degree. It was great to enjoy lunches with the girls and not feel guilty if she left the office at a reasonable hour.

And then there was Christian. This tall Australian with the broad shoulders and mop of blond hair excited her. He wanted and desired her, and he showed her how much over and over again in the sensual language of love and in the little things – a certain look he threw her when they were in the midst of a crowd, a warm squeeze of her arm when he came across to join her, the feel of his hand in the small of her back as he guided her across to a restaurant table. A kiss on the back of her neck. Their Friday night meals and Saturday night drinks were sparkling with anticipation of the hours they would spend together in bed, where she would lose herself in his arms, enjoying the glorious sensation of making love, getting to know his body, allowing him to know hers, and revelling in the way she wasn't afraid to arch herself seductively towards him to better allow him fill the aching depths of her. Which he did, over and over until she felt she had melted into him.

Bouyed up by her new-found confidence, she'd had her hair styled shorter and softer, and she went back to Harbour City and shopped until practically every outfit in her wardrobe was replenished. She didn't buy a single item of clothing unless it had the wow factor and made her feel sexy. Out went a collection of blouses (the kind, she admitted, that not even Vivienne would have worn) and in came soft cami tops and whispery silk shirts. Her charcoal-grey trouser suits were replaced with more feminine, curvy skirt suits in soft dove grey and emerald green. She replaced trousers and jumpers with softly flowing skirts, and cotton tops, layering the effect in a casual, feminine way. She bought chic dresses that could go from the office to the restaurant with a quick change of accessories. She spent a fortune on designer jeans and had great fun updating her lingerie, choosing delicate and frothy satin, bras, knickers and thongs, all highly indulgent and far more expensive than her usual selection from Marks & Spencer. The best fun of all was watching Christian's face as he slowly undressed her.

It wasn't all a dream, she told herself. It was real and it was her. Most importantly of all, it was *now*.

Sometimes, as she came through Harbour City clutching a raft of carrier bags, she had the uneasy feeling that it was all too good to last, that she didn't deserve to be enjoying such happiness, especially when her sisters were in such trouble with their own lives. Sometimes she wondered if it all might come to an end. Occasionally, when she woke up before him and stared at Christian's sleeping face, she pinched herself and wondered what he saw in her.

He knew a lot about her background and childhood by now, and she knew a lot about his, thanks to the cosy intimate chats they enjoyed both in and out of bed, but he still didn't know how her sisters had always overshadowed her. And she was nervous of revealing to him how Ellie had scuppered her love-life once too often. Although he didn't need to know, did he?

'Hey, beautiful, how long have you been looking at me?' he'd asked one morning when he opened his eyes to catch her studying him.

'Not long,' she'd said, loving the way he clasped her to him. 'Am I beautiful?'

'Yes, you are,' he'd said, nuzzling her neck. 'Kind, beautiful and great in bed. I bet you were watching me snoring and asking yourself what you were doing with a hairy gorilla like me.'

'You're not a gorilla.'

'So in other words I'm hairy?'

'Sort of, but I'll live with it,' she'd teased, running her finger-nails through the hair on his chest.

'And I'm not far off a gorilla because I feel some animalistic behaviour coming on,' he'd grinned, kicking back white cotton sheets, making her laugh as he tickled her soft spots with his raspy chin, then making her gasp as he nudged her legs apart and lay between them.

Too good to be true? She'd wondered what would happen if she were totally honest with him about her past. It could be awkward, but it would certainly be embarrassing. So, she'd ignored the little voice inside her head as Christian stirred up all of her senses and she was overwhelmed with desire for him. She'd put aside the nagging whisper that, going on past history, this wouldn't last if Christian ever met Ellie.

That wouldn't happen, she'd vowed.

And, occasionally, when she thought about Lucy and Johnny and how Ellie must be feeling, she surprised herself by being a little short on sympathy, because she couldn't help thinking that what goes around, comes around.

Chapter 33

$\mathcal{N}$o one was going to know about her meeting with Ian, Lucy decided. Sasha would only start making a big thing out of it, and tease her mercilessly. Rebecca would talk in serious tones about there being a conflict of interest, blah, blah, blah, and that Lucy had better watch her step.

The whole point of meeting Ian, she said aloud to herself, as though she was rehearsing her defence, was to find out if there was any way he could help manage her profile or effect damage limitation if she fell out of line again. Or better again, generate some positive publicity for her.

She'd opted to meet him for a casual evening drink, figuring it was less formal than a lunch appointment. She pulled on a jade-green shirt over her Gucci jeans and tied back her tumble of hair, wondering if she looked any different as she stared in the mirror. She wasn't getting any younger. Even at twenty-one, she was conscious of her age and the army of sixteen- and seventeen-year-olds coming up behind her; beautiful, confident, climbing all over each other in the race to the top, and more than ready to stab her in the back and step into the five-inch Gucci stiletto boots she was pulling on.

Only the few world-famous supermodels had any kind of longevity in the modelling industry. She had the looks, Lucy told herself as she slicked on Dior lip gloss and generously sprayed herself with Flowerbomb. But she'd have to start thinking serious strategy if she wanted to be part of that elite and start believing she could do it.

She stared at her light grey eyes in the mirror. Sometimes, she found that the hardest thing of all to do.

Just before she left the apartment, she tugged up the collar of her aviator jacket, tucking her hair behind it, and pulled a peaked cap over her head. Not much of a disguise, but it helped her from sticking out like a sore thumb as she walked into the quiet, out of the way pub on the outskirts of Chelsea, chosen because it was a far cry from her usual trendy haunt and less chance she'd be recognised by the clientele. The pub was quiet, with a few customers sitting by the bar and others watching a football match on the wall-mounted television. Ian was already waiting. He jumped up as soon as she arrived, almost knocking over his drink in his eagerness, and leaning over he kissed her a little awkwardly on the cheek.

Not exactly the polished performance she'd expect from a PR consultant, she thought, swallowing a tiny sliver of annoyance.

'A mojito?' he asked, his eyes darting towards the bar. He lifted his jacket and scrabbled in the pockets for his wallet. His rummaging was in vain though, for he eventually located his wallet in his jeans pocket and gave her a sheepish grin.

'No, I'll just have a beer, thanks,' she said as she slid out of her jacket and pulled off her hat. She sat down on the leather seat, reminding herself that it was important to keep her wits about her and the less alcohol she drank the better, especially as Ian was drinking sparkling water. He wanted to be on his best behaviour, she assumed. Getting Lucy Morgan all to himself like this was a big break for him. No wonder she sensed nervous energy sparking all around him.

'A beer?' he looked disappointed. 'Are you sure I can't get you a cocktail or a glass of champagne?'

'Oh, go on, then,' she said. He probably thought she'd never touched a beer in her life. 'Champagne it is, thanks.' She'd sip it very slowly.

She watched him head up to the bar, observing the contained, almost stiff way he walked and held himself, as though he was trying to keep a rein on his emotions. She wondered what he secretly thought about her. When he returned with the drinks, his face was inscrutable.

She took a sip of champagne, enjoying the fizz on her tongue and the warmth that slid into her chest. 'Right, where do we start?'

'I, um—' he took an iPhone out of his pocket and held it up. 'I'm hoping to record this, if that's okay,' he said, rushing his words a little. 'It'll save me making notes. But only, um, if you're entirely comfortable with the idea?'

'Doesn't bother me,' Lucy sat back and relaxed.

His mobile slipped out of his grasp and despite his best efforts to catch it, it clattered to the tiled floor. He bent down to retrieve it, banged his head off the table, and shot her an embarrassed look, 'That's if it still works.'

Lucy felt a tinge of irritation. He was almost freaked out with nerves and she couldn't remember the last time her presence had had such an effect on a man. Maybe this wasn't such a good idea. He'd be no use to her if he couldn't get his act together. In fact, he'd hardly be up to a public relations job and all the pressure that brought if he couldn't handle a routine interview. Obviously, there was a lot at stake for him as he tried to establish a footing in such a tough, competitive field. Still, she was here now, so she'd give him a few minutes and see if he calmed down.

'Ian, chill. It's fine,' she said struggling to keep impatience out of her voice. 'We're just going to have a chat, okay? It's not rocket science. Apart from your phone,' she said a little drily.

'Yeah, um, right.' He checked out his phone, gingerly holding it as though it was a nuclear weapon and about to detonate. He clearly wasn't used to the functionality because his face suddenly flashed with an irritation that put her on edge. As if he sensed her annoyance, he turned and gave her a guileless smile. 'Sorry about this,' he said. 'It's just new and I had the other one for so long ... this is light years ahead.'

'Okay. Why don't I tell you a bit about myself first, and what I'd expect from you in terms of damage limitation, and you tell me what you'd be able to offer. Then we can both go away and have a think about it.'

'Sounds good.'

She started to chat about her career then she broke off. 'Hey, why am I doing this?' She laughed. 'If you're any good you've already done your homework and you've googled me to death. You probably know me better than I do.'

'Yes, I've some background information, but it's incomplete and sketchy ...' he paused, the expression in his eyes suddenly boyish and vulnerable. She guessed he was in his mid-twenties but, right now, he could have been sixteen the way he was looking at her.

'Maybe I should give you a test to see if you're up to the job,' she teased, giving him a sidelong glance from under her lashes.

If she'd hoped he'd react to her flirtatious overtures, she was mistaken. He sat up straighter and became very businesslike.

'As I said, I don't have all the facts. However, Lucy, I want to be committed and professional in all my dealings with you. That means you have to trust me and we have to be honest with each other. I want to enhance your reputation, Lucy, not damage it. But it's in both our interests that I have a clear picture of your background and know what's going on in your life, for example anything that might prove to be a threat or easy pickings for the media.'

It sounded, Lucy thought, as though he'd rehearsed his speech and knew it off by heart. 'In other words you want me to bare my blackened soul,' she laughed again. 'I can't tell you absolutely everything because I don't want to shock you, but I think this calls for another drink,' she said, knocking back her champagne.

'I'm going out to the, um, bathroom. I'll get more drinks on the way back.'

Out in the bathroom, he gripped the cold, smooth edge of the basin and glared at his reflection in the mirror. How the fuck had he nearly blown it? How had he let his nerves get the better of him? And yesterday he'd practised with that new phone, switching it to record function several times to make sure he wouldn't make a fool of himself.

Seeing her stroll into the pub, with her strutting, cocky walk had angered him. She'd been hiding her face behind the upturned collar of her jacket so that she wouldn't be noticed. And why this pub? Nice and cosy all right, but hardly the place she'd frequent with her mates. She didn't want to risk any of her precious mates seeing her with him. Bollocks to that. He didn't want to be drawn into her fake kind of world anyway. But his anger had made him nervous and he knew she'd picked up on it.

Sitting there beside her, he couldn't help breath in her expensive perfume and notice her perfect face and clothes. Not that he knew much about designer fashion, but he could see money

283

written all over her shirt and jeans and those ridiculously high boots. She was so full of it all, so confident in the way she took it all for granted that it turned his stomach.

He wished he could have had his mother back again, just for one more day, even a few hours, so that he could bring her shopping, up along Oxford Street and into Mayfair, and treat her to fancy clothes. But that would never happen. He buried his face in his hands for a moment, closing his eyes against a black tide of memories, and then he sighed heavily and straightened his shoulders. He had work to do and more questions to ask. He put a smile on his face as he strode across to the door.

A freaky moment, all the same, he thought, when Lucy had started to flirt with him.

Lucy found that baring her soul, blackened or otherwise, to the accompaniment of another glass of champagne wasn't so difficult after all. In the beginning.

Ian listened attentively, and she saw him becoming more relaxed as she chatted away filling in her background for him, answering his questions with ease. It was a long time since anyone had shown such interest in her as a person, and not just a model or a product, and she found it heartening. In no time, Ian had caught up with her current career, the bad press she sometimes faced, and where she hoped to be in a year or two.

It was only when he began to ask about her childhood that Lucy felt her gut instinct rebel.

'What's my childhood got to with anything?' she asked with false insouciance.

'I'd say it has everything to do with it,' he said, looking at her intently.

She laughed. 'That's ridiculous. I am who I am, here and now, full stop.'

'I just need to get a complete picture of you,' he said pleasantly, as though it was no big deal. 'Like, did you always want to model? Did you like school? Were you happy growing up?'

'Wow. I'm impressed. You like digging deep,' she said. 'Maybe you'll be good at your job after all. I was as happy as anyone else, I suppose.' *Anybody, that is, whose Dad didn't bother with them*, a little voice at the back of her head piped up. Lucy ignored it and chatted to him about what it was like to have a successful actress mother and two ambitious sisters who were older than her. 'I didn't even attempt to follow in any of their footsteps. I was the baby of the family, and I was spoiled,' she said this proudly, as though it was something to celebrate, determined to mask her sudden defensiveness.

'Spoiled in what way?'

'I soon figured out that I only had to lift my little finger to get whatever I wanted,' she said with a giggle. *Except for the one big thing that had been impossible to get*, the little voice whispered again. And naturally she'd wanted it more than anything else. She didn't even notice fresh drinks arriving, as they seemed to materialise on the table in front of her. She sipped more champagne, needing to calm her jangling emotions.

'Hmm. That's the kind of thing I'd keep out of the press,' Ian said. 'If you want people to warm to you, and generate positive feelings towards you, it's better to show you've had to work hard and struggle to get where you are. It's good to have the common touch and some kind of vulnerability, and preferably a childhood that was far from idyllic. Look at icons such as Madonna and Oprah, and even take Cheryl Cole ... they all came from humble beginnings, and had a few knocks in life, but they had their dreams to sustain them.'

Lucy grasped at his words. 'Hey, are you saying I have something in common with them?'

'Look, with respect Lucy, we're ignoring the elephant on the table in front of us. I don't want to intrude, but where did your father fit into your life?' He went on in a quiet, respectful tone, 'We need to be honest and there's no point in having this whole conversation if we're not going to talk about him.'

She felt a brittleness on the inside that was difficult to conceal. 'Guess what, Ian?' she said, with a hard edge to her voice. 'You probably know more about him than I do.'

'It's bound to be a sore subject with you because of his death. His anniversary was all over the media recently and that must have been hard . . . I certainly don't want to make light of it in any way, but can't you see it gives you an instant hook?'

'Well, that's obvious,' she said with alacrity. 'At the start of my career, my name was always bracketed with Zach Anderson. It gave me a little cachet and a leg-up of sorts, but I was glad when I finally became recognised in my own right. And if you want to know the real truth, all that crap about his anniversary did my head in.'

'I know you were hounded a bit by the media, but if that happened in the future, I would advise you to turn it to your advantage. Like, instead of running away from the cameras, stand your ground. Admit your heartbreak. He was your father. People would empathise immediately if you showed them how upset it all made you feel. They'd love you for it.'

'Hang on a minute,' Lucy shook her head. 'Is that thing still recording?'

'I'll switch it off if you're not comfortable.'

'Please do. Because this is strictly off the record.'

Ian seemed to be fumbling for ages with his phone and she didn't resume until he had put it away in his pocket.

'Right. Off the record,' he picked up his glass of water as though he was unconcerned about turning off his phone, but she knew by the tension in his face that he wasn't.

'Truth is, as far as I'm concerned, my father was the biggest prick going.'

Ian hadn't been expecting that. He spluttered on his drink. 'What?'

'He so totally did not want me. He ignored me.' Her voice shook and she didn't care. 'I was never in his life, nor was he in mine.'

Ian's eyes narrowed. 'You must have seen him sometimes, maybe you forgot, you were very young when he ... died—'

'Do the maths. I was thirteen months old. Sounds like a big sob story. He went to Canada before I was born to work on his new album in peace and quiet, and he was too busy to come back to see me.'

'Are you sure?'

'Of course, I'm sure.' Lucy shrugged, wearing her bravado like a coat of armour. 'Mum used to tell me he loved me, but how could he? Sometimes—,' she gulped, and tried to turn it into a laugh. She looked at Ian, as if to make him understand. 'Sometimes, when I was a kid, I fancied he wrote that hit song for me, 'Forever My Angel'. Sometimes I sang myself to sleep with it, especially the bit where he said, "No matter what the world might say/I hold you in my heart ..." Silly, really,' she finished with a wobble.

Ian was silent for a long time. She was beginning to feel uneasy with his sudden withdrawal until he said, 'How do you know for certain that he didn't come home at least a couple of times to fuss over you?'

'I stopped talking to Mum because I had the feeling she was being evasive and knew it must be upsetting her. So I began to pester my older sisters Ellie and Miranda. They didn't want to talk either. But they couldn't remember him coming back at any time. Miranda told me, years later, that it had been very hard on

Ellie that our mother had taken up with him so soon after their dad had died. That's why they don't like talking about it. So it's a big family skeleton that we all avoid.'

'I didn't expect to hear any of this. It must have been very tough for you.'

'It was. And the mention of his name makes me more angry than upset. So you see, Ian,' her voice broke again and she snatched a gulp of champagne. 'I don't know how you'd turn that around to make it more acceptable to the media. Of course, I could always do the "little girl lost" thing . . .'

He looked into space as though absorbing this information. Then he turned back to her. 'I'm sorry if I upset you, asking those questions. And all that stuff about his anniversary . . . it must have brought it all back to you.'

'Yeah, well, it did, I suppose.' She frowned, remembering the wreath, and instantly deciding not to mention it to Ian because she didn't want him to know how much it had freaked her out.

'What's the matter?'

She shook her head. 'Nothing. Is there anything else you feel you need to know?'

'Just a couple of things to help me work out the best angle for you. I presume Zach Anderson provided for you? Especially with the success of his song after his, um, accidental death?'

'Well, that's another thing . . . I don't know if it was an accident or not,' she said, her voice trembling.

'Don't you?'

'Mum always said it was, but that could have been to spare me again. I mean, how do you live with the knowledge that your father did away with himself, not caring that he had a child?'

He was silenced by what she'd said. They were just words. And they flowed off her tongue into the cosy ambience of a neighbourhood bar in Chelsea, as if they didn't weigh too heavily, didn't really matter, didn't mean anything, anything at all.

'I don't know,' he said, his voice subdued, looking desperately unhappy himself, as if he totally sympathised with her.

'Hey, lighten up,' she said with forced jollity. 'You can guess what I mean about tiptoeing around all this. It's like a conspiracy of silence in the family. In the end I looked Zach up on the internet, when I was about twelve. There wasn't much, but some articles said there were rumours that he'd done himself in on purpose. And I certainly never got one single penny from his music. Actually, that's a very good question. I don't know what happened to it.'

'You must have had some sort of right to his estate. Next of kin, and all that?'

'Next of kin?' she laughed. 'You mean result of a quick shag. A biological urge that had long-lasting consequences. Look, forget it,' she shook her head. 'I'm not talking about it anymore. I am who I am, what you see is what you get, and that's it.'

He fell silent for a moment. 'Another drink?'

'No, thanks, I've had enough.' She'd had more than enough to judge by the way the pub was all hazy around her and Ian's features were a little indistinct.

'Just one, and then I'll take you home. Promise. I want to keep an eye on you for a little longer to make sure you're all right and don't feel too bad.'

'Thanks.' His concern for her well-being warmed her. He seemed to be a nice enough guy, and that wasn't just because she was seeing him through the end of a bottle of bubbly. She sensed he had a real understanding of what it meant to be Lucy Morgan in a way no one ever had before.

'Do you see much of your family?' he asked, when they were walking back to her apartment. It was just over a mile and he'd suggested getting a taxi, but Lucy preferred to walk and clear her head a little. It had rained when they were in the pub, the streets were quiet and the pavements were wet and shining here and there with reflected light from fast-food restaurants and shops and the air was scented with rain.

'I go home to my mother every couple of months, for a weekend or whatever, depending on my schedule,' she said.

'You're from Dublin aren't you?'

'Yes, Dún Laoghaire.'

'You'd better give me your mother's details, as your next of kin, just in case, seeing as you drop over so often.'

'I'll text them to you as soon as I get home,' Lucy said. 'Mum's still hanging on to the family home, even though my sisters think she should move into something smaller. It's very handy for the city-centre nightlife, so I'm not complaining. I usually end up treating the house like a hotel and going out most of the time, catching up with my friends when I'm over.'

But all that had changed, she realised coldly. Her attention had been that focused on her father and how to gloss over it with Ian that she'd forgotten all about Johnny and Ellie, and what she'd done. How much she'd hurt her sister. Now it came back to her with a force that wrenched at her heart and winded her. She tried to breathe slowly and evenly as they strolled along and she was glad he was with her, to distract her from herself.

'Dún Laoghaire,' he said, mispronouncing it a little with his Scottish accent that she found attractive. 'That's by the sea, isn't it?'

'Yes, and our house is along the coast road and has lovely views of the bay from the upstairs window.' The house that had always been welcoming and there for her whenever she needed it. Her room ready and waiting. Always. Everything soured and tainted now thanks to her crappy behaviour.

'Sounds nice,' he said. 'I should go to Dublin some day.'

'You've never been?' she said in surprise, concentrating on him as they strolled along and not the image in her head of her mother's house.

He smiled at her, his face shadowed against the street lamp. 'Not yet.'

She paused at the steps of her building and put her hand on his arm. 'Would you like to come in for coffee?' she asked, hoping he'd accept. She felt a connection to him and could easily see herself enjoying the comfort of a kiss and a cuddle and maybe more . . . Especially tonight when every part of her head seemed to hurt. Some of it was withdrawal symptoms from the champagne, but most of it was from images chasing around in her head and looping endlessly over and over. Her and Johnny, Johnny and Ellie and pictures of a deep Canadian lake. Her mother, by her bedside when she was about six, in a room over-looking the sea, telling her that of course her father had loved her.

Loved her? Her mum had surely been lying to her, evading the truth, glossing over everything that was important. As if none of it mattered.

But of course it mattered. Everything about it mattered.

Ian stepped away, out of her reach. 'I won't, thanks,' he said.

'Right. Okay,' Lucy said, surprised at how rejected she felt. She'd fully expected him to jump at the chance to come up to her apartment. Most men would. It seemed Ian didn't even want to kiss her goodnight because he backed away as she began to walk up the steps to the hall door.

'I have to start working on a package for you.'

'Straightaway?' She was halfway up the steps by now and it started to rain again. She looked down to where he stood with his hands in his pockets and could have sworn he looked relieved.

'Yes, I work best at night with no distractions. Don't forget to send me your mother's details, for my file.'

'Okay. Give me a call in the next few days.' She didn't bother turning to wave as she opened the door and went into the hall. She had to remind herself that if they were to have any kind of a business relationship, everything else was off the agenda. Still, it had been so intense between them that evening that her apartment felt ridiculously empty and she was bowled over by a wave of loneliness and longed to put her head on his chest and be wrapped in his arms.

God. Her life was turning into a right mess. She'd always thought that when you were grown up, you'd understand everything and your life would unroll in a straight enough line in front of you, leading the way towards rewards and success and secure happy-ever-afters. She'd never thought it would be like this, resembling nothing short of a snake-pit of snarling contradictions that seemed impossible to resolve. Suddenly, she wanted to know what kind of person Zach Anderson had been. Why had he gone as far as Canada to work? Had there been some sort of a row? Why had he never come back to see her? She thought of all the elusive answers she'd allowed her mother to get away with over the years. Her mother must be hiding something. Was it anything to do with her greatest fear, the one that whispered that Lucy didn't deserve to have a father? The silence only helped to reinforce her thoughts, as though she didn't even deserve to know the truth, however cold and unpalatable it might be.

He strode back to Fulham in the murky night, heedless of the rain spitting in his face, oblivious to the swish of tyres and glare of oncoming car headlights, and he didn't know whether to laugh in self-derision or cry from frustration.

All his grand plans had hit the dust. All his preparations had led nowhere. He'd worked so hard to get close to her. Ordinarily, she'd never have looked at a guy like him so he'd had to dip his toe in her world of ultra glitz and look as though he belonged. It had been nerve-wracking, but he'd done it. For his mother's sake. And it had all been in vain because Lucy knew nothing about her father. She didn't remember him and he'd never even seen her. Funnily enough, even though he hated her guts and her expensive clothes, and the whole glam image she put out there, he'd believed her.

In fact, he was astounded to realise that in a moment of weakness, he'd even felt sorry for her. *Sorry* for Lucy Morgan! He'd felt almost protective towards her, and he must be going soft in the head for that hadn't been on his agenda at all.

His mother would have liked her, he sensed.

And he should have told her the truth about that song, the one he'd heard his mother singing on and off, right back to his childhood. He should have told Lucy who he really was, only he'd feared it might shut her up completely and he'd never find out the truth. He hadn't come this far to give up. He couldn't – wouldn't – let his mum down. He'd been looking in the wrong place all the time.

The following morning he cleared out of the Fulham flat and took the train back to Edinburgh, working out another plan of action as he travelled north. A few days at home would soon sort his head out. Then it would be next stop Dublin or, more precisely, Dún Laoghaire.

Just as he'd asked, Lucy had texted him all the details he needed.

Chapter 34

'Are you sure you don't mind me dragging you around the shops?' Megan asked.

'No problem, I'll enjoy this,' Ellie said, feeling the warmth of the sun on her face as they stepped out onto the pavement. She checked out Megan's loose cotton top, leggings and flat, sequinned sandals, and smiled. 'Glad to see you're dressed for comfort and quick changes.'

'I can do comfort all right, it's the rest of it I need help with! This will be the wedding of the year in Leitrim and I'm not going to let the side down. The bride was my room-mate in college, and she's invited all the gang to witness her snagging Mr Most Eligible. I badly need some eye-popping style.'

'What date is it again?' Ellie asked.

'The end of June,' Megan said. 'I'll need a whole weekend wardrobe. The castle is booked out for three nights, with a pre-wedding buffet, the wedding itself, and post-wedding barbeque. I thought Ireland was supposed to be in a recession.'

'It is, so it's all the more important to spend some money

if you have it. You'll be gorgeous, Megan, I'll make sure of that.'

There was nothing like New York for shopping, Ellie decided, especially on a bright spring Saturday, when the sky above Manhattan was a pristine blue and even the towering steel and glass skyscrapers looked beautiful in reflected sunshine. It was fun shopping with Megan, scouring Fifth Avenue as they chose her outfits for the wedding. Ellie felt the proverbial spring in her step as she and Megan swanned in and out of stores, sifting through rails of glitzy designer wear, displays of alluring shoes and sparkly sandals. She scrutinised Megan carefully as she sashayed out of dressing room after dressing room in chiffons that flowed around her body, taffeta that accentuated her curves, satins and silks that skimmed her figure. Ellie cast a professional eye over the cut and finishing, and stroked sensual fabrics and textures between the pads of her fingers.

She felt something else, too, a palpable excitement, a rush of recognition, as though she was stepping back into a familiar skin that had been neglected. She caught sight of her reflection as she passed a boutique mirror, surprised to see a glint in her green eyes that had been missing for some time. She wondered if Ben had anything to do with the new animation she felt stirring in her blood. She smiled quietly to herself – of course he had. She'd joined the walking group on Friday, surprised to hear herself laugh and joke and give as good as she got from him, keeping in step with him as they marched through Sheep's Meadow, around by The Pond and up along the avenue under a periwinkle sky, while springtime blossomed all around them.

Then Ben had invited her to join some friends on Saturday night for a meal and some drinks.

'Who'll be going?' she'd asked.

'Me, Megan, some of our friends . . . Irish and American.'

'I might. I'll see,' she'd said, trying not to grin too widely, but knowing her eyes were sparkling. *Jesus, she was flirting with him. And she liked it.*

From the way he was smiling at her, he seemed to like it too. 'I hear you're going out to buy up the town with Megan tomorrow. I'll make sure she reminds you.'

At Ellie's advice, Megan tried on a strapless, apricot Donna Karan sleek column dress.

'This isn't me at all,' she protested at first.

'Go on,' Ellie shoved her into the changing room, knowing how stunning it would look on her.

Right enough, Megan glided out, her face a picture of amazement.

'How did you know? This is perfect. Ellie, you're brilliant!' She went on to help Megan select a cream lace mini-dress with peep-toe heels for the buffet, and a scarlet jumpsuit with ribbon-tie sandals for the barbeque. Then casual outfits of jeans and shirts for daytime wear, when the wedding guests would take advantage of walks in the nearby woods or around the lake. They went for lunch, laden down with exclusive bags. Later, Megan treated herself to some sexy nightwear, necessary, she joked, in case she was lucky enough to find herself sleepwalking through the flag-stoned corridors of the castle. Even Ellie got in on the act, picking up some perfume and lingerie. She didn't dare ask herself what she was thinking, as she handed over her Visa card and watched the assistant swaddle drifts of gossamer silk in whispery tissue paper. And to round the shopping trip off, they went for cocktails in the Plaza, juggling even more designer-logoed bags.

'Ellie, you've been a total star,' Megan said, clinking her margarita glass to Ellie's. 'And incredibly patient. I can't thank you enough. You really have an eye for what suits a woman.'

'It was fun, I enjoyed it.'

'You're coming out on the town with us tonight, aren't you? Ben said it was an order.'

'I guess if he ordered it, I can't refuse,' Ellie smiled.

She felt a bit strange at first as she hit the town on Saturday night with Ben, Megan and their friends, most of whom she'd already met at the party in their apartment. She felt a prickle of delight that there was no sign of Susan. She knew she looked good in black leather jeans and a softly draping cream top. Her dark hair was loose, one side caught back in a crystal slide that matched her earrings and necklace. There were eight of them altogether, and they met up in a noisy Italian. After a meal, they moved onto an Irish bar for drinks, and then they bundled into yellow cabs, Ellie delighted to find herself squeezing up beside Ben as they drove through the glittery night-time streets and went on to Pacha, one of the hottest clubs in New York.

'I didn't think this was your scene,' she shouted to Ben above the loud beat of the music, when they found themselves together by the bar.

'It's not,' he said. He was wearing a dark shirt over his chinos. Ellie felt a charge inside her every time she looked at him, which was far too frequently. All night she'd been painfully aware of him, as the group had moved from the restaurant to the bar, to the nightclub. She felt like she had an aerial attached to her head, which registered every time he laughed and talked to someone other than her. Which he seemed to be doing a lot of, much to her annoyance.

But how come she felt so drawn to Ben from Leitrim? Was she trying to get back at Johnny, or prove to herself that she was still sexy and desirable after his treachery? It could be she was enticed by Ben because he was so different to Johnny and the kind of men she had dated before, men who had always come running if Ellie Morgan so much as crooked her little finger. Ben wasn't exactly falling into her lap. He was a challenge – maybe that was why she found him so attractive.

'If it's not your scene, then why are you here?' she asked.

'I'm keeping an eye on you.'

'Oh?' A bubble of hope.

'Sure. I have to make sure you behave and that you don't drag a stranger back to Laura's flat.'

Laura. Her bubble of hope burst. She'd forgotten that Ben was supposed to be mad about her. He sounded like he was only concerned about Laura's flat and she was piqued, as it wasn't the answer she'd hoped for. What *had* she hoped for, though? *I'm keeping an eye on you because you've snagged my interest/I find you attractive/I can't help wanting to be near you . . .*

'You never know, I might bring *you* back,' she blurted, feeling a little heedless after the mixture of wine and cocktails. She stirred her straw around in her glass to give her something to do with her hands.

'Really?' He stared at her for ages, the dark pupils in his eyes seeming to bore into her, but betraying nothing, and even though she felt a quiver of anxiety at the way she'd put herself out there and by the fact that he wasn't responding, she found it impossible to look away.

Eventually she laughed and said, 'Just so you can make sure I'm keeping it clean and tidy for Laura, of course.'

He tossed back the last of his beer. 'So you're not inviting me back for coffee, then?'

'Whatever gave you that idea?' Had she been that obvious?

'I must have misread the signals. What a shame.'

He was playing with her. She shrugged and said, feeling on the defensive, 'Hey, come on, Ben, you hardly think I want to be just another string to your bow.' Her voice was raised and even as she said the words, she realised how tacky they sounded. Too late. He recoiled, as if highly offended.

'That's a pity,' he said, 'I could have sworn we were on the same wavelength.'

'What wavelength?' she asked, a hollowness spreading out from her heart. She'd felt that too, somewhere inside her, hadn't she? But she'd decided she was just being fanciful.

Her shoulder tingled where he put his hand, and he leaned in close to make sure she heard him above the din as he said, 'I thought we clicked somewhere, and that maybe you were . . . that I could . . . but no worries.' He threw up his hands in defeat, moved away from the bar and pushed through the crowd.

'Ben, wait!'

Either he didn't hear or he pretended not to. Ellie stood frozen for a moment until Megan came looking for her, and she barely had enough time to finish her drink before Megan dragged her onto the floor and into the thumping, gyrating melee. She stuck a grin on her face and pretended to be having a good time, furiously trying to get a grip on herself.

What had that been all about? One minute she'd been enjoying Ben's attention and feeling close to him as they stood together by the bar, the next, he had gone off in a huff – and somewhere in between, there lay a whole load of smart words and comments that had become confusing to say the least. She couldn't bear to think that she had hurt Ben in some way. The Saturday that had started out so full of expectation had turned sour. She was sorely tempted to go back to the bar and order fresh drinks, but she knew she'd already had more than enough. Too many to face getting into a cab by herself, which meant she had to hang on until Megan was ready to leave – after all, there was safety in numbers – yet not enough, never enough, to camouflage the sinking feeling in her heart.

She rose early the following morning even though it was Sunday, because she was too agitated to stay in bed. She'd come to New York to get away from her heartbreak, to sort herself out, yet here she was causing even more problems for herself. As she was sipping her orange juice, something Miranda had said came back to her – about being with yourself wherever you went. She wondered what had happened to make her sister file away that little bit of wisdom. She showered and dressed and it was only when she realised she had put on her tracksuit that she knew where she had intended going all along.

The park was busy, and she automatically retraced the steps she'd taken the previous Wednesday, looking for the calm she needed to soothe the dark, rough edges of her heart. What was she doing here, really? How was time in New York going to change her direction in life or make her whole again? Would Ellie Morgan behave like a child the next time she came up against a personal challenge?

Down by the meadow, in through the woods, along by the serenity of the pool, dappled in morning sunlight, until she was halted by the sight of a familiar figure coming towards her from the opposite direction. Her heart leapt into her throat.

'Thought you'd be sleeping off your hangover,' Ben growled when they drew level.

'I beg your pardon, I don't have a hangover,' she said haughtily, looking into the space over his shoulder.

'Pity. I was hoping you were half-cut when you shot me down last night.'

'I shot *you* down? That's hilarious, that is.'

'What about your wisecrack about the strings on my bow? What kind of a sex maniac do you think I am?'

'I never mentioned sex,' she said, amazed she managed to sound cool when her heart was thumping at the mere mention of the word. 'But aren't there other women in your life?'

'What women?'

'Well, er, Laura, for one? You seemed so concerned about the well-being of her apartment that you must care very strongly for her personal well-being. And what about Susan?'

She could have kicked herself when she saw the wide grin spreading across his face.

'So that's what this is all about. You're jealous!'

'I am not.' She was far too old to be jealous. That went with being sixteen. Didn't it?

'Yes, you are!' He gave a rich, contagious laugh. 'Laura and I are good friends. Nothing more. And Susan? She's a nurse in Mount Sinai who works with Tina and happens to be my second cousin.'

Ellie felt as though she was going to cry.

'Hey, I don't mean to be laughing. I like this side of you,' he said soberly. 'I like the idea that you might be—'

He didn't finish his sentence. She saw him looking at her mouth.

'This is what I should have done last night,' he said. And there, on the pathway where the light was softly diffused by the overhead trees, he pulled her into his arms and kissed her.

It was a proper kiss. Not just a butterfly touch. It was soft, yet skilful, deep and soul searching. It reached into her so that something sang in her heart and she responded as fully as she could. After a long time, he drew away and they stood staring at each other, Ellie's breath straining in her chest, her head whirling, her lips tingling and wanting more.

'Come on,' he said, catching her hand, 'I'll buy you breakfast.' He held up their joined hands. 'I'm just making sure you're safe crossing the road,' he said.

'That's okay.' It was a friendly gesture that made her feel warm and sheltered. She might be Ellie Morgan, ambitious fashion supremo, but not too sophisticated to hold hands crossing the road, and she liked it. A lot.

She hardly remembered what they chatted about over breakfast of omelettes, fruit juice and coffee. It was one of the best meals she'd ever shared with a man, but mostly it was a blur as they chatted and laughed, on account of the hot undercurrent pulsing between them. Afterwards, he asked her if she was in a hurry home.

'Not particularly, why?'

'I thought it might be fun to take off for the day and do a few sightseeing things together.'

'Yeah ... good.'

They spent the day together, like a couple of kids let loose in New York for the first time. Ellie had seen most of the sights already, but today everything was coloured with the magic of sharing it with Ben. Never mind the excitement swirling in her tummy. He made her pulse run a little faster every time he looked at her, and his kiss had left her wanting much more and wondering what it would be like to sleep with him ... wanting to sleep with him. They caught the subway down to Battery Park and strolled on down to catch the Staten Island ferry, scrambling on board before hordes of tourists arrived and the queues were intolerably long. She let the breeze tumble through her hair, watching the glint of choppy grey waves and feeling the shift of the boat as she stood by the rails with Ben beside her. A warm glow spread out inside as she caught his eye and they smiled in silent conspiracy at some of the more outlandish comments of the other sightseers as the Statue of Liberty came into view. Later they came back up to Greenwich Village and had lunch in a quirky little café, the kind she'd never have found by herself. Then it was on up to the Empire State Building where they picked out landmarks in the blue grey distance and Ben took photos of her on his mobile. And some time after, they stepped into the reverent solemnity of St Patrick's Cathedral, and even though she wasn't particularly religious, Ellie lit some candles, feeling humble as she sensed the echo of the many millions of heartfelt prayers that had whispered around the beautiful cathedral over the years.

And her prayer, if she was to ask one?

A few months ago, she would have looked for success and recognition. Today, she wanted love and affection, the kind that would touch the empty spaces inside her.

'So how are you feeling now?' Ben asked, as they strolled along Fifth Avenue in the late-afternoon sunshine.

She looked back at the striking, gothic facade of St Patrick's, thinking that everything seemed to point heavenwards into the blue infinity. 'Calmer,' she said automatically, realising immediately it was a mistake when he looked at her thoughtfully.

Nervous, excited, wondering what might happen next – she should have said, knowing what she wanted to happen next.

'How about we go for a drink before we go back home?' he said.

'Good idea.' She wanted more of this magical day. She wanted it to go on and on.

They went back to the wine bar they'd been to the other night and this time Ellie watched Ben's face as he talked of his childhood growing up in Leitrim, and the numerous wild escapades he'd enjoyed. He sounded as though he'd had the total freedom of the countryside along with his brother and three sisters, something Ellie found herself envying.

'I'd nothing like that,' she admitted. 'We had fun growing up all right, and family holidays in Ireland and abroad, but far less freedom than you had. Our lives were lived under the spotlight because of our mother, even though the media wasn't half as invasive as it is nowadays. We had to behave like little ladies. And then, the year after my father died, my mother went and lost the plot completely.' She paused, not wanting to remember.

'In what way? Ellie, you can't leave me hanging here . . . '

Ellie laughed hollowly. 'It's common knowledge, but it mightn't have crossed your radar. She had an affair with a rock musician – Zach Anderson – he's long dead now. There was some fuss recently with his twentieth anniversary.'

'Wasn't he the guy who went into that lake in Canada? The rock ballad . . . "Forever something".'

'That's him. My mother had a brief relationship with him a couple of years before he died. It didn't go down too well with me. And it resulted in my half-sister, Lucy.'

'Yeah, I see,' his eyes roved slowly around her face, with a mixture of empathy and understanding. 'That must have been a bit rough.' He gave her a half-smile. 'Still, the upside is you have another sister.'

Ellie shook her head. 'Yes, but unfortunately Lucy and I have never been all that close and I have to come clean and say much of that was my fault. We clashed sometimes and all that started with me.'

He looked taken aback at her confession and Ellie realised it was the first time she'd actually said this aloud to anyone. Nonetheless, she sensed he wouldn't stand in judgement of her, or make little of it, as Johnny might have. Easygoing Johnny would have laughed it off under the general heading of sibling rivalry, telling Ellie to get a life, heedless to how much the soul-baring admission would have cost her.

'*Your* fault?' Ben said, looking at her with concern.

She sighed, realising there was no fudging this issue. 'Sometimes, I was a little awkward around Lucy. And I didn't have much patience with her childish dramatics as I had my nose to the grindstone establishing my career, but I think I could have spared her a little more time and consideration. I kind of kept a distance from her ... but before you break out the violins, Lucy doesn't deserve that much sympathy because she was the reason for my break-up with Johnny.'

'Uh-huh?' He waited, expecting her to elaborate.

She waited for a moment, looking down at her hands, reluctant to voice the words, knowing it would change things between them. He would know, exactly, the humiliating way she'd been made a fool of. He might feel sorry for her, or look at her with pity, and that she couldn't stand. She took a deep breath, forced herself to look him in the eye and went on, 'Yeah, I found them in bed together. My bed. My sister and my – so-called – loving boyfriend.'

'Jesus, Ellie, really? That's a load of horseshit.' He whistled.

'Isn't it just.'

She liked the look in his hazel eyes. It wasn't pity or embarrassment, thankfully. Instead, his eyes were full of respectful concern, and it melted around her like a soothing balm.

'So that's why you were ...' he hesitated.

'Acting like a crazy lady from time to time?' she supplied quickly.

'No worries. You were allowed to go off the rails a little,' he smiled.

'I came to New York to get over it,' she half-laughed. 'But there's no such thing, is there? You can't switch off your emotions like a tap. Another thing,' she said, a little desperately, hoping he would understand, 'I don't feel I can work anymore. When I try to lift a pencil, it's as though everything inside me has dried up. I've no ideas, no passion.'

'Ellie, that's bound to have happened,' Ben said reassuringly. 'You've had a shock to the system. You need time to lick your wounds. Eventually, you'll bounce back. I know you will. Are you still in love with, um, Johnny?'

'The truth?'

He nodded.

She paused as she gathered her thoughts. 'I don't think I was ever truly in love with him. I was in love with the idea of being with him, of having fun, laughing a lot, skimming the glitzy surface of the best that the Dublin celeb scene had to offer. Parties, balls, whatever. But love as in happy ever after? No.' She stared into space, not seeing the bar around her. Seeing, instead, Johnny's face when she'd laughed about marriage, covering her slivers of uneasiness with banter, refusing to take him seriously so as not to change the status quo. 'You see, he asked me to marry him and I couldn't give him an answer. I kept stringing him along, wishing we could just stay the way we were. So what does that say about us?'

'You didn't want to marry him,' Ben said immediately.

'No, I didn't. From a male point of view, would that hit at your ego?'

'I can't comment on what might have gone wrong in your relationship. Only you and Johnny can answer that question. However, speaking as an objective third party, I guess nobody likes rejection of any kind. It can be hard to take.'

'So, you see, Johnny was pissed off with me and so was Lucy in her own way. And they picked the best form of revenge or payback, whatever you like.' She gulped, her mind sliding away

306

from the vision of them lying together on the tangled sheets of her bed. She would have to get rid of that bed, when – no, *if* – she ever went back home.

'A particularly horrible form of revenge, all the same,' Ben said, catching her hand and giving it a squeeze. She thought his eyes were suddenly sensual as they slowly scanned her face and lingered on her mouth. 'Wish I could make you feel better.'

'I don't know how we got talking about all that,' she said, shivering a little at the unexpected sparks that were fizzing inside her. 'I've been trying to parcel it away and get on with things. And now, it's been a great day, I enjoyed it, but I think we'd better get on home,' she suggested lightly, conscious that she'd sounded a little dismissive, but, all of a sudden she was terribly nervous of the effect he was having on her, as though every single cell in her body was vibrating with some kind of achy need that only he could fill.

What was happening to her?

He gave her a smile tinged with regret as he let go of her hand and they finished their drinks, before they strolled home together through the mellow night, Ben with his hands firmly in the pockets of his jeans. Ellie was too focused on holding herself together to try to bridge the sudden coolness between them. Then of all nights, he insisted on getting into the cramped lift with her, and it meant she had to hold her act together in the narrow space as they lurched to the fourth floor.

'So now you know why I came running away to New York with my tail between my legs,' she attempted a joke as they stepped out of the lift and she rummaged for her key.

'I think you've been very brave.'

'Brave?' she opened the door and looked back at him. 'I'd no choice. When I arrived in New York all I wanted to do was cower down under the duvet, sleep forever and blank out the whole goddamn world, but guess what,' she grinned at him, 'some bolshie guy from Leitrim started knocking on my door and bugged me to get out and about and start living again.'

'Was that good or bad?' he asked, leaning against the door jamb, watching her. His focused concentration alarmed her. It was there again – that look in his eye. As though he saw himself slow-kissing every inch of her skin. God, she couldn't bear much more.

'It was good, of course,' she said, struggling to keep an ordinary smile on her trembling mouth.

'Glad to help.' He began to move away, and her heart plunged with disappointment. Then, as though he sensed it, he changed his mind and turned back to her.

'You're special, Ellie,' he said, in a soft voice. 'There's something very lovely about you. If you weren't pining for Johnny, I'd be tempted—' he paused.

'What? What would you be tempted to do?' She could hardly get the words out, her throat was so full. And there was only one place they were leading. Right then, she could think of nothing better than to lie in Ben's arms and give in to the hot ache of desire streaming through her body.

'Do you really want to know?' he asked, looking at her mouth.

She nodded, because speech was so difficult.

He leaned in close and pushed back her hair with gentle fingers, his touch sending spirals of pleasure around her body. Then he murmured in her ear, 'I'd be tempted to do what any hot-blooded Leitrim man would do if they had a beautiful woman like you in front of them. I'd whisk you off to a cabin in the woods and take you to bed.'

Something flashed through her, almost like a pain. 'Does it have to be a cabin in the woods?' she heard herself whisper. 'How about a big comfy bed in an Upper West brownstone?'

His hazel eyes glittered with desire as he looked at her. 'Sounds wonderful, Ellie, but are you sure?'

She put her hand on his face, feeling the slight roughness across his chin, and sudden nerves coupled with sensual excitement shivered violently inside her. 'I can't think of anything I'd like more,' she said, running her index finger across his mouth.

It was like putting a spark to dry tinder.

Ben stepped into the apartment and locked the door. Then, they were in each other's arms. He splayed his fingers in her hair and pressed tender kisses all around her face before he finally locked on to her mouth. She closed her eyes and strained towards him, kissing him back as a flame of desire shot through her.

She couldn't recall the last time she'd felt like this. If ever.

In one easy movement, Ben took off his sports top, flinging it to the floor. He pulled her against his hard chest, deepening the kiss and dipping his hand up the back of her shirt to release the catch of her bra. She was floating somewhere hot and exciting away from reality, as he peeled off her shirt, and her bra, and Ben was staring at her breasts. He led her through the living room and into the bedroom. He pulled away for a minute and as if in a heat haze, she watched him open the buckle of his belt and slide it through the loops of his jeans. Her heart jolted as he looked at her with a quirky yet intimate smile while he opened the catch, pulled down the zip and kicked his jeans away and just as easily hooked his fingers under the waist band of his boxers, and then they too were gone, flung in a heap beside his jeans. Something like liquid fire flooded through her when she looked at his physical beauty; the taut sweep of his shoulders, his powerful rib cage and, straining rigidly between strong thighs, his large erection.

Her throat almost closed over and something molten pooled

inside her groin. She couldn't wait to feel him deep inside her. This was what she'd been looking for – this mind-blowing desire and sense of wild abandon. An urgent passion she'd always known existed. It was here, in this room, with this man. Ben reached for the catch of her trousers and she put her hands on his shoulders to balance herself as she hastily stepped out of them. He took her hands and held her at arm's length, and standing in her lace panties, she watched his eyes spark as he drank her in. Then he pushed her across the bed and she felt his fingers on her skin and then his mouth, as he began to kiss her all over, fever-ishly and hungrily, as though he couldn't get enough of her.

The hot core of her, behind a small triangle of lace, pained for his touch and she opened her legs. He lifted her knee and ran his mouth up along her soft, inner thigh and she gave a low moan when he put his hand on her crotch and slipped his fingers under the lace.

'You're gorgeous, Ellie, absolutely beautiful,' he murmured, his fingers circling her sensitive, aching bud.

Then, suddenly, it was over. One minute, she was lost in the bliss of the moment, every nerve ending on fire as she antici-pated the ultimate pleasure he would give her, the next her heart was ricocheting painfully in her chest and she was pushing him away. 'No, Ben, no.'

He sprang off the bed. The electric passion that had swelled between them vanished in an instant, leaving a painful vacuum.

'I can't,' she said, her voice a whimper. Her fingers were like jelly as she scrabbled for the duvet, bundling it around her. She sat up in bed and buried her head in her hands. 'I'm sorry, I can't,' she said through her fingers. She made herself look at him, too shocked to cry. 'It's just . . . ' her husky voice trailed away as words failed her.

Ben's face was dark with embarrassment. He picked up his

boxers and stepped into them. Then he pulled on his jeans. 'It's okay, Ellie,' he said. 'Probably too soon for you.'

'Too soon,' she heard the whispery echo of her voice, wondering how that could explain the depth of the raw vulnerability that she was feeling right then.

He was very kind. He came over to the bed and gently kissed the top of her head. 'It seemed like a good idea, but you're not ready yet. Hey,' he went on, ruffling her hair as he would a child's, 'it's fine, I understand. Don't get all in a heap over this. I still think you're beautiful. And special.'

'Ben – look—' she grappled futilely for words.

'It's okay. No worries. Take care of yourself. Get an early night and I'll see you tomorrow outside Central Park, as usual. Okay? I'm leaving now, so make sure you lock the door after me.'

He went quietly, and she remained sitting on top of the bed with the duvet bunched around her as she tried to make sense of what had happened and the moment she'd called a halt. What demon inside her had made her push Ben away? Hardly the memory of Johnny, for anything she'd ever experienced with him had been nothing but a pale shadow of the frenzied excitement that Ben had whipped up. Johnny had never touched her soul in the way Ben did.

And she'd never before felt so ready to abandon all control and lose herself completely, yet she'd stopped on the brink. What had held her back? Once again, she dropped her head into her hands. She thought she'd reached rock bottom before. She thought every layer of Ellie Morgan had been stripped back to raw bone, but those moments had never felt as shattering as this.

It was a long time before she rose to her feet, slid off the bed and padded across to lock the door.

Chapter 35

*I*n the end, it was very easy, and more than anything it told
Miranda just how far she had come that she felt able to con-
fide in Christian.

It didn't happen in one of those intimate, heart-to-heart
moments, before, during or after bed. Neither had she prepared
any words in advance, or was stylishly dressed to give herself a
confident edge, let alone had the benefit of any make-up cam-
ouflaging her face. She'd taken a day's leave from work and was
spending it in her apartment catching up on some spring cleaning and freshening up her small kitchen. Then coming up to
lunch-time, her door bell had chimed unexpectedly.

She had been reluctant to answer it until her mobile rang and
Christian's name flashed across her screen.

'I'm outside. Aren't you going to let me in?'

'Christian! God – I wasn't expecting you until this evening.'
She looked frantically around her living area. She'd just emptied
everything out of the kitchen cupboards, and the table and chairs
were covered with precariously balanced crockery and food

stuffs. Then she looked at herself. She was wearing an old pair of jeans that had somehow escaped her wardrobe cull, her hair was clipped back and covered with a conditioning masque, and her face was bare of make-up. Great.

'Hey, who are you hiding in there?' he called through the door.

There was nothing for it but to let him in.

He stepped into her living area, brandishing a bulging supermarket bag and wearing a beautiful suit that was totally at odds with her rather tatty appearance. 'I missed you in the office today and I thought we might share some lunch?'

'We could, but there's nowhere to sit,' she grinned, a mixture of dismay and exhilaration washing over her. Dismay that he had caught her on the hop, and exhilaration at the fact that she was allowing herself to surrender to the moment, and finding it amusing. Also because he didn't look the least bit startled by her appearance.

'You've a smudge of dust on your nose,' he smiled. His gaze roved across her face. 'Is this what you look like when you're busy with women's work?'

She knew by the devilish gleam in his eye that he was blatantly teasing her. 'Yes, and you can take it or leave it,' she said with a new bravado.

'I'd very much like to take it,' he said. 'I can't believe how honest-to-God cute you look.'

'Cute?' She was bemused. 'I don't think I've ever been called that before.'

'Haven't you?' He strode across to the sofa and pulled over a low table. He proceeded to empty the grocery bag and take out chicken bagels, strawberries and fruit juice, looking as though he was quite at home setting up lunch on her low coffee table in his good suit, but she knew by the way he kept glancing at her that he was keenly waiting for her reply. Christian had already told her that he'd had several girlfriends, some of whom had been good friends, but none of whom had intrigued him like Miranda. It was the first time that any hint of Miranda's previous men had arisen between them.

'I've been called lots of things,' she said, eerily calm as she watched him, 'but never cute.' She'd already thrown caution to the wind in allowing him to see her with all her defences down, so to speak. It was a small step then to let herself fall through her usual safety net. She heard herself say, 'That word was always reserved for my youngest sister.'

'Lucy?' He looked sideways at her in the act of grabbing some plates off one of the kitchen chairs.

'Yes, Lucy.'

'So if Lucy was the cute one, you must have been the beautiful sister,' Christian said. And she knew him well enough by now to spot that he was falsely nonchalant as he went across to take some cutlery off the table. She was temporarily amused that he might be imagining a long list of lovers admiring her beautiful body.

'No.' She was falling further, down to the depths. 'Beautiful was always reserved for my older sister, Ellie.' She knew the words, delivered in a light, casual voice, held a wealth of meaning. She was amazed at how easy it was to express what had defined her life in Dublin, and to abandon herself to whatever he might think.

He didn't look at her. He was silent for a few moments as he arranged the cutlery and fetched two glasses. Then he sat on the sofa and patted the space beside him. And, finally, he looked at her.

'So, if Lucy was cute, and Ellie beautiful, what was Miranda?' he asked, his voice soft, his eyes warm with sudden understanding.

'Miranda was the brainy one, caught between two spirited sisters,' she said, laughing as if it didn't matter.

'Why don't you tell me about it?'

She sat down beside him, in her gungy hair and shabby jeans, and she picked on a chicken bagel and drank some juice. He listened as she spoke, not self-pityingly or reproachfully, but choosing her words with care as she described what it had been like to shadow Ellie's glittering and outgoing personality, to keep a sort of peace between her and her mother, and then between Ellie and Lucy.

'I never got much of a look in,' she said. 'I was too quiet, I suppose, for my own good. I felt I couldn't compete with Ellie's nature and beauty, so I didn't even try.'

Christian shook his head. 'Miranda, darling, I'm glad you're the way you are, warm and loving, kind and caring. We get tired of the boisterous, "me me" personalities.'

'But, see, I understand where Ellie comes from, it's not that she's selfish and doesn't care, and some of the time I think her confidence is put on, for she never got over our mum having a relationship – an affair – very soon after our father had died, and that has shaped her into the person she is.'

'There you go again, it's you I want to talk about. Your life, your childhood. I'm not interested in your sisters.'

'You might be interested in Ellie, if you saw her.'

Her ultimate fear. Now there was nowhere for her to run or hide.

He gave her a look that went straight to her heart. Then he took her hand. 'And what makes you think that?'

She was silent.

'Miranda? Has it happened before? Your boyfriends being interested in Ellie?' His blue eyes were softly concerned.

She looked away. 'Yes. Lots of times. Ellie doesn't know. I always told myself they weren't really meant for me.'

'You were right and I'm glad that happened.'

Startled, she said, 'You're *glad*?'

'Yes, because it means you're now in Hong Kong with me instead of – God forbid – back home with one or other of those very short-sighted, incredibly stupid men.'

'Do you mean that?'

He pulled her close. 'Do I heck? Miranda, don't you realise how absolutely perfect you are? How lovely you look? You need a lesson in love – lots of lessons, I think.'

A lesson in love.

Christian said he didn't care if his good suit got stained because her hair was matted with deep conditioning gunge, or if he was late back to the office after lunch.

Or, he said an hour later as he kissed her face, if he never went back that afternoon.

'Hey, Lucy, Rebecca's been looking for you. Didn't you get her call?'

Lucy adjusted her bag and clamped her mobile closer to her ear as she darted through the crowds of shoppers strolling down Oxford Street in the sunny morning. It had been pure luck that she'd heard the ringtone in the first place, as it was burrowed in the depths of her leather tote bag and the street was noisy with a slow-moving line of red buses.

'Hi Sasha, I can just about hear you, what's up?'

'Rebecca's looking for you. All morning. Get your ass over to the office pronto. She sounds upset. You've been warned.'

'Thanks, Sasha.'

Lucy ended the call and saw that she had three missed calls. She checked her message minder and right enough, Rebecca wanted to see her in her office. As soon as possible. Like, now.

Shite. Lucy's brain raced. What had she done wrong? She

stared at her reflection in Selfridge's window, feeling horribly gloomy despite the sunny morning. She looked okay in her navy D&G jeans, white top and short trench jacket. Her hair was loosely held back in a Swarovski hair slide. Standard dress down for a model going shopping on a day off. She felt she'd pass muster with Rebecca, but that all depended on what she'd done wrong, of course. She nipped into the large department store and circled the cosmetic counters, helping herself to a generous spray of Allure, and lightly touching up her face with samples of foundation, mascara and lipstick, because naturally enough, she mocked herself, this morning of all mornings she'd left her cosmetic bag at home.

Outside, the London city traffic was still bedlam, so instead of getting a cab, she hurried to the nearest tube station, rushing down to the Victoria line. As the tube rattled through the underground, she furiously cast her mind over the previous week, trying to pinpoint what she could have done that might have attracted Rebecca's displeasure.

Right enough, she'd been snapped coming out of a Notting Hill club at three in the morning and despite her best intentions she'd unwittingly given the camera an eyeful of her boobs as she stepped into a taxi when the tape holding her skinny vest top in place had let her down. Still, there had just been a tiny crescent of nipple on show. You'd think she'd deliberately flashed her boobs to judge by the caption.

Then, two days later, she'd been caught coming out of a sex shop in Soho. She didn't realise the photo had been taken until she saw it tagged on Facebook. Now, that she could have done without. She'd only gone in for the laugh with Sasha and she hadn't even bought anything, but according to the commentary she'd emerged with several bulging bags and was clearly all set to make a night of it. To her fury, the photo had been cropped so that she just appeared from the waist up, and from the angle it was taken, the name of the shop ran around her head like a halo. Naturally, there had been no such photo of Sasha, who'd come out of the shop directly behind her. Lucy had been beside herself with rage, and even more annoyed that she'd tried to get hold of Ian several times, but he seemed to have disappeared off the radar.

Where was he when she needed him? Despite leaving several messages on his phone he hadn't got back to her. She searched through her bags for his business card, the one he'd given her when she was first introduced to him – or had he actually given it to her? She was confused. She could always google him, but still . . . for someone who'd been mad keen on getting some PR experience, he was losing a valuable opportunity and she was losing opportunities to limit the damage.

Her heart was thumping as she breezed by the reception desk and the booker's office and went on up to Rebecca's office. The door was already open.

'Lucy. Come in,' she said straightaway, 'And close the door please.'

Close the door. Double trouble. Rebecca's office often resembled a railway station with bookers and models constantly coming and going. The door was seldom closed. Lucy's eyes were riveted to Rebecca's glass table, where her portfolio was open. Her insides churned.

Rebecca sat with her elbows on the table and rested her chin in her hands. 'I'm in a bit of a dilemma, Lucy. Sit down, for God's sake,' she added impatiently, when Lucy continued to stand there like a frightened rabbit.

Lucy sat on the edge of a chair, prepared to march out of the room as soon as Rebecca uttered the words that would terminate her contract.

But she didn't.

'It's about the Venetia campaign. As you know, you were on the shortlist, but you didn't make the final cut. Sasha, Beatrice and Carla were chosen. But now I have a problem with one of the models . . . ' she paused, looking thoughtfully at Lucy.

Hope soared through Lucy, making her dizzy.

'It turns out that Carla won't be available after all.' Rebecca pursed her lips.

Lucy dug her nails into the palm of her hand, not caring that she broke off two false nails. Rebecca's magic words could change everything.

'The company have decided that you fit the bill, Lucy. But—'

'But what?' Her voice came out like a squeak.

'There are some reservations. *I* have reservations. You have the looks, there's no doubt about that, but my problem lies with your attitude. We've had this conversation already and I haven't seen any improvement. Still, the Venetia guys have decided that you're perfect for the job, and are willing to give you a chance. The contract is generous, apart from giving you positive and valuable exposure. So,' she looked Lucy straight in the eye with her laser stare, 'the contract is yours. Provided, of course, you manage to stay out of any kind of trouble for the next few weeks. Shooting starts at the end of the month. In Switzerland. Before then, there will be lots of meetings and fittings, and mock-ups that you'll have to attend. Starting with a team briefing on Tuesday afternoon. You must keep a low profile during this time. No bad press whatsoever or the contract is shredded. Do you read me?'

'I do, oh, I do. I'll be on my best behaviour. I didn't really buy up that sex shop—'

Rebecca put up her hand. 'Please. I don't need to know. You can be thankful that your name came up for consideration before that ridiculous incident and I doubt if even Facebook has managed to penetrate their ivory tower. But from now on ... I suppose you could say this is your last chance, Lucy. For your own sake, don't mess it up. If you do, it'll be the end of your career with us.'

'I won't, promise. Cross my heart.'

Rebecca smiled. She passed a document across the table. 'Now go home and read this. Make sure you're happy with it before you sign.'

'Can I not just sign it now?'

'No way. At least be seen to examine it. You have to know exactly what you're signing up for. I'm happy with it anyway. I think you should be too.'

Lucy paused at the doorway. 'What happened with Carla? Or can't you say?'

'I guess you'll all know soon enough. She's pregnant.'

'*Pregnant*?'

'It happens,' Rebecca said. 'I'm putting my trust in you, Lucy. Make sure I don't come to regret it.'

'You won't, I promise. This is a fantastic opportunity for me.'

Outside, it was still a sunny London morning, but now the sunshine was dazzling and uplifting, and glinting all around her like a golden aura. Funny how life could change in the space of a few minutes. Her hands shook on her mobile as she put a call through to Sasha. And even though she knew she looked silly, dancing around the street like crazy as she broke the news to her friend in between her giggles and laughter, she didn't care.

More than ever, she needed to talk to Ian, to make sure she got through the next few weeks in one piece.

That evening she googled him, trying to remember the name of his new firm. There were lots of entries for an Ian Douglas, but none of them matched his details. She tried his mobile again, but just got a message to say it was switched off. Later she went for a celebratory drink with Sasha. They'd agreed it would strictly be a couple of cocktails and no mad session. She went to the same pub where she'd first met Ian, the pub he'd called his local, but there was no sign of him. So for someone who had been so enthusiastic about working for her and getting his foot in the door, it was all very strange. If anything stupid had happened to him, like an accident, she would surely have found a news item during her internet search. Or would she?

Funny all the same. It was as though he had simply vanished without a trace.

Chapter 36

As the last notes of Andrea Bocelli's 'Canto Della Terra' powered to a finale, Vivienne sighed and roused herself out of her trance. She pulled off her silk-covered eye mask, raised a wet slicked arm out of the depths of the lavender-scented water in her claw-footed bath, and reaching out to the pile of soft, thick towels arranged on the heated rail, she dried her hands. Then she carefully removed her ear plugs and switched off the iPod that was sitting on a rack across the bath. She picked up a crystal glass from the rack and drained the end of the chardonnay. She was reluctant to lever herself out of the warm embrace of the water, but neither could she lie there all evening and watch her skin turn to the texture of a prune.

Relaxing in the bath, swaddled by the silky water and listening to the rich warm tones of one of her favourite singers, she had lost herself in a dreamlike trance. She thought she'd heard the doorbell at one point but it was so far in the distance that it had been easy to ignore it. A long soak in the bath was a great way to unwind, and had been recommended by her cardiologist.

He'd ordered this along with the usual boring reminders of regular walks, a good diet and plenty of sleep. She found his bath suggestion the best recommendation to follow because her bathroom was somewhere rather special. Several years ago, she'd knocked the wall between the bathroom and a fifth, adjoining bedroom to give a much more spacious area for her deep, free-standing bath, vanity basins, heated rails and linen cupboard.

This evening, however, she didn't feel as relaxed as she would have liked. The music had been beautiful, but it had made her feel hauntingly sad at the transience of it all. Life, love, sex, motherhood – nothing ever stayed the same. Her recent brush with mortality had brought that home to her with a vengeful force. As well as that, sitting in the waiting room of a cardiologist's office was one sure-fire way of seeing what was important and what was insignificant.

And there was still so much to be reconciled in her life that it wasn't funny. So much to sort out with Ellie and Lucy.

They had *all* been very quiet over the past few weeks. *Too* quiet. Somehow or other, chatty phone calls had dwindled to bland texts. She brushed aside the thought that they were avoiding her. She smiled to herself at including Miranda along with Ellie and Lucy. It was as if her usually biddable middle daughter had decided to behave like a recalcitrant child and see how long she could put off talking to Vivienne before she was pulled up by her mother. She'd expected Miranda to get back to her straight away after she had phoned Ellie, to tell her how her sister had reacted to the news about Johnny, but there had been silence from Hong Kong, which was unusual for Miranda. God knows what Ellie had said to her on hearing about the gossipy article.

Ellie. Somebody else who was ignoring her calls. She guessed her eldest daughter was still fuming over the news, but she felt hurt that she hadn't bothered to talk to her about it. It made her feel that Ellie didn't want her in her life. In a way, though, that had always been the case, ever since she had invited Zach into her life. The rift it had caused between her and Ellie ran like an invisible crack through their lives and had never been resolved, something that made Vivienne sad. Sometimes she felt she was still paying the price and would do so until the day she died.

And as for Lucy ... she was still kicking up a storm in London. Vivienne made it her business to keep up with everything, and she was amazed Lucy was still in a job with such a prestigious modelling firm considering the way she generated plenty of trashy fodder for the gossip columns, both online and tabloid. Although maybe all that free publicity was to her advantage.

Despite everything Vivienne had done to give her some stability, Lucy had always been a rebel soul and fought with life, questioned it, argued with it, rather than learning to go with the flow and live it on its own terms. Vivienne sometimes admired her feistiness but often wondered if her youngest, attention-seeking daughter would ever be truly happy. Although happiness was elusive, wasn't it? Peace of mind and contentment was the ultimate holy grail. But try telling that to a fiery, headstrong Lucy. She had too much of her father in her, and also something of her mother in the way she thumbed her nose at the conventional masses.

Just as well her own life was busy, Vivienne decided, as she eventually climbed out of the water, pulled the plug, and wrapped herself in a warmed bath sheet. She was just starting rehearsals for *Big Maggie*, which gave her plenty to keep her occupied. She dried herself, snuggled into a luxury terry robe and slid her feet into her furry mules. She picked up her glass and the bottle of chardonnay, deciding to finish it off down in the living room.

She came out onto the landing and paused. Shafts of late evening sunshine streamed out through open doors from the bedrooms with west-facing windows. Suddenly, the stairwell and the empty rooms were full of whispers. As though it was running in a parallel reality, she saw Ellie and Miranda as carefree children bobbing up and down the stairs, and heard the excitement in their raised voices.

Look, Santa Claus has come . . .

Is it really my birthday today? Did I turn into eight when I was asleep?

Hey, Mummy, how many dolls can I bring on holidays? Ellie says there's only enough room for one.

Then she saw Edward smiling at her as he caught her hand and led the way up the stairs to their bedroom, and she felt a lump in her throat.

That was before everything had gone wrong.

She *had* spent too long in the bath, Vivienne thought crossly. And she shouldn't have been listening to such heart-tugging music. It was making her far too nostalgic, something she couldn't afford to wallow in.

Downstairs, she went on through to the living room beside the kitchen at the back of the house, poured more chardonnay and picked up her script.

She knew all her lines by now and was almost word perfect. It would be a demanding role with all its conflicts and undercurrents, and probably her finest hour on a Dublin stage, but it didn't seem like any of her daughters would be around for her opening night and that made her feel lonely. Other years, the three of them would have been there for her, beautifully turned out and rooting for her, understanding the nerves that churned in her stomach until the first act was well under way, then, afterwards, plying her with champagne and smiling for the press photographers. Together, they were all so striking and beautiful that they always made the diary pages.

Vivienne didn't like the niggly feeling that they might be deliberately ignoring her. Though, she reasoned, they were as busy as she was, even more so, especially Miranda, finding her feet in a completely different city and getting to grips with a new job. It was half past seven in the evening now, too late for calling Hong Kong, she guessed, but fine for London and New York.

Lucy cursed when she picked up her mobile and heard her mother's voice at the other end. She'd been on Twitter, unable to stop herself broadcasting the triumphant news of her contract for Venetia, and her friends in both London and Dublin had been so busy calling her that she'd snatched up her mobile and answered it without checking the display, assuming it was another of her mates. She cursed silently a second time, realising that Vivienne had probably overheard her first expletive.

'Hi, stranger,' her mother said cheerily. 'Thought you had vanished off the face of the earth.'

'I texted you last week,' Lucy said, immediately on the defensive, her mind racing furiously. Her mother didn't sound as though she knew the gory truth about her and Johnny. Was it possible that Ellie hadn't told her? Oddly enough, that didn't make her feel any better.

'Yes, you did. And the week before. Actually, that's all I've had from you in while,' Vivienne said, betraying nothing with her bland tone. 'So it's nice to hear your voice. Can't remember the last time we talked.'

'I've been busy, you know? And,' Lucy swiftly decided it was safe to proceed, 'you'll hear soon enough, I have some great news. I'm about to sign the Venetia contract. It's very high profile, with print and television advertisements. We'll be shooting snow scenes up in the Swiss Alps.'

'But that's wonderful. Well done, darling.'

She definitely didn't know the part she'd played in Ellie's break-up. Somehow that put Lucy on edge, as though the words might spill out of their own accord. *By the way, I slept with Johnny and that's why Ellie has run off to New York. I thought Johnny liked me but he didn't waste any time finding someone else.* As she recalled this crucial fact, the humiliation of it all swept over her, brushing away for a moment her delight in the contract.

'Have you told Ellie and Miranda?'

'No, I just found out today.'

'I thought you'd be on to them straightaway, never mind me.'

'God, Mum, I need time to get used to it.'

'Still, it's great, Lucy, and I'll understand perfectly if you're not here for my opening night.'

'Flip, I forgot all about that. I doubt if I'll make it—'

'No worries,' Vivienne said cheerfully. 'Once you're happy, I'm happy.'

The usual mum-speak. She hated hearing this, Lucy decided. It was like some kind of passive blackmail, as though her mother's quotient of happiness depended on Lucy. It made her feel under a compliment and reinforced her guilt at not being around for her mum's opening night. Then again, if her mother knew what Lucy had done, she wouldn't want her around at all. She certainly wouldn't be happy. She had the childish urge to tell her, to shock her out of her calm contentment, to lash out at her in some way.

And then see if it was possible for her to be absolved.

'Do you really mean that?'

'Yes, of course, why?'

'Well then, there are some things I'm not happy about,' Lucy said.

'What is it, Lucy?' Her mother's voice was carefully patient, as though she'd heard it all before. At the last minute Lucy changed her mind about confessing about Johnny and blurted out the deep-down questions that had always been swirling around in her dark consciousness, and a couple more that had bothered her since the night she'd talked to Ian.

'It's my dad,' she said. 'What would make me happy is to know exactly why he went off to Canada, whether or not his death was really an accident and if he ever made a will.' The words tumbled out of their own accord and she hardly knew where she'd found the strength to say them. 'And what about all those royalties that must have come from his chart hit? Like, did he bother to make any kind of provision for me? Or didn't he care?'

In other words, did I deserve his love? For how can I be a person in my own right if I didn't even deserve a father's love? She knew by the dead silence that her mother was completely taken aback. To her shame, Lucy felt a twist of gratification that her heart-wrenching questions had found a mark.

Then, eventually, her mother said in a very quiet voice, 'What brought this on?'

'Nothing. Everything.'

'Lucy, come on, it's ancient history and we've been over and over it hundreds of times already.'

'Maybe I'd like to go over it again.'

Vivienne sighed loudly. 'Your father went to Canada to work on new material, he kept meaning to come home, but somehow the months passed and he never found the time. And of course his death was an accident; after all, he had so much to live for. As for his estate ...' another silence, this time so profound that Lucy knew it was big, whatever it was. She heard her mother give a slight cough before she went on, 'There isn't loads of money, but his records did generate posthumous royalties, and there will be more with the re-release. I was going to tell you about this in another two or three years, when you had matured a little.'

Lucy gasped. 'What? Is this for real? Why the hell wasn't I told this before now? Jesus, Mum, this is mega. Fuck's sake! And you kept it from me?'

'Hang on, Lucy, there's not that much money. Remember this was twenty years ago. The red tape was all very messy after Zach died, and probate and taxes and lawyers' fees gobbled up a lot. Because you were just a baby, I acted as your guardian. I didn't want to tell you just yet for your own sake. Look, we really can't discuss this over the phone—'

'Why not? I have a right to know. How dare you keep this from me!'

'I didn't want to tell you about it just yet because I thought it was better for you to make your own way in the world, to see what it's like to work towards what you want rather than having it falling into your lap—'

'*You* thought? What gave you the right to think for me?'

'Come on, Lucy, you haven't exactly been the easiest. A lot of that was my fault because I spoiled you too much. This was something I decided to hold back for your own good, just for a couple of years. You regularly hit the headlines for all the wrong reasons. You drink too much and for all I know you take the odd recreational drug—'

'So the gloves are off. How dare you assume that about me!'

Her mother ignored this and ploughed on. 'Lucy, I'm only telling it like it is. Add the expectancy of coming into a sum of money into the mix and you have a recipe for disaster. I know I should have told you when you turned eighteen, but I did what I thought was for the best. Look, I know this has been a bit of a shock—'

'A *shock*? I can't believe what I'm hearing! This so totally stinks. And you've one helluva nerve—'

'Lucy, calm down. Most young women of your age would be delighted to know they had a financial cushion to help set them up. When your modelling career slows down and you're looking for another direction, it could give you a start, maybe go towards a home of your own.'

'Jesus, you're even telling me how to spend it. And assuming my modelling career will be over in a couple of years' time. Why wasn't I contacted by this lawyer – whoever he is – as soon as I turned eighteen?'

'He was a Canadian lawyer who looked after Zach's affairs, and he passed away several years ago. I have all the paperwork put away carefully. I was going to choose my moment to talk to you.'

'It's not about the money. You kept something from me, some important and legal acknowledgement from Zach himself, that I was his daughter. Even if it came second hand through a lawyer.'

There was a long silence. Eventually, Vivienne said in a shaky voice, 'Is that what this is all about? Acknowledgement?'

'Christ, I thought that was pretty obvious,' Lucy stormed. 'I've been looking for this all my life, even if Zach fecked off and didn't give a damn about me.'

'Lucy, I told you Zach didn't know I was expecting you when he left,' Vivienne gabbled. 'It's not that he didn't give a damn about you. Anyway, he left because of me.'

'*You*?' For a moment Lucy thought she'd misheard. 'But I thought he went to Canada to work on new material. I didn't know you'd *asked* him to leave. So that's what you've been hiding from me as well as everything else,' she said bitterly.

'Look, I'll have to see you, to talk to you—' Vivienne sounded rattled and Lucy pressed home her advantage.

'Talk? No way. So far, you've done a perfectly lousy job. I'll never, ever, forgive you for this.'

Lucy's hands were shaking as she ended the call and threw her mobile across the bed. The room whirled around her as she digested her mother's words. Her glittering, new contract was forgotten. How could her mother have kept something so important from her? Zach Anderson had provided for her, in some shape or form. It was the next best thing to the man himself acknowledging her existence.

And – oh, God – it was her mother who had asked him to leave. Her *mother*!

Confused, disorientated, feeling an ache in her heart that shocked her with its depth and intensity, she threw herself down onto her pillows and bawled her eyes out.

Vivienne sat for a long time with the phone gripped in her hand as the evening dimmed and shadows lengthened across the room. She saw the quarter full bottle of chardonnay sitting on the low table in front of her and wondered how it had got there. She picked it up and stumbled out to the kitchen, feeling she had aged about ten years since she had sat down.

The doorbell pealed, and she looked up the hallway, frowning at the interruption, eventually registering the sound. Slowly, she walked up the hall, as if on auto-pilot. Her fingers fumbled with the door handle and, after a minute, she freed the lock and pulled back the door.

There was a man standing on the steps outside.

'Vivienne?'

She didn't recognise the voice.

'What is it?' she asked irritably, belatedly realising that she was in her dressing gown and slippers. Knowing too she shouldn't have bothered answering, and – clever girl, Vivienne – she had totally forgotten to use her security chain, as Ellie had always advised her.

'I've disturbed you.'

'Yes, you have,' she said sharply. 'It had better be in a good cause.' Her hand fumbled with the light switch. She cursed the fact that she hadn't got one of those automatic sensor lights, something else Ellie had told her to get, particularly as she was living alone most of the time.

'I think it's an excellent cause.'

She found the switch and light sprang on in the hallway behind her and flooded out onto the steps. Rather tall and thin, he was young and well groomed, and he smiled at her as though he knew her.

'Do I know you?' she asked.

'You should,' he said, lifting an eyebrow.

She felt suddenly nervous as he continued to stare at her. Then he moved closer, up as far as the top step, under the light; she looked him in the eye and she felt she was looking at a ghost.

'What do you want?' Her voice was a whisper. Her heart thumped painfully. First Lucy asking after her father, and now his ghost at her door. All her sins were coming back to haunt her. All the lies and the deceit. And if anyone deserved retribution, she did.

He leaned in against the door jamb and murmured in a quiet voice, 'I was hoping you'd invite me in and tell me everything I need to know about Zach Anderson.'

'The hell I am,' Vivienne said enraged. 'If you don't leave immediately I'll call the police.'

'And why would you do that?' he smiled at her. 'Unless you have something to hide.'

She realised he was very good looking when he smiled, but somehow his friendliness was menacing. As she pushed at the door, she felt a tightening in her chest that spread out across her back and into her neck. God, no, not now. She tried to get a grip on the door knowing that Ellie would be furious when she found out how careless she'd been.

Ellie, oh, Ellie. These were her last thoughts as she sank to the ground before warm darkness overwhelmed her.

Chapter 37

*E*llie sat quietly on a bench outside the Rockefeller Center in the Monday evening sunshine. She breathed slowly, allowing the energy flow all around her, from the ceaseless tide of visitors and shoppers, to the laughter of children, to the towering skyscrapers, which held countless others going about their daily lives. So many people and all so busy and everywhere teeming with life.

The funny thing about hitting rock bottom, she decided, was that it was, actually, a place where you could exist. That even if you felt every bone of your body had been blanched clean and the marrow removed, you could still move around in a vacuum of detachment. She'd actually slept after Ben left her apartment on Sunday evening, even though she'd thought she'd never sleep again. She'd got up and showered that morning, even though she thought she could never face another day. She hadn't gone to Central Park for the usual walk, but instead of chiding herself for avoiding Ben, she followed her gut instinct and went for a solitary walk along by the Hudson, walking for miles, her senses absorbing the surge of the grey glinting river, smelling the salty breeze, feeling it on her face, and breathing it in slowly and evenly, the simple act of getting air into her lungs making her feel alive and keeping any panic at bay.

And now, sitting on the bench, she was still wrapped in comforting numbness when her mobile buzzed and in an instant, everything changed.

Her mother's number came up on the caller display, but it wasn't Vivienne, it was Sheila, her neighbour, using Vivienne's mobile. At first Ellie's mind refused to absorb what she was hearing. She had to ask Sheila to repeat herself. She pulled out her notebook to write down phone numbers, Sheila's mobile and landline, the hospital. Then she was sprinting through the warm, spring-like afternoon, zigzagging sharply through the throng of shoppers and tourists, half-convinced she was in some kind of nightmare. There wasn't a minute to lose so she hailed a cab to take her back to her apartment and when she caught glimpses of Central Park flashing past in the near distance she felt she was looking at pieces of a life she'd enjoyed once upon a time that were already in her past.

As soon as she was in the quiet of her apartment she phoned Miranda. She didn't know what time it was in Hong Kong, but that was irrelevant now.

Miranda sounded groggy. 'Hi, Ellie, what's up?'

'Miranda.' Ellie tried to compose her thoughts, but it was impossible. 'It's Mum,' she said bluntly. 'She's been taken ill and she's in surgery right now.'

There was a sound from the other end as though Miranda was talking to someone. 'What happened? How is she? Ellie, are you okay?'

Ellie realised she was freezing cold. 'No, I'm not. Mum collapsed at the hall door and Sheila, her neighbour, found her.

She's not sure how long she was lying there, but she called an ambulance straightaway and Mum was whisked into hospital. It's her heart. She needs to have some valves replaced. They're preparing to operate on her now and it's serious.' Ellie couldn't continue as her teeth were chattering so much.

'Jesus.'

Ellie swallowed. 'Sheila got my number on Mum's mobile and called me from the hospital. Sheila's there now with her husband and will contact me as soon as she has any more news. But Miranda— I can't believe this . . . '

'I can't either.' More sounds as though Miranda was talking to someone.

'You're with someone?' Ellie asked, unable to believe that this bothered her while her mother's life hung in the balance.

Miranda didn't answer her question. 'Ellie, I'm getting up now and I'll arrange a flight home as soon as I can.'

'Same here as soon I finish this call,' Ellie said, her mind running ahead of itself.

'What about Lucy? Does she know?'

'I haven't talked to her. I was hoping you might.'

'Okay. I'll do that now. She should be able to get home before either of us. Call me the minute you hear anything.'

By now it was seven o'clock in the evening and Ellie gave up trying to calculate the time difference between New York, London and Hong Kong, beyond working out that it was Tuesday morning in Hong Kong. She called the Dublin hospital at the number Sheila had given her. They had very little information other than to tell her that her mother was in theatre and likely to be there for at least three hours. Miranda texted her to say she'd had to leave a message on Lucy's mobile because she wasn't answering and Ellie felt a bolt of annoyance. They needed Lucy to get home pronto, so that at least one of them was at the hospital in case anything happened. She had to shut all negative thoughts out of her head as she checked flights on the internet. After a lot of scrolling around, she worked out that a direct flight home from New York the following afternoon was her best option. It would get her into Dublin in the early hours of Wednesday morning. Then Miranda texted to say she was getting a late-night flight out of Hong Kong, coming through Amsterdam, and would also arrive in Dublin on Wednesday morning a few hours after Ellie.

Don't let anything happen before Wednesday unless it's good, Ellie silently beseeched. She paced the apartment, her mind skittering senselessly around, unable to settle to anything until finally, at ten o'clock that evening, the hospital finally called to say that Vivienne was out of surgery, it had gone as well as could be expected and she was holding her own.

'Oh, thank God,' Ellie said, her legs giving way so that she had to sink to the green sofa.

'She's in recovery and will be held there while they get a bed ready in intensive care,' the nurse told her.

Intensive care. A new and frightening landscape, where everything else was superfluous.

'We have your number and will call you if there is any change. She's stable for now.'

'Thank you so much for your help,' Ellie said. 'I won't get home until Wednesday morning, but my sister from London should be there later on today. I presume it's Tuesday in Dublin?'

'Yes, it's after three in the morning,' the nurse said, sounding quite matter of fact.

Ellie pictured a busy, artificially lit hospital theatre where day and night blended into one. She called Miranda to bring her up to date. There was still no word from Lucy and by now Miranda was in her office. 'I'll keep trying her. I'm tidying up loose ends

337

before I leave,' she said. 'Then it'll be home to pack some stuff. I'll see you soon, Ellie.'

Miranda sounded very subdued. That was another thing Ellie realised as she put down her mobile one more time and pulled her case out from under the bed. Any quirky idea she'd had about staying on in New York was well and truly knocked on the head. In just over twenty-four hours, she'd be back where she'd never wanted to be again — facing Lucy, maybe even running into Johnny, in the most traumatic circumstances possible. Now that she was about to leave, her little refuge gleamed like a small piece of heaven, out of kilter with everything else, a golden hiatus that had lifted her out of herself, save for that final encounter with Ben.

Suddenly, she wanted him to know why she wouldn't be around anymore. And mixed with this was the sickening knowledge that she wouldn't see him again because he couldn't leave America. She stepped over her empty case, grabbed her keys and mobile and without thinking any more, went downstairs.

'Ellie?' He answered the door looking so normal in his stocking feet that she longed to cling to him. His face changed to consternation when he looked at hers. 'What's wrong?'

'Oh, Ben, my mum's very sick and I have to go home.' Ellie put her fist up to her mouth. He opened his arms and she went into them, shaking silently. He held her in the hall for several moments, his grip solid and reassuring, and then he brought her into the living room.

'Megan's out for the night,' he said, 'I think this calls for a shot of my special Irish whiskey.'

He continued to hold her close long after she'd told him the news in between sips of fiery liquid, which helped to calm her. Later, he brought her back to her apartment, taking her key out of her shaking fingers to open the door and locking it after they went through.

'I'm spending the night with you,' he said, his hand stroking her cheek. 'Just in case you get a call you don't like.'

'Oh, Ben! Thank you!' She'd been dreading the night, with the alarming prospect of a shattering telephone call. Then her face coloured when she remembered the last time he'd been in her bedroom. 'But—'

He gave her an easy smile. 'No worries. I'll sleep on top of the bed. In my clothes.'

'So will I. Not that I'll get any sleep.'

In her bedroom, he pushed her case out of the way and told her he'd help her pack in the morning. 'And I'm coming to the airport with you.'

'Are you sure?'

'What are friends for?' he said. 'Now go clean your teeth.'

They took off their shoes and sat on the bed together, like two children. Ben plumped up the pillows and picked up a chunky throw, tucking it around them. Then he curved an arm around her shoulder and drew her head onto his chest. She reached out and put her arm around his waist.

'Tell me about growing up in Leitrim,' she said, her voice muffled against his chest.

'That could take all night,' he joked.

'That's fine by me.'

It didn't take all night. She didn't stay awake that long. Ben told her funny stories and kept her safe and warm in the circle of his arms as the night closed around them both and her eyelids drooped and eventually she slept.

Lucy woke with a start. She'd been having a crazy dream, which she couldn't recall, and the last shreds of it dissolved as she lifted her head off the pillow. Or she tried to, because the room swam around her and her head was hammering so much it felt like it

339

was about to split in two. She turned it around gingerly on the pillow. She wasn't alone. Lying beside her in bed, the duvet falling away from his bare torso, was Justin.

Oh, yeah. Justin. Her favourite photographer and occasional bed mate. She'd a vague memory of calling some of the crowd last night and a few of them had met for drinks, and when Justin had said he'd see her home, she hadn't refused, even though she knew it meant bed. Then, with a thunk, she remembered her meeting in Rebecca's office just yesterday, and the fantastic opportunity she'd been given.

So why had she gone out and got blotto last night? She badly needed to stay on the straight and narrow. What had made her call up the gang and invite Justin into her bed? Of course. The row with her mother. All the stuff about her father that she hadn't known. It came back to her in a rush, sending a sour wave through her stomach that rose up into her throat.

Naked except for a pair of black panties, she stumbled out of bed and went into the bathroom, getting to the toilet bowl just in the nick of time, where she puked up everything she'd ingested the evening before. *And* everything she'd drunk. She rinsed her sweaty face and her hands. She cleaned her teeth and swigged a capful of mouthwash. Then she swallowed two codeine tablets.

Brilliant. Great. Well done, Lucy, she told her reflection in the mirror. There was a meeting scheduled that afternoon in the offices of the media group heading up the Venetia campaign to outline the timetable of events, including shooting and all the scheduling. And, of course, Lucy Morgan, supermodel extraordinaire in waiting, had already sabotaged herself by going on the piss the night before.

How else, though, had she been supposed to cope with the revelations about her father? Important things she should have known. Mega things that had been kept from her. Her mother's words came back to her – '. . . hitting the headlines for all the wrong reasons. You drink too much and for all I know you take the odd recreational drug'.

Fuck that. On top of everything else, her mother had no faith in her whatsoever. So why not live up – or down – to her mum's expectations?

She felt numb as she went back to bed and flopped down. She plucked her mobile off the bedside table and glared at it. Three missed calls from Miranda. She must have fallen into a very deep, alcohol-induced sleep not to have heard them. Then a text message asking her to phone Miranda as soon as possible, it was about Mum. Lucy stuck out her tongue at the display. Well, prim and prissy Miranda could go to hell. She'd obviously heard from Vivienne, knew she was upset, and wanted to give Lucy a piece of her mind.

No way.

'Hey, babe.'

Justin was awake. His hair was all messed up, his chin dark with stubble and his eyes grinned lazily at her. His hand snaked out and clamped around her breast. Under the duvet his leg looped itself around her thigh.

'Mmm, Justin,' she said, playing for time. He wasn't Johnny. He wasn't even all that great in bed. But he'd been there with her last night when she needed him, distracting her from herself and her horrible thoughts. He pulled her to him, pressing his naked body against hers.

'Why don't you seduce me all over again,' he said, his hands running across her breasts and slipping down past her stomach to the join of her thighs. He slid his hand in under her panties and cupped her groin and, leaning closer, he kissed her neck.

Lucy's mobile buzzed.

'Ignore that,' Justin said, nibbling her ear, pressing his erection against her.

'I will,' she grinned, making up her mind. She reached for a condom from the packet on her bedside table and passed it over to him. Then she peeled off her panties, straddled his hips, and lightly bit his shoulder with her white teeth as she lowered herself onto him. She closed her eyes as she balanced herself against the bedstead and rocked her hips to and fro, holding him tightly inside her, willing the feeling to come, the mind-blowing ecstasy she'd had with Johnny. It had to be there, somewhere, just beyond her reach. Maybe if she pretended this was Johnny, she might recapture some of that magic. She arched her back and took him deeper, just as Justin clutched hold of her buttocks, gasping loudly as he came.

'How about you? Was it good?' he panted.

Lucy groaned and faked an orgasm, then flopped down beside him. She rolled under the duvet and curled it around her body like a cocoon. 'Yeah, it was great.'

'You're still as hot as ever,' he said, swatting her bum.

'Am I?'

'I'd love to stay here all day, babe, but I've things to do.' He got off the bed and headed for the bathroom.

'Aww.' She pretended to be disappointed. She lay there while Justin showered, and then he dressed swiftly and left, kissing her forehead and telling her he'd see her around. Her head still hurt and she was vaguely let down. Let down by herself.

Why hadn't she been able to accept what her mum had to say calmly and rationally? Okay, it had been a shock, but she'd over-reacted by going on the tear, and almost put what was left of her reputation on the line. She shivered in spite of the warmth of the duvet. Just as well it had been Justin, he was okay and she could trust him to keep his mouth shut. When her mobile buzzed again she grabbed it impatiently. If this was Miranda, she was going to tell her to fuck off and leave her the hell alone.

It was indeed Miranda. But after her sister's opening words, Lucy sat bolt upright in bed, all traces of a hangover forgotten. Her breath froze in her chest and she felt light-headed. For a long moment, she saw her glittering future sitting like a big silvery bubble in the palm of her hand and then it dissolved as she heard herself tell Miranda that, of course, she'd be home as soon as possible. Ten minutes later, she was in the shower, and an hour later she was sitting in Rebecca's office, telling her she had to return to Dublin immediately.

'Home?' Rebecca's brows drew together in disbelief. Then she laughed. 'Lucy, is this some kind of a joke? You do realise that this afternoon is the team briefing. You can't just tear off home on a whim. Besides, I've pulled strings for you—'

'It's not a whim. My mother's sick, ill, I dunno . . . ' she faltered, feeling weak, hardly able to believe she was saying these words. 'She's had major heart surgery. She collapsed at home last night.'

'Oh dear. I see.' Rebecca studied her from the other side of the desk, looking somewhat concerned.

It was beyond cruel, Lucy decided, being handed her biggest dream on a plate, then a just a day later having to hand it back. She felt that a door had irrevocably slammed shut in her face. But far, far worse was her mother's illness. She had to get home to Dublin, contract or no contract, dream or no dream. Eating away at her was the fact that she hadn't picked up Miranda's calls. Anything could have happened in the time she'd been having lacklustre sex with Justin. 'My mother's stable but the next forty-eight hours are critical. I'm getting a flight out late this afternoon. I'm not sure how long I'll be home for,' she said, her voice wavering.

She tried not to think of Sasha, busy getting ready for the first stage of her golden opportunity. She heard Carla's mocking voice in the back of her head, asking her if she really thought she was going to capitalise on her misfortune. Who the hell did Lucy Morgan think she was anyway?

'Lucy.' Rebecca sighed and shook her head. 'You always manage to confound me. Just when I think I have you figured out, you do something to surprise me. I would have thought you'd put yourself first before anything else. I thought you were very hungry for this contract.'

'I am— was,' Lucy said in a quiet voice, dizzy with the way she had to forego it, and wishing Rebecca would get off the subject.

'I think . . . ' Rebecca paused, and pursed her lips. 'Most other agencies would think I'm mad, but I'm impressed with your loyalty to your mother and I'm glad you're not just a heartless bitch. It's important to be single-minded in your career, but not to the exclusion of your nearest and dearest. So, Lucy, I'm not going to do anything for now. I'll explain that you can't be with the team this afternoon, you go back home and see how your mum is, and then we'll talk. Of course, if your absence is likely to be for any length of time, I'll have to reconsider, as deadlines are tight.'

Lucy was dumbfounded. '*What*? You mean, you— but why?'

'You have something, Lucy. A sparkle, an edginess, but it's mixed with a kind of vulnerability that the camera picks up, which is very engaging. If it's okay to mention his name, it's not unlike the sexy kind of vibe your father put out there. I wish you'd believe it yourself. And if you mixed those ingredients with a little bit of that warm heart you're always hiding away, you could go places, even beyond your modelling career.'

Tears sprang into her eyes. 'Are you serious?'

Rebecca smiled. 'Go home. See your mum. Talk to me

tomorrow. And one thing, Lucy, I know you're in a heap right now, but please don't turn to alcohol. You've done more than enough hiding behind that.'

As she left the office and stepped out onto the street, Lucy had to pinch herself. Her glittering future wasn't all over just yet. And Rebecca thought she had some of her dad in her. His sparkle and edginess. It made her realise that it hadn't all come to a horrid end in the cold darkness of a Canadian lake. It was running through her veins, alive and well. She'd never known him, but she was part of him and had some of his good genes. She should be happy with that.

In the meantime, she thought, there were important things to do. Like getting to Mum as soon as possible. And coming face to face with Ellie. And maybe even Johnny.

Christian wanted to take her to the airport, but Miranda refused.

'I want to spend as long as I can with you,' he said.

'No, really, I'd far rather say goodbye here.' Here, in her apartment, where she could have a good bawl as soon as he left. It was eight o'clock in the evening and she was heading to the airport in less than an hour.

'I wish I was coming with you.'

'I'm glad you're not.'

'Why? Don't you want me?'

'I do, it's just—'

'What? Tell me.' His hand sifted through her hair, sending delicious ripples around her scalp.

'Nothing. Look, I don't know what I'm going home to face. It could be messy.'

'All the more reason for me to go with you. Can't you see I want to be by your side?'

Miranda sighed and hung her head. 'I'd rather go home alone.'

He lifted her chin. 'I know what this is about. It's about your sister. You don't trust me.'

'I do trust you—' she avoided his eyes.

'You don't, Miranda. After everything we've been to each other over the past few months, surely you know how I feel about you? I'm crazy about you. Do you place such little value on us that you're afraid of old history? I thought we were above all that. I thought I'd dispelled all your little fears, and I'm disappointed.'

'Christian, please,' she shook her head. 'I didn't expect this to happen. I was sure we'd have more time before ...' Before what? The threat of facing Ellie? Yet what difference would another couple of months have made?

He turned away from her and walked to the window. 'I didn't expect you to push me away. I thought you had more faith in us – and trust in me. Haven't the past few months meant anything to you?'

'Christian, don't be like this, please,' she said desperately.

He'd told her she was warm and charming, but he didn't know Ellie with her sultry sexiness.

He wheeled back around, 'Hell, Miranda, I was beginning to think we might have had a future together. I can't believe you're letting your sister come between us.'

'I'm not. Look—' she began in a hoarse voice. But she had nothing more to say, no words to bridge the rift that had so suddenly opened between them. To her embarrassment, tears pooled in her eyes. He was looking at her silently and images of the past few months flashed in front of her. His warmth, his kindness, his love-making. Was she was going to let Christian slip through her fingers? And all because of Ellie? Just like she had other men? Those other men, who were never meant to be the one, perhaps, but not Christian too?

346

'I do trust you,' she said, a fighting spirit she hadn't known she possessed suddenly sparking inside her. 'I trusted you enough to bare my soul and tell you something I've never told anyone else.'

Then, in the next minute, Christian was by her side and curving his arms around her.

'God, I'm sorry,' he murmured. 'I'm being selfish. Your mum is ill and I'm fighting with you. Go home. Do what you have to do. And when you come back, I'll be waiting.'

'Oh, Christian,' she sighed, melting into his arms.

Chapter 38

There is some kind of fog clouding her brain, but, behind that, Vivienne is not lying in a hospital bed hooked up to a forest of tubes and beeping machines. She is just forty years of age. Feisty, flirty forty. Her life can begin again. How wonderful.

He is sitting opposite her in the green room, while they wait to be summoned into the glare of the television studio for their respective slots with Ireland's premier chat-show host in front of a live, studio audience, as well as Ireland's Friday night invisible armchair audience.

It is the first time they meet.

He is dressed from head to toe in tight black leather. He sits with one leg cocked up at an angle so that the foot of it rests against his other knee, showing off the most outrageous pair of studded, high-heeled, python-skinned boots. His unruly dark hair sweeps the collar of his jacket. His eyes are a dark, broody grey. He reeks of attitude and bold things in bed and the full force of his sexuality takes her breath away. And there is something else in the depths of his eyes that goes straight to her heart, some kind of uncertainty – it's barely perceptible, but she picks it up. It reminds her of how uncertain she felt when she met Edward's parents for the first time – and every time after that. As though he is trying very hard to fit something, an image, a persona. Her face betrays none of this as they watch the monitor where a blustering politician is being grilled on the woeful state of the economy. They are the final two guests of the night.

'That'll be a hard act to follow,' Zach says laconically, raising an eyebrow. He's already told her he is a famous Scottish musician. She didn't tell him that he couldn't be all that famous because she'd never heard of him. Although that wasn't too surprising because for the previous year she might as well not have existed in the world. She tells her he's hoping to follow in the footsteps of his idol, Mick Jagger, albeit as a solo artist.

'You're up next,' she says unnecessarily. She doesn't need a mirror to know that her face is caked with an excess of television make-up and this guy must think she needs it as some kind of pollyfilla. He's at least ten years younger than she is, but more than a generation removed in terms of the gap between them. After all, there is no possible meeting point for a forty-year-old widow with two daughters and a Scottish rock musician who is smouldering with raw sex appeal. Still, it's the first time in a year that she's noticed that particular attribute. Something flutters deep inside her.

He fixes her with those dark-grey eyes. She finds them disturbing, but in a nice way. A sensual way.

'They must be keeping the best until last,' he says.

'I wouldn't say that,' she smiles self-deprecatingly, immediately annoyed with herself.

'I'm just going to warble a song,' he says. 'You probably have a dance and a recitation up your sleeve.'

'I'm not wearing any sleeves,' she says primly. Again, annoyed with herself.

'No, actually, you're not.' His eyes rove across her fitted cobalt blue dress and linger for a moment on her cleavage.

She should be outraged, but she's not. And she likes his Scottish accent. It's warm and sexy – like the man himself.

Shortly afterwards, she watches his performance on the monitor, and he throws himself into a raunchy routine that would put Mick Jagger in the shade. She feels he's singing for her, his eyes staring at her through the television camera, knowing full well she is watching. Zach tells the studio audience he's here in Ireland for a few weeks to devote himself to some songwriting in quiet, peaceful surroundings. He has rented a house in the depths of a Wicklow valley to ensure total privacy. Again, he looks directly into the camera lens, and to Vivienne, his eyes are alive with possibilities.

She'll never see him again, Vivienne tells herself, as she watches him stalk off the stage. She is the final guest on the show, and if the presenter thought he was going to charm her into opening her heart about the pain of her husband's sudden death, he is mistaken. On the other side of the camera, Ellie and Miranda are at home, sitting in the television room of their Dún Laoghaire home, watching this with Florence, her mother. Behind the camera, an unseen audience of hundreds of thousands are also watching. Nothing about Edward's death is suitable for public disclosure and the consumption of the masses. No way is she going to bare her soul about the heartbreak, the sheer, dogged loneliness, the moments of utter despair. The anger at finding herself a widow before she was forty.

Funnily enough, she feels a lot more animated after her encounter with Zach, as though a fuse has been lit deep inside her, and she has the confidence to draw the focus around to her career, where she is taking up the reins again after a year's break with a pivotal role in one of Ireland's new soap operas.

'Well, Vivienne, you're a very brave, courageous lady,' the presenter says as he winds up the interview, throwing her a warm, questioning look as though she might have some comment to make to back up what he has said.

'Thank you,' she says graciously, still refusing to be drawn on her private life.

She has to wait in her seat while he wraps up the show and dips his hand into the middle of a bath-sized container overflowing with postcards, selecting one as the winner of the prize car. When she walks out into the foyer, itching to take off her cake of foundation, Zach is waiting.

And this is the start of their whirlwind romance.

She is ready for it, hungry for it, pining for love and lust. The milestone of her birthday coming a year after Edward's sudden death is telling her that life is far too short. Too short to waste time wondering what people will think. Too short to waste time in a cat and mouse game of flirtation. Too short to waste time when Zach is looking at her across a table after a candlelit meal with hot desire in his brooding grey eyes on their third date. He will be here for two more months, no more. Then back to London and into a recording studio, although his big dream is to conquer America. So there is no time to waste. She knows exactly where she sits on his agenda. A little Irish dalliance, some fun, no strings, a taste of hot passion, which will give him a distraction during the time he is in seclusion, deep in a valley in Wicklow.

And her? He makes her feel alive again, even if it is just a temporary madness. The house in Wicklow is perfect for a lovers' tryst. It has wonderful views across a vale, a cosy kitchen and living room, a first-floor bedroom with a huge bed adorned with white silk sheets. He gives her a spare key so she can come and go at will. He plays his music for her and she lies in the bed with the white silk sheets watching his long fingers pluck the notes out of his guitar, bringing it alive as though it is magic. Bringing her alive again as they make long, slow love and she feels all her senses on fire.

But there is nothing clandestine about their friendship. Zach calls to the house in Dún Laoghaire, quite openly. He comes for meals, trying to draw out a subdued Ellie and answering Miranda's innocent questions easily. He treats the girls with presents and takes them to the cinema. Her head turned with a powerful lust, Vivienne tells her daughters he is just a friend, like the new friends she is now making on the set of the soap opera. She senses Ellie's displeasure, but she tells herself it will be over before she knows it and she is going to grab a slice of happiness while she can. When Zach has left, in the late summer, she will bring the girls on holidays to France or Spain, as soon as she has a break from filming. In the meantime, she is enjoying the desire that flows between them, the hours she spends in his arms.

Then, when Zach has just three weeks left, and she is beginning to count down the days until he leaves, Vivienne finds out she is pregnant.

Not this, now, no way. Her mind recoils against the absurdity of a forty-year-old widow becoming pregnant in these circumstances. It is one thing to have a brief fling, in an attempt to plaster over the gigantic hole in her life. It is another thing to have a baby for this mercurial rock musician, who has most likely left a trail of broken hearts trampled under his sexy leather boots and will undoubtedly leave more in his hunger for success.

In a panic, she decides there is only one solution and she flies to London for the weekend, leaving the girls in the care of her mother. Then, at the last minute, she knows she can't go through with it. They are very understanding in the abortion clinic when she changes her mind. She arrives back in Dublin early on Sunday morning and instead of going home, she drives to Wicklow.

Zach will be gone soon, so there's no time to waste. She needs to make love to him, to take away the fear and self-loathing of the weekend. She uses her key to let herself into his secluded house, stepping out of her high heels in the hallway. All is quiet, and she guesses he is still in bed. As she runs lightly up the stairs, she's already opening her blouse, slipping it off her shoulders, undoing her bra, to surprise him.

And this is the moment it all goes horribly wrong.

Chapter 39

*E*llie's heart was pounding somewhere in her throat as she followed the nurse through the security doors and down the length of the corridor. Her head reeled with disbelief as she pulled a white, plastic apron over her head, fumbled with the ties, and swabbed her hands with disinfectant before entering the Coronary Care Unit and the alarming world where her mother now belonged.

The ward resonated with understated urgency. It had beds on each side surrounded by impressive banks of equipment, where teams of crisply uniformed staff moved around, looking quite at home in these alien surroundings. Ellie was startled to hear the murmur of prayers and the shuffle of footsteps behind one curtained bed. She saw another empty cubicle space being washed down, and then, with a fresh shock, her mother, her face so pale and motionless on a pillow that it was scarcely recognisable.

It didn't seem right. Ellie saw her swanning out onto the stage clad in a blue velvet gown, her unique presence and compelling voice holding her audience in the palm of her hand. She saw her sitting in the kitchen in Dún Laoghaire with her friends, laughing and pouring coffee, her reading glasses perched on her hair. She saw her sipping champagne and surrounded by fans after a successful opening night in the Abbey. She wanted to spin back time and put her back in those places so that Vivienne Morgan wasn't lying in a bed, white-faced and somehow reduced, clad in some kind of makeshift cloth gown, and hooked up to drips, monitors and clicking machines.

'I'm Gillian and I'll be looking after your mum today,' the nurse introduced herself, picking up a clipboard. 'She regained consciousness after surgery, but just briefly. Don't worry about the look of all these machines. We're closely monitoring the activity of her heart and lungs, her blood pressure and respiration, and she's still on a ventilator to help with her breathing.' She explained the functions of each machine to Ellie.

'It's all very high tech,' Ellie said, still finding it impossible to grasp.

'She's in the best place anyhow. The cardiac consultant and his team were around earlier this morning and they're happy with her progress. They've already spoken to your sister, she's just taken a break and gone out to the canteen.'

With a leap of relief, Ellie assumed Miranda was home, before she realised she was still somewhere in transit, and the nurse was referring to Lucy. Something else that had to be faced.

'How long before she's fully conscious?' Ellie asked.

'I can't say. That's up to the lady herself. Right now, she's sleeping and that's fine. It's her body's way of giving it a chance to heal. She was in surgery for over three hours, so it was quite serious. Hopefully, we'll get her off the ventilator and moving in the next twenty-four hours.'

Ellie's heart clenched as she looked at her mother. She was so far removed from her normal flamboyant self that it was impossible to visualise her sitting up, let alone moving around.

'Yes, I know it seems impossible,' Gillian read her thoughts. 'But it's amazing what twenty-four hours can do.'

'It is indeed,' Ellie said, pulling out a chair and sitting down. She watched her mother's white, still face, the tube of oxygen snaking into her mouth and the flickering machines, alert for any kind of change. Then images of the previous twenty-four hours rose up in her mind.

Although she'd only left New York yesterday, the colourful energy of the city and the life-affirming beauty of Central Park was already a far-flung planet. Ben had travelled out to JFK with her on a gloriously sunny afternoon, and inside the busy airport he'd stayed right beside her until she'd come to the security barrier.

'This is it,' she'd said, turning to face him. 'Thanks for everything.'

'You take care of yourself,' he'd said, looping his arms around her and drawing her close.

She'd allowed herself the bliss of leaning forward and cradling her head into the nook of his neck. She'd absorbed the scent of his skin and the solid strength of his body, heartbroken to think it was now all over.

'Sorry I can't come with you,' he'd said, stroking her cheek, concern all over his face.

She hadn't known if he was just being kind or if he really meant what he said. She, who had always been confident where men were concerned, had found herself unsure and at a loss. Ben would never be able to leave the States without facing possible deportation and being refused re-entry. He was among the thousands of Irish there who were caught, unable to go home to attend weddings or funerals.

'I understand,' she'd said, feeling bereft that they had come to a sudden end like this.

It had been torture to step away from him, to loosen her fingers from his grasp, and pass through the barrier, every footstep widening the distance between them. She'd swallowed back a sudden spurt of tears and set her wobbly mouth in a grim line as she continued on through the formalities until she reached the departures lounge. Neither of them had referred to the night they'd almost made love, and memories of the way she'd pulled back from the brink swirled around her as she passed up on the in-flight movies and pretended to eat airline food. Then, somewhere over the dark Atlantic ocean, she'd mentally said goodbye to Ben and turned her thoughts to Dublin and her mother. Had Vivienne known something was wrong? Had she felt afraid? How come she'd been found at the hall door? Ellie was puzzled by the chain of events but still found it impossible to grasp that her effervescent mother was lying in a hospital bed.

As soon as she'd arrived in Dublin, she'd phoned the hospital and on hearing that her mother was stable, she took a taxi home to her house, where she'd dumped her case in the hallway and taken her car out of the garage. Then, crawling with tension, feeling fatigued and disorientated, she'd driven to the hospital.

It was only when Gillian nudged her gently that Ellie realised she'd nodded off.

'Hey, Ellie, you've just come in from New York, is that right?' Ellie nodded.

'Why don't you go home for a few hours and catch up on your sleep? There's nothing you can do here. You'll be more use to your mum when she's starting to recover. If there is any change we'll contact you immediately.'

'I'll wait until Miranda gets here,' Ellie said, her mouth tasting stale. She'd had to switch off her mobile phone inside the unit, so she'd no way of knowing if she'd landed yet. Time seemed interminable as the minutes ticked by, yet it was just a half an hour or so before there was the sound of different footsteps coming up the ward and Ellie turned to see Miranda.

She blinked. For Miranda looked so different that Ellie was quietly amazed. Her hair was cut in a soft, chic style, and as for her clothes . . . behind her plastic apron she was smartly dressed as always, but more feminine as though she wasn't afraid to show off her figure, or spend a fortune on looking good. After all the times Ellie had advised her to update her wardrobe, Miranda had gone and done it for herself. There was something soft and glowing about her and Ellie sensed immediately she was in love.

She hugged her sister. 'Miranda! Thank God you're here.'

Miranda's eyes fastened on the bed. 'How is she?' she asked in a subdued voice, moving closer and putting her hand over Vivienne's.

'Holding her own,' Ellie said. She introduced Miranda to Gillian and drew over another chair and the sisters sat for a while watching their mother as Gillian went across to the nurses' station. Ellie brought Miranda up to date on everything Gillian had told her, feeling like a pro as she explained what some of the machines were for.

'It's a nightmare, isn't it?' Miranda said, tears in her eyes. 'What I can't figure out is what Mum was doing at the hall door in the first place.'

'I've been asking myself that question and can only think she must have felt weak and was trying to get help.'

'But why didn't she use her mobile to call someone?'

'I don't know. Sheila found it on the kitchen table when she checked the back door before she left in the ambulance. I can only think that Mum opened the hall door because she knew she was about to pass out and was afraid it might be difficult to break down. We won't know the full story until she wakes up.'

'It's all a bit odd.' Miranda shook her head.

'Lucy's here, but she's off out having coffee,' Ellie said after a while, her voice a little hard.

'She's outside in the waiting area,' Miranda said. 'I met her coming back from the coffee shop and she offered to keep an eye on my luggage because I came straight here from the airport. I can't go home without her, I've no key. Ellie . . .' Miranda paused, 'she's as scared as we are about Mum, but she's also afraid of what you'll say after what happened between you—'

'That's for another day,' Ellie said curtly.

'Yes. I'm staying clear of it anyway.'

'That's fine by me,' Ellie said, a little hurt that Miranda wasn't taking her side. Surely, she was the wronged one? Or did she expect Ellie to forgive and forget on account of Mum being ill? No way could Lucy's betrayal be brushed aside so easily. 'Will you be staying in Dún Laoghaire?'

'I have to. I left clothes and things there before I left because I've leased my apartment.'

'And how long are you home for?'

'Who knows? It all depends . . .' Miranda said, her eyes roving around the bank of machines.

Silence fell between them until Ellie eventually asked, 'So, what's been happening to you?'

Miranda smiled. 'This and that.'

Whoever he was, she wasn't saying. 'You look fantastic. The best I've ever seen you.'

'Thanks.'

Ellie was intrigued. Again, Miranda had the calm confidence to accept the compliment rather than shrug it off. Her new man had done wonders for her. She swallowed an unaccustomed pang of envy. 'If this is what a few months in Hong Kong does, I want some of it,' she said.

Even her sister's reply was different from normal. Her sister wasn't flustered, or making little of her reinvention. Instead, she gave a gentle laugh and said, 'Now, now, Ellie, let me have something of my own without wanting it for yourself.'

Ellie didn't have time to fully absorb the meaning of her words before there was a prolonged beeping from one of the machines and Gillian was there in an instant. Ellie jumped to her feet. 'What's wrong?'

'We have to clean out the lines,' Gillian said, clicking buttons and switches. 'It's nothing to worry about, but it'll take a couple of hours. My advice is to go on home and get some rest. We'll call you if there's any change, or you can call us at any time. Your mum looks very stable to me, so there's no immediate cause for concern.'

'I just want to be here if— when she wakes up,' Ellie said.

'Of course you do. But there's no knowing when that might be. And she'll probably be conscious for just a short while at first, given her medication.'

They had no option but to leave and Ellie's heart was heavy as she leaned across and kissed Vivienne's pale cheek. She felt as though she was leaving a vital part of herself behind as she left the ward with Miranda, and walked out of the Care Unit and through to the main part of the hospital. A wave of exhaustion washed over her, reminding her that she'd had little or no sleep in the past twenty-four hours. And she'd temporarily forgotten about Lucy, until they reached the waiting area, where worried-looking relatives were huddled in knots waiting for news, and Lucy was sitting near a soft-drinks machine with Miranda's luggage. As soon as she saw them, she jumped to her feet.

'Any news? What's happening?' she gabbled, looking worriedly at Ellie, shadows under her eyes telling her how little sleep she'd also had.

Ellie gave her a baleful stare. It was ironic, she thought, that despite the vow she'd made never to set eyes on Lucy again, they'd been thrust into this new reality where she couldn't possibly avoid her. That didn't mean she had to talk to her. Neither did it mean that Lucy was going to get away scot-free for her behaviour, she decided, uncaring how childish that was in the circumstances.

The three of them were attracting curious glances from the scatter of people who were seated in the area.

'Let's go,' Ellie said, ignoring Lucy. Turning to Miranda she said, 'I have my car with me so I can drop you home.'

'Am I coming as well?' Lucy asked.

'Of course,' Miranda said smoothly. 'We'll talk in the car.'

Ellie drove with a grim determination, avoiding Lucy's eyes in the rear-view mirror, trying not to think of all that happened since the night she and Johnny had collected her from the airport. All that stuff about Zach seemed to have died a death. She wondered briefly if Lucy had ever found out who sent her the wreath, but it was something she'd probably never know. Just as well Miranda was home. She would have felt forced to talk to Lucy, but, as it was, Miranda was doing all the talking.

She dropped her sisters in Dún Laoghaire, then popped next door to have a chat with Sheila, who insisted on making tea for Ellie. Unfortunately, she couldn't throw any light on why Vivienne had been found at her hall door.

'It was late-ish and we let the dog out as usual,' she said. 'But instead of coming back he stood at Vivienne's hall door barking his head off and that's what alerted us. Otherwise, Ellie, your mum could have been lying there all night. I found her just inside the hall door, as if she'd opened it and collapsed straightaway. I don't know what she was thinking. I said as much to Lucy when she arrived home yesterday evening.'

Ellie gave her a warm hug. 'Thank you for finding her and for all your help. Miranda is home now and will be staying next door with Lucy. So we're all around for the moment, until we see what happens.'

'It'll be fine,' Sheila said warmly. 'Vivienne is strong and I know she'll come through. It's great you're all together and can be a support for each other. And if there's anything I can do, just call.'

Back home in Laurel View, Ellie was totally disorientated. In a fog of exhaustion, she unpacked her case, moving between her en-suite, her bedroom and the laundry basket. During her absence, Marta had come in a few times and her bed was freshly made up and invitingly arranged with crisp sheets, plump pillows and cushions. Ellie had a shower and crawled under the duvet, remembering at the last minute her vow never to sleep there again after Lucy and Johnny.

To hell with them, her thoughts fluttered as her eyelids closed. She wasn't going to let them deprive her of a decent sleep in her own luxury bed. She deliberately focused on Ben and the sooth-ing way he'd wrapped his arms around her on her last night in New York. He'd texted her a couple of times – warm messages, full of concern – and she felt his tenderness enfolding her again as she drifted into sleep.

Chapter 40

*L*ucy was glad to have something to do, even if it was the mundane task of putting away the groceries she'd had delivered by the local supermarket. Although it seemed ludicrous to be filling the fridge and freezer with convenience food and topping up the fruit bowl, given that their mum lay gravely ill. Still, they had to eat and neither she nor Miranda would be in the humour for cooking.

Mum! It was all so scary. Yesterday afternoon, when she'd arrived in from London, had been the stuff of nightmares. As she'd been the first of the family to arrive on the scene, she'd suddenly had to grow up a little as she spoke to doctors and nurses and answered some questions about her mother. Miranda had suggested she contact Maeve, Vivienne's agent. Lucy would never have thought of it otherwise and Maeve had been very helpful, making the necessary phone calls to Vivienne's acting colleagues and the theatre, and offering support wherever it was needed. Still, Lucy was so relieved to have Miranda home. Right now, she was back in her old bedroom, sleeping off the after-effects of her flight.

But having Ellie home was a different story. Lucy had hated the way she'd ignored her in the hospital, but an angry pride inside her had refused to let Ellie's cold disregard upset her, even though she knew she deserved it. She *had* behaved very badly. Seeing Ellie again had brought it all back. She wondered if she was some kind of monster because she'd found it so easy to park it all to one side and get on with her life in London. Then, even though she knew it was selfish, she wished heartily that Mum had never collapsed and she was still over there in the thrust of it all, full of excitement as she geared up for the Venetia campaign. She hadn't phoned Rebecca just yet, half-afraid that she'd pull the plug on her contract.

She glanced through the newspaper she'd had delivered, cringing when she saw a small photo of her that had been snapped as she'd entered the hospital the previous evening.

Word about her mum's collapse was out, and even though Maeve had issued a discreet press release, naturally the paps were ready to jump on the bandwagon, heedless of how upsetting it might be to Vivienne's daughters. The caption said that Lucy had walked away from her modelling career to fly to her ill mother's bedside. Ellie was bound to think she'd engineered it, hungry for any kind of publicity. 'Yeah, well, I didn't,' Lucy scowled.

When the doorbell rang, she wasn't going to answer it, until she realised that Miranda would be disturbed if it continued. So she stalked up the hall and flung it open, fully expecting it to be a reporter – but it was Johnny.

'Johnny!' She flew into his arms, instinctively seeking the comfort of his embrace.

'Hey!' He hugged her close, and then held her at arm's length. 'Are you okay?'

'What do you think?' she sprang back, awkward and

embarrassed, biting back tears at the suddenness of seeing him before she'd had a chance to prepare herself.

'Of course you couldn't be okay.'

'What are you doing here?'

'I want to find out how Vivienne is. The hospital isn't giving out any information.'

She brought him down to the kitchen, switching on the kettle to boil while she finished putting away the groceries.

'Miranda's upstairs sleeping off her jet lag. Ellie's home as well,' she said guardedly. 'Why aren't you over at Laurel View?' she asked, testing him.

'Do you think she'll talk to me?' he asked, sitting down at the scrubbed pine table.

'I dunno. You didn't waste any time finding a replacement,' she said. She turned away to put a carton of eggs into the fridge, not wanting to watch his face while he digested this.

'That was another mistake.'

Another mistake? Her heart sank. That's all she'd been to him. A mistake. How had she ever thought otherwise? Avoiding his eyes, she made tea and brought the pot over to the table, assembling sugar, milk and mugs. When she poured his tea, her hand shook so that it spilled on the table.

'Here, let me,' he said, putting his hand over hers and guiding the teapot safely back down. 'I shouldn't have taken advantage of you,' he went on quietly, reading her thoughts. 'That's the mistake I made with you. You're lovely, Lucy. You're sweet—'

'Sweet! Hah! I've been called lots of things but never that.' Her voice cracked and tears threatened. *Sweet*! How old-fashioned. She sat down opposite him and put her elbows on the table, resting her head in her hands.

He reached forward and pushed back tendrils of her hair. His touch filled her with a delightful panic.

'I'm sorry,' he said. 'You're upset over your mother and now I've made it worse. What I'm trying to say is you're far too good for the likes of me. If you take Ellie out of the equation, what happened between us was special, but it was a once-off, Lucy. I'm old enough to be your father. Anyway, you have a modelling world to conquer and years of carefree life to enjoy.'

'I think you have the wrong end of the stick, Johnny,' she gave a laugh, her pride once more rescuing her. She sat up straighter and flicked back her hair where he'd touched it as though wiping it away. 'I'm upset over Mum. Nothing more. As you said yourself, you're old enough to be my dad, and,' she went on in a careless voice that she summoned out of where she didn't know, 'I'm more than happy that our quick shag was a once-off.'

'Ouch,' he said, his eyes looking at her a little regretfully. She stared at him defiantly, back in control of herself.

'How is your mum?'

'Stable.' Lucy brought him up to speed on what had happened so far. 'We've spent the morning in the hospital and we're heading back in early this evening. Ellie is picking us up.'

'I'd better make myself scarce, so.'

He looked so anxious to be gone that Lucy felt a flash of annoyance. 'I never thought you were that much of a scaredy-cat,' she said.

'I don't want to upset her,' he said, a little shame-faced.

It did nothing to endear him to her. 'That's no excuse,' she said tartly. 'You were with her for two years. I've had to face her, although she's still not talking to me. Thank God Miranda's home. She's acting as a go-between, almost like an interpreter between two foreigners. Come to think of it,' Lucy continued in a reflective tone of voice, 'I guess she's always been the middle-man where Ellie and I are concerned.'

*

Miranda paused on the carpeted staircase, glad she was soundless in her bare feet as Lucy's words floated up to her through the open kitchen door. Then she turned around and tiptoed silently upstairs.

It was odd being back in her old bedroom after ten years of independent living. The room bore no trace of all the time she'd spent in it. After she'd moved out, Vivienne had had it completely redecorated and turned into a guest bedroom and it had that empty feel as though no one had used it for a long time. She'd been glad about that at first – she was a stranger here and wanted no reminders of the past. Lucy's assumption that she'd fall back into her usual role of keeping the peace between her two sisters had annoyed her. Much as she loved them, she couldn't allow herself to be pulled back into that place where she was swamped by them.

Yet was she being totally selfish in thinking like this? Right now, they needed the old Miranda, who'd do anything to keep the peace. For all her good intentions, she'd come home at a time when everyone was upset and out of sorts, including herself. She sat down in a white wicker chair, and her blood ran cold as she thought of Vivienne lying in a hospital bed surrounded by complex machinery, the engines of which were supporting her life. It was a sight that had been almost impossible to bear. Panic gripped her as she wondered where it would end. And mixed with that, she was full of regret that the promise of her new life was stalled.

More guilt.

She checked her mobile again but there was nothing from Christian. She'd texted him as soon as she'd arrived, and spoken to him after she'd seen her mother. Then she'd taken a deep breath, stepped out of her comfort zone and texted him to say she was missing him, but he hadn't replied.

An old insecurity gnawed deep inside. Why did she fear the worst? Or consider for a moment that he'd already forgotten about her? She stared around the four walls of the room. The colours might have changed but the contours were familiar. Like herself. She might think she was a stranger here – and that she'd turned over a brave, new leaf – but she'd been kidding herself. Some things were impossible to get away from, such as the old, familiar contours of her own self-doubt.

Chapter 41

*B*y the time it came to Thursday evening, the scents and sounds, and even the staff of the Coronary Care Unit were so familiar to Ellie that she felt as though they had always been an intrinsic part of her life. Ben had followed up his texts with a phone call that afternoon, his voice warm and caring. It was painful to realise that she felt light years away from him, the weeks she'd spent in New York a muzzy dream.

Johnny had sent her a text, full of warmth and apology and concern for her mother, and she hadn't deleted it. Nor had she replied. Sooner or later, she would have to face him. Already she felt a little removed from the hot rage that had consumed her before she'd gone to New York, but she didn't know what it would be like to see him face to face. Claire had spoken to her as well, but Ellie told her there was no point in trying to see Vivienne as only immediate family were allowed to visit, and only two at a time.

Which meant that she, Miranda and Lucy were performing an elaborate dance, tacitly ensuring that Lucy and Ellie wouldn't be left alone together, either in the waiting room or by Vivienne's bed. Throughout all this, her mother looked the same, a small figure in the bed dwarfed by the immensity of the high-tech equipment around her. It was simply a waiting game while her body recovered, and Ellie felt stretched, like elastic about to snap.

And it became more stressful when Lucy refused to leave the unit later that evening. Miranda came out to find Ellie, shaking her head.

'She's crying and clinging to the bed rail,' Miranda said. 'She won't come home, even though the nurses have said there's nothing she can do, and they'll phone us the minute there's any change.'

'Let her stay all night if she wants to,' Ellie said ungraciously.

'The staff aren't too keen on having her in the way. Obviously, if Mum was in any danger they'd accommodate us. Lucy will only wear herself out.'

Ellie shrugged. 'She'll do whatever she wants to do, as usual. Bold child.'

'Come on, Ellie, she's hurting, just like you and me.'

Miranda was still refusing to take any sides, Ellie noted, allowing herself to be talked into a cup of coffee. The mezzanine café was busy with visitors and patients. It was easy to spot the visitors, they stood out like bright, lively creatures amongst the patients, who were invariably muffled in shapeless dressing gowns over pyjamas. Some were in wheelchairs and others on crutches, and a couple of them hooked up to mobile drips. Ellie cleared a small table of the previous occupants' detritus of abandoned coffee and unopened sugar sachets while Miranda joined the queue at the counter.

'I'll give Lucy half an hour then I'll go back in for her,' Miranda said, when she returned with a small tray and passed a cup of coffee over to Ellie. Ellie took off the plastic lid and stirred the froth with a plastic spoon, thinking how sad and depressing it all was, even down to the tasteless coffee.

Miranda switched on her mobile and checked it, biting her lip.

'What's up?' Ellie asked.

Her sister's face flooded with colour. 'Nothing. They seem to be coping without me okay in Hong Kong. I left in such a rush I wasn't sure . . . ' her voice trailed away.

Ellie wondered why she was pretending to be checking up on her job when it was surely a man causing that colour in her cheeks and look of anxiety in her eyes. The same man who, no doubt, had encouraged her to be wearing that softly contoured cream shirt and olive-green trousers with a fabulous belt cinching her waist. The man who had been in bed with her when Ellie had phoned. So far, for some reason of her own, Miranda was keeping him strictly under wraps. Ellie was tempted to say it was four in the morning Hong Kong time, but something about Miranda's air of despondency stopped her.

And when Miranda went back into the unit, returning some time later with a teary eyed, woebegone Lucy, who looked more like twelve than twenty-one, with all the attitude of that sassy, sexy model stripped away, Ellie surprised herself by feeling a wash of emotion for both her sisters. They were all hurting in one form or another. The one thing they all had in common was love for their mother. And, right then, they all hoped and prayed for her recovery. So, later, when Miranda suggested she come in for a while, as she drove them home to Dún Laoghaire, Ellie agreed, ignoring Lucy's look of panic in the rear-view mirror.

'Ellie, I'm so glad you're coming in, but I don't know what to say to you,' Lucy began to babble as they all went down to Vivienne's big roomy kitchen and Miranda opened a bottle of wine. 'You didn't reply to any of my texts and that made me feel ten times worse.'

'What did you expect me to say? Thanks for jumping into bed with my boyfriend? Get real, Lucy. Anyway I don't want to discuss it now,' Ellie said. 'Mum is ill and that's more important. We've enough to cope with as it is.'

Fat tears pooled in Lucy's eyes and rolled down her cheeks. She was wearing a nutmeg cashmere cardigan, against which her hair was a rich, riotous flame. Her pale, drawn face looked haunted and her agitated fingers twisted and stretched the edges of her cardigan. 'Oh, thanks, Ellie,' she cried. 'You've no idea how badly I feel because it's all my fault—'

Ellie put up a dismissive hand. 'I said I don't want to discuss it. Not now. And don't wreck that lovely cardigan.'

Lucy's fingers worked faster. 'No, I'm talking about Mum. It's all *my* fault. I made it happen. I made her ill.'

'Relax, Lucy,' Miranda said, handing her a glass of white wine. 'Don't upset yourself.'

Lucy's teeth chattered against the glass. She eventually managed a big gulp of wine. Miranda gave her a job to do, cooking the microwave pizza and putting out crackers and cheese, while she arranged slices of brown bread and slivers of salmon.

'I know we're grazing all over the place,' Miranda said, 'so tomorrow I'm making a big chicken curry and a lasagne or two to keep us going.'

'I'll help,' Lucy said in a quavery voice, telling Ellie she was still on an emotional edge.

They picked at some food, Ellie scarcely tasting hers. Afterwards, she was sorry she hadn't gone straight home, or left while there was still an uneasy truce between them, because as Miranda talked about Vivienne's prospects for a good recovery, Lucy gulped more wine, and became increasingly upset.

372

'Do you think she'll ever recover?' she asked, her hand shaking as she lifted a slice of pizza.

'That's all in the lap of the gods and her own state of mind,' Miranda said. 'She has to want to wake up.'

'That's not good, because she was very angry with me. I have to talk about it before I go mad,' Lucy said, putting down her untouched slice of pizza. 'We'd a huge row, me and Mum, earlier that night. I was the one who caused her attack.'

Ellie sighed. 'Could we have less of the drama queen, please? I doubt if what you said put Mum in hospital.'

'I'm not being a drama queen,' Lucy rounded on her. 'I said some terrible things and I need to get it off my conscience.'

'Okay. What did you say?' Miranda asked in a tone of voice that told Ellie she didn't believe Lucy could have done anything wrong.

'It was about Dad,' Lucy said, her voice catching.

'What about him?' Ellie asked sharply.

Lucy stared into her wine glass. 'I started asking about him, like why he really went away, how come he'd died so suddenly—'

'For God's sake, hasn't this come up time and time again over the years? Why now?' Ellie fumed, unable to believe how annoyed she felt with Lucy.

'Why not now?' Lucy lifted her chin, her eyes challenging. 'I always felt that Mum was holding something back, and it turns out I was right. I never asked her much about Dad because I was afraid to ask too many questions *and* because I was afraid to find out the truth.'

'You mean Mum always spoiled you and you didn't want to upset the apple cart,' Ellie said cuttingly. She was quietly horrified that after all her best intentions, she was arguing with Lucy. But trust Lucy to turn things around so that she was centre stage. Maybe she should have followed her mother onto the stage, she thought blackly.

'I didn't want to upset her and I ended up doing just that,' Lucy said quietly, pushing away her plate.

'I still don't know why you had to start badgering her in the first place,' Ellie said, conscious that she'd be better off changing the subject.

Lucy gave her a mocking glance. 'No, I don't suppose you do. It was all right for you, Ellie and you too, Miranda. You didn't have a dad who ignored you.'

'Lucy, don't start playing the victim role again,' Ellie said. 'Worse things happen to families and people. Sometimes life is shit.'

'So? This is my life I'm talking about,' Lucy said. 'I know I was spoiled by Mum. Even that made me feel the odd one out, as though she was giving me special treatment because she was making up for something. Well, she was.'

'We lost our dad too,' Ellie said, tension on top of exhaustion making her feel ill. 'It was a difficult time for us, and made ten times worse when Mum took up with Zach. Isn't that right, Miranda?'

Miranda shook her head. 'Don't drag me into this. I'm not taking any sides.'

'It wasn't as bad for you as it was for me,' Ellie retorted. 'A lot of it went over your head. And you, Lucy, have you any idea what it was like to be in a classroom full of hormonal teenagers, where your mother's love-life was the topic of sniggering taunts?'

'So you must have really hated me when I came along. A constant reminder,' Lucy said softly, her grey eyes wide as she stared at Ellie.

'For God's sake, you two, stop carrying on like school kids,' Miranda finally snapped. 'And that's a bit much, Ellie. From what I remember, in those days you were the queen of your classroom. You were tall and beautiful, and even then you had a

374

special quality that set you apart. I find it hard to believe your classmates managed to get through that veneer.'

'Hah! You have it all wrong,' Ellie said. 'I didn't feel remotely beautiful. I was set apart from everyone else all right, but for all the wrong reasons. I wasn't part of the in-crowd, and was so painfully self-conscious it wasn't funny.'

'You could have fooled me. Have you any idea of the way I used to look up to you? I always felt like a second-best version of you, as though I was a very pale imitation. Still do, some-times . . .' her voice trailed away.

Ellie looked at her, confusion spiralling inside her. Where had this come from? Miranda was giving her a level look, and she knew from her sister's convincing tones it hadn't just been a remark spat out in the heat of the moment, but something that had quietly festered.

'Don't be ridiculous,' she said. 'There's no reason for you to think like that. I'm no more beautiful than you are.'

'Well you've always had something. A kind of sheen, a gilt-edged quality that men find attractive. You only have to bat your eyelashes at them to have them eating out of the palm of your hand.' Miranda was smiling at her, but it was a strained smile that made Ellie uneasy.

She laughed, to cover her disquiet. 'That's nonsense. Look at Johnny – Lucy only had to wiggle her hips to make him eat out of that and forget about me.'

'You didn't want him,' Lucy said defensively, hugging her arms around herself. 'He knew that and I knew that. It's the only reason we got it together.'

Then to Ellie's complete surprise, Miranda said, 'I guess you could say that what goes around comes around.'

'What do you mean?' Ellie asked, her scalp prickling.

Miranda was silent for a moment and the kitchen crackled

with tension until she said, with a half laugh, 'I've never admitted this, but my love life is littered with a trail of men who took one look at you and found they preferred the gilt-edged Morgan sister to me.'

'*What*?' Ellie's head was spinning. Miranda's features danced in front of her. All Ellie could make out was the honesty in her sister's eyes which bored through her like a painful laser.

'That's why I went away to Hong Kong,' Miranda said calmly, as though she was talking about going shopping and not a huge problem she'd had with Ellie all these years. 'I needed to get away from feeling stuck between the beautiful Ellie and pretty model Lucy, and start off somewhere anonymous. And it worked, or should I say it *was* working. I was feeling good about myself at last. As though I was finally me. Until, well, hello, here I am, back in Dublin and nothing has changed. I'm still piggy in the middle, trying to keep the peace, and stop you guys from killing each other.'

'Stop it!' Lucy begged. 'Miranda, I can't bear to hear you talking like that. I love you to bits. You're my soft, gorgeous sister. The one person I can turn to no matter what happens. I'm sorry I was to blame for dragging you back home.'

'What happened to Mum was an accident,' Miranda said.

'No, it was *my* fault. That's what I'm trying to tell you. I found out things about my dad that I hadn't known and I raged at Mum.'

'What did she tell you?' Miranda asked.

'I was left an inheritance. Would you believe that?' Lucy said desperately.

'But that's good isn't it?' Miranda said slowly.

'Yes and no. Mum kept it from me all these years because she didn't trust me to be able to handle it. But at least it's some form of acknowledgement from Dad.' Lucy's voice was thin and it grated on Ellie. 'But that wasn't the worst of it,' Lucy went on. 'The worst of it was the real reason he went away. Mum let it slip and I told her I'd never forgive her and now she could be dying.'

Ellie finally found her voice. 'What did she say, Lucy, about why your dad went off?'

Lucy gave her a mocking glance. 'I bet you knew all along and you never told me either.'

'What do you mean?' Ellie asked sharply.

'You must have known if they were having rows or just got sick of each other. I was reared on the fairytale that my father went to Canada to work and I assumed he just wasn't bothered with me. But I was wrong. Because he was *sent* away – by Mum.'

'Did she say why?'

'Does it matter?' Lucy glared at her, her eyes glinting with a sheen of tears. 'He didn't even know she was pregnant with me when he left, and he never got a chance to come back, but it was her fault that he went away and that's why I told her I hated her.'

Then Lucy burst into a storm of weeping and threw herself into Miranda's arms.

Chapter 42

As Ellie drove up the lane towards Laurel View in the gathering evening, every bone in her body was on fire with tension and exhaustion. A bath, a generous brandy and bed – in that order.

But it wasn't to be. As she turned in at the gate she saw Johnny's Mercedes parked in the corner of her driveway. Her heart sank and she willed him to vaporise into the shadows shrouding the garden. Thanks to the heated words with her sisters, she was already stretched to breaking point, and hadn't the energy for anything else. As she came to a halt, he climbed out of his car and gave her a nervous smile.

If she had been through the wars over the past few weeks, then so had he. His eyes were apologetic and tentative, and his handsome face was taut, his mouth turned down at the corners. The debonair aura he usually flaunted like one of his dress jackets was subdued, the cocksure composure finally bruised.

'What do *you* want?' she asked.

'Just a quick chat,' he said soberly. 'Sorry if I've caught you by surprise, but I thought waiting here was the best chance of seeing you.'

'You're right,' she retorted. 'I'd scarcely have picked up your call or answered the door.'

All along she'd wondered how this moment would feel, but in spite of the relationship she'd had with this man and how much they had meant to each other, it was as though there was a sheet of glass between them. Or maybe she was still too raw and shocked after the evening, never mind the past few days, to feel anything more.

'You'd better come in,' she said, not wanting to have words with him out in her front garden.

'Thanks, Ellie,' he said in a sober voice, crossing the threshold with an overly exaggerated hangdog look. This was a new, über-contrite Johnny. He was just short of wearing a sackcloth and ashes and, to her surprise, it saddened her. It didn't suit Johnny Tyler to look defeated.

'There's no need to play the prodigal son,' she said a little smartly. 'It won't wash with me.'

'Ouch. You Morgan sisters know how to give as good as you get.'

She raised an eyebrow. He had clearly been talking to Lucy as well, and she wondered what her sister had had to say to him – nothing good, by the look of him. Down in the kitchen she stood with her back to the island counter and folded her arms. 'Tea? Or coffee?'

'No thanks.' He shook his head. 'I just wanted to say – I guess it's far too late to say I'm sorry? For what it's worth, I am. Deeply.'

'I accept your apology,' she said smoothly.

His eyebrows shot up, as though he had never expected her to capitulate so easily. 'Do you? Really? I don't suppose . . . ' he gave her a hopeful look while he left the rest of his sentence hanging in mid air.

'Not a chance,' Ellie said firmly. 'Don't even go there for one moment. I'm not accepting your apology to make you feel any better. Or because I want to pick up where we left off, and if you had that nonsensical idea, for however briefly, then you're a bigger eejit than I thought.'

Johnny looked crestfallen, but Ellie ploughed on. 'It's more for myself. To help me move on. I'm not saying I'll ever forget what happened, but I do forgive you.'

Forgive us our trespasses as we forgive those who trespass against us – wasn't that the way the prayer went? Karma. As Miranda said, what goes round comes round. And around and around . . .

'I thought we were good together, Ellie,' he said, his voice tender. His bedroom voice.

'We were.' For a moment, she felt something inside her waver. She forced herself to remember Lucy and her alabaster limbs as she scrambled off the bed.

'I thought we were in love.'

'When you stand back, Johnny, you'll see that we were both buying into an image,' she said tiredly. 'We were in love with the image of us in the golden circle of Dublin celebrity la-la land. We fed each other's ego. We were handy for each other, good press, convenient, a habit.'

'A habit? I can't believe that's all I meant to you? I loved you, still love you—'

'You don't.'

'Hell, Ellie, I even asked you to marry me . . . surely that meant something?'

'Only because you thought it was time for marriage. It wasn't because you couldn't live without me.'

'Would wanting to wake up beside you every morning not count? Or simply being there for you when you're tired at the end of a hard day? That's what I wanted, Ellie, to share every single part of your life.'

She shrugged. There was no point in saying that nobody could share anyone else's life to that extent. 'If you'd really loved me, you'd never have slept with Lucy out of spite.'

'I fucked up, didn't I? I'd hate to think our relationship was always going to be defined by that. It was the worst mistake I ever made.'

'It was,' she agreed, marvelling at her coolness – but that was only on the outside. Underneath the calm exterior, her chest was paining her. 'Sometimes, mistakes can be very costly,' she went on. 'Even the silliest, most heedless mistake can do all sorts of irreparable damage. Because, you see, you can never undo them.' Tears pricked the back of her eyes. Her head began to thump.

'I've no comeback, have I?' His mouth smiled crookedly.

'No.'

'I didn't mean to hurt you,' he said, again in that tender voice. 'You might have forgiven me, but I'll never be able to forgive myself.'

In the bleak look he gave her, the last traces of his jauntiness were gone and the pain grew and moved up and expanded into her throat so that it was difficult to breathe. This was it, the end of it all. They moved awkwardly up the hall, like two strangers, and she didn't wait until he had fired the engine of his car before she shut the door, her hand trembling. She couldn't even cry, she was so tightly wound up, but she knew she had done the right thing. Johnny had never been enough for her. There had always been something missing.

She now knew there *was* such a thing as feverish, exhilarating sex. The kind of passion that caused you to abandon all control. She hadn't been imagining it. She knew exactly what it felt like, looked like, tasted like.

Ellie didn't think she'd be able to sleep after the upset of Johnny's visit on top of Lucy's tears and drama, never mind Miranda's startling revelations, but as soon as her head hit the pillow, she fell into a deep, dreamless sleep. She woke around three o'clock in the morning and she slipped out of bed and went to the window, absorbing the shimmer of the cityscape in the near distance.

She stood for a moment watching the panorama of thousands of lights glittering iridescently as far as the horizon, like a breathtaking, magic carpet. She wondered how Ben would compare it with the high-octane sparkle of the New York night-time skyline. Or the deep, soulful stillness of a dawn-lit Leitrim countryside. She guessed he'd come down on the side of his beloved Celtic roots. Not that she'd ever know for sure. He'd scarcely have a chance to see it, stuck in New York as he was. A pang of regret hit her and she went back to bed, leaving the curtains open and plumping up the pillows before she settled herself under the duvet once more. Somewhere in the night, she had a vivid dream of them making love, but this time she didn't hold back. This time she allowed herself to get lost in the feelings surging through every cell of her body, soul and spirit, just the way she'd always known love-making could be. She stirred a little, and opened her eyes long enough to see the stars winking through the skylight. She imagined Ben's face against that glittery backdrop.

It fitted in perfectly.

Lucy stretched in bed as she heard Miranda and Ellie talking quietly downstairs. Before they left for the hospital Miranda came up to warn her that there was a photographer skulking around outside, just a few doors up the road.

'Ellie spotted him, and he dived down pretending he was checking the wheel of a car.'

'I'm not going anywhere,' Lucy said. 'I'll be here waiting for you to come back with the news.'

'Right. Enjoy your lie-in, you need it. See you later.' Miranda blew her a kiss.

Lucy heard the soft click of the hall door behind them and from the street outside, the engine of Ellie's car starting up, before it accelerated away from the kerb.

Miranda and Ellie were seeing the consulting team that morning to discuss their mother's prognosis, and they had agreed it was best for Lucy to stay at home and have a lie-in as it didn't need the three of them to talk to the doctors. Lucy had said she was happy enough with that, so long as they told her the exact truth. She was privately relieved that she was spared a hospital visit that morning. She knew it probably meant she was selfish and uncaring, but she badly needed a break from long hours spent watching her mum hooked up to frightening-looking equipment.

She fervently hoped the doctors would have good news to report but no matter what they said, she would have to talk to Rebecca that afternoon, whether she liked it or not, even if it meant waving goodbye to a lucrative contract. Her mother came first. She hadn't told her sisters about her golden opportunity. It seemed all wrong to be thinking about her career with their mum so ill. And they were all down in the dumps and at loggerheads with each other.

Take last night. She wasn't quite sure what had gone wrong. For starters, she'd almost lost it from guilt and anxiety. But something else had gone wrong between her sisters. She'd been shocked at Miranda, of all people, having words with Ellie and she'd fully expected Ellie to go in, all guns blazing, and demand a proper explanation for Miranda's strange comments. It was obvious Miranda was feeling the strain, so Lucy had managed to change the subject around to her father and after a short while, Ellie had simply put on her jacket and left.

Just like that.

Which made her wonder what the hell was really going on between them.

After a while she got up, showered and dressed. Down in the kitchen, the sun was streaming in, a cheery yellow beacon brightening up the whole room. Suddenly, Lucy felt a lift of hope and was gripped with the belief that it would all turn out fine. Miranda's words came back to her, about their mum being determined to get well, and her utter conviction that her heart had been weak to begin with, and that Lucy hadn't caused her collapse. She hugged that to herself as she poured a glass of orange juice.

When the doorbell chimed, she thought at first that it was another of the many bouquets of flowers that had started to arrive for her mother from her friends and acting colleagues. Unless it was Miranda ... fear gripped her ... unless something was wrong. She hurried up the hall and opened the door. To her complete surprise, the person standing in the porch was Ian.

Chapter 43

'What did you make of that?' Miranda asked, feeling a little down as she and Ellie left the small room beside the Coronary Care Unit, where they'd spoken to a member of the cardiac team. It had taken less than ten minutes for the consultant to tell them what they already knew, courtesy of the vigilant, experienced nurses.

'They can't guarantee the extent of her recovery either way,' Ellie said, her voice strained.

'At least Mum is off the critical list,' Miranda said, trying to sound more positive than she felt. 'And she could wake up at any moment. The sooner the better.'

Today, Ellie was wearing an ivory cashmere jumper and black leather pants. Her dark hair was caught back in a jewelled barrette. Miranda thought she looked beautiful in spite of her emerald eyes clouded with worry and her skin pale and tight as though she'd been awake half the night. So far, Ellie hadn't referred to her outburst of the previous evening, which suited Miranda.

385

She'd been secretly horrified to hear herself in full flow, baring her worst fears to her sister and admitting the shabby truth about her love life. She knew her usual reticence had deserted her because of the shock at seeing their mum so ill, and anxiety at the way Christian was ignoring her. He still hadn't replied to the texts she'd sent him and her heart was heavy. Outside, it was a beautiful spring morning and sunlight poured through corridor windows and threw oblongs of light across tiled floors. It was a day for walking along a beach with the breeze on your face, or taking a stroll through a woodland glade. Not a day for being confined within the sterile walls of a hospital. Miranda was beginning to feel claustrophobic. In a few short hours her whole life had shrunk to this airless corridor with the pale blue walls, the waiting area with the drinks machine and endless huddle of anxious relatives waiting for news, and the heart-wrenching room where her mother lay, her life even more on hold than Miranda's.

They weren't allowed through to the ward to see Vivienne. Gillian was on duty again and she explained that Vivienne's condition was much the same, she was sleeping and peaceful, but the ward was closed off to everyone except critical visitors while cleaning was in progress.

'We'll be freshening up your mother as well, so all this will take an hour or so. Come back later.'

'I guess it's coffee time again,' Miranda said. 'My insides are revolting against it, but at least we can phone Lucy from the café.'

'I'll need a colonic irrigation after this,' Ellie said drily as they sat drinking insipid coffee and nibbling on blueberry muffins.

'Same here,' Miranda said. She picked up her mobile and called Lucy, surprised that there was no answer.

'She's probably still asleep,' Ellie said.

'She was awake when we left, but she probably fell back asleep again. I'll send her a text.' Miranda sent her a brief message to say there was no real change, but their mum was off the critical list. She had just put down her mobile when it buzzed.

'Lucy,' she said, automatically assuming it was her sister. Then her whole body tensed as she glanced at the caller display. Christian. At last. She glanced at Ellie and hurriedly excused herself, rising to her feet and moving away from the table and down to the end of the café where it was quieter. She stood against the mezzanine rail and stared down onto the hive of activity that was the ground floor and entrance foyer of the hospital.

'Christian. Hi,' she said, feeling stricken with shyness.

'Hi, yourself,' he began, sounding very clear and very upbeat. 'How are things with your mum?'

'More or less the same. She's holding her own. We're still not sure what her ultimate prognosis is, not even the doctors can tell us that. But they're optimistic.'

'It must be a difficult time for you all.'

'It is,' she said in a quiet voice.

'Thanks for the texts by the way. I didn't reply because I thought it was better to talk to you in person.'

She wasn't sure if that was good or bad. She turned around to face the café, leaning back against the rail, and saw Ellie looking across at her with a puzzled face. 'Christian, I've no idea when I'll be back in Hong Kong. As soon as Mum is on the road to recovery—'

'I can't wait that long.'

Disappointment flooded through her. 'Sorry, but—'

'You don't get it.' His voice was full of warmth. 'I'm here,' he said, 'in Dublin airport. Did you really think I'd leave you to face this alone?'

'What?' All her senses whirled. She felt separated from the

activity around her, the queue shuffling along by the counter, a child crying to get out of its buggy, the hiss of the coffee machine and Ellie still watching her carefully.

Ellie, knowing Miranda's secret baggage. *My love-life is littered with a trail of men who took one look at you and found they preferred the gilt-edged Morgan sister to me.*

And Christian knowing her history and fears. Something thudded into her chest.

'So where are you?' He was still talking. 'I'm waiting for my luggage to come through, then I have to find somewhere to stay, grab a quick shower, and then I'm all yours.'

All yours.

'Let me think,' she said, her mind racing. Not the house in Dún Laoghaire, with Lucy and Ellie, especially Ellie, coming and going. Somewhere neutral. 'How about I book you into a convenient hotel? I should have it done by the time you collect your luggage. You'll get a taxi outside the terminal, and I'll meet you there.'

'That sounds perfect.'

'Call you back in a few minutes,' she said.

She felt like laughing ruefully at herself. There was no avoiding her fears now. They had been thrust upon her without any notice. Yet, right then, her joy at seeing Christian shortly lifted her so much that it outweighed her anxiety.

'Was that him?' Ellie asked, when she went back to the table. 'I know there's someone, Miranda. It was obvious from the minute I saw you walking up the ward on Wednesday.' Her voice softened. 'And I'm glad, you deserve it. I hope he's nice.'

'He is. And he's here in Dublin,' Miranda said slowly, watching for Ellie's reaction. 'He's just called me from the airport.'

'Oh.' There was a silence. Ellie pushed some crumbs around on her plate. Then she looked at Miranda and gave her a wry smile. 'About what you said, last night—'

'Forget it,' Miranda urged, knowing she still had this hurdle to contend with, and, of course, it was magnified now that both Ellie and Christian were also aware of it.

'I've been thinking about it, and you were right in some ways,' Ellie said. 'I guess I subconsciously set out to attract men as a way of bolstering my confidence—'

'*Your* confidence?' Miranda laughed. Coming from Ellie, this was hilarious.

'You'd be surprised,' Ellie said drily. She gazed into the distance for a while before continuing, 'But I never meant to pull your boyfriends or put a dint in any of your relationships.'

'Didn't you?' Miranda asked softly, holding Ellie's eyes with her own.

Ellie eventually looked away. 'Not intentionally. I suppose at a deeper level I was jealous because I didn't have a meaningful, exciting relationship myself. Not even with Johnny.'

'That's a surprise to me.'

'There was always something missing. I thought I found it with someone in New York . . . but I don't know if it was just because he didn't seem all that interested in me or because I knew I couldn't have him . . . the lure of the unobtainable. You see, Miranda,' she smiled wistfully, 'deep down, I wonder if that's how I get my kicks. Wanting what I can't, or shouldn't, have.' She compressed her empty coffee cup in her hand. 'And this is a ridiculously heavy conversation to be having at this hour of the day.'

'I always consoled myself by saying those guys couldn't have been right for me,' Miranda said. 'And I don't think you were flaunting your inner temptress on purpose. Unfortunately for me, they just took one look at you and I was history.'

'That won't happen anymore because you look radiant,' Ellie said. 'Not just your hair and your clothes, but everything about you. It's as though you finally believe in yourself. I didn't think I'd ever say this, but getting away from us all was the best thing you ever did.'

'It was hard, especially at the beginning. I was terribly home-sick, but I knew I had to do it to save myself from drowning in misery. And, right now, I'm going to love you and leave you because I want to meet Christian. I'm booking him into the Merrion and I can get a taxi outside and be there when he arrives. There's nothing I can do for Mum this morning.'

'Go on then, off with you,' Ellie smiled.

'I'll see you later and call me if there's anything.'

'Of course I will.'

Ellie watched Miranda pull on her jacket and grab her bag and mobile and tried not to be envious of her sister's excitement. Be glad for her, she told herself, that there was someone called Christian in her life who had encouraged her to crawl out of her shell. He must love her if he'd followed her home to Ireland.

There was no chance of Ben being able to do that for the foreseeable future. He'd been texting every day, and his messages were funny and warm, just like he was. She missed him. She still hadn't got over the huge wrench it had been to leave him in New York.

Her mobile chimed and it was Lucy. Awake at last.

'Didn't you get Miranda's text?' she asked straightaway, still feeling she was on awkward ground with Lucy.

'Thank God you answered, Ellie, I thought you might have been in the ward. Is Miranda in there?'

'She's gone off for a couple of hours. I'm on my own in the hospital café.'

'I need your help, Ellie.'

'My help? What for?'

'I can't tell you over the phone. I'll tell you when I see you. Can you come home? Now?'

'Lucy, don't tell me we're back to drama-queen tactics?' Ellie said in a cold voice. 'Get off the stage. We had enough of that last night.'

'Please, Ellie. I need you to come home, now, immediately. Then it'll all be explained. Promise.'

Lucy ended the call. Ellie fumed. Trust her youngest sister to start throwing a tantrum, even with Mum ill in hospital.

Ellie left the café and stalked back to the waiting area outside the Coronary Care Unit and the theatre suites. She pressed the bell for the nurse and when she was told that the ward was closed for a further hour she decided to go home to Laurel View for a while.

Lucy could go to hell, she thought as she stabbed her parking ticket into the machine and waited for the barrier to rise. She didn't owe her any favours, especially after the way she'd betrayed her with Johnny.

What goes around comes around. She remembered Miranda's words from the night before and suddenly she saw Lucy's defensive attitude in a different light. It reminded her of the time she too had used defence tactics to cover up her vulnerability. She closed her eyes for a millisecond and remembered how Lucy had sounded on the phone. Nervous. Shaky. She clutched the steering wheel tightly as she accelerated out onto the main road and turned towards Dún Laoghaire.

Chapter 44

'I told you she wouldn't come,' Lucy said.

'Well you're just going to have to try again,' Ian said.

Lucy shivered. She was sitting at the table and Ian was leaning back against the kitchen counter, arms folded in front of him, and although he hadn't looked at them, she knew he was aware that there was a block of kitchen knives within reach. His face was pale, making his stubble look darker. He was casually dressed in dark jeans and a thin jacket over a light-grey top. She tried not to think she was memorising these details in case she needed to give his description to the police. She was afraid, too, that if she made a move in the wrong direction, he might reach for a knife. She wondered then if she was being overly dramatic. Ellie would surely think she was.

At first, Lucy had been delighted to see Ian at the door. She'd welcomed him like a friend, assuming he had finally seen her messages and had decided it was best to come to Dublin to talk to her. She'd brought him down to the kitchen, but he'd asked so many questions about her mother's condition and prognosis, and he'd been so obviously on edge, that Lucy had begun to feel there was something not quite right.

'What is it, Ian? Why do you need to know so much about my mum? And, no, she hasn't come around yet. Is there something going on that I don't know about?'

'Who found your mother?'

'The neighbours. That's a funny question. How did you know she . . . ' her voice had trailed away. *How did you know she'd been found*, she was about to ask. *How did you know she didn't just phone an ambulance herself, or happened to be with friends when she fell ill?*

Then she'd remembered that she hadn't even texted him since she left London.

'Jesus! Were you here that night when Mum collapsed?'

He'd remained silent, just staring at her, and she'd continued, anger flaring inside her at the injustice of it. 'You *were* here. How dare you leave her alone? She could have *died*. And you would have killed her. I'm going to call the police.'

Lucy had reached for her mobile, but he had been quicker, and he'd plucked it off the table and moved along the counter, nearer to the block of knives. Lucy's blood had run cold. There was no mistaking his threat. The back door was locked, with the key put away. She'd tried to judge the distance to the hall, but had known she would never make it.

'I'm not a murderer,' he'd said.

Not yet, she'd thought.

'Some crazy dog started barking so I guessed she'd be found. Where's Ellie?' he'd asked.

'I don't know who you're talking about,' she'd said.

'Come on, Lucy, I know she's your sister.'

'I hardly talk to Ellie, I don't know where she is.'

He'd scrolled through her contacts page on her mobile until

he came to Ellie's name. He'd pressed the call button and had put the phone to Lucy's ear. 'Tell her to come home. Just that. No more.'

And, of course, Ellie had refused, thinking Lucy was wallowing into another tantrum. After listening to the conversation for a minute, Ian had taken her mobile and disconnected the call.

Now she watched him putting it down on the counter, beside the block of knives. So near and yet so far away. And nothing about this made any kind of sense.

'Why do you want to see Ellie?' she asked.

'I think she can answer some questions for me. Questions you couldn't answer and your mother wasn't able to.'

Lucy sat, cold with shock. 'You're not in PR, are you?' she said, realising why she hadn't been able to find him on Google. His company didn't exist. 'Why the pretence? What's all this about?'

'I had to find a quick way of getting close to you so that you'd talk to me. If I'd just walked up to you in the street, or in a pub, how far would I have got?'

'I dunno,' she shrugged trying to look nonchalant, although her heart was hammering.

'Come on, Lucy. You inhabit such a different world to me, we're poles apart. I'm a car mechanic who left school at sixteen. Look at you, a glamorous model with the world at your feet. You're always surrounded by hot-shot people and celeb-chasing paparazzi. I wouldn't have got anywhere near you.'

She sat there, letting the silence lengthen between them, knowing there was some truth in what he said. She thought of how they'd met, how willingly she'd accepted him as part of her glittering world because of his false image. Something to think about later.

'It was you who sent me that wreath,' she said, taking a wild guess into the dark, still trying to figure out who he was and what he wanted.

'Clever girl.'

'I don't understand. What was the point? That didn't scare me.'

'Didn't it? I heard you hot-footed it home pretty quickly.'

'You were following me.'

'Not literally, not until the about three weeks ago.'

Jesus, whatever he wanted, this was serious. 'You weren't very professional. I knew I was being followed. Even here. I went to the police and they're keeping an eye on me.'

'Oh, yeah, they'll come to your help, just like your sister, I'm sure.'

'I liked you,' she said, desperately. 'I was all set to hire you as my trusted PR guy. I even felt we had a connection.'

He smiled, and it unnerved her. 'We do have a connection, Lucy. Haven't you figured it out yet?'

She looked at him, her brain galloping furiously. 'Is it something to do with my father?'

'You're getting warm.'

'Who are you?' she whispered.

Again that smile, but it was empty of real feeling. 'Zach Anderson was my father too.'

His father too. That meant he was her half-brother. 'Fuck. Aaargh!' She jumped to her feet. 'I almost kissed you. I even thought about sleeping with you. Jesus *Christ.*'

'Sit down,' he said. 'I wasn't going to let that happen.'

She sat down, recalling the night she thought she'd been rejected by him. The hastily turned cheek, the feeling of being let down. Bloody hell. Nausea rose inside her. 'How do I know you're telling the truth? I've never heard of you before.'

'No, because I'm somebody else that Zach Anderson decided

to ignore. So well that I'd no idea he was my dad until a few months ago. And I can't prove it conclusively, other than I'm supposed to have a slight resemblance to him. I knew you'd never listen to me if I just sprung it on you, so I had to find a different way to reach you and get you to talk to me.'

She stared at him for long moments, taking in everything he'd said. She recalled old photographs of her father, but she found it difficult to spot any resemblance. Maybe around the eyes . . .

'Why the wreath though? What was behind that?'

'I arranged that because I wanted to rattle you and get some revenge.'

In spite of her nervousness, Lucy felt a sense of outrage. 'What have I ever done to you?'

'When I started to google Zach, you were all over the references like a rash, your name coupled with his, up there in lights. I was angry, like someone possessed. Everywhere I looked, you were recognised as his daughter. It was the kind of recognition I never received. I was hoping too that it would shake you up enough to talk to the press about him and his anniversary. That you might have used it for publicity. Appearing in the tabloids seems to be one of your major pastimes—'

'I can't help that,' she said defensively. 'But I know little or nothing about Zach Anderson.'

'I didn't realise that until after we had talked,' Ian admitted. 'So I came over here to see your mum and I was wondering how I'd get her to talk to me when I took a chance at knocking on the door on Monday night. I didn't expect her to answer.'

'Mum doesn't usually answer the door to strangers. Especially at night.' Monday night. Lucy bit her lip. The night they'd had a row. Mum's guard must have been down. Oh, God.

'What did you say to her?' she asked.

'Not much. She took one look at me, said she was going to call the police and then she collapsed.'

'You must have threatened her or something.'

'I didn't. But I got the feeling that my very presence was a threat. Has she something to hide? Hmm, Lucy?'

'I told you already, I don't know.'

'I heard her whispering Ellie's name as she fell. That's why I came back this morning. I need you to get Ellie back here so that I can talk to her.'

'That's a laugh. I told you she wouldn't come. We've had a row and she's not talking to me so she's hardly going to talk to you. Hey – this is about the money, isn't it?'

'What money?'

'The money that's held in trust for me. The royalties from Zach's song—' She broke off at the sound of the hall door opening and footsteps coming down the hall.

Then Ellie walked into the kitchen.

Chapter 45

*I*an had seen photographs of Ellie on the internet but nothing had prepared him for how beautiful she was in real life. Different from Lucy's obvious prettiness, more like a famous movie star on the lines of Angelina Jolie, she exuded an inner sensuality and polished confidence. It came from everything about her, the way she glided through the door, the way she tilted her head to one side and gave him a calm, expectant look, and the graceful way she sat down as though she was quite relaxed in her own skin.

And not in the least bit fazed by him, even though she had taken in the situation in one appraising glance.

'Hi, sis, we have a visitor,' Lucy said.

'So I see. What's going on?' she asked in a soft, melodious voice that surprised him and somehow calmed his jittery nerves.

He saw her beautiful eyes sweep over Lucy as though to say, *It's fine, it'll be okay* and, funnily enough, he clutched to that reassurance himself. For the situation he was finding himself in was becoming more tense by the minute. He'd never envisaged those months ago that his anger-fuelled quest for the truth about his father would turn out like a low-budget thriller, with him standing in a Dublin kitchen, near enough to a block of knives to appear alarming to his half-sister, having scared her mother enough to induce a heart attack.

If his mother could see him now.

Mum! He felt the familiar pain in his chest when he thought of her. She'd have words with him and they sure as hell wouldn't be complimentary. But he was at a loss as to how he might extricate himself, without bringing the wrath of Lucy down on his head, never mind the possibility that she'd call the police. And he still was no nearer the truth.

Ellie was talking. 'Is this why you called me, Lucy?'

'Yes, I didn't think you'd come. What made you change your mind?'

'You said you needed my help.'

He saw the two sisters looking at each other as though some other meaningful exchange was going on under the surface. For a ridiculous moment, he wished Ellie would look at him like that, as though she truly cared.

'I don't think you've ever actually said that to me before,' he heard her say to Lucy.

'Ian wants to talk to you,' Lucy said.

'Ian.' Ellie's beautiful eyes were focused totally on him. He found her attention disconcerting. 'What can I do for you?' she asked, in that calm, soft voice he somehow found encouraging.

'I want to know the truth about how my father died.'

Ellie knew who he was the minute she walked into the room and looked at those heavily lashed dark-grey eyes.

Zach. She'd seen those eyes smile at her mother across the kitchen table. This man could only be Zach's son, but he was missing his father's magnetic charm and raw energy. It was as though a very pale version of Zach Anderson had come back from the dead. What she couldn't figure out was what he was doing here, in a rather menacing situation. How had he known where Vivienne lived? Why had Lucy let him in? Lucy was sitting at the table, pale faced but calm and composed despite the way he was leaning against the counter, his right hand far too close to the block of knives for Ellie's liking. Her mobile phone was beyond her reach. Well done, Lucy, she thought silently. Her sister was holding it together and hadn't given in to her dramatic impulses.

Ellie tried to work out her options. She could take a run at him, and urge Lucy to fetch help, or she could run for help herself. In both scenarios, he'd have enough time to grab a knife and inflict damage on Lucy's lovely face – although he didn't look like the knife-wielding type. He looked ill at ease and rather sad. It was best, she decided, to play along with him. The answers to her questions could come later.

'So you want to know about your father?' she asked. 'That's fine. I'll tell you everything I can.'

'You know who I am?' He seemed pleased with this.

'Yes, you have to be Zach Anderson's son.'

'I am, and I want to know how and why he died. Like, whether it was deliberate on his part, or an unfortunate accident? Or—' he stared at her, 'could it even have been murder?'

She hesitated. 'Why don't you start by telling me what you know, and we'll work from there.'

'I know very little. I only found out recently that he was my dad.'

'Oh?' She made herself smile encouragingly. Keep him talking, isn't that what they advised you to do if you were in a difficult situation? Let him get it off his chest.

'I looked him up on the internet, but there's only general information about his early career, his relationship with your mum and, of course, loads about Lucy. But I can't figure out how he ended up in Canada, when he had planned to go back to Scotland. Or how the hell he found himself at the bottom of a lake. Reports said he died in questionable circumstances. That could mean anything. Somebody, somewhere must know more.'

Ellie stared at him, feeling a little faint. 'Zach's relationship with our mother was very brief,' she said. 'When it had ended he chose to go to Canada because he thought the wonderful landscape would be inspirational,' she said. 'As well as that, it was a convenient back door into America. He'd planned to take America by storm, but, well, that didn't happen. And we certainly didn't know he had a son.'

'He knew he had a son, but he ignored me.'

'How come you only found out about your dad recently?' Ellie asked in a quiet voice.

Ian's eyes darted nervously around the room. 'My mum told me.'

'Your mum?'

'Yeah, Heather Douglas. She told me just before— before she died. About Zach.'

Lucy swallowed a gasp. Ellie noticed that Ian was breathing hard. She threw Lucy a reassuring look and strove to be calm. 'I'm very sorry to hear she's passed away. You must be missing her.'

'Missing her?' He looked blank now, as he stared at her, but she sensed he wasn't really seeing her at all. 'It's much more than that. I can't even start to get my head around it.'

'I can imagine how you feel,' Ellie said.

'No, you can't. You haven't a clue,' he snapped. 'All along I thought my father was the asshole she'd lived with, who'd died

401

of alcoholic poisoning when I was five. The guy she'd moved in with before I'd been born and put up with just to keep a roof over our heads because her parents had kicked her out when they found out she was pregnant at sixteen. Can you imagine what that was like?'

'No,' Ellie swallowed.

'After he died we moved into a poky flat. We never had much money, it was always a struggle. I left school at sixteen and was glad to bring home a few bob. Just when she was beginning to have a bit of a life, she got sick. By the time she went to the doctor, it was too late. The cancer had spread all over and she had six weeks left. Can you imagine that?'

He didn't wait for an answer. 'That was when she told me about Zach. In the cancer ward. With the curtains closed around her bed.'

'Ian!' Lucy cried, her eyes wide with dismay.

Ellie shot her sister a look as though to urge her to stay still, but Ian went on as though he hadn't heard her.

'He was her hero from the wrong side of town,' he said. 'He saw himself as the next Mick Jagger, waiting for stardom to knock by playing in third-rate clubs in Edinburgh. She believed in him, and spent hours with him, just listening to his music. She was two months gone with me when he was discovered by a talent scout. He was whisked to London to be groomed for fame and fortune. Before he left, he told my mum that a pregnant girlfriend wouldn't be good for his hip, rock image, not while he was establishing himself. She told him to follow his dreams and he promised he'd come back to her eventually. But she never saw him again, because he never had a chance to keep his promise.'

Ellie opened her mouth to say something soothing, but words failed her. Lucy was transfixed, her eyes wide as they fastened on Ian.

'It could have been so different,' Ian raged. 'She could have been with my dad, living the high life, enjoying his success. Now, I don't know if he ever meant to come back to Edinburgh – to Mum and me.'

'I hope you're not blaming our mother for that,' Ellie said. 'She didn't know anything about you or your mum.'

'But Mum knew all about his fling with Vivienne, and then she learned all about Lucy from the newspapers. She had this foolish, romantic notion that Zach might have ... done himself in because he had a broken heart after being unfaithful to her ...' his voice faltered.

'Were you behind his anniversary vigil?' Ellie asked, her eyes once again cautioning Lucy to stay calm as she pieced together his story.

'Yeah, I was.' He went on, his voice edged with anger once more, 'I'd been saving, little by little, to bring Mum away on a surprise holiday, but she died before I had the chance. I ended up using the money to see if I could find out the truth about Zach and how he died. I didn't care if I spent it all, so long as I knew the truth. I'd hoped that the vigil might get some interest going, and maybe after all these years, someone might talk. Like, if he'd left a note or confided in anyone. Or if he had any enemies or stalkers who might have wanted to take him out. You know, like how John Lennon got killed. But I found nothing. Lots of people turned up, but none of them had actually known him in person. They were just mad about his music.'

'I don't think any of us will ever know for sure what really happened that morning,' Ellie said. Ian was watching her closely, and she was glad to see his attention was more on her than the knife block close to his hand. She fervently hoped she'd managed to say the right thing.

'You see?' he said, his hand beating a staccato on the worktop. 'It's like there's a conspiracy out there.'

'Unfortunately, Ian,' Ellie said smoothly, 'when someone like Zach dies, in tragic circumstances, lots of theories and conspiracies spring up. I see where you're coming from with the John Lennon theory, but I'm not sure I'd agree. Zach was a good musician and composer, but he was a far cry from Lennon's genius. He actually became more of a cult figure after he died, because the tragic way it happened turned him into a rock legend overnight. I'm sorry if this is not what you want to hear, but we all came to the conclusion that it had been a most unfortunate accident.'

'I can't believe it might just have been a stupid accident,' Ian said heatedly. 'That his motorbike brakes might have failed or he misjudged the end of the pier? How could all that raw talent and promise be obliterated in one fucking instant? Gone? Just like that? It doesn't make sense.'

'There are lots of things in life that don't make sense.'

'Tell me about it,' he glowered. 'But someone of his age, with everything he had going for him, and all those dreams to fulfil . . . Christ.'

'Would you rather someone had tampered with his brakes? Or that he had taken his own life?' Ellie asked, pretending a bravery she didn't feel as she confronted him.

Silence fell. She heard the echo of her voice in the kitchen and sensed that Lucy was holding her breath.

'I'd prefer it to have been an accident,' Ian said eventually. 'It's the only thing I can live with, even though it seems so crazy and senseless. I couldn't bear to think he might have ended his own life, in spite of knowing he had a son he'd never seen. Didn't I mean anything to him at all?'

'I feel the same as you, Ian,' Lucy said in a small voice. 'It

404

would be easier to live with. I've had that baggage as well, only I've had it all my life, not just a couple of months. Believe me, it soured lots of things.'

Ellie cursed under her breath. The last thing she needed was an aggrieved Lucy, trying to compete with Ian in terms of fatherly rejection. But again, Ian was too angry to hear her.

'I can't accept . . . the randomness of it all,' he raged. 'If only he hadn't gone to Canada. If only he hadn't met your mother . . .'

'Ian, life can turn on the briefest of moments,' Ellie said in an even voice, trying to bring down his anger and remain calm her-self. 'If he hadn't decided to go for a spin on his bike that morning . . . if the talent scout hadn't been in that Edinburgh club to hear him singing that particular night . . . how far back do you go?'

'Yeah, but it's so final . . . that's what I can't get my head around,' Ian said. 'I feel so fucking angry it's not funny.'

There was a thick silence that seemed to go on forever. Then, from the depths of Ellie's bag, came the sound of her phone.

Lucy froze. Ian's head jerked up and his hands gripped the back of Lucy's chair. Very slowly, Ellie reached into her bag, took out her phone and glanced at the display.

'I have to take this call,' she said. 'It's the hospital.'

'Mum?' Lucy breathed.

Ellie listened to the voice at the other end. Then she smiled at Lucy. 'It's good news. The best. She's starting to come around. They're running some tests and we can see her in an hour's time.'

'Oh, thank God,' Lucy said, tears glinted in her eyes as she slumped in her chair. She turned to Ian, 'I guess that means you're in the clear, with Mum at least. You won't be held up for murder at any rate.'

Ellie stiffened. 'What do you mean?'

'I found out that Ian was here the night Mum collapsed,' Lucy said softly. 'She could have died and Ian was afraid I was going to call the police.'

Suddenly, the menacing situation they were in made perfect sense to Ellie. She stared at him over the top of Lucy's head. He stared back at her.

'What did you do to our mother?'

'Nothing,' Ian said. 'She just looked at me and collapsed.'

'And he was behind that horrible wreath,' Lucy whispered.

The wreath that had badly shaken Lucy and the catalyst for everything coming after that. And *Mum*. Oh, God. Some kind of fury lent Ellie a razor-sharp impulse. She brandished her mobile phone.

'How dare you intimidate this family,' she said, 'I'm calling the police.' She registered Lucy's shock and Ian's momentary confusion as she swiftly pressed the keypad. Then she lifted her hand and lobbed her mobile into a corner of the kitchen away from Lucy. Ian dived after it. And in one bound Ellie hurried across the kitchen to Lucy and secured the knife block.

'Get out of this house,' she said, glaring at Ian. 'How *dare* you threaten our family! You've frightened my sister and caused our mother to become dangerously ill. If you don't leave this instant I *will* call the police.' She picked up Lucy's mobile.

Ian turned to face them, breathing hard, his face a mixture of sadness and anxiety. 'Look,' he threw out his hands in a futile gesture, 'I didn't mean ... all this. I'm just so angry and it's fucked me up. I can't stop thinking of it. One minute Zach is zooming up a deserted pier at the crack of dawn, full of life and energy. One minute Mum is there, breathing, alive, her eyes looking at me, seeing me, then there's nothing at all. Nothing. They're just *gone*.'

There was another long silence that weighed heavily in Ellie's heart.

'Then, when your mum collapsed ... I just freaked out,' he said.

'We understand you've been through a tough time,' Ellie said, 'and it's very sad about your mother. I appreciate how you feel and I think you should get some help to work through your grief, but there was no need to use scare tactics. Now just leave us in peace.'

Ian gave them a haunted look, hesitated as though he was about to say something else, then obviously thought the better of it. Then, head bowed, he walked up the hall and out the front door.

Lucy threw herself, weeping, into Ellie's arms.

Ellie still felt shaken when she phoned Miranda to tell her about Vivienne. Then she made mugs of strong, sugar-laden coffee while Lucy went to the bathroom to tidy herself up.

'How are you feeling now?' she asked, when Lucy returned to the kitchen looking a little better despite her pale face and red eyes.

Lucy hugged her tightly. 'So grateful that you came to my rescue. And love me enough to take a risk.'

Ellie hugged her back. 'Isn't that what sisters are for?'

'Thank you. How did you manage to stay so calm?'

'I breathed really slowly and it helped. Someone showed me that tip in New York when I got a bit panicky one day.'

Ben! Ellie smiled to herself as she wondered what he would have made of her kamikaze sprint across the room.

Lucy put her hand on her arm. 'Well, you were brill. I'm sorry about the scene I caused last night, you know, Zach and all that. When I see it from your point of view, it must have been difficult for both you and Miranda. And I can live with Mum having sent him away. Knowing Mum, she wouldn't have done that without good reason.'

'No, she wouldn't.'

'There must have been a mega row between them and I wouldn't like to have witnessed that,' Lucy said. 'I'm glad Ian didn't find any trace of a suicide note and that Dad's death was an accident. I'd hate to think he had deliberately—' Lucy shivered. She sat down and took a sip of her coffee. 'I'd hate to be as bitter and unhappy as Ian,' she went on. 'I kind of feel sorry for him. He must be a little unhinged after his mother died.'

'Yes, it happens.'

'I'm so lucky to have you and Miranda and Mum.'

'We're lucky to have each other. And as for your dad,' Ellie hesitated. 'Neither you nor Ian will know for sure if Zach intended to come back. You can let that eat away at you, or you can park it to one side, get on with own life and follow your dreams. And something else, Lucy,' she continued softly, 'you're never just gone. People live on in our hearts. And how they live on depends on the way we think of them.'

Lucy looked as though she was finally listening to Ellie and not instantly rebelling against her as she usually would.

'Hey, yeah,' she said. 'I've been offered that contract, Ellie. My agent actually said I was a bit like my dad. But in a good way. That I had his kind of vibe. So if I stopped bashing myself up about him and just carried that part of him with me and got on with my life, I guess he'd always be there in a good way,' she finished with a little gulp.

Ellie smiled. 'Of course he would. So you clinched the contract? Well done.'

'It's a long story, and I nearly didn't make it.' Lucy stared into space for a minute, looking suddenly vulnerable, Ellie thought. 'But I'm in danger of losing it if I spend too long in Dublin.'

'We won't let that happen,' Ellie said. 'Come on, it's time to go and visit Mum. She should be over those tests by now.'

In the hallway, Lucy paused and said, 'Oh, Ellie, I had the strangest feeling when I came into the kitchen this morning that everything would work out fine. And now it has.'

As Ellie looked at Lucy's shining eyes, she crossed her fingers behind her back and vowed that Zach Anderson's secrets would stay dead and buried. Forever.

Chapter 46

*E*llie and Lucy were allowed in to see Vivienne for ten short minutes. She was tired and disorientated but, according to the watchful nurse, beginning a slow climb back to recovery. After the brief visit, Ellie stepped out of the Coronary Care Unit just in time to see Miranda appearing at the end of the corridor, arm in arm with a tall, blond guy in pale grey chinos and a white shirt. Christian.

Miranda's skirt swirled around her knees and her soft cream cardigan was open, revealing her lacy camisole top. Her hair was messy in a cute way, her whole body glowing with love so that it projected itself like an aura around her. As they walked up the corridor towards Ellie, she imagined she was looking at a slow-motion sequence in a feel-good movie – the couple were lit by blocks of sunlight beaming in through the windows and they looked so picture perfect and tightly knit together that it brought tears to her eyes. Ellie guessed immediately that her phone call had disturbed their love-making. She stalled where she was, captivated by the image they made, and any envy she might have harboured was totally superseded with delight that Miranda looked so fabulously happy.

'Hi, Ellie,' Miranda said, finally reaching her and giving her a hug. Her sister exuded a fresh, clean scent and tendrils of her hair were still damp from the shower. Then she stepped back and introduced the guy by her side. 'This is Christian.'

'Hi, Christian,' Ellie said, accepting his firm handshake. If Miranda was nervous at introducing her boyfriend to Ellie, she hid it well. Although she need not have worried because as they chatted for a few moments, he was kindly polite to Ellie, but nothing more. It was clear to Ellie that Christian only had eyes for Miranda. Even his body language was focused on her in the way he touched her lightly when he spoke and seemed acutely aware of her to the exclusion of everyone else. He was so wrapped in Miranda that she had no inclination to flirt with him, however mildly.

'Is Lucy still in with Mum?' Miranda asked.

'No, she's gone to call her friend, so the two of you can go in to see Mum. She's conscious, but very tired and isn't talking much yet. I told the nurse to expect you and she'll let you in for a few minutes.'

Miranda turned to Christian, 'Although maybe you don't want to come in? It's not the most pleasant place in the world.'

Ellie liked the way he looped his arm around Miranda's shoulders and gave her a squeeze.

'Of course I'm going in with you,' he said.

Lucy came back and there were more introductions all around before Miranda and Christian disappeared through the security doors.

'I think it's best not to mention Ian for now,' Ellie suggested to Lucy as they sat in the waiting room. 'Christian doesn't need to know our family drama. Not yet. We'll tell Miranda quietly and let her decide when to tell him.'

'And what about Mum?'

Ellie shook her head. 'We'll wait until she's fully recovered. Then I'll pick a good moment to talk to her.'

'Mum still looks very weak. How long do you think she'll be in there?'

'As long as she needs to be,' Ellie said. 'Don't let that stop you from getting back to London. You're not that far away if we need you.'

They were still chatting when Miranda and Christian came through and, once again, Ellie was struck by how right they seemed together. Ellie drove them all back to Dún Laoghaire and they spent a pleasant hour having lunch in a restaurant close to the harbour, everyone in high spirits now that Vivienne was out of danger and on the road to recovery.

When Christian went up to the counter to pay the bill, despite everyone's protests, Miranda turned to Lucy. 'Christian is staying in the Merrion so, if it's all right with you, I'm going to join him.'

'Thank God for that,' Lucy smiled. 'He's one hell of a sexy guy and I don't want to be kept awake listening to the jingle of bedsprings or screams of ecstasy.'

'Lucy!' Miranda blushed prettily.

'I'll drop you both into town before I go back to Laurel View for a while.' Ellie suggested. 'And take a break from the hospital tonight. I'm sure you want to catch up with Christian. Lucy and I will visit Mum.'

'Are you sure? Christian is going to hire a car tomorrow so we can come and go more easily.'

Christian . . . we . . . Miranda hugged the words to herself, feeling a nugget of happiness. The unthinkable had happened. Christian had passed the Ellie test.

He'd been overjoyed to find her waiting for him in the foyer of the Merrion Hotel and she'd been equally overjoyed to see him. Here, on her home ground, he seemed a little different. Taller and broader, and attractively foreign in the way he carried himself and spoke, yet all hers, and the Christian she knew and loved when he took her to bed and they made blissful, passionate love.

Then the phone call from Ellie, and the hurried shower together before they'd dressed, left the room and dashed down the hotel steps straight into a taxi to take them to the hospital. She was glad it all happened in a rush, because she'd no time to feel nervous about Ellie and Christian coming face to face until it actually happened. She'd watched him covertly in the hospital and during lunch, but there had been no trace of the little but important signs that had heralded the death knell of other relationships – the glazed looks other boyfriends had bestowed upon Ellie, attempts to sound ultra witty and clever in order to impress her, a heightened consciousness of Ellie that meant a slight withdrawal from Miranda.

If anything, Christian had been even more loving and considerate towards her, treating Lucy and Ellie like kind friends and no more.

So, when they sat at a quiet table overlooking the garden terrace that evening, having cocktails before their meal, Miranda's heart jolted when he reached across to grip her hand in his, and said they needed to talk.

Needed to talk had always, only, ever meant one thing – it was over. Something chilly ran down her spine and she shivered.

'Hey, don't look so sad,' Christian smiled gently at her.

She tried to see if there was a smidgen of regret in that smile.

'I had two reasons for dropping everything and coming to Dublin to see you,' he said, interweaving his fingers securely through hers. 'I wanted to be with you to support you when your mother was ill. And by the way, your sisters are lovely but not half as lovely as you. I also need to tell you – and this is the hard part—'

She braced herself for the worst and wondered how he managed to look so gorgeous as he broke her heart. 'What is it, Christian?'

He took a deep breath, gave her a rueful smile, 'I'm going back home to Australia at the end of next month.'

The end of next month ... in six weeks! Dear God, whatever she had anticipated, it hadn't been this.

He heard her gasp and tightened his grip on her hand before continuing hurriedly, 'Before you ask me if I shall miss you, of course I will. I'll miss everything about you. But, the thing is, I don't want that to happen. I'd love it if you came with me, Miranda. Back to Byron Bay. I know this is a bolt from the blue. Let me explain all about it.'

Miranda felt light-headed as she sipped her cocktail and pictured him back in Byron Bay, Australia. Thousands of miles away.

'My father's taking early retirement,' Christian explained. 'It was always expected that I'd return home to manage the family yachting business, but it's happening sooner than I planned as Dad wants to hang up his deck shoes, lifejacket, whatever, a few years earlier than intended. He's had one or two scares with his health recently and wants to make the most of everything while he can. He wants to go travelling with my mom, back to Europe to find his roots ... then Cambodia and Vietnam ... flashpacking, stuff like that. He has asked me to consider coming home by the end of next month to allow for a handover period.'

It was really happening. He was serious. Miranda stared out the window at the evening sunshine falling gently across the pretty garden terrace and felt nothing but dread inside her.

'Hey, Miranda, come back to me. I know I've surprised you,' he said, 'but I'm hoping that you might come home with me. I know that's probably a crazy step for you to consider just yet, seeing as we're only together two months or so. I can't expect you to give up your career and follow me, just like that. I hope you'll agree to come on a long holiday as soon as you can, and maybe you might like it enough to stay? With me? Look, this isn't what I planned on happening,' he continued, when she remained silent. 'I knew it was on the cards that I'd be heading home eventually, but—'

'But what?' she found her voice and was raging that it trembled. Where was the new svelte Miranda? That confident woman who'd discovered herself in his arms? Somehow, she couldn't summon her up and the old Miranda with the fragile self-esteem was whispering that he'd been playing with her all along because he knew he'd be going home eventually. Inviting her for a holiday was just a cover. He was letting her down in the nicest way possible. He knew she was from Ireland and Australia wasn't exactly next door. All this crashed through her head as she stared at him.

'I thought that by the time I'd be going home you and I . . . that we'd be in a long-term relationship, and maybe even engaged.' He shook his head. 'I shouldn't be piling this on you. The last thing I want to do is to force anything. I thought we were pretty hot together. And not just sex. But that too . . . Sorry.' He grimaced. 'This is going all downhill very fast.'

'Yes, it is,' she agreed with him. 'I didn't expect this either.' *Long-term relationship . . . engaged . . .* easy to say and talk about when he had a cast-iron way out. She wouldn't have been able to compete if he'd fallen for Ellie's charms, but it was impossible to compete with the reality of Christian returning home to Australia.

'So, what do you think?'

'I don't know,' she was amazed to hear her laughter flutter and wondered why she was putting on an act when she wanted to cry. Why had she gone back to being the perfectly behaved Miranda instead of ranting and raving at him, and bawling her brains out?

'It's your family, isn't it? You don't want to be so far away. I can understand that. Or it's me. You don't love me enough.'

Love? He hadn't mentioned this before. It hadn't been part of their language.

'Yes and no . . .' Her voice cracked. She *could* live without her family. She'd felt freer than ever during the past few months. She'd even pictured never going home again. She loved Ellie and Lucy and their mum, but she was well able to exist without them. She didn't actually need them to give her a sense of who she was. Did she love Christian enough to follow him? Yes, she did.

'I've picked a very bad time with your mother so ill,' he said, 'but I couldn't pretend, Miranda, and I couldn't wait until you came back to Hong Kong in case that left me with fewer weeks in which to persuade you. Hell, I wish we were in our room so that I could show you how much you mean to me. How much I love you.'

She stared at him, beginning to come around to the rather startling but wonderful idea that he might be speaking the truth. He *could* have waited until she got back to Hong Kong to drop his bombshell. Instead, he'd come to see her. That wasn't the action of a man who wanted to end it between them. His eyes were warm and full of desire as they looked at her. Could this be really happening?

Yes, it was, she told herself, something bright and sparkling in her head silencing forever that old, outdated voice as she leaned very close to him and murmured, in a daring and most un-Miranda way, 'In that case, I think we'll have to delay dinner and go to our room.'

Chapter 47

*E*llie was glad to see Vivienne's eyes light up when she and Lucy visited that evening. Her mother had more colour in her cheeks, she was breathing unaided, and someone had washed her hair. Gillian was on duty and she chatted away brightly, telling Vivienne not to wear herself out by trying to talk too much, and reminding her that if she kept recovering at this rate, she'd be up and about in no time.

They were so lucky, Ellie thought, glancing around the ward as Lucy went around to the side of the bed closest to Vivienne. Not everyone made it out of here. Already there were new faces in some beds, new family members clustered around in the waiting area outside, lives changed utterly in the space of a single phone call. It was all so totally random, this thing called life. In a way Ian had done Vivienne a favour, for if she'd collapsed on her own at home, which she could have at any stage, she might have lain undiscovered for several hours. He'd done Ellie a favour too, bringing her closer to Lucy.

Not that *she* had done either of them any favours.

When Lucy moved back from the bed, Ellie suggested she go outside straight away and call Rebecca.

'I just want to chat to Mum for a few minutes,' she said pleasantly. 'You go and tell Rebecca you'll be back in London by next week. I won't be long.'

'Okay, see you tomorrow, Mum,' Lucy leaned in to kiss Vivienne's cheek.

And when Lucy had strolled back down the ward, reaching behind her to undo the ties of her plastic apron, Ellie moved closer to the bed. She put her hand over her mother's. Vivienne's skin felt velvety soft.

'You don't have to talk,' she said. 'I don't want to tire you. But I just wanted you to know that everything is fine.'

Vivienne frowned.

'We know how you collapsed,' Ellie said quietly, 'and who was at the door. It was Zach's son. You recognised him, didn't you?'

Vivienne nodded, her eyes sad. 'Yes, immediately,' she murmured in a hoarse voice.

Ellie pressed her hand gently. 'He must have given you a shock.'

Vivienne nodded again. 'He did.'

'We spoke to him, Lucy and me, this morning, and it's all okay, so I don't want you worrying about it. His mother was a childhood sweetheart of Zach's. But everything's fine. You needn't even think about it. You just have to relax and get better. I'll tell you all about it when you're feeling a little stronger. I spoke to the two of them and although I didn't tell them the whole truth, I didn't tell them any lies either. We've all agreed that Zach's death was a terrible accident.'

Vivienne smiled. It was a smile of love and it wrenched Ellie's heart. She took a deep breath and went on, 'We've never talked of this before, Mum, and I thought I'd lost my chance, and it's years too late—'

'Shh.' Vivienne frowned and made a dismissive gesture with her hand as though to stop what Ellie was going to say. They'd scarcely talked about Zach over the years, only when the subject couldn't be avoided, but they'd never once acknowledged the harrowing moment in Zach's bedroom that had fractured their relationship and always lurked between them.

Ellie took another deep breath and said, 'I just wanted to tell you I'm really sorry for what happened. I didn't know that you and he were . . . ' her voice faltered.

Vivienne shook her head and smiled as though there was no need for Ellie to apologise, and Ellie felt tears well up in her eyes and squeezed her mother's hand. There *was* need. She knew now that she had to acknowledge the past to be able to put it aside. For sins needed to be forgiven before you could be free of them.

Especially big bold sins like Ellie's.

Chapter 48

W hen Ellie got home to Laurel View, she poured a glass of wine and sat outside on her patio in the fragrant night-time air. She thought of the shock she'd got that morning when she'd looked at Ian and seen Zach's eyes. The eyes that had smiled at her mother across the living room in Dún Laoghaire; that had swept around that room to include both her and Miranda, before sliding back to her and lingering on her face, dropping to her breasts, then giving her a warm, secret smile, when her mother wasn't looking.

The memory that had suddenly surfaced and held her back as she lay in bed with Ben. For it had been the only other time she'd ever lost control and allowed herself total abandon.

But that time had ended in disaster. And she'd never forgiven herself.

Now she stared at the shimmering city lights below as she peeled back the layers with a delicate hand. She recalled the excitement that had made her feel both hot and cold. And alive for the first time in her life, as though everything up to now had been in dull monochrome. The bright, feverish intensity of it all, the depth of which she'd never since experienced, except with Ben.

'How old are you, Ellie?' Zach asked, when they had a moment alone in the house in Dún Laoghaire.

'I'm fifteen, almost sixteen.' She was three months off sixteen and it mattered. In those days, fifteen was a no-man's land in between the last rites of childhood and emerging adulthood. Fifteen was gawky and insecure, long awkward limbs, a body holding the secrets of a woman, but not yet comfortable with its flickering sensuality. Finding it alarming when feelings took over and were so, so intense that your body gave you away, staining your cheeks with red blush at the wrong moment, making you fumble and be clumsy and bursting with secret, urgent longings, instead of cool and confident.

She was torn in two. Missing her father dreadfully, she hated the way Zach had now come into their lives. Hated her mother for forgetting her father so quickly. How could she be seeing this man who was ten years younger than her? He came for meals as though they were a happy family. He chatted to her mother as though they were great friends.

Yet when he began to look at Ellie and his eyes said she was beautiful, it was balm to her soul. It soothed the ragged edges of her father's death. It honeyed the bitchy remarks of her class-mates and put her somewhere they couldn't reach. It was her secret, their secret. And it was one up against her mother, getting back at her in a way for forgetting their father so swiftly.

She felt the attraction pulsing between herself and Zach like an invisible touch. They found opportunities to talk whenever he was in Dún Laoghaire. But whenever Mum or Miranda were around, Ellie was very careful to hide her startling feelings under a sulky mask. She knew she wasn't fooling Zach, by the way his eyes stole teasing glances at her.

And then the evening came when the four of them were sitting around the table and her mother said, quite casually, that she was off to London for the weekend to see some film people, and that Granny Florence was coming to stay with Miranda and Ellie. She was afraid to look at him, because she felt sparks were coming out of her eyes, even her whole body, and she knew . . . she *knew* exactly what was going to happen.

It was easy to tell Granny Florence that her friend Gemma was having a sleepover for her sixteenth birthday. Granny was taking Miranda to the movies. Ellie was to enjoy herself, she said, smiling kindly. Ellie knew she should have been deeply ashamed of herself as she packed a small bag, but she wasn't. She paused by the mirror of her girlhood and looked at her face. She felt like a woman possessed.

She felt like a woman.

He was waiting for her down by Dún Laoghaire pier and the drive to his secluded retreat in Wicklow went by like a dream. She wasn't afraid, but full of a nervous, high-flying excitement. They had food, but she can't remember what they ate. Then he took out his guitar and played to her.

Later, he brought her upstairs and began to take off her clothes – slowly, very slowly, seeking permission with his eyes and his soft, tender voice.

'Is this okay, Ellie?'

At first her blouse fell away, then her jeans.

'Are you sure, Ellie?'

He brought her across to a chaise longue covered in red velvet, and laid her across it, so that she was posing like someone in a drawing.

'Can I do this, Ellie? I can't wait to see all your incredible beauty.'

He stared at her and took out his guitar again. He had written a song especially for her. Didn't she know she was his muse? She gave him inspiration. She haunted his dreams. He sat at the end of the chaise longue and sang to her, and she tried to hold on to snatches of his lyrics, but they slid past her as though she was catching rays of sunshine in her cupped hands.

'*In my dreams I feel you close / I see your perfect face / I've never known a love like this.*'

She was the one in a dream, a golden, scintillating dream.

After a while he led her across to the bed. She watched him undress, mesmerised by him, a glittering seducer, and she felt as though she was Sleeping Beauty, asleep all of her life. Until now.

She lost all sense of time. It didn't count in this room, on this bed, with this man. And she, abandoning herself and responding instinctively as though the knowledge of it all had been embedded into her soul, lifting her head and kissing him back, hot skin sliding across hot skin, and the feverish excitement of it all blended with the euphoria of discovering and relishing her new power.

The room grew dim and she felt sweat on her forehead and in her hair. A long time later, when it was dark, he lit candles and brought her into the bathroom and carefully bathed her, drying her body with huge soft towels. She felt alive like never before. They ate more food, and went back to bed and their bodies were coiled around each other the following morning when her mother came through the door, half-undressed, and Ellie saw her horrified face above the weave of their limbs.

Chapter 49

*J*ust before dawn on a pearly Monday morning, he parked the rented car at the end of the lane. He climbed out of it and went around to the boot, lifting out the small wooden box. Then he locked the car and took the track that led to the edge of the lake.

The depth and breadth of the landscape on this hushed morning took him by surprise. The pristine sky arched loftily above him, a tender milky blue. The lake, stretching off into the immense horizon, was calm and still, as though it was silently embracing the glorious new day. He stepped onto the deserted pier, disturbing two swans in the rushes. With gracefully beating wings, they rose into the tranquil air. He thought this was a good sign. In their wake, water whispered gently against the wooden joists, sending tiny ripples swirling across the mirror-like surface. When he reached the end of the pier he paused, feeling like a tiny speck in the magnitude of the sea and sky.

He was amazed at how calm and peaceful it all was.

Then he opened the box and wheeled his arm in a wide,

curving arc, releasing his mother's ashes so that they flickered into the clear blue infinity. One minute they were dancing on the air, silhouetted against the dawn sky, just like Zach had been, before they sank down into the secretive, silent lake. He took a flimsy piece of paper out of his pocket, the kind of page that belonged in a copy book. It had been folded and refolded and was full of scribbles and scrawls and crossed-out words, and he could only make out some of them:

In my dreams . . . feel you . . . touch your perfect face . . . you will always rest in mine . . . forever my angel . . .

He'd found it amongst his mother's papers, soon after she'd died, and had known exactly what it was. Draft lyrics to 'Forever My Angel'. The song that Zach had written. It was all about Heather Douglas. He held the page aloft so that it fluttered in the air, and then he let it go, watching as it was snatched away by the playful breeze. Then it, too, flickered on the air stream for a while like a spirited kite, before it fluttered down to meet the surface of the lake. It drifted on the water, dancing with the current, and then it became sodden as the lake slid over it.

He stood for a moment in the silence.

What had it been like, he wondered, to zoom at speed, in a Harley Davidson, along this pier, on a pristine morning such as this? You would have felt powerful, like some sort of Greek god. You would have felt a connection with the immensity of the universe, and that in this wonderful silvery kind of morning there was nothing you couldn't have accomplished.

That all your dreams could come true.

Chapter 50

'Thanks for this,' Lucy said, sitting in Ellie's car on Monday evening as they surged down the M50 towards Dublin airport.

'Nonsense, I have to see you off in style,' her sister joked as she overtook a lorry.

'You think Mum will be okay?'

'She'll be fine. They're moving her to a convalescent home at the end of the week. And she's talking about going to Boston for a short holiday as soon as she gets her mojo back. Her own words. She says she's not going to let the rest of her life pass her by. She's going to live it to the full.'

'Good for Mum. What do you think of Miranda! She could be following Christian back to Australia.'

'I hope she does. I'll miss her, but they're so right for each other, and we can always visit. It's only a day away. And I'm glad you're going back to London in time for your new contract.'

'I'll pop home for a weekend as soon as I can,' Lucy said.

'The best thing you can do is get your career back on track.

Make the most of this opportunity. Keep away from the press. And any mad parties. Don't blow it this time, Lucy. You owe it to yourself to make the best of you and become the next super-model. And,' Ellie grinned, 'that's the end of my lecture.'

'It's fine,' Lucy said. 'I like it. Thanks for your support. I will behave. Promise. I feel so much better about everything now. As though I'm at peace with myself instead of always fighting. You know, I sensed all along that Mum was keeping something from me. I didn't like it when she spoiled me, because I felt she was trying to compensate for something. I know this sounds child-ish but I used to think that if I pushed her enough and rebelled she'd get angry with me and admit that Zach had gone off because he hadn't wanted me.'

Ellie moved into the slip lane for the airport. 'Well you know for certain that he didn't.'

It was now or never, Lucy decided, clenching her hands. 'Ellie, I – I still can't believe the way I messed things up with you and Johnny,' she said, needing to say it, now, before she was back in London and caught up in the busyness of her career, where time would march on and the moment would be lost. That was the main thing she'd learned about her mother taking suddenly ill. You just never knew when it might be too late to say any-thing important. 'You don't know how sorry I am,' she continued, 'and I wish there was something I could do to fix it.'

She stole a glance at Ellie, but her sister was facing the motor-way ahead and her eyes were hidden behind her sunglasses.

Eventually Ellie said, 'Look, darling, just forget all about it. If you hadn't broken us up, something else would have sooner or later. I wasn't in love with Johnny. Not deeply. And not enough to spend the rest of my life with him.'

'You're not just saying that to make me feel better?'

'Absolutely not. It's over, behind us, and I totally forgive you. So don't let it bother you or affect any of your future relationships.'

Lucy felt relief pour through her. 'Ellie, that means everything to me. You've no idea how grateful I am to hear you say that. I hope you fall madly in love with a really nice guy and have lots of lovely children. You'd be a great mum.'

'Do you think so?'

'Of course!'

Ellie's mouth smiled as she pulled up in the set down area for departures, but Lucy still couldn't see her eyes.

'Stay where you are, I'll organise my case,' she said. Leaning across, she kissed Ellie's cheek. Then she jumped out of the car, hooked her bag onto her shoulder and pulled her case out of the boot.

Ellie zapped down the passenger window as Lucy began to wheel her case towards the terminal building. 'Hey, sis,' she called out. 'Love you!'

Lucy halted, and felt a smile breaking across her face. 'Thanks, I know you do!'

And with that Ellie peeled off her sunglasses, jumped out of the car and, hurrying forward, enveloped her in a big, warm hug. 'Love you lots and lots.'

'Is Lucy gone?' Vivienne asked.

'Yes,' Ellie glanced at her watch. 'She must have arrived in London by now.'

Vivienne gave a deep sigh and felt herself relax against the pillows. 'How was she?'

'She's fine, Mum, grand. She's going to be so busy over the next few months and caught up in the excitement of her new casting that things will settle down. So everything's fine.'

'Good.'

428

They both fell silent. Earlier that day, Vivienne had been moved out of the intensive care unit into a private room in the general coronary ward. She turned her head, glad to be here and to be able to look out the window at the late-evening sunshine, watching the way it flickered off the soft, green leaves unfurling on the trees outside, feeling as though she'd never really seen this miracle before. She'd been in hospital for a week, but it had been the week in which the spring had finally made way for a bright new summer. More momentously, the week in which she and Ellie had begun to mend a rift that had caused friction between them for over twenty years.

She was full of gratitude.

Now she turned back and smiled at Ellie.

'Ellie, darling, I'd love to think you'll be fine. I want you to be happy. I don't want you to feel in any way to blame for what happened.'

'God, Mum, of course I did,' Ellie said. 'I always thought that, only for me, Lucy might have had her father around. That has always nibbled away at me whenever she brought up his name. Funny thing is, Lucy thought I resented her for reminding me of your relationship with him. She has no idea that deep down I felt more guilty than resentful, and that was why I was tense and awkward around her.'

'And now? Has that changed at all? Especially in view of the drama that happened in my kitchen while I was stuck here?'

'Yes, it made me realise that if Zach so easily abandoned his son and girlfriend in search of fame, he could just as easily have abandoned Lucy.'

'Remember, Ellie, Zach never intended to hang around but I was the one who told him to get as far away as possible. I warned him that if he dared to darken the doors of Ireland or even Great Britain again, I'd ruin his reputation.' It had been difficult for her too, Vivienne thought, for she'd chosen to protect Ellie by banishing Lucy's father, something else she'd had to make up for. 'As for Ian,' she sighed, 'what a sad story.'

'He's already texted Lucy sending deep apologies for everything. He said he's going to talk to someone in Edinburgh,' Ellie said.

'Good,' Vivienne said, her voice a little stronger. 'The other thing you have to remember is that Zach's sights were set on nothing else but his goddamn quest for fame and his obsession with his music. And we both know where that led him. That was his choice entirely.'

'Yes,' Ellie said quietly.

'And I hope you're not blaming yourself for that either,' Vivienne said, trying to sound as strong as possible for Ellie's sake.

'No,' Ellie said. 'I think his note made his intentions pretty clear.'

'That's why I showed it to you at the time. You had to know his death had absolutely nothing to do with you. And Lucy doesn't suspect?'

'No, nor does Ian. They both said it was easier to live with the idea that his death was an unfortunate accident.'

'Some secrets are better off being kept for everyone's peace of mind. Especially when there's nothing to be gained by revealing them,' Vivienne said as she lay back, recalling the contents of the letter from Zach that had arrived in Dún Laoghaire a few days after his death.

It was a letter she had shown just once, to a silent, guarded Ellie, before destroying it, but every word was engraved on her memory. In it, Zach had admitted that he'd been horribly dejected when his dreams of conquering America didn't come to pass.

'There's only one song going around and around in my head, and my inspiration has dried up. When I think of all the beautiful women I've loved and lost, in order to follow my dreams ... I messed up ... those dreams have turned to dust right now, but there is one way, the ultimate way, to make sure my music lives on and I'll become a legend ...'

'Zach was caught between his ruthless ambition and his desires,' Vivienne sighed. 'And his ambition won hands down. I think he was always a bit of a lost soul. And let's leave it at that, Ellie. Leave him in peace. Leave it all in peace. Otherwise, we'll be going around in circles forever. Life is too short for putting some things under the microscope.'

Ellie smiled at last, 'You're right. But there are still a few things I'd like an explanation for.'

'Such as?'

'All those bouquets of flowers that have arrived in Dún Laoghaire, addressed to you. You seem to have a lot of admirers. Mum?'

Vivienne smiled. 'Well you know that flowers aren't allowed into the hospital.'

'Come on, Mum!'

'Didn't I say some secrets are better off being kept? Anyway, getting back to the most important people in my life, my daughters – Lucy's set to conquer the catwalk, Miranda's madly in love, so what about you?'

Ellie hesitated. 'I'll be fine. I hope to get busy again with Ellie Belle. Claire has been holding the fort for me, and there have been lots of new enquiries about my designs, which is great, including enquiries from an Irish-born movie actress—'

'Wow,' Vivienne interjected.

'She seems very interested, but I'm not holding my breath just yet,' Ellie said cautiously. 'And I need to get back to my drawing board. I haven't felt much like it recently,' she admitted.

'Of course not,' Vivienne patted her hand. 'You needed some time out.' She still didn't know who or what had caused Ellie to break up with Johnny, but mindful of Ellie's self-respect, she wasn't going to pry. 'And tell me this, before the nurse throws you out and orders me to rest, how was New York?'

'New York was—' Ellie fell silent. Then her eyes took on a faraway look and her mouth curved in a big smile that warmed Vivienne's heart. 'It was good,' she continued. 'And that's all I can say for now.'

A couple of days later, Ellie opened the door to her studio, paused on the threshold and looked around. Everything was just as she had abandoned it, weeks earlier, and the atmosphere was tired and faded, as though time had stood still. It was the one place in the house that was off limits to Marta.

She took a deep breath, stepped into the room and she thought it welcomed her like an old, long-lost friend. This was the place where her success had taken root and flourished. It was still a reference point and her passion, and an intrinsic part of who she was. She threw open the window and began to tidy, feeling a lift of energy as she worked methodically, going through her desk and ridding it of anything that wasn't useful or inspirational, organising her sketchpads and pencils. She cleared her room of old magazines, patterns and samples of material that were no longer of use. Picking up a dead, dried-out spider plant, she apologised for neglecting it as she dumped it into a black sack. As she worked, her thoughts drifted, flitting first to Lucy, who had already sent her excited texts about her upcoming modelling assignment in Switzerland. Ellie felt a warmth in her heart when she realised that her capacity to forgive her sister was, in turn, helping her to forgive herself. What goes around comes around, Miranda had said. When Ellie had heard her words, she'd immediately applied them to both her and Lucy's betrayal, but they were equally relevant to good, positive things.

Then she thought of Ben. He had begun to phone instead of just texting, and she enjoyed the chatty conversations that reminded her of their time together.

It took just over two hours to expel the stale, tired feeling and breathe new life into her studio and by the time she was sweeping the floor, she felt more energised than she'd felt in a long, long time.

Later, she took up her pencils.

It took several false starts, and then something began to shape and form, for she just had to think of Ben and the passionate way he'd spoken to her of his native Leitrim. All the colours and textures she needed were there, from the sparkling silver of a salmon river, to the deep velvet green of a hidden valley, to the lacy froth of a crystal waterfall. Purple mountains fringed with a golden sunset. A field of springtime heather, rippling in the breeze. All images waiting to be recreated into beautiful Ellie Belle clothes.

But now she knew this was just one of her dreams, and no longer her all-consuming lodestar.

Epilogue

Six weeks later

'Right everyone,' Lucy said, as she went across to the television. 'This is it. And it's very short so keep your eyes on the screen. You especially, Mum!'

'I can't help it if I keep looking around,' Vivienne said. 'It's so long since I had my three daughters, at home, all together. I never thought I'd see this wonderful kind of evening again.'

There was a short silence and Ellie bit back sudden tears. She smiled across at her mother, who was relaxing on the sofa. A slightly frailer Vivienne, Ellie had to admit, but still as mentally spirited as ever.

'I'm ready and waiting,' Miranda said, sitting beside Vivienne.

'I'm ready too,' Ellie said.

Lucy stepped back, pressed the remote, and fast forwarded through jumbled images of various outtakes. 'This is just a rough proof,' she said. 'I'm not supposed to have it.'

'How did you manage to get hold of it?'

Lucy grinned. 'A friend of the cameraman got it for me. I want to show it to Miranda before she leaves for Australia.'

Ellie noticed the almost imperceptible way Vivienne's hand reached out to Miranda's. Her sister had flown in from Hong Kong the day before and was spending two weeks at home in Dún Laoghaire before heading out to her new life with Christian. She was looking happier than Ellie had ever seen her.

'And it's great that I caught you too, Ellie,' Lucy said. 'Before you head off to New York in the morning.'

'I'm only going for a few days,' Ellie reminded her.

'There you are, look!' Miranda said.

It was indeed Lucy on the screen. Clad in a House of Venetia calf-length coat, her flame hair glinting against the snowy white slopes of a Swiss mountain range. She was joined by two other models, both wearing different winter coats, and they laughed and joked and bumped into each other as they began to make a snowman.

'That's Beatrice and Sasha,' Lucy said pointing to the screen. A light snow started to fall, white flakes lingering in Lucy's hair. There was a close-up of her laughing face and her smoky grey eyes before the camera panned away. She looked softer yet beautifully vibrant, Ellie thought.

'That falling snow was fake,' Lucy said. 'In reality the sun was splitting the trees. We were boiling hot in our winter coats and doing our best not to squint.'

The scene changed and Lucy appeared again, this time standing against the lantern-lit balustrade of a Swiss chalet, wearing a Venetia sequinned dress and sky-high heels, a cocktail glass in her hand. She glided elegantly into a reception room, where she joined her glamorously dressed friends by a magnificent Christmas tree and they raised their glasses to each other.

The final clip showed Lucy in a leather jacket climbing into a sleigh. She smiled warmly at the camera as the sleigh pulled away, its bells jingling.

'What do you think?' Lucy asked, somewhat nervously, Ellie thought, as though she valued their opinion. Her youngest sister had grown up a little.

'You look brilliant,' Ellie said, leading the congratulations.

'You're beautiful, Lucy,' Vivienne said.

'I'm not sure how the finished commercial will appear, but that gives you an idea,' Lucy said, pink with pleasure. 'When I get back to London next week we'll be shooting indoor stills.'

'It's wonderful, Lucy,' Miranda said. 'You look fantastic. It makes me feel all Christmassy even though it's the middle of summer. I wonder if I'll miss that kind of a Christmas this year,' she continued in a teasing voice.

Once again, Ellie caught a quiet exchange between Miranda and her mother.

'No, you won't,' Vivienne said to her. 'You'll be too busy enjoying your new life with Christian. He's a lovely man and I'm really happy for you, Miranda,' she went on. 'Besides,' she looked around the room, smiling as she caught both Ellie and Lucy's eyes, 'it'll do you good to get away from being squeezed between your bossy sisters. Don't think I haven't noticed the way they've always ordered you about.'

'Now it's my turn to make demands. Everyone is to come out and visit me, or else,' Miranda said, with a sparkle in her eye.

'Try keeping us away,' Ellie told her. 'I'll be back from New York next Saturday so I'll have a whole week with you before you fly out to Oz, and we can start planning then.'

'The best of luck with your trip,' Miranda said. 'Sorry I can't go with you, but I've stuff to sort out before I head off myself.'

'Yeah, Ellie,' Lucy said, 'Me too. I'm needed in London next week, but I hope it all goes fabulously. Hey, we might even see you on television swishing up the red carpet.'

Ellie laughed and shook her head. 'I don't think so.'

She tried to ease her sudden nerves as the plane touched down in JFK the following evening. New York glinted in sparkling June sunshine as the cab whisked her across to a Manhattan hotel. Ellie ordered room service, and then had a relaxing bath before pulling the blinds and going to bed. She slept the night through, waking early the following morning, refreshed and alert. She lay in bed for a while, thinking of the day ahead.

This evening was the premiere of *Ruby Tuesday*, in the Lincoln Center. It was being hailed as the summer's must-see film and, when the leading actress stepped out of a limousine onto the red carpet, she would be wearing an Ellie Belle linen and lace creation.

Although she'd known about the initial enquiries, Ellie had been stunned to hear confirmation of the order. Everyone had urged her to go to New York for the occasion, including the Irish-born actress herself, who had sent Ellie invitations to the premiere as well as the after-show party in the Russian Tea Rooms.

'This is mega-mega,' Lucy had decreed.

'You deserve it, sis,' Miranda had told her. 'A foothold in the States!'

Ellie didn't know where it might lead, or what opportunities it might bring, but it was a fantastic boost for Ellie Belle. She wasn't even sure if she wanted to rub shoulders with the high-octane glitzy people that evening – it was so far removed from the peaceful ambience of her workroom overlooking the Dublin city lights.

But she couldn't resist the opportunity to revisit New York.

After breakfast, she left the hotel and headed up Columbus Avenue in the heat haze of the morning. She crossed at suddenly familiar traffic lights, the memory of those few short weeks she'd spent in the city swirling around her and causing her heart to flutter in her throat. She increased her speed, afraid she might be too late. Wondering, too, if she was making a fool of herself – he wouldn't be expecting her.

But she wasn't too late, and she didn't make a fool of herself.

She reached the 79th Street entrance in time to tag along as the group briskly strode into the dappled sunshine of Central Park. There were about a dozen people ahead of her, and just as he always had, Ben did his trick of turning around and half-running backwards while he checked everyone was following him.

Then, above the bobbing heads he saw her. And slowed his pace. 'Hey, Ellie,' he called out, grinning broadly, 'you showed up just in time.'